Behind every great fortune lies a great crime.

—Honoré de Balzac

PROLOGUE

Rome, 2019

A sleek black Maserati moved quickly through the darkened streets of nighttime Rome. Inside were two men, two pistols, and six pounds of diamonds that no one believed were missing.

Every thief has a story about a perfect crime.

For once, it was actually true.

But Vito Verrazano was nervous.

His palms were wet, and lines of sweat moved down the side of his face. He prayed the other man in the car, the man driving, didn't see it. Vito rubbed his hands on his pants. If Rusty noticed his discomfort, he didn't say anything. Rusty was focused on the road.

The Maserati Quattroporte GTS slid through the dark streets of Rome like a black lozenge, slippery and elusive. It was approaching one in the morning, and the streets were not quite empty. Vito was still trying to process the day, wrap his mind around the sheer absurdity of it all. The illogic, the unbelievability of it, stretched the fabric of his mind to its limits.

At eleven that morning, Vito had walked into the Commerce

Bank of Rome wearing a business suit and carrying forged papers identifying him as Aldo Grassi, an old alias of Niccoló Bartolo, his onetime boss in the notorious School of Turin thievery ring. Vito asked for the bank manager and told him he'd like to access his safe-deposit box. The man took his identification, looked him up in a computer, and said that they hadn't seen him in some time. Sixteen years, Vito told him with a practiced smile. He was taken down to the vault and given a private room they had for their preferred guests, and the box was brought in. When the curtain was pulled aside, Vito opened the box.

Inside, there were over six pounds of finished diamonds worth approximately one hundred million dollars.

Vito greedily scooped most of the diamonds up and placed them in a velvet sack, which he then secured and placed in the briefcase he carried. Vito left about a fifth of the stones in the box. He had to eyeball it, but it needed to equal about twenty million. That was how much the Antwerp Diamond Centre claimed Bartolo actually got away with when he originally stole these in 2003. Leaving an actual fortune behind was insane to him. He had to fight himself not to pocket a fistful—Christ, what would that be? Five million in rocks?

But that twenty million he left behind would be their escape plan. That's what would make the police believe they got everything back.

Vito handcuffed the briefcase to his wrist, closed the box, and gave it back to the manager, who was waiting in the vault. Vito thanked him for his time and walked out of the bank with eighty million dollars in his right hand.

Then the day got weird.

Rusty, Jack's man, who seemed to be able to conjure up handguns, passports, and high-end sports cars with a magician's flourish, picked him up in a black Maserati, and they drove to a hotel where they waited for Jack's call.

They watched it happen on TV.

Four men—ex-Serbian special forces and Jack Burdette—

attempted to rob the Commerce Bank just hours after Vito was there, and it went sideways in every way possible. Of course, Jack was on the inside making sure that it did. He got out without getting killed and ended up in a shootout on a Roman street, him and a bent Italian cop against Aleksander Anđelić and what was left of his Serbian goon squad. Jack escaped that too, and Vito began to wonder if Burdette was part cat and what the count of nine lives was up to.

They picked Burdette up in the Maserati, the same car he and Rusty sat in now, and they fled to Rome-Fiumicino, where they boarded a chartered plane, Vito didn't know what kind, and flew two and a half hours to Alicante, Spain. He and Rusty remained on the aircraft with the diamonds for about an hour. Jack returned with Enzo Bachetti, a safecracker and alumnus of the School of Turin. Enzo was worse for wear. He was bloody, and he'd been tortured.

They didn't talk for a time.

Jack drank.

They'd watched a man die. Vito still didn't know who pulled the trigger, but he knew Jack hadn't stopped it. Nothing else was said.

Something else died there too, in that hot Spanish night, but Jack wouldn't speak of it.

He only drank and rifled through a thick collection of files they'd brought back with them from Aleksander Anđelić's house.

They split up at Rome-Fiumicino airport, Vito and Rusty in the Maserati and Jack and Enzo in another car. Jack said they were going to meet Giovanni Castro.

Castro. He was the cop who busted up the School of Turin in 1997. Jack and Enzo had gotten away. Bartolo had gotten away. Vito didn't. Vito only did five years, but when he got out, he looked up Bartolo, asked him what he had going, and Bartolo said they couldn't work together anymore. Vito was an ex-con. The police knew where to find ex-cons.

Then Bartolo robbed the Antwerp Diamond Centre.

If it weren't for Castro, the original School would have been in on that job, including Vito. Instead of grabbing the diamonds now, sixteen years after the fact, he would've been living high on the fat. He'd never have stolen anything again.

If it weren't for Castro.

If it weren't for Castro, the School of Turin would have pulled that job, not the practice squad, and they would have gotten away with it.

And there wouldn't have *been* a Castro if it weren't for Jack.

Vito told him there were no hard feelings. That he'd forgiven.

But that wasn't true.

There were *only* hard feelings.

The time you spend in a concrete box, you never get that back.

Vito was nervous, exposed wires in the rain.

Vito pointed to the left side of the car and said nonchalantly, "Vatican. Always looks pretty at night."

Rusty looked over at the illuminated circular columns that enveloped St. Peter's Square like the arms of God.

Vito had never believed in God, but he was Italian, and that made him a Catholic.

"We haven't heard from Jack," Rusty said, "so I'd like to stop by the hotel first before we find our place. Just want to make sure everything is okay."

"That's fine," Vito said. He pointed straight ahead. "This road will take us right by there."

Rusty drove through a traffic circle and continued down the street, which eventually split into lanes falling on either side of a tunnel entrance. The road was slightly elevated, and as they descended to merge with the tunnel traffic, they could see the Tiber, a black ribbon across the glowing city. It was too dark to make out the water, but Vito saw the illuminated bridge stretching across it. Rusty slowed to a stop, the third car in a line at a red light. The other two appeared to be taxis in front of them.

Now. Now was the time.

Vito pulled the .22-caliber Beretta Bobcat from his pocket and held it against his chest. Rusty, focused on the road and his mind apparently elsewhere, still hadn't noticed.

"Sorry, kid."

That got his attention.

Vito fired twice.

Not believing in God doesn't mean you don't believe in remorse, it just means you don't have any place to put your guilt.

But he was also seventy years old, an ex-con, and not living off the promised fortune of a job he should have been on sixteen years before. That left little room in his heart for anything else.

Vito liked the kid. Rusty was damn good at what he did, and he was crafty. In another life, perhaps.

Vito reached into the back seat and grabbed the diamonds, now in a bag he could sling cross-body. He got out of the car and closed the door, never looking back. Vito slung the bag across his chest. A .22 was a small-caliber weapon, and when fired from inside a car, the sound wouldn't carry far. Vito doubted that the shots would even register as anything more than a backfire or blown tire to the cab drivers, especially if they had their radios on. To anyone on the street, if there was anyone at this time of night, it'd just look like a guy got out at a stoplight.

Vito moved quickly down the Piazza della Rovere, the dark waters of the Tiber on his left and a wall of seventy-year-old, five-story stucco to his right. He disappeared quickly into the inky half-light of the Roman night. Vito turned down the first street he came to and snaked deeper into the outer edges of the city, away from Rusty. He still didn't hear any sirens.

When he'd walked for about ten minutes and was certain that he wasn't followed, Vito pulled out his phone and dialed a number.

When the person on the other end picked up, Vito said, "It's done."

"Good," the voice on the other end said.

Then Vito Verrazano went to ground.

PART 1

THREE CAN KEEP A SECRET...

ONE

October 2021

Jack stepped from the cool, dark interior of the low barn into the hot afternoon sun. The yeasty smell of fermenting grapes abated some when he left the tank building, but it still hung heavy in the air. He loved this time of year. It was always a gamble with growers trying to push the harvest as long as possible to soak up the dry, late summer sunshine and cool mornings. The trick was to time it so that you completed the harvest before the October rains, which would destroy whatever crop was left on the vine. It was incredibly stressful. If the rains came early, entire crops could be lost.

There was little danger of that, it seemed.

It was early October, and there was no sign of rain in the forecast. It had been another dangerously dry year, and wildfires burned throughout the state. They'd had several near misses with fires and the last time could see flames from the property.

The unfortunate irony was that as the climate had warmed, the harvest was starting earlier and earlier. A dry growing season was ideal, but if it was too hot and too dry, the veraison, or the process of ripening, started in early August now in some parts. This meant that the vines would cease growing and starting to push sugars into the grapes. That began a clock of approximately six weeks for when harvest needed to begin. For the estate fruit here in Alexander Valley, which was at the northern end of Sonoma County and enjoyed a cooler microclimate, they hadn't had to harvest much earlier than previous years. But Jack also owned a tract of vineyard in Napa Valley that supplied the fruit for their signature Cabernet, "the Kingfisher," and that harvest started in August. They would have a much smaller yield this year, but hopefully they'd be rewarded with more intense flavor from the smaller grapes. That fruit, from the legendary Sine Metu vineyard in Napa, was one of the most storied plots of land in California wine country and produced some of the state's highest-quality grapes. What fruit he didn't use for the Kingfisher Cabernet, he sold to other vineyards and turned a significant profit from it.

Megan handled the crush. She oversaw all of the winemaking operations, managed the day laborer harvesters, all of which had to be done by hand, and she was ultimately responsible for the bottling. That was several full-time jobs in itself. Jack handled everything else. Most of his grapes were here at Kingfisher, at the very northern end of Sonoma's Alexander Valley, among the black oak and with a gentler climate that favored more European-style wines.

They'd survived the last two years, but it had been lean.

Most of the money he'd made on his last job was gone, funneled into the winery to keep it going during the bleakness of 2020. Of course, there hadn't been that much money to begin with. Jack, Enzo, and Rusty all walked away with about a million three, and that was what they'd been able to steal from the Serbian gangster Aleksander Anđelić. It was supposed to be much, much more.

Jack thought about Vito's betrayal often.

When it first happened, it was a raw and festering wound. It felt like a hot poker behind the eyes. Jack felt such a primal fury, such uncontrollable anger, that for a while he even scared himself. He didn't know where to put his rage; it just seemed to batter against the sides of his consciousness, trying to be let out. He slept little in those early, dark days.

Megan McKinney had met him in New York when Jack cemented his deal with the Justice Department to plea to several counts of passport fraud in exchange for avoiding prison and agreeing to help the FBI with several ongoing trafficking investigations. She wasn't fully back in his life in those first months but saw the change in him, saw the darkness taking over. She told Jack that she loved him, but he had to banish whatever those demons were if they were to be together. She didn't ask to know what was troubling him but promised that he could tell her if he wanted. She would listen and she wouldn't judge.

Jack told her.

He and his crew targeted one hundred million in finished diamonds that no one was looking for. They made the painful decision to leave about twenty percent of those diamonds in the safe because they knew the police needed something they could believe.

The plan was perfect. Jack had made his deal with the government. He would help them capture the Serbian war criminal-turned-thief Aleksander Anđelić, and in exchange, the government wouldn't press charges on a litany of damnable offenses. Jack would be a free man and would have twenty million in untraceable diamonds.

The one thing they hadn't counted on was an inside threat.

Vito Verrazano, one of their own crew, double-crossed them. Vito shot Rusty, left him for dead, and disappeared with the diamonds. Eighty million gone in the blink of an eye.

And there was nothing Jack could do about it.

Because his deal involved a guilty plea for passport fraud, he could never hold another passport again. Not legally, at any rate. He still had one expertly forged passport that he could use should he ever need to escape. The other was hidden in his villa in Tuscany, which he obviously couldn't get. At least not without incredible risk.

Jack told Megan this and, to her credit, she didn't judge him.

Megan knew who and what Jack was and had accepted it. Jack came to realize that the source of his rage wasn't just that he'd lost an actual fortune in stones but that someone had outsmarted him. For Jack's entire professional career, he'd earned a reputation for staying several steps ahead of the competition, ahead of the law. Now, one of his own, a cagey seventy-year-old no less, pulled the one move Jack never anticipated. That burned him as much, if not more, than being arrested by the FBI.

When it first happened, Jack, Enzo, and Rusty spoke daily. They were searching for Vito. Rusty scoured the dark web for any trace of the double-crossing bastard from his recovery bed in Switzerland. The plan was that Jack would use his last passport, they'd steal the diamonds back, and then they'd slowly sell them off over a number of years so they didn't arouse suspicion. But when Megan reentered his life, Jack finally admitted to himself that he had something to lose.

Jack never shared this to his partners, but it became a simple calculus of risk versus reward. Before Megan, he was prepared to run. If Jack's passport was burned, he could leave his winery and his "Frank Fischer" life behind. It would hurt, but he could do it. But Megan McKinney was the one thing he wouldn't trade. She loved him not for who he had been but for who she believed Jack was now and who he had the potential to be, a person she wanted to see him become. Their relationship over the last ten years was confusing, a hot and then cold affair that was equal parts elation and gut-wrenching pain. When he thought about it, Jack likened it to what it must be like to land an airliner in bad weather. It was hope and despair, usually, it seemed, in unequal amounts and anchoring on the latter. But Megan was back now, and it felt like this was permanent. Jack had exorcised the demons of his previous life, the thing that had kept her away.

That didn't end the pain of betrayal, and it didn't make it any easier to accept what happened. But it did force Jack to acknowledge that he now had something to lose. More than that, it forced him to take stock of what he *did* have: a way out. Jack had a real life, a new identity, and a business that both employed many and made many more happy. He was making something.

The worst, though, was the guilt. Rusty was nearly killed over the diamonds. Enzo, Jack's oldest friend, was tortured by Anđelić's men while Jack, Vito Verrazano, and Rusty were stealing the stones from the bank. Rusty and Enzo paid a debt in blood that Jack could never repay. He owed them. A three-way split of eighty million dollars would have gone a long way to settle those scores. There were times when the guilt was crushing.

Eventually, the daily calls with Enzo and Rusty became weekly ones. Then, less frequently than that.

It's not that they had moved on. Enzo had a woman and a small olive orchard in Calabria overlooking the Mediterranean. Jack had met her once. They didn't live together, Enzo would probably never trust another woman that far, but he seemed happy enough most days.

Rusty, less so.

He'd lost everything on their last job. The State Department's Diplomatic Security Service was actively pursuing him, as was the FBI, for his passport-forging operation—not to mention whatever the FBI was after him for already. Rusty had a very lucrative business in Europe working as a fixer and troubleshooter for criminals like Jack (and, on occasion, certain intelligence services). That was all gone now. Rusty was a full-time fugitive, and the entire time he was recovering from the gunshots Vito left him with, he was thinking about nothing but payback. Even the diamonds were secondary.

Then the world stopped. They found Vito in that lost year. Ultimately, it wasn't hard work for Rusty, himself an ex-FBI agent and counterintelligence specialist. They initially tracked him using his cell phone to the shores of Lago Maggiore in Italy's lake country, not far from the Swiss border. Then, shortly after he arrived, all trace evaporated. Vito had ditched his phone. From there, Rusty started looking at other indicators, for example, property that was purchased in late 1997 or early '98. Jack knew that was when Vito was supposed to have been arrested along with the rest of the School of Turin, but instead they learned he had paid off a corrupt judge and disappeared. They were able to use that data point and others to figure out where Vito was living and under what alias.

Rusty, who was hiding in Lucerne, showed extreme restraint in not showing up at Vito's door and exacting revenge.

With the world locked down, the three of them agreed to wait. Verrazano couldn't move the stones even if it'd been safe to travel. Vito had been a crew dog in his prime, a working thief who moved from job to job. He didn't have the kind of connections that one needed to safely and securely fence a score that size. Time, it seemed, was on their side. Though Jack hadn't yet told his friends that he wouldn't possibly take the risk of traveling abroad, wouldn't risk losing what he'd gotten back. Jack spent so much of the last year weighing his options. Vito betrayed them, and that was a sin that couldn't go unpunished, but Jack also couldn't reconcile what he'd have to risk to get the diamonds back. Back in Rome, when all he had was the score to think about, Jack had been prepared to leave everything else to get them. Now, it was exactly the opposite. It wasn't that he had something to lose, he had *everything* to lose.

That weighed on him daily, dragged him down and caused him as much internal strife as how to keep a winery in business during a year when no one could visit it.

Megan appeared at his side, a soft hand on his shoulder. There were two plastic water bottles in her other hand, one of which she handed to Jack. He opened it and took a drink.

"Thank you," he said, with smiling eyes. Megan was the rare woman who didn't defy age but assumed it gracefully and grew more beautiful every day. Her auburn hair was tucked beneath a dark and dirty ball cap with the pony tail extending out the back. Even with her face shadowed by the hat, Jack saw the playful line of freckles running across the ridges of her cheeks. She wore a UC Davis T-shirt and dirty, ripped blue jeans over boots. Megan was splitting her time between overseeing the last throes of harvest and the crush, the process of extracting the juice from the grapes they harvested.

"Are you going to call Eagle Ridge today? That guy has left about four messages on my phone. Today," she added ruefully.

"Yes," Jack said at length. "I've already contracted the rest of the Sine Metu allotment, though. I've told him as much." Jack took another sip, and his gaze traced out to the black oaks that surrounded the property and to the neat rows of vines that gently climbed the rolling hills of their estate. "Told him in July."

"You have to do it," Megan said. "Negotiating is the only thing around here you can do better than me." Jack saw a smile crack the right side of her mouth.

"True. Your version is, 'I said there's no fucking grapes.'"

"I'm not *that* bad."

"Well," Jack said, drawing the word out.

"Okay, I've got to go check on Lincoln. I'll see you at round-up." Round-up was their end-of-day meeting with the heads of the various teams that ran the winery. It usually started in mid-August as they were getting ready for harvest and continued through October when harvest and crush were finished. They circled up to review the major events of the day and cover what needed to happen the next. Everyone enjoyed a glass or two of whatever bottles were open in the tasting room, leftover from that day's service. Megan gave him a playful kiss and headed off for the vines.

"Oh, I almost forgot. Corky is trying to get ahold of you. They are a little short-handed in the tasting room."

Jack patted his pockets quickly and realized he didn't have his phone on him. Another sign of changing times.

"See you," Jack said as she left. Though they were still figuring out what exactly their relationship was, Jack and Megan could at least admit to themselves what everyone at the winery had known for a decade—that they were wildly in love with each other and were the only person that the other could tolerate.

Jack finished his water and tossed the bottle in a recycling bin, enjoying the moment of solitude. He walked across the road to the winery's main building. It was a two-story, mission-style construction with the tasting room on the main floor and winery offices above. There was a large patio they'd put in about two years ago, using much of the money Jack had from the Andelić job (he'd told people it was a divesture from an old business venture). The patio was a wide semi-circle of dark granite with a low wall, about three feet tall, that separated it from the parking lot. There was a roof of reclaimed wood, built in a ramada style, over the patio with slowly turning ceiling fans.

Jack cut a quick path through the outdoor tasting area. It was a Saturday, and they had a good crowd today. He greeted a few guests, recognizing a few regulars and club members. Jack also made a point to seek out some new faces to welcome them as well, introducing himself as Frank Fischer. Megan knew Jack's real name, knew that "Frank Fischer" was a cut-out, and when Jack first told her, about eight years prior, it was an obvious (and understandable) fracture in their relationship. But, over time, she'd come to understand why he chose to keep those lives separate and decided that it was simply part of the package.

So long as Gentleman Jack Burdette stayed retired.

She called him Jack in private and Frank everywhere else, and she didn't seem to mind the duality.

"Hey, boss," a jovial voice called from behind a counter in the center of the tasting room. He had a round face, bright eyes, and steel-colored hair.

"Corky," Jack said, smiling. Corky was a nickname he'd picked up while serving in the Air Force. He'd never explained to Jack what it meant, just that Jack wouldn't get the story. Corky was one of their first employees. Originally, he'd worked part-time, just looking for something to do now that he'd retired from the military, but eventually he promoted to running the tasting room and now was in charge of all hospitality operations and the wine club.

He diverted his attention momentarily to pour a tasting flight for a small group of customers at counter. "This is our Osprey, which is our Cabernet that we grow here on the estate. Our wines get warm sun throughout the growing season, but the marine layer comes in at night and cools everything off, which really helps the grapes rest and produce more sugar. You should pick up blueberry, black cherry, and a little chocolate on this one." Corky turned back to his boss. "If you have twenty minutes, could you do the tasting for that couple at the end of the counter? Jenny is outside helping, and they're both double-covered. I tried to get someone from Megan's team to help pour, but she yelled at me."

Jack laughed. He scanned the bar behind Corky for what was open and interesting, not necessarily what matched their scripted tasting. Jack sold more wine on the stories behind the bottles than he did talking about tannin or flavor profiles. Jack also grabbed a glass for himself. It took him a couple trips back and forth to get everything set up.

"Hey, folks," he said with a wide, genuine smile. "My name is Frank Fischer, and welcome to Kingfisher. I'm sorry you had to wait a little. If you don't mind, we're going to go off-script a bit, and I'm going to share some of my favorites with you..."

Jack put the thoughts of diamonds and urgency out of his head. He didn't know why he stressed about it as much as he did. The one thing he could take comfort in was at least he and his partners were all on the same page.

Wait it out until they had time to make the right play. This wasn't the sort of thing you should rush.

TWO

Lago Maggiore, Italy

The son of a bitch lived well, but this was not a home for a thief.

There were far too many windows and too many blind corners.

The house itself was two-story Mediterranean style, the color of an unripe peach. It was built on a terrace that overlooked Lago Maggiore from the west. The home was long and somewhat narrow, with the main living and dining areas extending out in a curved fashion that must have afforded incredible views of the lake. From where Enzo crouched beneath the stone arches surrounding a covered patio beneath the curved part of the house and facing the lake, he could see a small pool. A waist-high iron fence ran the length of the lawn. It was hard to tell because it was dark, but Enzo guessed it was a straight fifty- or seventy-foot drop from there. There was a steep slope and more trees that all spilled toward the lake. There was a Z-shaped stone staircase that led down to a dock. It was lit, but not well.

Vito at least had security spotlights installed down below that shone up from the lake level.

Enzo guessed the house was at least forty years old, perhaps more.

The neighbors were close. Vito's property butted up against them on both sides. The house next to Enzo, a yellow villa about half the size of Vito's home, was dark and had the look of a vacation property. The one on the other side, Enzo hadn't gotten a good look at. There were trees between them and a bit of a gap, but he could still jump from Vito's wraparound balcony to the other one. Even at his age.

Earlier that day, Enzo had driven by to get a look at the front. The house was built on the strip of land between the road and the cliff, along a two-lane north-south road that ran along the lake. Vito's driveway was about as long as a stubbed-out cigarette, just enough room to pull in and enter the gate code. If the police or any of his enemies showed up one day, the only fast egress Vito would have was by boat, and even then, it required running through the house, exiting the patio, navigating those stone steps (God only knew what they'd be like in the rain) and then down to the boat at the dock.

All that to say, it was a bad house for a thief.

It was a house for a man who didn't think he could be found.

Enzo had been staking it out for two days.

It rained off and on throughout the afternoon and the sky was still thick with dark clouds, creating a velvety blanket around the area that seemed to absorb all light. He'd made his way along the lakefront starting around eleven that night, and once he'd determined that Vito didn't have any security cameras or motion sensors down here, Enzo snuck through the bushes to the stone staircase and quickly ascended, finding more than enough shadow. The house had been designed to maximize the views of the lake with as little obstruction as possible. So far as Enzo could tell, there was nowhere in the house one could actually see the stairs that descended to the water. Once he was up there, he moved along the rounded stone exterior to the covered patio and made sure that Vito wasn't having a late-night swim or a cocktail.

There were exterior lights here, which appeared to be more for decoration than security, but none of them were on. Enzo had seen

Vito leave and return earlier that day. Enzo wanted to follow him, but he wasn't practiced in tailing people and knew his limitations. That was hard enough to pull off with a single car, harder still in an off-season resort town. When he'd driven by the house earlier, Enzo slowed to make sure that Vito's two cars were still there. One was a black Maserati Levante, the automaker's luxury, high-speed SUV. The other was a Ferrari 246 Dino GTS in metallic midnight blue. The Dino was the first car that Ferrari produced in large numbers, and most aficionados believed it was one of the finest sports cars produced in the 1970s, with its sweeping and elegant curves. The car looked like a high-end escort. An interesting choice for someone with a nearly unlimited amount of money to spend. Or would have, once he could get access to it. Between the house and the cars, Enzo was beginning to wonder whether Vito had found a buyer.

Once he was sure it was clear, Enzo moved to the iron gate that led to the house. It was locked, but he picked the lock and opened the gate in less than ten seconds. The metal door was old and needed oil. When you were trying to be silent, every noise sounded like a scream, and this one sounded like a particularly aggrieved, unquiet dead. Enzo slid through the gate and closed it but didn't engage the lock, just in case he needed a fast exit. There was an actual door on the other side of the gate, and at least this one had a high-quality lock. That took Enzo about twenty-five seconds.

There was no security system. No cameras, no wires.

The absence of a security system didn't surprise him. Last thing a professional thief wanted was a device that sent a signal to the cops, but Enzo didn't understand the lack of cameras.

With the tools he carried, tightly packed in his backpack, Enzo could have made it through most home security systems, though the serious, professional-grade ones were beyond his ability. Enzo's speciality was safes, and there were few better than he.

There were no lights on in the house, and Enzo couldn't see a damn thing in the hallway. There were no windows. His eyes were semi-adjusted to the dark already from being outside, but this was like staring into deep space. Enzo waited a few more moments, breathing slowly and quietly to calm his heart rate, but it was hard standing here in a dark hallway with no cover.

He had no idea of the layout of Vito Verrazano's house, no idea where a safe might be.

Jack normally planned these things, worked out the details. Enzo's job was the safes; the rest he left up to others.

Left up to Jack.

He wished his friend were here, was sorry that he wasn't. But Jack wouldn't listen to reason. And he was dead wrong to let these diamonds just sit here in Vito's safe for two years. Maybe Jack was right and it would be very difficult, almost impossible, for Vito to move them, but "almost impossible" wasn't certainty. The hardware in the driveway suggested that. Enzo knew he should have done this a long time ago. They'd waited way too long in trying to figure out a way to get the diamonds, and every day that ticked by was one more that said Vito Verrazano was going to find a buyer. You didn't do something like he did on a whim.

But always with Jack was, "We gotta wait."

Jack, he couldn't trust something that he couldn't control himself. If *he* couldn't be here to plan the job himself, move the stones himself, then none of them were going to fucking do it. That kind of meticulous attention to detail probably kept them both out of prison over the years, but it hadn't done them any good in a situation that none of them saw coming.

Worse, Enzo feared what was really happening was that Jack was losing his edge.

So, Enzo took the decision off the table.

He was going to steal them back from Vito. Jack would be pissed, fucking furious, no doubt, but when Enzo handed him a six-pound bag of goddamn diamonds in a few days, Jack would forget all about being angry.

Focus, Enzo told himself. There was a door to his left and a hallway to the right. He doubted the safe would be down here, and he could discount the doors to the right. There's no way Vito would put a safe in a ground-level room with a window. Enzo tried the door handle next to him. It was unlocked, so he pulled the door open just enough for him to slide through. The room inside was cold and completely, utterly black. He paused several long seconds, listening for breathing. Hearing nothing, Enzo took out his penlight and turned it on. He'd dialed in the lowest setting beforehand. The tight beam of light revealed a wine cellar.

Not a bad place for a safe, honestly, if it wasn't so close to a door. Still, it was worth a look.

The wall to his left curved outward in a semicircle, following the contour of the exterior wall. Wine racks, mostly full, lined the walls, and there was counter, boxes stacked on top. Enzo moved over and checked the counter and the cabinets, testing for false bottoms or back panels. Even with the low light, he determined quickly that Vito wasn't stashing anything here but Tuscans. It didn't follow, anyway, with no lock and it being steps away from an exterior door, but with no advance intelligence on the job, Enzo had to be thorough. Satisfied, he turned the penlight off, slithered out the door, and closed it behind him.

With his eyes fully adjusted now, Enzo could see the fuzzy outline of the staircase leading up to the main floor. He was grateful to find it was tile. That wouldn't creak like wood. Slowly, inexorably, Enzo made his way up the stairs. He moved cautiously, pausing every few steps to listen for signs of movement. Hearing nothing, he continued. The top of the staircase was a rectangle of dark gray light; the windows on the main floor must be open.

Enzo paused at the top of the stairs to listen again. Hearing nothing, he crept into the hallway. There was an open door directly across from him. Even in the darkness, Enzo could discern the depth and size of the room, could see the large bed in the center of it. This would be the master. The bed was empty and looked made. On the far wall, there was a glass door that opened to a balcony that faced the lake. The curtains hung by the side of the window, silent guardians.

A bedroom was a common location for a home safe. People wanted the psychological security of having their treasured property close to them. In America, he knew, it was just as common for them to be built into the floor and hidden by carpet. Not in Europe, however, where floors tended to be tile and covered by rugs rather than wall-to-wall carpet. No, Vito Verrazano would have a wall safe or a larger standing model, though Enzo found that unlikely. Most thieves tended not to advertise that they had something to hide.

The walls in the master bedroom were spartan. Either Vito didn't spend a lot of time in here or didn't value decoration. The point was that there wasn't anything on the walls that would hide a safe. Enzo turned from this room, dismissing it for now, and continued down the hallway. He paused at the next door, this one on his left, which meant that it would also face the lake. The next room down the hall would be the floor's main living area. There was no door, and Enzo could see the dark gray half-light drifting into the hallway, giving some ghostly shape to the larger room beyond.

Enzo paused again to listen, and he heard no sound but his own breathing. He should've at least heard Vito sleeping, passed out in a chair or something, if he wasn't in his bed. But there was nothing. Enzo was starting to get concerned now because he'd staked out the front of Vito's house for several hours and saw no sign of the son of a bitch. Enzo sat, parked in the driveway of a vacation home that he knew was unoccupied, until night fell. Vito's lights went out a little after ten, and Enzo assumed that meant he was going to bed.

All that said there should be some sign of Vito Verrazano in the house, but Enzo found none.

Maybe Vito went out for the evening? Called for a ride instead of driving? Was it possible to leave in the time it would take for Enzo to make it from the front to where he'd accessed the shoreline? If so, that meant Vito could be home at any time.

You're spooking yourself, he scolded himself. The mind had a way of playing tricks when you were creeping around a place that you weren't supposed to be.

Enzo could practically hear Jack lecturing him about already being in this place too long, about never doing a job in someone's house and sure as hell not while they were in it. Or if you didn't know for certain when they'd be home. He could hear Jack saying, "This is why we're not burglars."

Well, doing it Jack's way got us into this.

The door was closed, so Enzo grasped the handle, the metal cold to his touch. He turned it slowly, and the sound of the lever disengaging was like spring-loaded thunder in the silent house. Enzo pushed the door open and slid inside, closing the door behind him but not all the way.

This was where it would be.

The room was small, with a floor-to-ceiling bookcase running from the door to the far wall. Vito had a small writing desk next to the glass door that, like the bedroom, led out to the patio that wrapped around the semicircular portion of the house. There was a patterned rug on the floor, for which Enzo was grateful because it would mute some sound. There was a painting on the wall behind the writing desk, which would be large enough to conceal something, but Enzo decided to start his search with the bookcase. The bottom row was a series of small built-in cabinets. Enzo knelt down, chose the center cabinet, and opened it.

And there it was.

Enzo retrieved his penlight and inspected it.

The safe filled the cabinet, which suggested that the bookcase was built around it. The sides of the safe were flush with the cabinet, and Enzo figured he could slide a few pieces of paper between the safe and the cabinet but little else. It would be anchored to the back wall with masonry screws and a plate. He couldn't tell the make or model; the manufacturer's branding didn't appear on the exterior, not that it mattered much. The safe was a traditional dial-combination entry. Enzo never trusted electronic safes. There were techniques to figure out which buttons were pressed most often, and from there it was a relatively simple process of determining what the right combination was. Which one usually got from some basic research about the target—most of the time it was a meaningful date or other number. It was actually amazing the number of people that had their combination written down and stashed in a desk drawer so they wouldn't forget it. There were newer models that incorporated biometric security, such as fingerprints, but those too could be spoofed. That was a more involved process and usually required being able to lift a fingerprint off another surface. Enzo had the capability to do that, but it was messy and time-consuming. Most home safes were designed to protect against run-of-the-mill burglars, not safecrackers.

Enzo shrugged his backpack off and set it on the rug next to him. It was a tactical-style pack that allowed him to access the contents while it was lying flat. Enzo's tools were organized by type and secured to the interior in pouches with MOLLE webbing.

Given enough time and force, any safe could be opened. What separated licensed safecrackers from thieves was time, noise, and ambient lighting.

And permission, Enzo noted ruefully.

On that latter score, this was an admitted gray area, since Enzo was just stealing back something that was his and his friends' already.

Enzo's tool kit was as simple as his approach. There were no high-tech gadgets to use, no computers, no plasma torches (not that one would fit in his bag, but he knew people that used them). Somehow, he'd known Vito wouldn't have an electronic safe, wouldn't trust it. That was wise. The irony was, the more technologically advanced a lock was, the more tools there were to crack it. That theory had upper limits, of course, but for what even a wealthy person could afford to put in their home, it didn't. The tools were a safety net in case he couldn't open the safe by hand. If he was forced to use a drill, he'd first need to find and subdue Vito so that he would be free to make noise. As much as Enzo wanted to tie Verrazano up and make him watch, Enzo knew revenge moves were stupid and only gave you away.

For this, Enzo would just use touch.

Which was not to say it was fast.

It took him about twenty minutes—longer than normal because he was working in the dark—to be sure that he had all of the numbers. Then it was another five to get the correct number of spins in each direction before disengaging the lock. The fastest way would be an acetylene torch, which technically was portable, but it wasn't the kind of thing one could sneak easily. Enzo wouldn't risk using that unless he knew that Vito wouldn't be home. There would be no mistaking the sound, or the smell, when it was powered on.

The silence in the house was deafening.

Enzo's pulse pounded and his heart raced, nearly drowning out anything else he might hear.

He could feel the last tumbler fall into place, and he rotated the dial back to zero. On this model, he'd learned that you had to turn past zero one full rotation before coming to a stop and then opening. If he was found, it would be then. In a quiet house, there would be no mistaking the sound of pulling the handle down and opening the safe door.

Enzo paused. He wasn't sure if he heard something or not, but the hairs on the back of his neck raised up. He reached over and quietly retrieved the compact Beretta he'd stashed in the pack. The gun was clean; Rusty had gotten it for him on a previous job. Enzo had driven here, all the way from his home in Calabria on the southern tip of Italy, so that he could bring the gun and his safe-cracking gear. Those sorts of things tended to draw attention at airports.

Before he opened it, Enzo made one last check for wires around the safe, trying to determine if there was a secondary alarm on it. He'd checked once before, but best to do so again. Finding none, he proceeded with the final step.

Enzo rotated the dial, and the lock disengaged. He knew it was his imagination telling him that the sound was thunder, but it still sounded goddamn loud to him. He pulled the handle down, which also sounded like a cacophony, and opened the door.

He had to bite back the words, the spiteful *gotcha* phrase he wished Vito would hear him say. To know Enzo had gotten the better of him, had gotten him back. Had equalized.

He paused again, listening for any movement in the house in response to the safe opening. Enzo patted the gun, just to reconfirm its location again in his mind's eye. He didn't think he heard anything, but it was so eerily quiet in that house, he felt like he was hearing nothing rather than there being nothing to hear. Enzo took in a shallow breath and shone the light into the open safe.

It was empty.

That was when the lights came on in the room.

THREE

Jack liked to stay late at the winery, particularly during the summer and early fall, before the rains started. When the lights were off, looking above the inky outlines of the Mayacamas, the heavens opened up and it seemed as if you were staring directly out into space. It was breathtaking and incredible. Jack relished the solitude.

Though it was quite warm during the day, the temperature fell quickly when the sun went down. Jack pulled a black leather bomber jacket on for his usual evening walk through the vineyard. Jack poured a small glass from one of their tasting bottles and stood near the barn, looking out at the rows of vines. They were now just dark shapes against a background of darker shapes. His phone jangled—a different tone than the standard ringtone, this one sharp and jarring.

This would be a call through the encrypted messaging app Jack, Enzo and Rusty used to communicate safely.

Jack checked the phone. It was Rusty. It would be early morning in Switzerland.

"Hey, Rusty," Jack said. "What's up?"

"We have a problem."

Jack was in the middle of asking the obvious reply when Rusty simply continued.

"I got an alert on an old bank account that you and I used to use. It wasn't one that I set up for you, but you used to pay me from it."

"Wait. How did you get an alert on one of *my* bank accounts?" Jack had anonymous accounts tied to shell corporations or false identities in banks across the globe, dozens of them, if not more. Most of them he hadn't bothered closing down because they would be impossible to trace back to him.

"After the Carlton job, when everything started going sideways and you figured out Reginald was working against you, I created a back door into the offshore accounts that I knew about. Once we figured out that Reginald was an informant, I was concerned that he might have given some of that information up to the authorities."

Anger welled up inside him, and Jack bit back words. This was wrong and a complete betrayal of trust. Not the action itself—that was smart. It was the fact that it was almost a decade later and he was just hearing about it now. Jack had worked with Rusty for a number of years leading up to the Carlton InterContinental heist in 2013, but it was strictly professional and transactional. When Jack needed something—a clean car, a weapon, a way out, he'd call Rusty. He'd paid for the services rendered with a wire transfer from one quiet account to another. Their relationship had been professionally distant for years. It wasn't until Reginald double-crossed him and Jack knew that he needed help that he brought Enzo and Rusty in. Though Jack and Enzo went back almost twenty years at that point, Rusty was more of a business associate at the time. Their friendship didn't develop until later. Jack was furious that Rusty would do that without telling him. Even angrier that he never figured it out.

Or thought to check. There would be time for that later. First, he needed to understand what exactly the problem was that Rusty called him about.

"Jack, Reginald is the only person I know of who had access to that account. He created the dummy corporation that set it up."

"But he's still in prison," Jack said. "His sentence is barely halfway through."

"No. He's out *now*."

"What?"

"I just found this out. He was moved to a minimum security prison in 2018 and then released the following year on parole. I started digging into this when I got the alert on the account. According to court documents, given his age and status as a 'model inmate,' Reginald was deemed to pose no further threat to the public."

"He's been out of prison for two years and we didn't know," Jack said. Whatever anger he felt toward Rusty faded well into the background as he tried to process what he'd just learned. Reginald LeGrande was free. He'd been sentenced in 2014 for fifteen years for embezzlement and passport fraud.

Rusty continued. "The bank account was registered to a Consolidated Holdings International. Someone just dropped a hundred and fifty thousand dollars into it and used that to charter a plane from Rome to Los Angeles. I've been up since about four tracking this down. Once I saw the transaction in the account, I called the company, Cirrus International Aviation, to confirm the flight. Told them it was a security measure." Rusty paused to give Jack a chance to ask questions, but he didn't have any. "The customer is Vito De Angeles and two other passengers, Tommaso Benedetti and Lucio Greco. So, the question is, why is Reginald LeGrande using a shell corporation to charter an airplane from Italy to the United States? I think I know the answer to this, but I'll let you have the honors."

Jack exhaled. He turned and began walking back to the tasting room. It was the only light in the murky indigo of the long dark matte painted by the mountain's shadow and the drooping black oak trees that surrounded the property. "Vito De Angeles is obviously our Vito." Having lived and worked so long with aliases, Jack understood the psychology all too well. The hardest part was getting the first name down, because you're conditioned your entire life to go by that.

It took Jack years of practice, and at one point, he actually studied method acting, of all things. A common trick that criminals used when working with false identities was to only change the last name so that they would reduce the risk of an accidental slipup. "Because Reginald and Vito know each other," Jack said finally. "They worked together as far back as the eighties. They were on the Knightsbridge job together."

"Knightsbridge?" Rusty said. "I'm not familiar with that."

"In 1987, a crew tunneled into a security deposit in Knightsbridge in London. They had someone on the inside who helped out with security. They made off with something close to a hundred million. I think Reginald and Vito each got about fifteen. Most of the crew was rounded up within months, but Reginald and Vito played it smart. Reginald told me they knew the other guys were a little shaky, his phrase for 'untrustworthy.' So, he and Vito stashed their money somewhere in London and left. Everyone else started spending money like crazy, and that's how they got pinched. Anyway, Reginald and Vito worked together on and off for the next couple of years. After a job we did went south in '95, Reginald bought me a plane ticket and sent me to Italy to study under Vito. That's how I ended up in the School of Turin." Jack walked across the patio, now cold and dark, and back into the glass-walled tasting room. He went to the counter and refilled his glass. He had a feeling this was going to be a long night.

"What happened to the Knightsbridge money?"

"I don't know. Reginald never told me how or if he got it. The reason they left it in the first place was they couldn't figure out how to smuggle the cash out of the country. Vito never admitted it, but I always assumed he moved it out by boat between England and one of the countries on the other side of the channel, then drove back to Italy. Maybe they figured out a way to launder it in London, that's always possible. I don't know."

"But if Vito stiffed him thirty-some years ago, why work with him now?"

"We don't know that Vito did. Reginald never told me about it. I assumed that's what happened, because when I asked them both, they told me not to ask. If that is true, could be this was a way to make up for it. Whatever they may have had against each other in the past, they've still got one thing in common. They both hate me more than anything." Jack leaned against the counter and took a deep drink. "If they are working together, this looks more and more like a long con. Vito convinces me he's been living hand to mouth for twenty years and that he *just* figured out where Bartolo hid the diamonds. We help him get the stones out of the bank and into the open, and then Vito steals them from us."

"Then Reginald helps him bring the diamonds to the US to sell them? I don't know, Jack, that seems like a long shot. The diamonds are in Europe now, and that's where half of the gray market is."

"That's true, but Vito doesn't have the connections with them. That's the one thing he told us that I do actually believe. Reginald wouldn't risk traveling abroad. He was convicted of passport forgery, among other things, and will assume he's on a watch list."

"He could slip in and out of the country pretty easy on a decent fake," Rusty said, challenging the logic. "You know that better than anyone."

Jack closed his eyes and thought. He knew Reginald very well. They'd worked together for so many years, Jack felt he had a good sense of how Reginald might try to play this. Jack knew how *he* would do it.

"Reginald just finished his second stint in prison and got out legally. He's not going to take the risk and travel abroad. Also, after being inside for six years *and* a snitch jacket, no one he used to know will talk to him ever again." Jack paused. *Think, Jack. Think.* He snapped his fingers. "They're going to move the diamonds legally. Well, sort of." His mind was getting ahead of his mouth. "The only reason to bring them to the States is they are going to try to sell them on the legitimate market. They'd just need to make themselves look like diamond brokers, which wouldn't be that hard to do—a website and some bogus incorporation paperwork? Importing gems into the US is so shockingly simple that most smugglers never think about it. You don't even pay taxes on gems coming in. As long as you have import paperwork, which can be faked, it's not that hard. Once they're inside...in my experience, most buyers will look the other way, or at least not ask questions." Jack stopped for a minute and tried to catch up with his thought process. "We also have to consider that these diamonds have been out of the news for twenty years. No one has stolen an amount like this, except for what I did in Cannes, and that was eight years ago. I doubt a buyer is going to question it if they can come up with a convincing enough provenance. They won't have thought that anyone could steal this many diamonds."

Rusty was quiet for a time, and Jack could hear him typing. "But how do they get them in the country? You keep them here in Europe, we have way more bulk diamond buyers than they do in the States, and it's a lot easier to smuggle them across borders. How do you sneak six pounds of diamonds on an airplane?"

Jack had never tried to move stolen gems in the United States, but he had to assume gem buyers the world over were much the same. Consumer appetite for previous stones was nearly insatiable and too often, buyers simply looked the other way or just didn't ask a lot of pointed questions when they were acquiring them. Except for those that were part of single supply chain distributors, some portion of the diamonds and other gems that were sold in Europe and Asia had, at one point, been stolen.

"That part is also not as hard as you might think, which is not to say that it's easy. But I've done it." Well, to be specific, Jack set it up for someone else to do. But when he was working steadily in Europe, he employed any number of methods to sneak his stolen goods across borders. One of the most successful had been to have a hardshell carrying case for sensitive and fragile equipment, such as cameras, modified with small lead-lined compartments that followed the contours of the case. On the airport X-ray, it looked just like the case walls. "Just speculating, I would guess Reginald would fall back on one of the techniques I used back in the day. *He* never moved anything himself. Alternatively, I suppose Reginald could have someone in Customs, but that seems highly unlikely. He did go up for forgery, so maybe he found a way to doctor an import certificate."

"This all seems like a long shot to me, Jack," Rusty said. "I get all of the things you're saying, but it seems like the risk of bringing these diamonds into the States would be too high. And there just aren't that many places that can or *would* do an eighty-million-dollar acquisition. I'm reading right here most of the big transactions happen at a couple large trade shows, neither of which are in Los Angeles."

"Maybe they aren't thinking about one big push. I wouldn't. They could be holding onto them for a bit and selling them off in small chunks like we planned to. But let's say for the sake of discussion that they wanted to move them all at once. Major supply lines have been significantly disrupted, and production isn't nearly what it was eighteen, twenty-four months ago. Somebody shows up with a massive amount of stones like that, offering in bulk, as long as they look legit enough, that lets a small company not quite corner the market but make a significant dent. All of a sudden, they're on par with De Beers. You don't think that a businessman is going to hold back on some of the questions he might ask for a situation like that? There are multiple importers and wholesalers in LA's Jewelry District. One of the biggest trade shows in the world is in Tucson, which is only four or five months out. They could be doing the prep work for that now, using diamonds like flash money and establishing their bona fides."

"Okay, now that I believe."

Jack paused again, trying to put himself in Reginald's shoes. What would he do in this situation?

"Look, neither of these guys are young. They may not try one big push, but they are also not going to sell a handful a year for the next two decades. I think they are going to try and do this in a couple of big moves, taking whatever they can get, and live the rest of their lives burning money."

"What's our next move, then?"

"We need to figure out where Reginald is living now. If he was released from prison early, he's likely on parole. See if you can't figure out an address. We have to figure a way to flush these guys out into the open." Jack took the phone off his ear and looked for new messages. Still nothing. "Where in the hell is Enzo?"

FOUR

When the lights came on in the room, Enzo could see the outline of a man standing in the doorway in his peripheral vision, but he was too focused on staring at the empty safe to give it much notice. It wasn't until the man said, "Don't fucking move," that Enzo broke his gaze. His eyes, adjusted for the darkness, were burning in the bright light. They flashed over to the man, but he didn't move his head. He saw the barrel of a gun that the guy was holding about waist height.

Enzo's Beretta was on top of the black backpack next to him, with the bulk of his body blocking it from view. Enzo snatched up the gun in his left hand, cranked his body around, and brought his right hand up to meet it. He squeezed off a shot before the other man even knew what was happening. The bullet landed right in the middle of his chest. The guy pitched forward, making gurgling sounds like a broken drain. If the man wasn't dead yet, he would be soon. Enzo didn't have time for guilt. He pushed everything into the backpack and urgently zipped it, then threw it onto his back, keeping the gun in his hand. Then he was on his feet and stepping over the crumpled and moaning man, careful not to get the pooling blood on his shoes. Enzo didn't bother checking for a pulse.

He needed to find a way out of this house and needed it fast. The way he came in was no longer an option. There were too many choke points, and he didn't know if the stairs or the back door would be covered. That left the front. It was the more obvious route but closer to where he'd stashed his car. Enzo didn't know anything about the layout of the house but could figure it out based on where he'd been. He ran left down the hallway. The next room, the one adjacent to Vito's office, was a large living room that faced the lake, and the kitchen was at the end of the hall. He could see all of this because the lights were all coming on. Enzo didn't take the time to count them all, but there were a lot.

The house's entry foyer was on the right at the end of the hall, almost to the kitchen. Enzo was maybe twenty steps away. He looked up and almost froze in mid-stride. There was a man in the kitchen, dark suit and dark shirt, whose features looked like they'd been chiseled out of rock. But it was the eyes that almost stopped Enzo cold. They were blank voids, empty black pits without any feeling, any recognition of humanity. It was the face of someone who would simply and casually kill you without explanation or hesitation, because that was the next action to take.

Enzo was so focused on the hallway that seeing this person jarred him and he almost missed the movement at the man's sides, almost forgot that he too had a gun in his hand. Enzo stopped his run, skidding across the tile, and brought his pistol up. He snapped off three rounds without aiming and then dove through the doorway into the entry foyer. There were shouts behind him now, movement, chaos. He didn't even remember opening the door but now he was moving outside—then he stopped. He was staring across the gravel carport at the closed gate and something wasn't connecting in his brain, adrenaline and flight instinct was clouding out his ability to solve problems. Then Enzo smashed the controls for the gate and ran.

Enzo's car was about a tenth of a mile away, hidden down the road. He'd have stolen one of Vito's cars but he didn't see keys on his way out the door. Enzo dashed across the dark carport, gravel crunching under his feet. He was halfway across when the place erupted into light. Vito had floodlights on the carport and ground spots aiming at the house. All of them seemed to be aiming right at Enzo's eyes.

The first gunshot cracked the night.

Enzo made the gate, grabbed a bar, and whipped himself around, nearly slamming himself into a car parked there.

Enzo ducked low and aimed his pistol at the BMW's rear left tire. He fired once, hearing the serpentine hiss of air escaping after the gun's report. Contrary to popular belief, car tires didn't explode when shot; instead they leaked like any other puncture until they went flat. The tire would probably hold enough air to get them a little ways down the road but not much more than that. At least he'd cut his pursuers in half.

Angry voices entered the carport, orders hurriedly shouted. Enzo stood and broke into a full run, passing a second parked car. The road was a tree-lined two lane in the foothills overlooking the lake with barely any shoulder to speak of. The road looked like a smear of black paint on a dark blue canvas, and Enzo, also wearing all black, was running down it at full speed. He could only pray that he wasn't struck from behind by a passing car.

He ran.

The sounds of a chase mobilizing behind him, shouts and ignitions.

Enzo had parked his car in the darkness beneath a tree alongside the road, where it widened just enough to count as a shoulder. A passerby would think he was a guest visiting the house it was in front of. He'd scoped that place out and, like several of the homes along this road, seemed like vacation property and didn't appear to be occupied. On his initial ingress to Vito's house, Enzo had snuck through this yard and descended the slope to the lake front and then made his away to Vito's. He'd rented a boat the day before and examined the route from the water to make sure that it could be traversed on foot.

Enzo found his car, which was a black Alfa Romeo Giulia. He'd purchased it from a contact of his in Rome. The car was clean and registered with plates from Milan. At least that was one thing he'd done right. The car lit up as headlights painted it and he saw two pairs in the side mirror as he was climbing in.

So much for the easy way.

Enzo powered the car up and mashed the accelerator just as the two cars were about on him. The Alfa's wheels spun for a second before getting traction on the damp asphalt, but once they did, Enzo rocketed forward. And just in time. He continued accelerating, quickly pulling away from the two cars. The Giulia was Alfa Romeo's entry into the luxury sports sedan market, and while it was quick enough, he didn't think it'd be a match for what his opponents were driving. The one advantage Enzo had was the Via Mazzini was a more or less straight line that followed the contour of the lake, but it would be dangerous to get up to top speed. He'd be in the next town quickly, and there was always the possibility that, even this late at night, a car could pull out of one of the residences that lined the lake. He blasted past a copse of trees, and Lago Maggiore opened up on his right, a long dark blotch in the night, marked only by the absence of light. Boats floating on the surface looked like bodies in space. In the distance ahead, he could see the lights of the next town along the Via Mazzini as well as those on the other side of the lake. Trees were more sporadic now with more frequent pull-offs so that cars could access the beach.

Enzo was doing eighty, and the mottled darkness blended into a single long blur on either side. In his rearview, he saw the headlights from the lead car drift to the left, putting them in the oncoming traffic lane. They were going to try to get next to him. Enzo put a little more to the accelerator. His pursuer's headlights jumped back and forth, as though someone picked the car up and shook it. A dark grin broke Enzo's lips. Their back tire would be just about out of air and the driver was just now realizing what was wrong. Enzo's eyes jumped between the rearview and the road, watching the headlights quickly shrink to pinpricks of light, only to be replaced by the second pair. The second car accelerated quickly, and Enzo could tell it was most likely an Audi from the headlights.

The Audi jumped forward and slammed into the back of his car. They were trying to run him off the road. Jesus, who the hell were these guys? Enzo took the car up to ninety. There were no streetlights here, and if another car pulled out onto the road, he might not see it until it was too late. Having bumped him once, the Audi was now trying the same thing that the other car did before they lost their tire, which was to get up alongside him, presumably so that the occupants could open fire.

The next large city was Stresa, which was about four more miles up the road. Four miles until he'd have a road he could ditch onto and attempt to lose his pursuers. At these speeds, they'd be there quickly, but probably not fast enough for Enzo.

Headlights appeared in the oncoming lane, and the Audi's headlights snapped back to the right side of the road. Enzo saw the headlights of the approaching car drift over slightly, and he couldn't tell if it was a curve in the road or if it was coming into his lane. He didn't pay it any other thought; it wasn't a thing he could control. Seeing their opportunity, the Audi closed again, ramming the back of Enzo's Alfa again, trying to drive him off the road.

The frequency of lights on either side of the road increased, and he could see by the small cluster of brightness up ahead that they were approaching the next small town. Enzo knew from his recon during the daytime that there would be a large hotel on the left and a group of buildings huddled by the roadside, bars, small shops, and a marina on the right. The possibility of someone walking across the road from the bar to the hotel or a car pulling out was almost a certainty. Enzo closed on the yellow-orange glow of streetlights; houses were already on either side of the road. He didn't have long. The Audi tried accelerating to his side again. Enzo weaved the Alfa into the other lane, cutting them off and jerking his car back just in time as angry horns erupted. A car appeared in the oncoming lane, he hadn't seen it, or if he did, it didn't register in his mind.

Enzo could see the hotel perched on the hillside on the left side of the road, bathed in light. The road curved to the left, following the contour of the lake. He was going way too fast. Enzo tapped the brake to back the Audi off. It worked, but it was the kind of trick he could probably only pull once. He could see them start to accelerate again.

There!

He saw his shot.

Enzo slammed on the brakes, and he felt like an invisible hand was trying to pull him through the car's front windshield. He cranked the wheel over, and the car screeched into the parking lot across from the hotel. Enzo stood on the brake. The car fishtailed, the trunk swinging wide to the left. Enzo brought the wheel back around hard to the left, reversing the slide's direction. He'd slid most of the way across the parking lot now. The car rotated, so he'd whipped it almost a full one eighty, but the momentum was still pulling it along its original trajectory. Enzo dropped his foot on the accelerator, wheels spun, and he shot out of the parking lot. The maneuver worked. The Audi overshot him by the length of the building, maybe a little more. He looked to the right and saw them pulling off into another parking lot that was on the far side of this cluster of buildings. He could hear them braking, tires practically yelling in protest. Enzo saw his chance. There was a small residential road entry across the street. As long as this didn't dead end, it might be his chance to lose them. Enzo floored the accelerator, not even bothering to clear for traffic, and blasted across the road.

The residential street ran perpendicular to the road he'd been on and quickly turned into a steep hill climb before curving right to run parallel with the lakefront road. Enzo accelerated but kept it around forty, as this was an entirely unlit residential street with large houses on either side. He checked the rearview and saw no sight of the Audi.

Through breaks in the trees and gaps between houses, Enzo could see the lakefront road to his right. A connecting road appeared on his right but Enzo held course, taking this street to the end. It angled down again, and Enzo could see the dark expanse of the lake in front of him with the lakefront road running alongside.

Now he had a choice to make. Did his pursuers take the bait and think he backtracked, or were they heading for Stresa? He didn't see any headlights behind him. Enzo decided not to double back. His pursuers would most likely go back and collect the others from the car with the deflated tire. He pulled onto the lakefront road, now called Via Sempione Sud, and headed toward Stresa. Just as Enzo got into the northbound lane, a pair of Carabinieri vehicles blasted past him in the opposite direction, lights and sirens flashing. No doubt they were bound for Vito's house, responding to the calls of shots fired. Enzo drove the last few miles to Stresa at a more lawful pace. Now bathed in yellow street light, Stresa's white buildings and orange tiled rooftops stood out starkly against the darkness.

Stresa was a thousand-year-old resort town, built on a low sloping hill that gradually climbed up from the lake. Looking out across Lago Maggiore from its many docks or shoreline, as Enzo had done earlier that day, one could gaze out over the widest part of the lake, their view encompassing the tree-covered Alps on either side and ribbons of mountains disappearing into the distance.

Enzo's hands shook with nerves shot through with adrenaline. He forced deep breaths but that didn't help. What he wanted to do was to stop the car, get out, and try to calm down, but he didn't dare. Instead, Enzo slowed his speed to match the street signs in town and checked the rearview obsessively for headlights, signs of pursuit. It was late on a weeknight and Stresa was quiet but not empty, and for that he was grateful. Ahead, just beyond town, Enzo saw the island Isola Bella blazing with light from its massive palazzo. Enzo missed the street he was looking for and had to pull a U-turn. He didn't dare use the GPS on this car, which he would be cleaning and ditching as soon as he put enough miles between himself and Lago Maggiore.

Enzo guided the Alfa up into the mountains and from there along the long, curving roads to Carpugnino, where he picked up the southbound Autostrada.

Enzo accelerated beneath the long, tall streetlights that illuminated the highway. He had only questions.

FIVE

Enzo didn't know where to go, so he simply drove.

He was in Milan by midnight and took one of the ring roads around the city to pick up the A1 Autostrada heading south. There were no further signs of his pursuers. As the lights of Milan faded behind him and the land flattened, Enzo pulled into an AutoGrill. He purchased a panino and a coffee and then found a booth. The restaurants, ubiquitous on Italy's Autostrada, were roadside rest stops that served food, tourist items, books, wine, and God knew whatever else. The dining area was in the center of the building with a lime-green crescent-shaped booth that ran the length of the food court. There were a dozen square and circular tables in the center. Enzo set his tray down at an empty table in the middle part of the booth so that he could watch both doors. The rest stop was located in the center of the Autostrada so it could service travelers in either direction.

Enzo sipped his coffee, his nerves having finally settled. He tried a bite of the sandwich, but the queasy feeling of adrenaline crash prevented him from taking another.

He couldn't have fucked this up any worse if he'd actually planned to fail.

Already, he was dreading the phone call he was going to have to make to Jack and Rusty. It was going to be bad enough that he'd have to listen to Jack lecture him about not following the plan. Or about the twisted Schrödinger's Cat logic that only thieves possessed of how if Enzo hadn't opened the safe, the diamonds would still be there.

Enzo's mind started to calm and the adrenaline faded, allowing him to think straight. But that gave him no insight into who was in Vito's house. Who he shot. He didn't stick around long enough to check to see if that man was still alive; he'd have been shot himself or captured if he had. Self-defense.

But self-defense was still cold blood.

Whoever they were, they were in there looking for Vito Verrazano and the diamonds.

But that didn't answer the question of who they were. Enzo needed to get an idea of that before he spoke to Jack. If they knew about Vito and they knew about the stones, they probably knew where they came from. That meant they could very well know about Jack...and Enzo. He didn't see any recognition in the man's face before he shot him, but it wasn't like he had the time to stare him down before he shot him either.

Enzo looked up from his white-and-blue Lavazza cup, realizing it'd been too long since he'd checked the doors. He made a quick scan of the AutoGrill food court and didn't see any groups of men, didn't see groups of anyone for that matter. He counted four other people, and none of them looked like a threat. But it was too bright in here, and the two exits were on opposite sides of the building. Enzo had to keep an eye on both. Enzo wrapped up his sandwich in the wax paper it came in and went back to his car. As he exited the building and returned to the cool, damp night, Enzo's hand went to his waistband and the pistol he had jammed in it. The parking lot was almost empty, only a few large trucks. Enzo scanned as he walked to his car and didn't see a black Audi. He'd made sure to park his car away from others so he could easily tell if something was off.

Enzo crossed the distance to his car quickly, checking left and right as he did. He had his hand close to his right hip, inches from the gun. Seeing no traffic in the parking lot, Enzo cast a surreptitious glance back over his left shoulder at the restaurant. No one had followed him out. He unlocked the car when he was about five steps from it, close enough that he could make it in a sprint but not so far away that someone could beat him to it. Enzo pulled the gun from his waistband, climbed into the car, and sat down. He placed the Beretta and the panini on the seat next to him, locked the doors, and then powered up the Giulia. Enzo wasted no time accelerating out of the rest stop.

He put fast miles between himself and Milan.

Enzo pulled off the A1 at a cloverleaf just before the city of Parma and connected with the A15, which would cut across the country and eventually take him south along the western coast. Once he was on the A15, he drove again in silence for a time, but fatigue and adrenaline crash started to weigh on him. Even with coffee, he wasn't going to make it all night. He left the Autostrada and turned onto a smaller local road. Enzo pulled off, finding a place that looked like it had a wide enough shoulder. It was hard to tell in the dark. Enzo cracked his window for some fresh air and placed the Beretta at the small of his back. Then he reclined his seat as far as it would go and closed his eyes.

A PASSING CAR WOKE HIM.

Enzo was up with a jolt, right hand immediately going for the pistol behind his back.

A jittery hand held the weapon in a shaking grip. Enzo exhaled and set the weapon down on the seat next him. The sky was lightening but dawn had yet to break over the horizon. Enzo shivered. Both he and most of the car's surfaces were covered in dew. He got out and pissed in the dirt behind the car. He stood by the roadside for a time to get his bearings, moving to get blood and warmth back into his extremities. He'd parked on a low hill, and from here, Enzo could see a rolling pastoral valley with haphazard squares of farm tracts. Looked like a broken chess board. A line of low fog hung over the valley above dark green trees, lighter green grasses and the yellow-brown of harvested fields. In the middle distance, he could see the gray ribbon of the A15 cutting across the landscape.

Enzo was cold and damp, and his muscles ached from sleeping in the car. The full realization of what he'd done fell on him as he stood there looking out at that valley. Enzo had killed a man. It wasn't his first. But the first man, a Serbian thief named Ozren Stolar, deserved it, cold retribution for murdering two of Enzo's friends. A debt paid.

He didn't know who the man he shot in Vito's house was.

A criminal, probably. If he was a cop, there would have been lights and sirens on the chase. Just being a crook didn't mean he deserved to get shot. He'd also be employed by the kind of people that wouldn't stop looking.

Enzo supposed that he should feel some kind of solace that there seemed to be no other options, but he didn't.

The diamonds were gone.

Vito Verrazano was gone.

And Enzo had no clue about where either might be. Worse, someone else knew about those diamonds and was there waiting. The second Enzo popped that safe, someone was on him. Who else knew that Vito had those diamonds? Who knew Enzo was going there to get them?

Guilt and failure were overpowering and crushing feelings. Once the fury of the moment wears off, one is left with the knowledge that they did something *wrong*. The world becomes gray. The guilty can see colors, but it seems as though they are meant for someone else. The guilty can only observe.

Enzo breathed deeply. It was time to make a phone call.

JACK SAT at his dining room table hunched over his laptop. He had a yellow legal pad with scribbled notes next to it. Jack had the sliding glass door open that connected the house's central room with his patio. Night descended on Sonoma, what was left of the day was an echo of firelight on the horizon and a deepening ochre in the sky. There was an open bottle of wine on the table, left over from dinner. He drank intermittently throughout the night, something to keep him occupied, but Jack also needed to keep his mind sharp, so he was careful to pace himself. He was compiling a list of all the places he thought Reginald and Vito might be able to sell the diamonds in Los Angeles.

What initially seemed like a flash of inspiration, the critical unraveling of a puzzle, now seemed farfetched and out of reach. Anyone that would attempt to vet Reginald too deeply would figure out that he was lying. No legitimate business was going to enter into an eighty-million-dollar deal with someone without digging deeply into their past and fully validating their credentials. Was Reginald really able to create a convincing background and a shell company that stood up to that kind of scrutiny? Jack wasn't sure.

Jack had been in this business for a long time. For years, he'd sold stolen gems to brokers in the legitimate trade who didn't care about the provenance of the acquisitions. That was probably less common in the States, whereas it was practically rampant in Europe and Asia. Less common, but not impossible.

Jack sighed in frustration and pushed himself back from the table. This kind of circular thinking had been plaguing him ever since Rusty told him about the flight Reginald chartered. Jack regularly vacillated from, "I've got you, you son of a bitch" to "There's no way they do this." He knew it was because they were trying to divine Reginald and Vito's plan with only a single data point. For all Jack knew, Reginald had made a connection with the Mexican Mafia while he was in prison and was selling the diamonds to them. Los Angeles's criminal underworld had about the same level of diversity as the UN General Assembly, so it was also possible that any of Reginald's old connections in Eastern Europe had links there. The simple fact that they were smuggling the diamonds into the United States only meant that they had a buyer or buyers here. It said nothing about the legitimacy of them.

Jack's phone beeped.

The call was coming on their encrypted calling app. Enzo. Jack picked up and said, "Where the hell have you been? Rusty and I have been—"

"I know," Enzo interrupted. "I know. I'm sorry, look, we…we gotta talk."

"What's going on?"

"I…I fucked up, Jack." Enzo sounded tired. No, that wasn't quite right. He was worn down, his voice stripped bare to just the ability to make intelligible sound.

"What did you do?"

"I was tired of waiting. Two years is a long time, man."

"What did you do, Enzo?"

"I broke into Vito's house. I was going to steal the diamonds back. I figured that I'd just get them to a safe place and then you and me and Rusty could figure out what to do about it. It's just that—"

"The diamonds aren't there, and neither was Vito."

After a long pause, Enzo said, "How'd you know?"

"The reason we've been trying to get you on the goddamn phone, Enzo. Rusty figured out that Reginald used one of our old shell corporations to charter a private plane from Rome to Los Angeles. We think that he and Vito are working together again. Probably always were. So, they're going to smuggle the diamonds into the US somehow and try to sell them here." Jack paused. He stood up from his chair and walked over to the sliding glass door, which he closed and locked. Then he drew the curtains. Walking back to the table, Jack said, "Enzo, you said you fucked up. If Vito is on his way to the States, he wasn't there when you tried to break in, right?"

"He wasn't, but someone else was."

"Well, who?"

"I don't fucking know," Enzo half shouted, his tone going from half-dead to anxiously agitated with explosive surprise. "But they knew I was there, man. I staked his place out. I saw Vito in town, followed him back to his place yesterday afternoon, and I didn't see him leave. I waited until it was dark and went in the back. His house faces the lake. I crept along the shore and then up these stairs he has. The house is up off the water a bit on a kind of bluff. Broke in through a downstairs door, made my way upstairs, and found his office. The safe was in there. It was good but not great. I was through it in a couple minutes, but Jack, as soon as I was in there, and I mean *as soon as* the lights come on, there's this guy just standing over me. Tells me not to fucking move."

Jack stayed silent and worked very hard to control his temper.

Jack had known Enzo for a long, long time, and in some ways, Enzo was the only true friend Jack had. But they were talking about an amount of money that would push any bonds of friendship to the breaking point. Was Enzo telling him this just because he failed?

Enzo continued. "He never told me who he was. I had a gun with me, he didn't see it, and I shot him. He had a pistol in his hand, but I just got the drop on him. Him or me. I didn't check to see if he was still alive or not, I just grabbed my shit and ran. But there were guys all over that house. Like I said, they waited until I had the safe open to flip the lights and come at me. I don't know if they were following me or Vito. Maybe they picked me up in town that day, I don't know, but it felt like a trap."

"So somebody else knows that Vito had the diamonds," Jack said in a flat tone. He wasn't asking questions.

"Looks that way. My first guess was that he was trying to sell them to someone and they got tired of waiting too."

"We need to loop Rusty in." Jack removed the phone from his ear and keyed the function in their secure app to add another party to the call. Rusty picked up right away.

"Hey," he said in a blank, distracted voice. It wasn't quite six in the morning for either Rusty or Enzo.

"You up already?" Jack asked.

"Yeah," Rusty said. "I've been up for a bit. I'm trying to find any of the accounts that Reginald might be using and seeing if there is anything else that he's doing with this one. I see there's a black card associated with this corporation now."

"Rusty, I've got Enzo on the line with me."

Rusty, far more even-tempered than Jack, said nothing. If he was irritated that they couldn't get ahold of Enzo for a few days, he didn't show it.

"So, Enzo has some news," Jack said in a loaded tone, trying to force some levity into his voice, to break the tension that he felt. Enzo spent a few awkward moments explaining what he'd done, but this time it was a rambling, roundabout telling. Jack could sense the guilt Enzo was putting on himself for betraying their trust, ignoring the plan, and most likely tipping their hand to some yet-to-be identified party.

"That wasn't smart, Enzo," Rusty said in an almost clinical tone. Rusty and Enzo had known each other since the Carlton job eight years before, but their association was limited and strictly professional until they went in with Vito to steal Bartolo's diamonds from the Commerce Bank of Rome. With Jack in FBI custody, it was Enzo that secreted Rusty out of that Roman hospital where he was recovering from the pair of gunshot wounds Vito left him with. It was Enzo that got him out of the country and safely back to Switzerland, where he could hide out and recover. They'd developed a friendship then. Jack knew they'd seen each other a few times before the world went to hell in 2020. Rusty had flown down to Enzo's place in Calabria, and they'd spent a few days drinking and looking at the Med.

"Rusty," Jack said in a cautious tone, "Enzo has been raking himself over the coals over this, and I've given him my share. What we need to do now is figure out what we're going to do next."

"Yeah," Rusty said, clearly focusing on something else. "What does everyone know?"

Jack summarized it for them. "We think Reginald chartered a

private plane from Rome to LA, and they're going to use that to smuggle the diamonds into the US. Enzo confirmed that Vito and the diamonds are not at his house and someone else was there. We can speculate that whomever that was, they knew Vito had the diamonds and were there to get them. What we don't know is whether they were following Enzo or not. If they were, that means someone else knows we're involved."

Enzo said, "I've been racking my brain, and I can't figure out who that would be. The guy who confronted me spoke Italian. My first thought was it could be Anđelić or some of the other Pink Panthers, but the man was a native speaker."

"Jack, any idea on where they'd try to sell the diamonds?"

"We're totally shooting in the dark here. Our assumption is that Reginald is trying to sell this on the open market to maximize their profits. Now, most large transactions with precious gems happen at the wholesaler's office or at trade shows. There are several large ones each year, Tucson, Vegas, Los Angeles, and I think something in New York. But in those instances, people aren't usually bringing millions of dollars' worth of product into a convention center. They'll bring a small sample, and then the deal will be conducted elsewhere."

"So where do we find these wholesalers," Enzo asked.

"LA's Jewelry District. On the West Coast, that's where most of the action will be. Honestly, I'm surprised that they aren't trying to do this in New York City, but Reginald has never worked there and doesn't have any contacts that I know of."

"All right, what do we do?"

"How quickly can you both get to Los Angeles?"

"Jack, I'm not coming to the US, you know that." The details on Rusty's past were still vague despite all the years they'd known each other. Jack knew Rusty had been an FBI agent and was either forced out or quit because of some scandal. But Rusty had admitted when they were together last in Rome that he'd been a counterintelligence officer and an operation against the Russians had gone very, very wrong. Rusty, whose real name was Scott Donners, was a fugitive just for that. Special Agent Danzig had also identified him as far back as the Carlton job and then later tipped Rusty to the State Department's Diplomatic Security Service, who was now after him for passport forgery. If Rusty was ever captured, he was looking at two decades in prison, and that was if he found a particularly benevolent judge.

"Rusty, I know it's a lot to ask, but I'm taking risks here too."

"It's not—"

"It's not the same, you were about to say?" Jack said, tension and challenge rising in his voice. "I'm on fucking *parole*, Rusty. We're talking about stealing, *again*, eighty million dollars. If I'm caught, I go to jail forever. Look, both of you, the diamonds are here, or they will be soon. If either of you want to walk away, tell me now. Rusty, I haven't worked in the US in twenty-five years. I have no contacts here at all. If I was looking for a clean gun or a clean car, I wouldn't even know where to start. But I'll figure it out if I have to. We're all risking a lot here." Jack paused, took a moment to breathe. "If you want in, you need to be here when the job goes down. Otherwise, our partnership ends now. You'll still get your cut. No hard feelings, but I have to know what I have to work with. Think on it, and let me know by tomorrow." Jack regretted his tone a little, but the sentiment was the same. Jack had been traveling internationally since he was twenty-five years old and never once on a passport issued under his real name. He wasn't really interested in someone being afraid to do so now, not if they wanted to be a part of this. They all risked exposure and arrest.

This would be a dangerous and risky endeavor, even under the best of circumstances. Escape in Europe was relatively easy. National borders were, at most, only a few hours away, and that always added complexity to any pursuit. It was much easier to disappear. European police forces, even national ones, weren't nearly at the size and scale of their American counterparts. But to do this in the US was a different order of magnitude entirely. Jack would need a full crew and half a dozen specialties. They wouldn't have those things, of course—they had the three of them. But there was no way they could pull this off with Rusty operating from the other side of the world.

"You're not pulling this shit, Jack, not now," Rusty said, his tone uneven. "And you can't have it both ways. For two years we've been hearing that we can't go after the diamonds because *you* won't leave the country. Now that that's flipped and it's me taking the risks, it's okay. You don't get to do a job like this only on your terms. If we're going to do this, it's equal risk. You need to be all in. You need to be a goddamn *thief*. You can't do this and have a foot in both worlds."

"Obviously, I am," Jack said.

"Are you? Or are Enzo and I going to put ourselves out there, and then halfway into this you decide that it's too dangerous, you don't want to risk your other life, and you pull out."

"I wouldn't do that," Jack snapped back.

"Wouldn't you? You need to tell us both, right now, that you're a hundred percent committed. If it comes down to it, which one do you choose?"

SIX

"Would you like a drink, sir?"

"I thought you'd never ask," Vito Verrazano said, and he had a Campari and soda in his hand before the aircraft had completed taxiing to the runway. Vito dressed the part. He wore an off-white linen suit and a bright blue shirt, with a black pocket silk featuring white dots. He understood the Americans had some stupid rule about not wearing white or linen this late in the year, and he had also read that they don't drink Campari after August. The Americans added to the stupidity because it wasn't their drink to begin with. Then again, Vito was flying in on the kind of aircraft that would allow him to make the rules up as he went.

Reginald had chartered him a Gulfstream 650, and it was a magnificent aircraft. Soft Berber carpet and buttery soft leather seats, each with its own window that had the shape of a squashed grape. Vito was seated in a chair with a small table unfolded in front of him. The flight attendant gave him a card with the menu selection for his meal when she returned with his drink. Vito chose to sit by himself. His two companions, Tommaso Moretti and Lucio Bianchi, were hired security. They dressed the part as well, black suits and crisp shirts without neckties. Their weapons were in the checked baggage beneath the plane, but they had forged permits to carry them for when they arrived at US Customs as well as identification showing them as being licensed private security for a company that didn't exist. In reality, both of them were out-of-work bodyguards for a Turin-based mafia don that Vito used to work for named Alberto Longo, who had been gunned down recently (no fault of theirs), and so when Vito found himself in need of protection, he contacted Tommaso and Lucio to see if they'd like to make a million each for a few weeks of easy work.

Vito selected his meal and wine pairing and then relaxed into his seat, taking a sip of his drink. He was trying to appear much calmer than he actually was. There was a lot that could go wrong on this. First of all, he and Reginald hadn't spoken in fifteen years when first Vito contacted him about Bartolo's diamonds in 2019. Reginald was just getting out of prison, and Vito was afraid he wouldn't want to take any chances. Then he learned that it was Jack who put Reginald in there, and Vito knew he was in. But there was the matter of Reginald being fresh out of prison and several years out of the game. Reginald admitted that his contacts were gone or they wouldn't talk to him. Vito also knew from the street that Reginald had been an informant for a long time. He didn't care about that, that shit could be useful in the right circumstances, so long as Reginald understood where that left the two of them. Vito was taking no chances. If Reginald tried anything, Vito wouldn't hesitate to shoot him.

The next challenge was the passports and the customs paperwork. Reginald hadn't forged so much as a driver's license in ten years, and now he was going to get Vito and six pounds of finished diamonds through customs as part of a made-up diamond wholesaler company for them to be part of? Vito wanted Reginald to be on the flight with him so that he would be there when they cleared US Customs and Immigration, wanted Reginald to be responsible for bluffing their way through, but Reginald told him it was all handled. The Gulfstream had the range to go from Rome to Los Angeles, so all they'd need was an overflight permit, which the charter company got. Reginald said he had someone to handle the customs process when they landed. He'd be there and it wouldn't be a problem.

Reginald said he just needed Vito to play his part.

Reginald also said he had US Customs handled. The paperwork, he said, hadn't been very hard to doctor. Reginald would be waiting on the other side. They were flying into a small airport that frequently—and quietly—handled high-profile passengers. Six pounds of diamonds probably wouldn't be the strangest thing they'd see that day.

The story they'd concocted was pretty good, and Vito believed he could sell it. Their legend was that Reginald and Vito owned a diamond import business and were attempting to undercut the larger, established names. They had been able to get a very large quantity of finished stones in late 2019 and were poised to make a fortune when the global pandemic hit and the market fell out from under their feet. Now they were sitting on this literal fortune and had nowhere to take it. They were both heavily leveraged and were just wanting to make their investors whole, take care of their employees that they'd had to let go—about fifty people. It was just believable enough, which was all that mattered. The story meant that they weren't knowingly trafficking in stolen goods and it was the kind of thing they could tell themselves to justify it.

Reginald did not want to get into detail on the phone. All he said was that they had several meetings set up in Los Angeles and they weren't putting all of their eggs in one basket. But he was cagey on what, exactly, the baskets were and said he wouldn't provide any details until he saw the diamonds for himself. Vito understood that too, and it didn't upset him. Neither of them owed each other anything.

Reginald told him that he'd made connections and he didn't think it would take them long to move the diamonds. A disrupted market was a hungry market, and Vito didn't need Reginald's constant reminders that America's appetite for diamonds would never be satiated. He felt they had a good plan, but Vito wouldn't be certain of it until Reginald made good on his promises. And if he didn't, well, Vito had two mafia hit men with him, and they would even that particular score.

Trust only went so far in this business.

The flight attendant refilled his Campari and soda as he waited for dinner and the aircraft leveled off.

They'd cleared the first hurdle. The diamonds were on the plane, and the passports that Reginald had made for Vito, Lucio, and Tommaso had worked. Vito could push those specific stressors to the back of his mind.

Then there was the matter of whatever the fuck had happened at his house. The Carabinieri in Stresa contacted him yesterday saying that someone broke into his house and that there was a dead man found there. Did he have any idea who would want to break in or how a man came to be shot? Vito, as retired Fiat executive Romano Valentini, told them that he was out of the country on business and had no idea who would do such a shocking, horrible thing. The Carabinieri could be in touch with his attorney, however, to manage the details. Vito's attorney, Carlo, had been cooking documents for him for years and helped him buy off the judge in Turin all those years ago. Carlo was the one who made it look like Vito spent five years in prison when in reality he'd disappeared to the house in Lago Maggiore. Carlo could make this go away. Vito wasn't planning to return to that place, anyway. Carlo was supposed to arrange it to be put up for sale before all of this bullshit happened.

Vito didn't tell the Carabinieri this, of course, but he knew exactly who broke into his house.

It wasn't an easy thing to sit on six pounds of diamonds for any length of time, but two years was interminable. When the world turned to shit and Italy, in particular, appeared to be leading that charge, Vito found himself in a dark place. A year ago, he and Reginald had a plan to move these stones, but that plan quickly fell apart. Neither of them knew if they'd survive or what the world would look like on the other side. So, Vito started working on a backup plan. He contacted Salvatore Cannizzaro and said he had a large score that he needed help moving. Vito had known the don from the old days, back when Salvatore's father ran the organization and they moved from Sicily to Rome to take advantage of the power vacuum there. They'd always been cordial, and Don Cannizzaro was happy to hear from him. The don told him he would look into it, would get back to him. Vito knew it was risky and, on a level, stupid. It was, after all, Salvatore Cannizzaro's bank that they'd stolen the diamonds from in the first place. Not that the don had any idea that there had been a hundred million in diamonds in his safe-deposit vault.

The don came back with an offer. He could move the score and take them all at once; for this, he generously offered twenty-five million. That was a fortune by any measure, though a fraction of their market value. The only thing was the don told him they had to wait until the world cleared up and it was safe to travel again. Vito never actually accepted or rejected the terms, but to Don Cannizzaro's mind, he'd made a gracious offer and therefore, the deal was done.

The don must have gotten tired of waiting for Vito to get back to him and decided to come get the stones himself. Well, that was fine. Don Cannizzaro couldn't affect things on the Amalfi coast, let alone in Los Angeles, so Vito wasn't worried about reneging on the deal. The don had called several times that day, but Vito hadn't answered. And wouldn't. In fact, he didn't even have that phone anymore. Vito didn't understand how one of the don's people came to be shot and killed in his house, however. That part didn't make any sense. But as far as he was concerned, it was now Carlo's problem to sort out. Vito had no intention to return to Italy after this.

Either way, Reginald didn't need to know about whatever happened back home. That was Italy, and Italy was the past.

Vito nursed the bottle he had with dinner over the course of the rest of the flight. He needed to be lucid when they cleared customs. He switched to coffee and water for the last hour before they landed in New York to refuel. They were ushered off the plane and into a private lounge, where they waited until the plane was ready. Tommaso slept most of the flight, and Lucio watched movies. Vito didn't think that either of them had ever been on a plane before. Lucio spoke English, though it was heavily accented, and Tommaso only spoke Italian, so Vito would have to interpret for them as they went through customs and immigration, though according to Reginald, that was all happening in a private lounge. They wouldn't have to go through the process like everyone else because it was a private plane and because they were importing diamonds. One of the reasons that Reginald selected the Van Nuys Airport just north of Los Angeles was that was where many of LA's elite flew their private planes out of, the movie stars, the rock stars, the athletes. Customs was a little more...forgiving there.

Somewhere over the vast swath of mottled greens and browns that made up the central United States, Vito slept.

Vito was shaken awake by a violent jolt, and it felt like God had slapped the aircraft himself. The pilot came on the intercom and explained that they would be experiencing a difficult landing because of turbulence from the Santa Ana winds, which he apologized for. He asked the flight attendants to take their seats for the remainder of the flight. True to his word, it was not smooth. But it was over quickly, and Vito tried to occupy his mind by watching them descend below the mountains that flanked the airport. They looked like someone had crumpled a giant piece of green-and-brown paper and then attempted to smooth it out.

The Gulfstream touched down, and the flight attendant welcomed them to Los Angeles. The pilot and copilot stood in the doorway, uniforms still crisp, and thanked them for flying as well. Both of the pilots had short, styled hair, dark tans, and square jaws and looked like recruiting-poster fighter pilots. Vito emerged from the aircraft and was immediately hit by the blast-furnace heat of an LA afternoon. Vito first found his sunglasses and then descended from the aircraft. There were two more flight attendants at the bottom of the stairs. They hadn't been on his flight, but they looked just like the ones who had served him the last thirteen or so hours—beautiful, elegant in their navy-and-white uniforms that showed just enough skin to edge the line between provocative and professional. "Thank you for flying with us, Mr. De Angeles. Welcome to Los Angeles. I guess you'll be right at home with a name like that."

"Buona sera, my dear," Vito said and smiled, then took her hand and kissed it. The flight attendant blushed and laughed. He smiled as he watched her cheeks darken. Vito was on the shorter side and slightly stooped, too many years hunched over things that he wasn't supposed to be getting into, he supposed. His once black hair was now mostly silver, but from the side looked almost like a metallic sunrise, silver-gray on top and fading to black around the temples. His skin was the color of a walnut, and his eyes, though hidden by the sunglasses, were just as dark as the lenses. Vito was still handsome and looked about ten years younger than he was. He was fit as well, having taken to swimming in Lago Maggiore, which stayed quite warm through the late fall. Vito was charming when he wanted to be and did well with the tourist women that frequented his town.

Vito looked back over his shoulder to see Tommaso and Lucio emerging from the aircraft. He apologized to them in advance before the trip began, hoping to mollify their fiery egos and quick tempers. The part they needed to play was servitude, they were security guards, the hired help, and Vito would be ordering them around when they were in public. Having worked for a mafia boss for so long, both were used to that and didn't think anything of it. Lucio said for what they were being paid, Vito could do anything short of question his mother's honor. They laughed at that, but there was a darkness in Lucio's eyes when he said it that told Vito there were indeed lines and those lines shouldn't be crossed.

As they'd agreed, Lucio and Tommaso waited for the luggage to be brought around. Charter company staff would handle their bags, and Tommaso would carry the case with the diamonds in it, which was a triple-locked Pelican. Lucio would walk next to him. Their weapons were locked in a separate case, and they wouldn't be permitted to retrieve their weapons until they cleared security.

The flight attendants who greeted them at the bottom of the plane escorted the three of them to the terminal entrance. The doors opened, and Reginald LeGrande appeared.

Reginald didn't look worse for wear given his stint in prison. He'd explained it was some kind of "minimum security" prison that was basically a shitty resort in the desert with barbed wire and ping-pong tables. It was a place for white-collar criminals, not hardened ones. Reginald explained this several times, but Vito simply couldn't grasp the concept. It was too alien for his mind to accept. Italian prisons were hellholes.

Reginald was taller than Vito, but below six feet. His once wavy blond hair was now almost entirely gray. When Vito last saw him, Reginald had a horseshoe mustache and a mullet. But now, he'd grown his hair out and wore it slightly slicked back, giving him the appearance of being a surfer past his prime. Reginald had grown the mustache into a full beard, which hid the sporadic liver spots on his face and neck. His mouth twitched slightly, like he was working something out of his teeth or maybe was about to speak but then thought better of it. Reginald was dressed well enough, for an American. He had black pants, a blue shirt with alternating dark blue and brown stripes, and a tan jacket with a white pocket square. Reginald had on a pair of Ray-Ban Wayfarers. There was a man with a briefcase standing next to him. He was dressed in a business suit.

Reginald closed the distance between them, and they shook hands. "It's good to see you, old friend," he said quietly. Reginald introduced the man he was with as their customs broker. He was the one who would get the diamonds moved through the process, which the man promised should only take thirty minutes or so. Reginald explained that he'd been allowed through customs and security because he was with the broker. Vito then introduced Tommaso and Lucio, using the names that Reginald had on the passports. Vito and Reginald agreed that for their aliases, they'd only change their last names, because that would be easier to jump in and out of character, prevent slipups. Reginald was "Reginald Burton" and Vito was "Vito De Angeles."

Vito and his two security guards met with a US Customs and Border Protection agent who was very polite, looked at their passports for a scant moment, stamped them, and handed them back. "Gentlemen, welcome to the United States." Reginald and the customs broker met them when they were finished with immigration and led them to a private lounge, where another customs official met with them. Vito and Reginald made small talk, not particularly interested in the process of clearing their diamonds. Mostly, Vito wanted something to take his mind off the biting anxiety. He could not believe it was this simple. But it was. Reginald told him before they left that as long as you had the paperwork in order, which was what the broker was there for, it was stunningly simple. There wasn't even an import duty, which Vito found amazing and shocking.

The entire thing took thirty minutes, just like the man said. Tommaso and Lucio retrieved their weapons from the case, ready to reprise their roles as security guards. After that, they were escorted out to the terminal, where they found two men with dark blue uniforms bloused into tactical boots, sunglasses, and radios on their belts that were connected to earpieces. Both of them were armed.

This is where it ends, Vito thought.

"Mr. Burton, are you all set?" the one said. It was then Vito noticed the patch on his uniform said "WorldSecure" rather than some law enforcement agency. The logo was a grid-like rendering of a globe with a key in the center. Vito gave his old friend a quizzical look. Reginald indicated the black Pelican case to the WorldSecure guards, one of whom took possession of it, and the other said quietly into his radio that they had the package.

Reginald led the group outside, where they were met by an armored car. The case was promptly loaded into the back by two more armed guards. Reginald turned to Vito. "WorldSecure is the world's leading precious gem and metals storage and logistics firm," he said, practically quoting company literature. "They help companies like us, as well as private collectors. Isn't that right, Jim?"

"That's what we're here for, sir," the guard said.

"They'll store the product in their secure facility, which consequently is located in the Jewelry District, until our transactions are complete." Reginald said something about arranging a tour of the facility, which he assured Vito was "very impressive" and thanked Jim for his time. There was another exchange of radio chatter, and the guards loaded up in the armored car and departed. Reginald had told Vito he had the storage worked out but hadn't wanted to provide any details over the phone.

And just like that, they smuggled eighty million dollars' worth of diamonds into the United States.

With the diamonds gone, they started walking to the parking lot.

"When you said you had storage taken care of," Vito said, "I sort of assumed you meant a safe-deposit box."

"Oh," Reginald said matter-of-factly. "It is, it's just in a much larger, more secure bank. Look, we wouldn't have these if it wasn't for that scam you pulled in Rome, but we don't want someone to be able to do that to us. They'll keep it until we make the sales."

"How much does that cost? It can't be cheap."

"It's not. None of this is. The plane was fifty thousand dollars, but I think you'll agree that was worth it. If we'd tried this on a regular flight, those would be sitting in a CBP warehouse right now under impound. The storage facility is tens of thousands, but we're not planning on doing that for long. I had some money." Reginald paused at a black Range Rover. "We'll square up later, don't worry. This is us," he said. "I'll drive until your guys figure out the lay of the land." They climbed in, and Reginald continued. "We have to look the part. No one is going to believe that we're gem merchants if we roll in looking like car thieves. But we've got to make a sale fast. Even if it's something small, because checks are going to start bouncing. I've been covering everything with a ghosted corporate card, but that's only going to work for so long."

"What's the plan, then?"

Reginald paid the parking fee and pulled out of the lot.

"I have some meetings set up. We just need one small sale, a couple mil, to hold us over until we can move the rest."

"And this logistics company, they handle the transport to and from?"

"That's right," Reginald said. "And do it securely. They'll move it in an armored car and under armed guard. It would take a SWAT team to steal those things."

The realization hit Vito that he'd just given up all control of the diamonds. He was trusting Reginald entirely now. If Reginald wanted to cut him out, he had complete possession. It was just a matter of three bullets.

Well, almost all of the diamonds.

Vito Verrazano learned a long time ago to never put too much faith in a single score. There was too much risk in this business not to have a backup plan. He had kept some for himself, probably five million worth, stashed in a box in a Swiss bank vault under a numbered account just over the border from his home. Call it a safety net.

After all, trust only went so far in this business.

SEVEN

Los Angeles traffic was light for a weekday, though "light" in this town was a matter of perspective. Jack picked Enzo up at LAX. It was an awkward meeting. Enzo had lingering guilt over the botched attempt to break into Vito's house, and there was still the matter of Jack's ultimatum at the end of the call. Words he now regretted. Rusty's challenge of "you can't have it both ways" seemed to hang over his shoulder and follow Jack like a specter. Despite the tension and the awkwardness, it was good to see his friend. There'd been too little of that lately.

They went to their hotel, the Ritz-Carlton downtown, to change. Jack dressed in a conservative navy suit from Brooks Brothers. It was the only off-the-rack suit he owned. Jack had purchased it in New York two years prior in order to appear before a federal judge and accept his plea deal, on the advice of Special Agent Danzig. She told him it wouldn't be a great idea for him to show up dressed like a diamond thief with expensive taste.

And for what Jack had planned for today, a five-thousand-dollar Canali would send the wrong message. He needed understated, professional, and bureaucratic.

Enzo, on the other hand, wore a Baltic-blue suit, silver shirt and silver tie, and brown slip-on shoes. Jack had told him, "Dress like Americans think Italians dress."

Enzo shrugged when Jack said this. "That *is* how we dress. Americans just lack style." This coming from a guy who wore a leather car coat in nearly any temperature. Jack made him shave, which pissed Enzo off. In their nearly thirty years of friendship, it was the only time Jack remembered seeing Enzo clean shaven. They both knew that by lunchtime, Enzo would have a dirty shadow underneath his chin.

Once they were dressed, Jack pulled his credentials out and slid them into the jacket pocket. Jack picked up a small ballistic nylon briefcase and asked Enzo if he was ready. Enzo had acquired his own credentials identifying him as an inspector with the Guardia di Finanza through contacts in Italy before he left. Both sets of credentials were surprisingly easy to get. Jack knew there were places on the dark web where one could get nearly any type of identification. In most cases, one could get a blank passport for about five thousand dollars. Credentials for a federal agent were somewhat harder to come by, but not impossible, and an agency with a lower profile than the FBI would be slightly easier.

Rusty initially argued against this, reminding them all that the penalties for impersonating federal officers were steep. Right now, all they were doing was stealing from thieves. If they were caught trying to pass themselves off as law enforcement, the hammers falling would be swift and severe. Even getting Rusty to agree to return to America took another phone call. Jack had calmly reiterated his previous and hastily delivered ultimatum, which was that Rusty was either in or he wasn't. Jack had this conversation without Enzo on the line. He respected his reasons for not returning to the US. The details were still vague after all of these years, and Rusty intended to keep it that way, but in a past life he'd been an FBI agent and counterintelligence officer. Apparently, he'd either chosen to or been directed to bend or break laws in order to roll up a Russian intelligence cell targeting

American service members in Europe. The FBI fired him and ordered his arrest when the story broke. Rusty had been a fugitive ever since. Could he slip past an overworked, semi-interested Customs and Border Protection agent at an airport? Yes, but that wasn't the part Rusty was worried about. Jack held firm, though: *Either you're here or you're out.* Rusty said he was willing to take that risk. Rusty said he'd be there. He needed to tie some things up in Switzerland and would be there in a couple of days.

Jack reassured Rusty, though, that while he understood and appreciated the stakes, Jack wasn't worried about getting caught. If the Federal Bureau of Investigation, with all of their resources, couldn't catch him when they had their chance years before, Jack didn't think some Los Angeles Police Department officer was going to get him today.

Jack and Enzo got their car from the valet. They might only be going a few blocks, but Jack had been in this business too long to not have a car right by in case they needed it. It was hot, desert dry, and it wouldn't do to show up with beads of sweat. No one would believe a federal agent walked. They got in their silver Chevy Malibu and drove the few blocks. Los Angeles's Jewelry District was in the center of what they called the Historic Core of LA. Most of the buildings were erected in the early twentieth century and were, at the time, limited to how tall they could be. They bore no resemblance to the ultra-modern glass and neon of the rest of downtown. Jack turned north on Hill and, after a few blocks, slowed. There was little traffic, and it didn't generate any attention from the few drivers behind him.

"What is it?" Enzo asked.

Jack pointed out the window to a building on the right as they rolled past.

"That's where it started," Jack said.

"What?"

"Everything. In 1995, that was an armored car depot."

"Oh." Enzo nodded. He knew this story.

It was Jack's first job as a member of an inside crew. Before that, he'd just been a wheelman for Reginald. Jack, Reginald, and four others, one of whom was a safety inspector who was about to get fired by the company, robbed the armored car depot. The job went south almost as soon as it started, "Fucked from the word 'go,'" Jack said at the time. One of them was shot and killed inside, another in the van. Reginald took one too. Case, the guy who planned the job, was arrested within days. Jack had made a crucial mistake. He was supposed to tie up one of the security guards, which he did, but not particularly well, and he didn't check the guy for additional weapons after they removed his service pistol. Turned out he had a snub-nosed revolver in an ankle holster. Jack and Reginald survived and managed to get some gym bags of cash out the door with them, only to have one of their own, a thief named Clint Sturdevant, turn on them and try to take the rest.

That ended badly.

After that, Reginald told Jack he needed "seasoning" if he was going to work with him again. He also thought it would be a good idea for Jack to be out of the country for a while. Told him to go look up an old associate of his, a thief named Vito Verrazano. So, Jack did as he was told. Six months later, he was a member of the infamous School of Turin, and he and Enzo were pulling scores all over northern Italy.

Jack cut across sixth to Olive, turned right, and parked their gray Chevy Malibu at a metered spot. They stepped out into a torturous Southern California afternoon. The buildings shielded them from the brunt of the Santa Ana winds, but hot zephyrs still curled about them occasionally, like random ghosts. Jack didn't wear his signature Persol Steve McQueen sunglasses, opting instead for a pair of bronzed Randolph aviators that he thought looked more "government."

They had four meetings that day, all in the same building, the International Jewelry Center building at 550 South Hill Street. It was sixteen stories of mirrored blue glass separated by bands of white concrete. It was what the architects of the eighties thought the future would look like. The bottom two floors were a sort of mall for retail jewelry, and the floors above were offices, primarily for those in the trade. They entered the lobby through a revolving door and found a stark, white modernist lobby. Tall succulents were positioned in white pots, strategically placed in corners and on the opposite ends of long leather benches. There was a security guard behind a circular desk. Jack told him where they were headed, and he indicated they could go up. Their first two meetings were very quick and essentially worthless.

The first made them wait about a half an hour until their corporate attorney was available, who turned out to be quite standoffish. He kept pressing for details on their investigation, and Jack distinctly felt like he was under cross-examination. Jack eventually got tired of it and took the offensive. He said they were attempting to shut down a major gem smuggling operation and were looking for cooperation from the industry, they weren't accusing anyone of anything, but if the attorney felt better, they could have this meeting down at headquarters and make "official." That backed him down a little, but they wouldn't confirm whether they were meeting with anyone or had been approached, saying it would betray the trust of potential clients who expect that in their business dealings. Jack thanked them for their time and left. The second meeting was a flavor of the first, though it was even shorter. A smaller firm, they didn't have an in-house counsel and respectfully apologized but couldn't meet with US Customs until their attorneys were present. Jack made a show of rescheduling for later in the week. When they were in the elevator to go to the third meeting, Jack told Enzo that these guys were clearly hiding something. "We might have to hit them on general principle," he said, but Enzo didn't laugh.

The elevator opened on the tenth floor to a long glass wall with double doors emblazoned with gold letters: INTERNATIONAL GEMS AND PRECIOUS METALS. Jack smiled at that. They used the same innocuous naming that he did with his shell companies.

Jack approached the reception desk and the young man sitting there. He was Black, close-cropped hair, wire-rim glasses, and looked like he didn't appreciate having to wear a suit or man a desk. He looked up from his computer as Jack's shadow crossed his desk. Jack quickly flashed his credentials and put them back in his jacket before the kid could ask to inspect them more closely. "I'm Harry Little with US Customs. This is Angelo Benedetti with the Italian government. We have an appointment to speak with Mr. Galbraith."

Eyes shot back to the screen and hands went to the keyboard. The kid pushed himself back from the desk and stood, buttoning his jacket as he did. "Right this way, please, gentlemen." Jack and Enzo followed him through a canyon of smoked glass offices, finally arriving at one that Jack could tell overlooked Olive. Jack had backgrounded Christian Galbraith the night before. Undergrad at USC followed by an MBA at Stanford with a focus on international finance. He was fairly new to the gem and precious metals trade, having spent most of his career putting together land deals overseas. Jack suspected that was how Galbraith got exposed to the gem trade. He was now the chief operations officer for International Gems.

Galbraith pretended to be busy with something on his monitor as the front desk kid escorted Jack and Enzo into the office and kept the charade up for a second or two after. "Mr. Galbraith, your ten o'clock is here."

"Thank you, James," Galbraith said, still pretending to concentrate on his screen. He slid back and then stood, flashing a smile that was so practiced it almost looked authentic. Galbraith was around six feet, athletic, and bald. His face was all sharp angles, precise geometry.

"Chris Galbraith," he said and extended a hand, having come around from the other side of his desk. Behind Galbraith was a floor-to-ceiling window that ran the entire length of his office. "You must be Agent Little," he said to Jack. "And that makes you Inspector Benedetti." Galbraith indicated a couch and two chairs that orbited an oval coffee table beneath a dark wood-paneled wall that had a stylized outline of a gemstone on it done up in chrome. "Please, sit."

"Thank you," Jack said. "We appreciate you meeting us on short notice, and I promise you, we won't take up too much of your time."

"It's no problem at all. I'm always happy to help out Customs," he said.

Jack opened his briefcase and drew out a folder. He set that on the table, opened it, and turned it to face Galbraith. Inside the left sleeve was an FBI wanted notice displaying Reginald LeGrande's picture, on the right was an INTERPOL wanted notice for Vito Verrazano. Rusty had created a pair of law enforcement notices that looked absolutely real.

"Mr. Galbraith, Inspector Benedetti and I are here because we believe that these men are attempting to make a sale of a large quantity of diamonds here in Los Angeles. The diamonds were stolen in Europe several years ago, hidden, and recently smuggled into the US. We believe they are attempting to sell them here because American law enforcement wouldn't be following this."

"Then how did you hear about it?"

"My agency, Italy's financial police, have been following Vito Verrazano for quite a while," Enzo said. "I am the...is 'case officer' the right term? We believe this is the work of a thievery ring that has been amassing wealth over time, small- and medium-size scores with the intent of trying to sell them on the legitimate market."

Galbraith concentrated on the photos and the notices for several long moments. Then he pulled his phone out and hammer-tapped the screen like a woodpecker drilling a hole. Jack watched his eyes jump between the phone and the notices. After a few moments of scrolling, Galbraith leaned back in his chair. "I'm scheduled to meet with a pair from an international brokerage later this week. Burton and De Angeles are their names. Reginald Burton and Vito De Angeles," he said. "Thursday morning at ten."

Reginald and Vito.

They didn't have the name Reginald used when chartering the flight—and that would be a bogus name anyway—but Vito De Angeles was the client on the passenger manifest. Jack looked over at

Enzo. "Those sound like our guys," he said, and Enzo nodded in grave agreement.

"So, how can I help?" Galbraith asked.

"For now, I'd like you to cancel the appointment."

"That's it?" Galbraith appeared visibly relieved. "You don't need me for a sting or anything?"

Jack gave him a perfunctory laugh. "Not right now, Mr. Galbraith. At this stage, we first need to verify that it's them. That means closing down some options."

"Well, wait a second. I'm running a business here. I can't just cancel appointments because Customs tells me to. If these guys are doing something shady, then obviously I want to help out. That's bad for our entire industry. But if you're wrong and they aren't your guys, then I could be passing up on a deal that one of my competitors is going to grab. I don't think you appreciate how competitive this business is."

Jack leveled a gaze on him that said, "You have no idea," but Galbraith didn't pick up on the double meaning.

"Mr. Galbraith, the most help you can be is to give us the phone number that they provided. This will allow us to check them out. If they turn out not to be our guys, then you can reschedule your meeting with our apologies. If this is a large deal, like you say, I'm sure it won't close that quickly."

"You'd be surprised," he said. But Galbraith provided both the office and mobile numbers for Reginald Burton and assured them that he would cancel the appointment. Jack admonished him that it was essential that he not give anything away, just to tell them that something came up. Galbraith probed a little more on the investigation, fishing for details, Jack suspected, so that he had something to give his chief legal officer as soon as this meeting was done. Jack remained cagey on details, giving him that age-old line that he was forbidden from talking about an ongoing investigation. They thanked Galbraith for his time and left.

When they got outside, Enzo asked why they didn't have the guy set them up. "He seemed like he was ready to jump, man, why didn't we just have him go all in? We could take them. Set up the sting like he said?"

"Well, I don't want to do anything until Rusty is here, because we don't have any additional support. But I'd be worried about Reginald being able to sniff out that something was up if it's their first meeting and the guy wants to buy all of the diamonds. It'll look suspicious. Besides, we've got the most important thing right now."

"What's that?"

"Reginald's phone number."

Even though they'd had the flight information and knew when Vito's plane landed in Van Nuys, they'd agreed that it was a bad idea to try to tail them. At that point, it was just Jack, and running a tail was very hard with just one person. Not to mention, Van Nuys was a small airport and the chances of Reginald spotting Jack were just too high.

So, Jack decided on this approach—posing as law enforcement officers to close off their options, force Reginald to make a bad, hasty decision, and take the diamonds. Their backup plan was to find out where the diamonds were being stashed and just steal them from there.

Jack's phone rang.

It was Special Agent Danzig.

EIGHT

Jack flew home.

Kingfisher was located on the northern end of Sonoma County, about a half an hour from the town of Sonoma. Jack told her that he'd meet her in downtown Sonoma, which would save them an additional hour in the car if they were driving up from San Francisco. Danzig told him it was no problem, they would meet him at the winery. When Jack pushed back on the idea, Danzig reassured him they were just coming to talk. She figured that's where he would be during business hours and didn't want to inconvenience him. He told her that he didn't typically have federal agents just come to talk, and he didn't want them raising unnecessary suspicion with the winery staff. But Danzig seemed insistent that they conduct the meeting at the winery, and Jack knew he could only push back so hard without it looking like he was hiding something. Like the fact that he'd been away the last two days and the questions that might bring.

Jack just didn't want the FBI crawling all over his place of business "just to talk." Danzig offered a compromise. She said that she and her partner would dress in casual clothes and they wouldn't drive a Bureau car. Jack reluctantly agreed, reminded her that everyone there knew him as Frank Fischer and that he took her advice and lived as Fischer, full-time.

With no other option, which, he recalled, was how Katrina Danzig did business, Jack agreed.

Things seemed to go poorly after that.

First, Jack had told his staff that he'd be away for a few days on business. He told Megan that he'd had something to take care of; she knew now not to probe too deeply in certain areas. Then, in the middle of this trip, Jack showed back up at the winery, unexpectedly, because he was going to have some guests and he wanted to show them around. It was a ham-fisted explanation, but the staff at Kingfisher knew that their boss was a bit of an eccentric who kept his own hours and would show up or disappear at the drop of a hat.

Jack asked Danzig to be there around ten so that he had time to finish whatever this was before guests started arriving. Then Danzig proceeded to be three hours late. Maybe they got a late start leaving San Francisco, misjudging the travel time. Maybe, also, they planned it this way. Conspiracy theories had a way of worming their way into a stressed mind. All of Jack's thoughts were on Los Angeles right now, how quickly he could wrap this up and get back there.

Danzig and another agent, whom Jack recognized from Rome, got out of their car. Choi, he thought the name was. Jack was watching from his office, which overlooked the winery's parking lot.

Danzig was in her mid-forties and very athletic. She'd grown her hair out since the last time Jack saw her. It hung to her shoulders now and curled in just slightly. She had large, piercing dark eyes that missed very little. They always seemed to be narrowed, just slightly, as though she was always focusing her stare on *something*. Danzig was dressed in jeans, a white blouse, and dark blazer. Choi was taller, a few years younger, and looked like he could run down an NFL quarterback. He wore a white polo and chinos. Both of them exhausted.

They both looked like federal agents who were trying hard not to look like federal agents.

Jack moved downstairs as quickly as he could, intercepting them before they got to the main building.

"Welcome to Kingfisher," he said in a dry tone.

"It's nice to see you again, Frank," Danzig said.

Jack's tension lowered a bit, automatically. Danzig was preserving his cover as a courtesy.

It was early afternoon, though it was a weekday in the fall, so they didn't have too many customers yet, and most of the ones they did have were inside in the tasting room. They had one group at a table on the patio. Jack spotted a couple on their honeymoon who'd finished their tasting and were taking a stroll around the grounds.

"Thanks for taking the time to meet with us. You remember Dan Choi?" Danzig said. "Is there somewhere we can go to talk?"

Jack looked to his left and right before he even realized what he was doing. Long years of staying a couple steps ahead of people like Katrina Danzig had taught him a few things, not the least of which was always knowing where the exits were. Danzig must have sensed this, picked up on his discomfort.

"I'm not here to bother you, Frank," she said. If Danzig wanted to cause him trouble, and God knew she had, she'd have used his real name and put him on his heels in public.

"Sure thing," he said. "You guys came all this way, would you like to try a glass?"

"We're on duty," Danzig said.

"Then just hold the glass while we walk around," Jack said in a low voice. "This is a winery. People come here to drink wine. People who don't drink wine don't come here."

Danzig nodded, and Jack walked over to the service counter on the patio, poured three glasses, and returned to his "guests." As he did, Jack introduced the wine for the benefit of anyone that might overhear them.

The patio was ringed by a low wall of dark granite that had openings at both ends and in the center. Jack led the two agents out the nearest one to the driveway that circled the tasting room. There was a line of black oaks on the other side of the road, whose long, leafy canopy hanging from gnarled, hand-like branches drooped low and covered half the road. Jack walked silently back toward the barn and the fermentation tanks. Reaching that, he stepped off into the grass.

"You've done well for yourself," Danzig said.

"I took your advice," Jack replied matter-of-factly.

As Jack was departing Rome to sign his plea deal two years before, accompanied by a pair of US Marshals to make sure he made it to Manhattan, Danzig told him, "Become Frank Fischer. Be a winemaker, live your life. Forget everything about Jack Burdette."

Well, he'd taken two-thirds of that advice.

"I'm glad," Danzig said.

Jack was genuinely surprised to hear that.

He'd been an obsession of hers for a decade, a master jewel thief that many in law enforcement debated even existed. That obsession nearly cost Danzig her career. But instead of being bitter, flaming out and blaming him for it, she learned from the experience. When the time came and she had the opportunity to arrest Jack for what would be—in contrast to the rest of his body of work—petty theft from a jewelry heist gone wrong, Danzig instead asked for a trade. Jack took a plea deal instead of prison, then helped the FBI and the Italian authorities break up a major criminal syndicate and jail a war criminal.

"I have purpose here," he said, and vaguely motioned at the rows of vines before them. "Look, I only ever stole gems because it was the thing I knew how to do. Over time, I learned something else."

That was mostly true. Jack reveled in the excitement. He lived for crafting an airtight plan and thrived in executing it. He loved outsmarting people like Danzig and Choi. Jack also recognized that about himself, however, and when he returned from the debacle in Rome, he applied that same philosophy, the same drive to winemaking. His people noticed the change immediately. Jack originally started this place as a way to launder the money he made from stealing jewelry. In time, he came to love it, love the people that worked here. But he still had no idea what he was doing. He made a lot of mistakes, some of which he paid for. He micromanaged. Jack assumed that because he was good at one hard thing, he was good at all hard things. But after Rome, he changed. He approached winemaking like a student, he listened, he took advice. The change in him was profound.

"I won't claim that this makes up for anything I've done in life, but I make a product that makes people happy. People come here and spend an afternoon with us, take a bottle with them, and make that turn into something special. We do weddings here now. It's something."

"That's really interesting," Danzig said flatly, and took a polite sip of her wine. "But I'm here to talk to you about diamonds."

"I'm retired."

"I'm not accusing you of anything, Jack." Switching to his real name now that it was just the three of them. "We need your help."

Jack said nothing for several long breaths. Instead, he looked out over the long rows of Cabernet grapes that climbed up the rolling Mayacamas foothills. The green tracts of grapes gave way to the lush green of the black oaks and other leafy trees in the mountains, with wide patches of wild grass that was golden brown now this late in the year. The wildfire threat was the highest now, and several other parts of the state were burning. A reminder, Jack mused as he flashed a sideways glance at Agent Danzig, that there was always danger even in peace.

"So, how can I help?"

Danzig took another sip. *So much for duty*, Jack thought. "This really is quite good," she said softly. "After we arrested Aleksander Anđelić, the Bureau put me in charge of a squad going after international gem trafficking operations. We, the Bureau, have been laser focused on counterterrorism for the last twenty years, and frankly, some other operations have slipped. Transnational crime is a big focus for us now. So, what does all that have to do with you?"

"The thought had crossed my mind."

"This is about your old friends, the Cannizzaros. Since we don't have the lawyers present, I'll just remind you that a condition of your deal was to assist any ongoing investigations about which you have specific knowledge."

Jack wanted to tell her he didn't have specific knowledge of anything at this point, but held his tongue.

Danzig continued. "You really kicked up a hornet's nest during the bank job. This is a fairly complicated situation, but we'll tell you what we can. We know from your depositions that they used extortion to gain access to an Italian shipping magnate. The Cannizzaro organization has been smuggling for years but over the last eighteen months has significantly ramped up their operations. They're into everything. They're buying guns in the Middle East, leftovers from the Iraq war, and selling them in Africa, mostly. Revolutionary groups, terrorist organizations, anyone with a checkbook. They're financing the arms trade primarily with stolen gems."

Choi spoke for the first time. "I was posted in Rome as an attaché at the US Embassy when you...when all of that went down. We were aware of the Cannizzaros even then and were providing some intelligence to the Italian law enforcement agencies. These guys have been trafficking for some time, but it looks like they've expanded considerably in the last two years. We think they're using a shipping company and moving things in container ships."

Trafficking precious gems was one of the primary ways that terrorist organizations and international criminal syndicates funded themselves and moved money beneath the eyes of governments. Gems had no serial numbers. They were a completely invisible currency, and consumer desire for them was practically insatiable. Most of the gems stolen in Europe and Asia ended up on the gray market, where they were acquired by unscrupulous wholesalers. Already cut and finished, these stones would then be sold back to jewelry makers at a substantial profit because the wholesaler didn't have any of the production costs. Everyone in the economy turned a blind eye to the dark economics of it because there was so much money to be made and, they rationalized, if we didn't do it, someone else would. However, the trend over the last twenty years was that an increasing number of precious gems spent time in terror networks before making their way back to the gray markets. This was because the world in general and the United States in particular had invested considerable effort in rolling up the dark money pipelines in the years following 9/11, eliminating the anonymous banking and offshore havens.

Danzig began her career in the FBI in financial crimes and chasing dark money before moving into gem trafficking. Jack had used those anonymous banks, mostly in Switzerland, and found that as the United States was more aggressively pursuing terrorist networks (and, to a lesser degree, criminal syndicates), he had fewer and fewer places to stash his money. The winery was born out of a need to repatriate his money so that he'd have access to it.

"So, the Cannizzaros are trafficking gems now? That's how you got involved?"

"Sort of. The Italian government reached out to the ambassador and asked if the FBI could help. They feel powerless. After Gio…" Danzig's voice trailed off. She took a drink.

Giovanni Castro was the other link between Danzig and Jack.

He was an Italian police officer and was the one who originally broke up the School of Turin in the late nineties on a lengthy undercover operation. Castro, while undercover, became close with Jack, and on the strength of that, Castro tipped Jack before the raid. Told Jack to run, change his life. Jack did not. Ten years later, Castro was working with one Katrina Danzig as part of a multinational countertrafficking taskforce—FBI, INTERPOL, Europol, and a host of other national agencies in Europe. They were investigating a string of unsolved heists in Europe, and Castro suggested they consider an enigmatic American thief known as Gentleman Jack.

Castro may have started as a noble cop, but he didn't end that way. Eventually, the pervasive corruption of Italian law enforcement got to him as well and he ended up on the Cannizzaro payroll. His job was to keep his agency, the Italian financial police, away from the Commerce Bank of Rome. Castro, again, spared his old friend's life and spirited Jack away from the bank after that botched heist that Aleksander Anđelić orchestrated.

Jack wanted to believe that Castro was bucking the Cannizzaros, had regained some measure of his righteousness, but he'd never know for sure. The Cannizzaros killed Castro that night, making it look like a suicide. Maybe they were worried Castro was changing sides, or maybe they were just plugging holes, Jack would never know that either. Jack had some complicated feelings about Castro, and instead of sorting them out, Jack tried to bury them with his friend. Danzig just brought all that back.

"What do you know about the organization?" Danzig asked.

Now Jack knew he was on shaky ground.

"Is my answer covered by my plea deal?"

"It is," she said flatly. "Nothing you tell me here can incriminate you, as long as you haven't done anything new and stupid in the last eighteen months."

Jack laughed, but there was no humor behind it. Then he said, "How much do you know about Italian mafia organizations?"

"A little," she said and looked to her partner.

"Probably a little more," Choi said, "but it'd be helpful to hear it from your perspective."

Jack didn't quite know how to take that but decided not to read into it.

"Okay, crash course is like this. 'Mafia' is a blanket term for an organized crime gang. Americans tend to assume 'mafia' means 'Sicily' because of so much of the American mafia had its origins there. Each region has their own—Camorra, 'Ndrangheta, Sacra Corona Unita, and, of course, La Cosa Nostra. Vincenzu Cannizzaro was a Sicilian mafia captain. His nephew was a thief named Niccoló Bartolo."

"Your old mentor and the head of the School of Turin."

"That's right. Bartolo and Cannizzaro's son, Salvatore, were very close growing up and worked together a lot. Now, there was a big civil war among the mafia gangs during the eighties. It was incredibly bloody. The Italian press called it *Il Mattanza*, 'the Slaughter.' The reason I bring this up is that after that, the Italian government cracked down hard on organized crime, to include trying to root out internal corruption. In no small measure because the Sicilian mafia murdered a pair of judges. The Italian government removed any mafia influence from Rome in the nineties.

"Sensing a power vacuum and knowing they had to get out of Sicily, Vincenzu Cannizzaro abandoned most of his operations and relocated to Rome. He somehow got controlling interest in a small Roman bank."

"That's the Commerce Bank?" Choi asked.

"That's right. I have no idea how he did it. Because there's so much internecine warfare within the regional mafia factions at this point, none of them noticed the Cannizzaros setting up shop in Rome. They kept quiet, focused on blackmailing politicians and money laundering. They also had this system where they'd use the safe-deposit boxes in the vault as a kind of dead drop. They could securely store and move small amounts of drugs, gems, money, information, basically whatever they wanted that could fit in a box."

"Interest in the bank died quickly after the Anđelić incident," Danzig said. "Italian law enforcement heaped everything on Anđelić and his organization, saying nothing about who actually owned the bank. We think it's because of how many local officials the Cannizzaros have in their pocket. So, the Italian government contacted us. The Cannizzaros had an inspector in the financial police, our mutual friend, which is a pretty high-ranking officer. The Italian government doesn't know how deep they've gone and how many cops are on the Cannizzaro payroll, so they want us to help. The idea is that the FBI tees them up and then their DIA will make the arrest."

"DIA?" Jack asked.

"Sorry, Direzione Investigativa Antimafia." Danzig said the words slowly and sloppily. Italian was not her strong suit. "It's a joint antimafia agency made up of their other police services. But everyone is thoroughly vetted and handpicked. Basically, the government's thinking is that if the FBI manages the investigation and makes an international thing of it, it'll force the respective police agencies to hold themselves accountable."

"That sounds risky," Jack said. "What do you think about it?"

"I think my job is to catch bank robbers and jewelry thieves and not to get involved in politics. Our squad is attached to the Bureau's Gem and Jewelry Program, and we specialize in countertrafficking. We're based out of the Manhattan office, but we spend a lot of time on the road. Given our previous experience with the Andelić case, we got the call. We've been detailed to the US Embassy in Rome for the last six months."

"Vincenzu Cannizzaro died about ten years ago or so," Jack said. "Salvatore took over and is running the organization now. I met him once in 1997, when they first took over the bank. Bartolo sent me down to Rome on an errand. Things were always tense between Vincenzu and Bartolo. Vincenzu thought anything Bartolo did was part of the broader Cannizzaro family, even if they didn't have anything to do with it. Pay tribute, that sort of thing. Vincenzu wanted Bartolo and the School to do jobs for him, and Bartolo refused. There was enough mafia in Turin already, and that would've touched off something worse. As it was, we could operate independently, kind of work for everyone. Anyway, once Bartolo defied him that last time, Vincenzu gave him the kiss of death."

Choi laughed. "Is that real? I always thought it was something Coppola made up for *The Godfather*."

"No, it's really real. Salvatore and Bartolo were very close once, but from what I hear, he keeps his father's vendetta alive. That's about the extent of what I know."

It wasn't. But the other parts, Jack wasn't bringing up.

Giulia Montalto. Bartolo's onetime mistress was the first woman Jack ever loved. They were together for two years when he was living in Turin. She betrayed him to Bartolo, and Nico almost killed him.

Then, when Nico went to prison, she somehow ended up under the protection of Salvatore Cannizzaro. Until she ended up with Anđelić. They were never involved, as far as Jack knew. There had been some political scandal in Rome, and Giulia was caught up in it. Jack didn't know what happened to her after that mess and didn't much care, as long as she was on the farthest side of the earth from him.

"Well, I hope this was helpful," Jack said. "Like I said, I only met Salvatore the one time. I wish you luck, though." This was absolutely something that could have been handled over the phone.

Danzig gave him a wry smile. "We're almost done. We have intelligence from an informant that Cannizzaro tried to buy a very large quantity of diamonds recently. Apparently, a thief by the name of Vito Verrazano was sitting on them from the heist, or a series of them, and couldn't sell them, so he asked Cannizzaro to move them. Cannizzaro lined up a buyer, and then this Verrazano up and disappeared."

"Does that name ring a bell to you, Jack?" Choi asked. "Verrazano?"

Jack was on very dangerous ground now. Danzig knew about Bartolo, and she knew about Turin. It was possible—in fact, highly likely—that Castro gave her the names of everyone in the School of Turin at one point. If Jack lied and she caught him in it, it would be obvious that he was covering up for something.

His mind raced.

The FBI and Italian DIA knew about Cannizzaro, had someone in his organization, and they knew about the diamonds.

"I know him," Jack said. "Or at least I did. I cut all ties with the School of Turin after Giovanni warned me off."

"Except for Enzo Bachetti," Danzig said.

Shit.

"Last I heard about Verrazano, he was arrested in '97 and went to prison with the rest of them. I lost track of him after that."

"So you don't know where Verrazano might have gotten a large score?"

"How much are we talking?"

"About eighty million," Choi said.

"It's interesting to me," Danzig said, "that after he was arrested, Niccoló Bartolo claimed to have stolen one hundred million from the Antwerp Diamond Centre in 2003. Before he changed his story. And he allegedly stashed those diamonds in a bank, which Aleksander Andelić and the Pink Panthers then tried to break into. Then Vito Verrazano, a onetime colleague of Bartolo's, is now trying to sell eighty million in diamonds to Salvatore Cannizzaro. The guy who owned the bank that the diamonds were stolen *from*."

"If Verrazano *is* doing that, he's an idiot. Very few people or organizations, to include mafias, have the money to make a purchase that large. And if they did, why spend the money? Why not just kill Verrazano and take the stones? That's one of the main reasons I never went after big scores. Maybe Cannizzaro did have a buyer or buyers lined up. If he's as deep into smuggling now as you say, there are lots of organizations that might try to buy from him. Not to mention, the gray market. But the part that doesn't ring true for me is the whole 'big score' thing. Those rarely work out in real life."

"Bartolo pulled it off," Choi said.

"He also never got to spend that money *and* he's still in jail. And he probably lied about how much he actually got. I think it's possible that Verrazano has something to sell. I think it's also possible that he may have a large quantity of precious gems to move that he's amassed over the years, but I have a hard time believing it's anything on the order of what you're talking about."

Jack saw movement out of the corner of his eye and turned his head. Megan had spotted them and was walking over. Jack cleared his throat. Danzig took the hint. Jack turned and smiled as Megan walked up, a puzzled look on her face.

"Megan, allow me to introduce you to Special Agents Katrina Danzig and Dan Choi of the FBI."

"What's she doing here, Jack?" Megan asked.

"She knows?" Danzig said.

"She does," Jack admitted.

Megan sized her up. "Katrina, huh? Fitting you'd be named after a natural disaster."

"Charming," Danzig said.

"Why are you here?" Megan asked.

"Consulting," Danzig replied. "Jack was offering me his expert opinion on a case I'm working on."

"Is that right," Megan said. "I hope that's all it is. Jack's paid his debt, and he's doing exactly what you told him to."

Danzig removed her sunglasses so there was no mistaking her expression. "Yes, and I expect he will continue to do so."

"Well, this is awkward and uncomfortable," Jack said. "Meg, can you give us just a minute, and I'll meet you inside for round-up?"

"You sure you're okay?" she asked. "I can get Hugh on the phone."

Jack winced at the mention and hoped it wasn't visible. Hugh Coughlin was once his close friend and mentor in the wine industry. A longtime attorney in Napa, Hugh helped Kingfisher out with any legal matters and consulted on any business dealings they had. Hugh was the first person that Jack revealed his identity to. That didn't strain their relationship, but by Rome it was obvious to Hugh that Jack wouldn't quit thieving, and he told Jack that he couldn't be around him anymore. Said he didn't want to watch Jack destroy himself. Hugh had helped broker Jack's plea deal, and that was the last they'd spoken. Megan knew all this and didn't mean it as a slight; rather, it was a shot across the bow at Danzig.

Megan hadn't asked a lot of questions when Jack said he needed to be away for a couple of days. She knew that was part of the deal, but Jack had also promised her that he was retired. When he returned here today, Jack told Megan the reason he'd gone down to LA was because he'd learned that Reginald was out of prison and Jack wanted to make sure that LeGrande wasn't going to try anything—like getting revenge on Jack.

Megan said she didn't like that and thought he was poking a hornet's nest, but also that she understood. Jack wanted to get Megan away from this conversation as quickly as possible so that she didn't slip and say something about Reginald, or worse, assume that was why Danzig was here.

"I don't think we need to do that," Jack said. "Katrina is just following up on some things we talked about during my deposition a few years ago to help her out with a case they're working on. I won't be much longer."

Megan had a fiery temper and was protective of Jack, of the winery, of what they were building and the relationship they had. It had been a long and difficult journey for the two of them to get back to this point, and Jack knew Megan wasn't going to let that go. But every second she stood here, Jack was worried that Megan was going to fire a shot off at Danzig, because she wouldn't be able to help herself.

Eight years before, the FBI had been no help in recovering the ten million dollars that Reginald LeGrande helped Paul Sharpe embezzle from the winery, a move that almost bankrupted them and forced Jack to take a very dangerous score in order to keep the winery afloat. They'd crawled out of that hole with more of Frank Fischer's personal fortune, but it left a scar on Megan, and she sure as hell didn't trust the FBI or much of the government anymore.

Megan looked at the wineglasses in Danzig's and Choi's hands. "Well," she said, "I hope you enjoy the wine." She touched Jack on the elbow, her fingertips lingering for a moment, and then turned to walk back to the tasting room.

Jack watched her go and had to force himself not to visibly exhale.

Jack guided Danzig and Choi back to their car. He made no attempt at small talk as he did.

"Thanks for your insights, Jack," Danzig said when they arrived at the car. It seemed like a long way to come for the substance of the conversation they'd had.

Choi asked, "One last question, Jack. Bartolo hid the diamonds in the Commerce Bank. Andelić forced you to break into the bank with his men with the intent of escaping through a tunnel and leaving you to take the fall for it."

"I remember," Jack said dryly.

"Since you have some expert knowledge of the bank, any idea how Vito Verrazano could have gotten those diamonds out? And do you think it happened before or after the Andelić incident?"

There was the trap question. Any answer he gave would be a jumping-off point for further questioning. Next thing, he'd be "invited" down to the FBI office in San Francisco for an interview.

"Dan, anything I'd say at this point would be pure speculation. I honestly have no idea."

"Try a guess."

"Under no circumstances," Jack said evenly.

An awkward few moments passed in silent standoff. Choi wasn't going to make his move until Jack did, and Jack was sitting this hand out.

Danzig let this play out for a bit longer than necessary. "If you hear anything from any of your contacts, I'd appreciate it if you let us know," she said.

"I don't have any contacts anymore," Jack said. "It's hard for me to say how accurate the information is, but in my experience, those big scores are very hard to move. Almost impossible to do it quietly in one fell swoop."

They thanked him again for his time and left.

There was only one reason that Danzig and Choi would fly all the way from Rome to San Francisco and then drive up here to talk to him in person.

Message received, Jack thought.

Jack made a quick scan of the patio. There were a few new customers sitting outside now, but they were all in the middle of tastings and all looked like tourists. Meaning, no one looked like a fed that was planted there to see what Jack would do as soon as Danzig and Choi left.

The FBI and Italian DIA knew about Vito and knew that he had Bartolo's diamonds. Danzig knew, or at least surmised, that the diamonds had been in Cannizzaro's bank two years ago when the Pink Panthers forced Jack to break into it. Danzig guessed those were the diamonds that Vito attempted to sell to Salvatore Cannizzaro over the last year but then didn't. She'd unraveled almost this entire scheme, and now Jack, Rusty, and Enzo were on very, very dangerous ground.

If Danzig learned that Vito was no longer in Italy, they would invariably start looking elsewhere for him. They were following the stones and not necessarily who was buying them. Jack couldn't be sure if Danzig knew about Reginald and Vito. Castro didn't know about that connection, but that's not to say she couldn't have gotten it otherwise. If the FBI refocused their investigation here...

Jack felt a cold, crushing sensation wash over him.

Reginald was all over the gem wholesalers in Los Angeles trying to put together a huge deal. That idiot was trying to sell those diamonds in one go. That was going to draw attention. Danzig said she was back in the FBI's Gem and Jewelry unit, which Jack knew all too well looked at smuggling operations into the United States and abroad. As such, they had contacts with the people in that supply chain. Contacts *and* sources.

Reginald was going to tip the authorities without even knowing it. In fact, the only thing they had going for them was the fact that Salvatore Cannizzaro had his goons tearing up the Italian countryside looking for Vito.

The last time out, Jack tipped Danzig to Aleksander Anđelić. Once Jack figured out Anđelić was trying to set him up as a fall guy, a cover for his bank heist, Jack turned himself in to the FBI and became their informant. That wouldn't work twice. If Jack went to Danzig now with the information he had on Reginald, not only would there be no way that he could pull another end around and still steal the diamonds, but Danzig would know that Jack lied to her when he said that he'd retired.

There were now a series of unacceptable choices before him.

They had to find out where Reginald and Vito had stashed the stones and steal them before Reginald's stupidity and haste alerted the feds. And they had to do that without tipping Reginald and Vito off that it was Jack, Rusty, and Enzo, because the first thing Reginald would do would be to give Jack's name over to the authorities in trade. And for spite.

Or Jack had to kill them both.

He'd shot a man once in self-defense, and it was a true him-or-me situation, but that didn't stop the nightmares. Jack still saw that man's face in his dreams. Radas was a Serbian war criminal, a member of the Pink Panthers thievery syndicate, and a murderer himself. He'd have shot Jack dead and not given it a second's thought. He was evil throughout, but that didn't make killing him easier to live with.

What if there wasn't any other way to get Reginald and Vito out of the picture?

And what happened when Reginald LeGrande and Vito Verrazano, two former associates of Gentleman Jack Burdette's, turned up dead in Los Angeles and Jack didn't have an airtight alibi?

Jack had told Rusty that this was a game he couldn't play from the sidelines. The same was true for Jack. He couldn't have a foot in both worlds and expect to pull this off. Or, at least, to do a job without consequences.

Jack checked the time. Rusty was due to have landed at LAX at noon. Jack called. They needed to talk, and Jack needed to think.

How far was he willing to go?

NINE

"I'm sure this is all just a misunderstanding," Reginald said in a voice that sounded like his words were dragged over gravel first. He was white-knuckling the phone with one hand and balling his fist with the other. "No, I absolutely understand and appreciate your concerns, but this is clearly a mistake. My firm is...I understand. Thank you for your time." Reginald wasn't sure if the woman on the other end even heard that last part. He lowered the phone and let out a thunderous, "Fuck!"

Vito and his two walking body bags were staring at him as Reginald emerged from the kitchen.

This place was far too small for all of them to be using as a base of operations. He had a four-hundred-square-foot apartment in Hermosa Beach. The rent was eye-gouging for an ex-con but was just affordable enough for someone trying to make an honest go of it. Reginald had money stashed away that the government hadn't touched when he went to prison in 2014, but he wasn't burning that on accommodations. Not just yet. Since getting out, he'd tried getting back into the underground scene in Long Beach, but he'd found that the game had changed and he no longer knew the players. Most of the people he'd worked with ten years ago as a fixer were out of his life, in jail, or dead. A decade is a generation in crime. Of the ones that were left, Reginald just didn't trust them enough to wade back in. He no longer had a pulse on who had been caught, who might be an informant. None of the cops that he used for information could be trusted now either.

Reginald had been an informant for California Highway Patrol for years, after his first stint in state prison for a botched jewelry store job in Beverly Hills in 2000. The CHP had become the state police in the nineties and were doing this big crackdown on robbery rings. So, Reginald played the part of the chastened ex-con and made his vast knowledge of the criminal underworld available to the police. What Reginald was actually doing over that period of eight or so years was tipping the CHP's robbery squad to his rivals. Reginald quickly became known in the thievery circuit as the guy who put these perfect jobs together. You followed his lead, did what you were told, and you weren't going to get busted. After all, he'd made Gentleman Jack Burdette.

Reginald dropped the phone on the counter and grabbed a beer from his fridge. He popped the can and walked into the living room, saying nothing for a time. Vito was sitting in a fold-out chair from a card table, and the two hired mooks he'd brought with him were sitting on Reginald's couch and stealing oxygen. According to Vito, they used to look after some mafia boss, but that guy was either dead or in jail, so maybe they weren't that fucking good at it. One of them didn't speak any English, and Reginald couldn't figure out which one that was. Reginald had tried to put them up in a motel down the street, nice old place that was a couple of blocks from the beach, but Vito wasn't having it. Reginald knew that he was pushing it, storing the diamonds in a place that Vito couldn't get access to, and he'd pushed it further doing that without telling Vito in advance. Vito told him that he understood those moves, but there was a cold front behind his voice, and Reginald knew not to press it any further. So, now he had someone sleeping on his couch and two others on fold-up camping cots that he'd bought at a sporting goods store. *That* was a fun conversation. Thankfully, that argument happened on the way from Van Nuys to his place in Hermosa Beach, and they were able to stop along the way.

"What happened?" Vito asked.

Reginald answered from behind his beer. "Cancelled the appointment. Just said they were no longer interested in talking with us."

"You said something about a misunderstanding on the phone."

"The other guy that cancelled on us said that the time wasn't right for the sale right now but he would keep us in mind for future acquisitions. I asked him why, and he just said their priorities had changed. Really vague. This lady told me that a US Customs agent was there and that she wasn't supposed to talk about it, was doing us a favor in letting us know. I told her it was a misunderstanding, and she said that it may well be, but they couldn't talk to us if there was a problem with Customs. She cut the call off before I could say anything else." Reginald took a deep pull from the beer.

"You don't think it had anything to do with our paperwork or that, what'd you call him, broker at the airport, do you?"

Reginald shook his head. "No. That's perfectly wired." Reginald's tone was flat, matter-of-fact. He'd planned this out to the last detail. The customs broker was someone he could trust. If there was a problem here, it wasn't on this end. "What'd you tell the people in Rome when you left?"

Vito shrugged his shoulders. "I didn't tell 'em anything. Nobody asked. We went to the private terminal, put our guns in the case, and got on the plane. That was it."

"Well, somebody fucking knows," Reginald shouted. One of Vito's bodyguards shifted in his seat like he was going to get up. Reginald caught Vito shooting the kid a glance, and he settled back in his seat. Reginald stepped back into the kitchen, set his beer on the counter, and got three fresh Sierra Nevada cans from the fridge. He passed them out in a kind of awkward showing of detente and then retrieved his own beer. "It just doesn't make any sense," Reginald said after they'd all had a quiet sip. "I have a lot of confidence in the broker. I mean, I guess it's possible that someone at Customs decided to look into it because of how much we brought over, but Mr. Walker, he assured me that wouldn't happen. They wouldn't ask any questions if the paperwork was legit. He said he handled a whole airplane the other day."

"Well, that's two down," Vito said. "What's left?"

"Day after tomorrow, that's the one we're waiting for. Word is, the prospective buyer is overextended in a big way. He's driving around in an Aston Martin, has a house in Palos Verdes that he can't afford and a wife he can't afford either. Has a side piece who knows how much money he makes. Certainly can't afford *that*." Vito's guy on the right laughed at that, so Reginald knew that was the one who spoke English. "Anyway, he's leveraged up to his forehead, and he's not making his numbers. I think he's desperate to make a big sale, because he needs the commission. He's agreed to meet with us and sounds excited about it."

"Great, so why are we meeting with all these other people?"

"Because very few people can stroke an eighty-million-dollar check, that's why. We want to move these diamonds in one go, we need to spread it around. But if we can sell a big chunk of them, say thirty mil or so, that buys us a hell of a lot of breathing room." Reginald looked around his apartment, taking in all four hundred square feet of it as he did. "This customs thing is definitely a problem, though," Reginald said, mostly to himself.

"How'd you find out about this buyer with the house and the expensive wife?"

"I was in prison with an old business associate of his. He went up on a tax evasion hit."

"We sure this is safe?"

"Vito, none of this is fucking *safe*," Reginald snapped and raised the beer can to his lips to hide the glower.

"Fine. So, this customs problem. You gonna call your guy? The broker? See if he knows anything about it?"

"Not yet," Reginald said, drawing an incredulous look from Vito. "We don't want anybody official looking into this, asking too many questions."

"I get that, but we also gotta know if your government thinks something is up. Customs can seize all of those diamonds while they investigate our made-up company. You yourself said that it wouldn't take a government investigator long to figure out that this is all bullshit."

"I know what I said," Reginald said, his lips curling around his teeth. But Vito wasn't entirely incorrect.

Reginald always knew this was a possibility. The odds were never in their favor. But Reginald planned this right, and their smuggling the diamonds into the country was as flawless an operation as he could hope for. Especially given what he had to work with.

Reginald wasn't surprised that Customs might start asking some questions. It was a huge amount of stones; that was bound to raise an eyebrow or two. Well, Reginald hadn't managed to stay alive in this game this long without having a contingency plan or two in his hip pocket. He'd considered this as a possibility. WorldSecure, the company that was storing the diamonds, had a worldwide transportation service. If they could make this first sale, the thirty-million-dollar one, Reginald would just move the operation overseas. He would pay WorldSecure to safely and legally transport his—*their*, he corrected himself—diamonds to one of their other locations. London was an option, and that brought them to the gray markets in Europe. But Singapore was another. And the underground gem trade was thriving in Asia right now.

"Listen," Reginald said and held up a calming hand. "I think this is all, probably, explainable. We're just fucking nervous. I think a customs agent is just trying to do his due diligence and call around, check up on us since we brought in such a large amount. These import houses and brokerages, they all do millions of dollars a week in business, sometimes more. Not all of that is over the table, if you know what I mean. What I'm saying is, these two that cancelled meetings on us, they probably just got spooked." Reginald was entirely bluffing, but it didn't appear that Vito had picked up on it. He actually had no idea how the legitimate gem trade worked or how any of these wholesale operations functioned. Vito didn't need to know that, however.

Reginald was burning through his cash reserves, his flight money, faster than he expected. Vito wasn't kicking anything in, said he'd done enough. They had to have this first sale go through, because they needed the operating capital and, most importantly, to continue to be able to afford the services of WorldSecure.

TEN

Salvatore Cannizzaro was a man unused to being upset. Today, he was furious. Salvatore was a reasonable man. He was a businessman, after all. He'd made a generous deal with Vito Verrazano and had expected Vito to honor it. Salvatore was going to purchase those diamonds for a reasonable price and all at once, which was impossible on the black market these days. Vito would become a rich man, and Salvatore would impress an important new business associate with his thoroughness and resourcefulness. And then Vito went silent. So Salvatore was forced to find him, because who were we if we did not honor our word?

Animals.

It took them a long time, far too long, to track down Vito Verrazano. Vito had never shared his location with Salvatore, which the don understood. If *he* were sitting on six pounds of diamonds, he wouldn't give out his address either. So, Salvatore engaged his network of informants and sent his soldiers looking. It took them months, and eventually they found him in a house in the lake district. He sent his men to Lago Maggiore to Vito's home, where they would force their way in and then make Vito give them the diamonds. Such was the price for going back on one's word.

When Constantino Fiore and his men arrived, he found that Vito was not there and he phoned Salvatore for instructions. Salvatore told him to enter quietly and wait. Vito would return home and they would be able to proceed with the operation as intended. Only, a thief arrived instead. They watched him sneak in from the back stairs. Constantino had a man on the window because Vito had a dock and though it was late, they didn't know if he owned a boat. The thief entered the home and found Vito's safe. In the retelling, Salvatore didn't have the opportunity to feel the same elation that Constantino must have felt at this development because he already knew the outcome. They waited until the thief opened Vito's safe and sprang their trap on him. If they didn't have Vito to force him to open the safe, this thief would serendipitously do it for them.

But this thief outsmarted them. He escaped the lure and then outdrove Constantino and his men. Salvatore's men were blunt instruments. He knew this. They were not professionals. This thief, he was a professional.

Constantino failed him, and the don was furious.

They never saw what exactly was in Vito's safe before it was opened. The thief shot their man and escaped, but he also didn't have much time to take anything.

Don Salvatore Cannizzaro reclined in his chair, and there was no sound other than ice melting, which caused the wine bottle to shift slightly, and the soft gurgle of the pool. He sat on his expansive back lawn, in a small circular patio that was a few feet from his pool, beneath an orange-and-white umbrella. A fifteen-foot hedge ringed the backyard, with large coniferous trees interspersed. Though it was probably unnecessary at this point, because who would have the audacity, but one of his soldiers patrolled the back line. His villa was a walled compound on the outskirts of Rome, a small village surrounded by forest and agricultural land. Salvatore kept to himself, and the locals assumed he was another rich man in a big house.

Moving from Sicily to Rome in the nineties had been a bold choice at the time. The Cannizzaros were members of La Cosa Nostra, the Sicilian mafia. No criminal organization could claim Rome, the city having been purged of its mafia influences after *Il Mattanza*. They were still close to the Camorra of Naples, and that required care, but the Camorra's influence did not extend that far. Salvatore's father was a visionary. He knew his country well and knew that the power vacuum that existed in Rome after *Il Mattanza* would eventually be filled. Nothing in Italy stayed free of corruption for long. But the elder Cannizzaro also avoided the perils of his Sicilian brethren. He didn't murder judges, for one thing. Instead, they bought them. But as businessmen, not as mafiosi. They used their fortunes to gain control of a small bank in Rome, and from there, they gained legitimacy. Then they had a vehicle to not only launder money but to quietly pay the politicians, judges, and officials they needed to stay in business.

Salvatore's father died with his dream largely realized. The one thing he wanted was for Salvatore to take the organization to the furthest heights, push them so far into the stratosphere that no one would ever question their origins, just that the Cannizzaros were great men.

Salvatore reclined and waited, occasionally sipping on the glass of wine at his side. Angelo appeared every so often and asked his don if he would enjoy some food as well. They had an exceptional chef. Salvatore calmly declined. He never ate on anger; it was bad for the digestion. Besides, he was waiting for his guest, who was late. This tension added to Salvatore's nerves. The wine calmed him to a degree, but too much and his fury would be exposed. He needed to find those diamonds and do it quickly. This deal would solidify the end of the Cannizzaros as a mafia organization and their beginning as a global smuggling empire.

Logistics, he corrected himself. They were now into logistics.

Getting control of Feretti and therefore Feretti's shipping business had been quite fortuitous, and for that, Salvatore was proud, despite his current troubles.

But if Salvatore was an impatient man, his buyer and new business partner (if such a term was even accurate) was far less forgiving than he. Salvatore's clock was ticking. His guest was, perhaps, the last chance to find them.

Constantino was a good soldier, but he was not a hunter. He was not a thief.

Salvatore needed a thief, and he needed the best.

But he was late.

If he didn't show, Salvatore would have expended the good options. There was also no guarantee that his guest would agree to the terms. There was much water under many bridges between them.

Angelo appeared at his side just as Salvatore lowered the glass of slightly effervescent lambrusco from his lips. The words of rebuke were forming on Salvatore's lips that he didn't want any goddamn antipasti, when Angelo said that his guest had arrived. Salvatore took several calming breaths and waited until two shadows appeared at the edge of his vision.

Salvatore stood and greeted his cousin.

For sixteen years in prison, he looked pretty good.

"Nico, it's very good to see you," the don said genuinely. Salvatore clapped Niccoló Bartolo on the shoulders.

"It's good to see you too, cousin," Nico said, and stepped forward to embrace his estranged relative.

Salvatore nodded to Angelo, who disappeared back into the house. Then he indicated a chair. "Please, you must sit and have some wine."

Salvatore knew how this must look to some of his men, most of whom had been with him since his father ran the organization. Since his father declared vendetta.

Nico looked like anything but a jewel thief.

Nico was taller than Salvatore and naturally muscled, even at what must now be sixty-three, sixty-four? Nico's face was slightly round with age, where he once looked years younger than he was, prison had closed that distance considerably. His eyes were dark and luminous and had lost none of their fire. When those eyes grew dark with anger, they were fathomless, and it was like looking into the depths of hell.

"I'm sorry that we lost touch for so long," Salvatore said. "It was unnecessary."

"Your father makes a convincing argument," Nico said in an offhand way.

Because they were blood, when Salvatore's father, Vincenzu, became don, he naturally assumed that everyone in his family was in his *family*, and Nico didn't exactly see it the same way. By then, Nico was living in Turin and making quite the name for himself on his own. Nico made one trip to Rome in the mid-nineties to try to patch things up between him and his uncle, for whom he still had much affection and respect. But the don insisted that Nico pay a very reasonable *piso*, a tax, just to show respect. Nico refused. Salvatore attempted to act as an intermediary, but his father was a passionate man and proud. Vincenzu declared vendetta. Nico's life was forfeit. Of course, he was in Turin, and there was very little that could be done.

There was an opportunity to repair the relationship after Antwerp, but Nico chose a different path.

So much water.

So many bridges.

Salvatore wanted to ask his cousin why he hadn't just accepted his father's tithe, shown the proper respect? It was the way of things. But Salvatore restrained himself. He knew starting off on this subject would gain them no ground and may just anger Nico, make him want to leave.

"I was sorry to hear of your father's passing," Nico said softly and genuinely. "He was a great man." Nico made the sign of the cross. Salvatore did the same. Salvatore admired his cousin and saw that he'd lost none of the old savviness, the cunning. With that move, he'd cleared the table.

Salvatore raised a glass and said, "*Salut*." They drank quietly for a moment. "Thank you for coming. And I meant what I said, it has been too long. For that, I am sorry." Because Nico had been imprisoned in Belgium, where Salvatore had no contacts, Salvatore didn't know exactly when he'd been released. Nico had returned to Rome a few months ago but hadn't attempted to make contact. That also meant that Salvatore had no idea how much Nico knew of what had transpired over the last year. The don didn't find himself at a disadvantage often. "Have you spoken with Giulia lately?"

"No," he said flatly. "I have not. Not since she..." Nico's voice trailed off and let what was unsaid speak for him.

Salvatore could tell his response was loaded, but he decided not to press it. Giulia was a dangerous card to play, at any rate.

"There is a situation. An opportunity. If you help me, I'll make you very wealthy, and you can live out the rest of your life on a boat so—"

"I'm already that rich. Or at least I should be," Nico said, and that dark glare came into his eyes.

The don wasn't used to being interrupted. He would forgive this slight this one time. After all, Nico had been in prison with animals for many long years. Likely, he'd forgotten his manners.

"Nico, you can lament about what *was*, or we can discuss what *is*. Vito Verrazano has your diamonds. He attempted to sell them to me and then disappeared with them. I believe to the United States. We can find them together, and I already have a buyer. I will pay you twenty million euros once I've sold them."

Nico scoffed. "Twenty. They're worth five times that, and anyway, they're already mine. Why would I share?"

"Possession is a curious claim, wouldn't you agree? It would seem that ownership is dictated by whoever holds them. But the other reason is that you've been in prison for sixteen years and any contacts you have are long gone. Where would you go? How would you sell them? What protection do you have? Where would you go that I would not find you? I'm asking you to be pragmatic, cousin."

"Pragmatic? You invite me here to give me money, a fraction, for what is already mine and act like I should be thankful for the favor. You're just like—"

Salvatore dropped the remnants of the smile he was feigning. For once, Nico shut his mouth before it got the better of him. Maybe he did learn something in prison after all.

"Nico, here are the facts. You pulled off one of the greatest thefts in history. But you got caught." Salvatore shrugged. "You hid the diamonds before they got you, which was smart, and putting them in my bank took balls. I'm honestly not even mad at you for that. But if you just would have kept your fucking mouth shut, you'd have been out of jail in six years instead of sixteen."

Bartolo's sentence was extended several times during his incarceration, most frequently for contempt of court and lying to the judges. There was one parole violation when he, inexplicably, flew to the United States and then one later for giving an interview to an American magazine—while still behind bars—about the heist.

"So, this is what you're going to do, Nico. This is what I'm offering. You're going to help me get the diamonds back from Vito fucking Verrazano, and I am going to make you a rich man for it. You're going to get a little bit less than what you would have if you tried to sell them yourself, but you and I both know there's no one that can or would write you that check. You're going to take this deal, or I'm going to make good on my father's promise. This would make my favorite aunt very sad, and I don't want to do that. Nico, I can give you twenty million euros, clean and in a bank. Money you can use immediately." Salvatore paused and took a drink, not wanting to overplay his hand.

Bartolo flashed that million-euro smile of his, the one that always turned the ladies up. Even after all that time in prison, he still had it. "Who is your buyer?"

Salvatore shook his head in response.

"Then at least tell me what happened," Nico said and rubbed the bridge between his eyes.

Salvatore refilled their wineglasses.

"Vito comes to me and he says he has these diamonds. He and that Burdette fellow took them from the bank when that Serbian tried to rob it. I'm not going to get into that, it was in all the papers, you can look it up."

"I know what happened," Nico said dryly.

"Vito tells me that he had plans for those stones, but they fell through. The lockdown prevented him from meeting with his buyer, so would I be interested. I offered him twenty-five million and his life, which he wisely accepted. Then, Vito, he disappears on me. I was very offended by this, so I did what any man of reason would do." Salvatore shrugged again and took a drink. "I hired private detectives, I hired police, I spared no expense. Eventually, we found Vito. He has a very nice place on Lago Maggiore."

"Why didn't you just do that in the first place?"

"Because we didn't know he was involved until he came to me. We tracked him down, I had my men break into his place in hopes of surprising him and reminding him of our agreement, but he wasn't there. Someone was, though. We found someone trying to break into his safe. At first, my men thought it was Vito. Like he figured out we were following him and was trying to get his diamonds out." Salvatore nodded at this, as any man of reason would. "Unfortunately, it was not Vito, and he escaped."

"If Jack Burdette was involved in getting the diamonds out of the bank in the first place," Nico said, "then it was very likely Enzo Bachetti in Vito's house."

"We suspected that as well. If, as Vito says, his intention was to betray Burdette all along, it would seem he wouldn't share his home address with them and it would have taken them some time to find him. Bachetti eluded us coming out of the lake district, but we picked him up when he stopped at an AutoGrill outside of Milan and followed him to Rome. He boarded a flight to Los Angeles. My men are following him now."

"So, I fly to America and get the diamonds from Enzo and my old protégé and return here? Then you'll pay me the twenty million?"

"Yes. We have assistance in America. There is a small Cosa Nostra presence in Los Angeles, friends of friends, and they have agreed to help. They have been able to get us weapons, cars, whatever we need. They picked up a tail on Bachetti while our people were in the air."

"I don't have a passport," Nico said flatly.

Salvatore laughed. "All I have to do is take your picture."

NICO WAS anxious to get to work, so he didn't stay much longer. Though, Nico wisely thanked his cousin for his hospitality and his generosity before he departed. Salvatore was pleased by this. Nico politely finished his glass of wine and went to see Salvatore's contact who would provide him a passport. He would be on a flight the following day. Salvatore would make contact with Constantino in Los Angeles. Then the hunt would begin. He had faith in his cousin. Nico had led the School of Turin, the notorious thievery ring. He had pulled the world's largest diamond heist in 2003, which he'd initially gotten away with but was eventually arrested and convicted for. Salvatore was angry and impatient. He was used to lording over his world, and it had been a long time since he'd encountered a problem that he couldn't solve through bullets, money, or some less desirable alternative. There was so much outside of his control, and that was something that Salvatore wasn't used to.

Salvatore had a week left to find and secure the diamonds. Perhaps he could stall for ten days, but that would be pushing it. Gennady Sokolov was a "businessman" in the same way that Salvatore was. He'd become rich enough that the people who mattered no longer cared about what he'd done in his past, which, if the rumors were half-true, was enough for two lifetimes. What Salvatore knew was that Gennady had been a Soviet intelligence officer who'd gone on to become a smuggler and an arms dealer. If it could be moved illegally across national borders, Gennady Sokolov could move it and sell it. But he was also not a man to be crossed. There was a man burned alive in Albania who would attest to that.

Or, at least, he would have.

Salvatore knew about Sokolov from early dealings with Ferretti's shipping concern, had even taken some of his cargo on a journey for him. So, when Vito approached him with the prospect of finding a buyer for his diamonds, Salvatore knew just who to speak to. Sokolov was very interested, Salvatore could tell. He feigned it, of course, that was his opener in negotiations, but Salvatore knew men and knew what motivated them. He could also read a newspaper. Sokolov, it seemed, was on the outs with his government and might be in need of funds. Salvatore might have been able to pay Vito the agreed price of twenty-five million euros, but it would have required the divestiture of significant assets, and he just didn't have that kind of cash lying around. So, when the opportunity to acquire them for free from Vito presented itself, Salvatore thought he would enjoy a substantial profit. His fortunes reversed, and he was now back to paying for them, but better to do that than disappoint his new business partner. Nico's little finder's fee would be better than what he had originally offered Vito.

Sokolov agreed to purchase the diamonds from Salvatore, almost at face value, which suggested that he would be able to sell them for considerably more. Or perhaps he simply needed assets that he could move around and use irrespective of borders. Whatever the case, Salvatore had given his word and arrangements were made. And if Salvatore couldn't deliver on time, there would be no forgiveness.

PART 2
...WHEN TWO ARE DEAD

ELEVEN

Rusty showed them how to track a cell phone with a handheld device, and they were able to trace Reginald to Hermosa Beach.

Rusty flew in two days after Enzo. Jack and Enzo continued their routine, meeting with many of the wholesalers in the International Jewelry Center over the last two days. Of them, Jack didn't think any were capable of writing an eighty-million-dollar check, and it seemed like a lot of wasted effort. Still, good to eliminate them as options. Of course, the more they pulled this routine, the more he was worried that he might encounter someone that actually did have a connection with US Customs and try to verify their story. But those they talked to were more cooperative, and having Reginald's and Vito's aliases to share added to Jack's and Enzo's legitimacy as cops. Enzo didn't agree with the strategy of closing off potential buyers, constraining them to just a handful, but Jack felt it was important to limit the number of people they interacted with in order to lower their profile and risk of exposure. Enzo's concerns had as much to do with every time they flashed a badge, they increased the probability that they would get found out as it did with disagreeing with the actual strategy. They argued about this often between meetings, and Jack was glad to see Rusty, if for nothing else than to break up the tension.

The bug was Rusty's idea.

It had a way of calming the nerves between Jack and Enzo because it meant they could focus on something besides impersonating cops.

Rusty arrived midday while Jack was still tied up at the winery. Jack was worried that the FBI might be watching SFO, and he couldn't get a flight out of Sonoma County Airport that went direct to LA, so instead Jack took an airport shuttle down to San Jose and flew out of there. He didn't arrive in Los Angeles until seven that night. While they were waiting on Jack, Rusty rented a car under whatever alias he was traveling on and picked up Enzo. They went straight to an electronics store that serviced private investigators and other security-related businesses that Rusty had scouted in advance. They picked up the GPS tracer and several recording devices. The amount of personal surveillance equipment available to the public was staggering.

The three of them met in Jack and Enzo's rented suite at the Ritz over a room-service dinner. Jack walked them through the conversation he'd had with Special Agent Danzig that day. As he played the events of the last several days back, Jack realized that while Enzo had been stupid and careless in attempting to steal the take from Vito's house, it didn't materially affect their plan. Cannizzaro knew that someone else was after the stones, but that in and of itself wasn't detrimental to the operation. Cannizzaro knew who Enzo Bachetti was, but his people did not, so Jack didn't believe that they would be able to make the connection that the "someone else" was Jack and Enzo. That thread was tied up, at least for now, in Italy. The danger would be if Cannizzaro's people figured out that Vito had come to California, but frankly, Jack didn't see how that was possible. Mafia organizations in Italy were so regionalized, they just didn't have that kind of reach. Certainly, the Sicilian Cosa Nostra once had very strong ties to American mafia families, but those days were long gone.

"This sounds off to me, Jack," Rusty said. "It seems like Danzig and her team are working in Rome right now, if indeed they are collaborating with the Italian government. I don't think she'd fly across country just to interview you. She sure as hell wouldn't fly all the way here from Rome to do it. I think something is up."

"Well, Cannizzaro doesn't know anything about us," Enzo said. "Jack and I only met him the one time, and that was, like, twenty-something years ago. I'm just saying that if they really do have an informant in his organization, they won't know shit about us. It's not like they asked me for ID when I was at Vito's place."

"I agree we're protected on that front," Jack said. "The bigger concern, in my view, is that if Danzig ever makes the connection between Reginald and Vito. If she starts looking here, we're fucked. And Reginald is already starting to light up the board by calling all over town, trying to put a huge diamond deal together."

"That seems pretty amateurish for him," Rusty agreed. "I thought he was a lot savvier than that."

"Desperate people do stupid things," Jack said and refilled his wine.

"You don't think this is some kind of false flag, do you? Reginald drawing all this attention?"

"I thought about it, but to what end? I mean, Anđelić did that to get the authorities to focus on me and not on him. But Reginald doesn't know we're involved. It doesn't seem like him to be that careless, but I can't figure out any other reason."

"Is it possible there's another crew involved?" Enzo asked.

Jack shrugged. A lot could happen in ten years, and who knew what Reginald said and who he said it to while he was in prison. But that didn't ring true for Jack. Not exactly. "It's possible, but I don't know how likely. If there is, the only thing we can do is outsmart and outmaneuver them. The thing we have to worry about is the feds."

"I agree," Rusty said. "Another crew might cause us some irritation, but they aren't going to be better. The real threat is the FBI."

"So, what do we do about them?" Enzo asked.

"For right now, nothing," Jack said.

"What?"

"What can we do? The FBI doesn't know we're involved yet."

"As far as *we* know," Rusty said.

Jack held out some steadying hands to both of them. "But we also don't have a way of finding out." Jack looked to Rusty. "Right? If we're going to pull this thing off, we need to do it as quickly as possible and get out. We can only worry about the variables that we can control. Our objective has to be getting the diamonds from Reginald and Vito without them knowing about it."

"But Jack," Enzo said, "even if we succeed, you know that we're the first place that they're going to look for them. And you basically live up the street. You also have something to lose. We all got pretty heated the other night, but what Rusty said was true. You can't have it both ways. You're either a thief or you're not. You're not going to walk away from what you have."

Jack nodded and knew his friends were right. He had something to lose now, too much, in fact. He'd let his anger at Vito get the better of him for far too long. Now that he could finally see it for what it was, he saw how clouded his judgment had become.

"Enzo and I talked it out," Rusty said. "I'm wanted, but nobody here knows who the hell I am or is even looking for me. No one knows anything about Enzo. Why don't you let us handle this. We still need you to broker the sale, but taking risk right now is stupid. If we get caught, Enzo and I can disappear, and it's basically just like it always was, only we can't come to America anymore." Rusty shrugged nonchalantly. "Reginald and Vito can both make you. Reginald has never met me in person, and it's doubtful he'd pick up Enzo. Vito is another matter, but he probably doesn't play that big a part in this."

"I've got to at least do something," Jack said with a protest that he didn't really feel. Rusty was right, of course. Jack's judgment would be completely impaired by the fact that he wasn't running away from

Kingfisher, from Megan. What he wanted, truly *wanted*, was to become Frank Fischer in more than just a name. This situation with the diamonds, he didn't see it for what it was at the time. Vito double-crossing them, Jack being outplayed wounded his ego on a level that he hadn't expected because it had never happened before. He wanted to get these diamonds back as much because it was like some kind of final victory over Bartolo, a man who once tried to kill him, as it was proving to Vito that he was better. Once they learned Reginald was involved, the stakes for Jack were raised so high that he couldn't see clearly.

In Rome, Jack risked his life and his freedom in a daring scheme no one saw coming to steal these diamonds right out from under his enemies. In the same sweep, he delivered Aleksander Anđelić to the FBI and brokered a deal that left him more or less a free man. For two years he'd quietly boiled over losing the diamonds because that plan, so audacious, so cunning, was just wiped away by an old man with a gun.

Jack could walk away now, and if Rusty and Enzo got the diamonds, then Jack would broker the sales, which would have to be spread out over a number of years to hide the diamonds' origin. That was how he would earn his share.

"No, you don't have to do anything," Rusty said.

"How about I plant the bug in Reginald's apartment? It'll be easier to tail them if you've got two eyes. I'll do that and then head home. You call me when it's over."

Rusty and Enzo exchanged glances, and Enzo nodded.

THE DEVICE LOOKED like a phone or a handheld radio. They could track Reginald's location using the GPS on the phone associated with that number as long as the device was on. Reginald wouldn't communicate with Vito and anyone else he might be teamed up with outside of their secure messaging app, and that wouldn't be available on a bare-bones disposable phone. Why he wasn't using a disposable phone for the communications with the various gem dealers, Jack couldn't say. It seemed out of character for Reginald, given the effort he usually put into maintaining his anonymity, but Jack wasn't going to question the break they got. Could be Reginald was slipping, could also be that he didn't think anyone would be onto him.

They used the phone tracker to find Reginald living in a shit-shack apartment in a pea-green building above a beachfront grocery store in Hermosa Beach. They found him that first day; Reginald was obviously on the phone quite a bit. The place was on Hermosa Avenue, about a block from the water. Part of Reginald's sentence, when he was finally convicted in 2014 of passport fraud and an embezzlement scheme involving Kingfisher's onetime accountant, Paul Sharpe, Reginald had to pay millions in fines. That cleaned out most of the fortune he'd had stashed away, but Jack always assumed that he had extra money hidden offshore for when he finally did get out. This place seemed like an odd choice to Jack because, given the proximity to the beach, it still had to be an expensive rental, which Jack confirmed on a real estate website. Two grand a month for one of the other properties in that long, two-story building.

But when he actually saw Reginald, Jack understood the logic of it.

Reginald was deeply tanned and had grown his hair out—it was long and had that salt-stringy effect from being so close to the ocean. He'd also grown a beard. He looked every part the retired surfer, beach bum. Reginald would never emerge from the scenery with a look like that; he would never register with anyone. The black Range Rover looked entirely out of place, though, but this was LA, after all, and someone driving a vehicle beyond their means was as common as sunshine.

The plan was to wait until Reginald and Vito left for the day, then Jack would break in and plant the listening device in his apartment. He didn't know where Vito was staying, but they saw that he had a pair of heavies with him, and all four of them were not crashing in a one-bedroom. But it would make sense that they would plan their moves here, because this was where Reginald would feel safe.

Jack cared less about the plan and more about learning where the diamonds were hidden, because there was no way they'd be here. He'd look, of course, but they were not going to hide their fortune here. Jack's guess was there was a bank somewhere, which was all he needed. He didn't want to pull *that* routine again. But knowing where that was meant they could plan to intercept them on the way to a meet. While Jack was planting the device, Rusty and Enzo would follow Reginald's Range Rover and make sure that they were going to be gone long enough for Jack to get the work done. The listening device had a pretty limited range—about a mile and a half, so they planned to take turns staking out.

They were half a block down from Reginald's apartment, parked on the right side of the street. The ocean was behind them, meaning Rusty wouldn't have to make a U-turn and attract attention when they started following the Range Rover. It was ten in the morning and already hot. They'd been in the car two hours, not wanting to miss anything. Vito and one of the goons walked outside around nine thirty and came back with breakfast. Thirty minutes later, all four of them descended the stairs, in suits and sunglasses, and climbed into the Range Rover. Reginald was driving. Seeing them walk down the apartment's exterior stairs to the sidewalk, Jack exited the car. He was wearing sunglasses, a ball cap, and casual street clothes, but he still kept his head low. Enzo's window was still down. He said, "Good luck."

The Malibu pulled away from the curb, about half a block behind the Range Rover. Jack walked in the opposite direction to where the road terminated at the beach. He stood beneath a couple of palm trees and watched the morning sunlight play off the water. There were still a handful of surfers riding out the last of that morning's swell, but otherwise the beach was quiet. After about ten minutes,

Jack's phone vibrated in his pocket. It was Enzo. "It's all clear," he said. "Rusty says it looks like they're heading for the four-oh-five, whatever that is."

Jack laughed. "It's a road. See you when I see you." He hung up. Jack traveled light. He had the listening device, which was about the length of his iPhone and half as wide, and his lock picks. Rusty had gotten them pistols the day before, but Jack left his in the car. He walked back along Hermosa Avenue, back toward the grocery store. The front door was open, and Jack had a line of sight to the person behind the counter. He could hear the radio from outside the store and saw the owner hunched over the counter, reading a newspaper. Jack turned to the staircase and took the steps two at a time until he was at Reginald's door.

This was the risky part. Because this was an outside unit, the doorway faced the street. There wasn't much foot traffic, though it was starting to pick up. Jack remembered seeing a car across the street with about four people in it and all getting out. Standing in front of the door, Jack made a quick scan for surveillance equipment or alarms. There was an alley next to the building, and it followed that the grocery store owner might have cameras, but if he did, there weren't any trained on Reginald's door. He pulled a pair of latex gloves out of one pocket, put them on, and then slid the lock picks out of his pocket and selected the probe and the pick that looked right for the lock. He was rusty. Jack hadn't touched his picks in two years. There were a lot of skills that he'd let slide. Why not? After all, Rome was supposed to be his last. *Focus,* Jack admonished. Luckily, this was a cheap lock and despite his fumbling, Jack was through it quickly enough. Time always seemed to pass slower when your nerves were up, but he did feel like he'd been standing out here just a touch longer than he could casually brush off if someone asked.

Jack opened the door, slid through, and closed it behind him. Jack couldn't tell how long Reginald had been living here, but it was clear that he was able to leave it at a moment's notice. There was no decoration to speak of, just a raggedy couch and a TV in the living room. The walls were off-white, but that might have been from grime, Jack couldn't tell. The front door opened to the living room, which overlooked the street. The kitchen was on the right. The living room and the kitchen both connected with a hallway that led to a bedroom at the back of the apartment. The bedroom had windows on two sides, which looked out over the alley that ran alongside the building.

Jack made a fast search of the living room before moving to the kitchen. Like he'd thought, there was nowhere here to safely hide the diamonds. And if there were, there was no way Reginald was going to trust that to a hardware store lock. Jack quickly opened all cupboards, finding only the barest of essentials—plates, thrift shop cookware, plastic cups, a few boxes of food. He looked for false bottoms, panels, but found none. Similarly with the refrigerator and freezer. He looked in the oven and the pullout tray beneath it. Jack tilted the small stovetop forward so he could peer behind it. Since that was located next to the refrigerator, he was able to get a look behind it as well but found it was flush against the wall. Jack removed the listening device and set it on top of the stove before moving to examine the bathroom and bedroom.

It took him perhaps an additional five minutes to determine that there was no possible way that Reginald was storing six pounds of smuggled diamonds in this apartment. Somehow, he knew they weren't getting off that easily, but it did reinforce Rusty's idea of planting the bug. There was a ventilation closet in the kitchen, and that would be the perfect spot. Jack opened it and removed the small package of adhesive putty that he'd brought. He fixed the listening device and then secured the microphone wire so that the tip was just below the vent. He placed a little more putty to make sure the wire stayed in place. This was a tiny apartment and the microphone should be able to pick up anything in the kitchen or the living room. Jack closed the thin metal cabinet door, which was painted the same off-white as the rest of the apartment. He picked up his things, placed them back in their respective pockets, and did a quick once-over to double-check that he hadn't left anything behind or something out of place.

Jack stepped back and made to leave. He was about four steps from the front door when he saw a shadow move across the window. Then another.

The door handle turned.

TWELVE

Jack would never forget those eyes as long as he lived.

Constantino Fiore was the first through the door, and Jack just stared at him, dumbstruck for a moment, but just as fast he landed on the question of what in the actual hell would *he* be doing *here*? There wasn't a continuity of events that Jack's mind could string together to make sense of this. Judging by the expression on his face, Fiore wasn't expecting to see him either. Fiore cursed in Italian and his hand went for a gun. Jack's hand went to the small of his back, where his holster should be, only to remember that he'd left the gun in the car.

Fiore was a heavy working for Salvatore Cannizzaro. He was their man in the Commerce Bank of Rome. The man who Jack disarmed in a very dangerous game of bluff and who did not take that well. He was the man who murdered Giovanni Castro, no doubt a reprisal for Castro not handing Jack over to the Cannizzaros for his part in the bank break-in. But it was the man behind Fiore that stopped Jack's heart cold.

Niccoló Bartolo.

"What the fuck are you doing here?" Bartolo asked.

Fiore's gun came up and a haphazard shot was off before Jack had a chance to react. It sounded like the loudest of thunders in the close confines. Luckily for him, it was effectively a hip shot and went wide, blasting the wall behind him. Jack had to move. He dropped back out of the kitchen and into the hallway, then darted down the hall to Reginald's room. He slammed the door shut behind him and quickly moved out of the way. Using the wall as cover, Jack pushed the lock to engage it. Two more rounds followed, piercing the door easily. He heard shouting in Italian. Jack ran around to Reginald's bed, which he grabbed the corner of and yanked. He pushed it across the wooden floor to the door, creating a makeshift barricade. It wouldn't last long, but it would give him a second to figure out how to get out of here.

Unfortunately, Constantino Fiore knew how to breach a door.

He fired a shot high and another low, aimed at the door hinges. The door bucked hard, and it sounded like Fiore kicked it to try to force it open. The door, braced by the bed, didn't open or fall off the hinges, but it wouldn't be long. That bed wouldn't hold. Jack's only choice was to go out a window. He opened one of the bedroom windows and punched out the screen. Jack stood there for a moment, trying to puzzle out how to go through it. The bed scratched across the floor as someone on the other side kicked the door with force. There was another gunshot, this one exploding into the wall next to him.

There was no more time to figure out a landing. Jack grasped the top part of the frame, put one leg through, and lifted his body up to make space for the second. Now he was sitting on the window with his legs dangling out. Jack kipped his body and pushed it through. He felt a shock of pain as his back scraped across the bottom part of the windowsill, then a free fall. Jack crashed down on top of a green and black dumpster that, thankfully, was closed. He collapsed into ball, bounced off the hot, heavy plastic lid, and rolled to the street. The sick, sweet reek of rotting garbage thick in his nose.

Jack looked up and saw Fiore at the window staring back at him with that same darkly confident expression he witnessed during their showdown in the bank. Jack remembered thinking at the time that this was a man that would murder you and then grab a coffee. Fiore's empty left hand rested on the sill for a moment, the pistol in the other as he calculated his odds, apparently.

Jack wasted no time.

He took off at a dead run down the alley. Another shot exploded out.

Then a second, which landed right next to him. Jack chanced a look behind him and saw Bartolo on foot in the alley. He must have run back through the house, down the stairs, and around to the alley, hoping to cut Jack off.

Jack broke left at the end of the alley, where it joined a small street. He was a block up from the beach and briefly thought about running that direction but rejected the idea almost as quickly. Neither Fiore nor Bartolo would think twice about murdering Jack in the middle of a crowd, if that was their objective. Jack dashed to the end of the block and across that street. Just as he was crossing it, a car screeched around the corner. This was a residential block, filled with long, two-story homes. Jack sprinted across the street and in between the gap between two of the houses. He heard a car screech to a halt, doors opening. He kept on running through the narrow, shadowed confine, jumping over a coil of garden hose. Jack emerged on the other side, sunlight blazing down. He ran across the next sunbaked street.

Jack again ran through the gap between two buildings, one a house and the other a squat, two-story apartment building. The apartment only ran half the length of the block, however, butting up against the back of a restaurant on the adjacent lot. Jack darted in the space behind the restaurant, changing direction. He was heading back toward the main road now and away from the beach. Jack moved down this alley and saw that it connected with two single-story homes next door. The alley continued on to Hermosa Avenue. Jack ducked around the corner and stopped to catch his breath and listen. His chest heaved. Jack was standing next to an air-conditioning unit, and that made it impossible to hear anything else. He couldn't tell if his pursuers were close.

Questions flashed through his mind almost as quickly as he sucked breath into his lungs.

How did they know about Reginald?

And how on earth was Bartolo part of that?

How was it they happened to be here at exactly the same moment?

Jack saw a blur of motion out of the corner of his right eye. He side-kicked low with his right leg and struck home. Jack turned to face his target. The man grunted in pain and collapsed on the injured leg. Jack had connected right on the outside of the knee. Jack didn't recognize him, but the gun told him he hadn't accidentally hit a store employee on a smoke break. He kicked again, striking the hunched-over pursuer just below his chin. The thug crumpled. Jack grabbed his pistol as it clattered to the ground, only then realizing he was still wearing the latex gloves from his break-in. He jammed the pistol in his front pocket and covered it with his shirt. Jack quickly checked the alley the guy had come down, and finding it empty, he kicked him one more time, sending the man back to the ground. He looked at him again to make sure it wasn't Bartolo. This guy was a heavy and wouldn't know anything worth forcing out of him. The risk wasn't worth the time it would take.

Jack turned his attention back to an escape route.

The house in front of him was a single story, white walls and a green roof. The space between the two houses was fenced off, but it was a low one and Jack mounted it easily. He crouched and ran the length of that space. The wall at the end was about his height. He trotted and then ran to gain momentum, leaping to vault himself over. Jack swung his leg up over the wall and his body followed. He came down in a carport and the pistol crashed to the pavement. Jack grabbed it and put it back in his pocket. He was facing Hermosa Avenue now. Jack leaned against the white wall at his back, heaving and gasping for breath. He didn't have long.

Behind him, he heard an astonished male voice ask, "Hey—who the hell are you?" Then there was a crashing sound. The homeowner must have seen or heard Jack running through his backyard and came to investigate, then found Cannizzaro's thug instead. Jack heard the sound of footsteps coming toward him. He also heard sirens piercing the air. Fiore's indiscriminate firing had summoned the police. Jack went to the sidewalk and checked the traffic on Hermosa Avenue, which he now realized was on an incline. He'd been running downhill this entire time and hadn't realized it. Jack sprinted across the two lanes to the median, where cars were parked on either side. He heard shouts behind him. Jack turned and saw Fiore's man, the one he'd kicked and relieved of his weapon, vaulting over the wall just as he'd done moments before. Jack stood there in the median and stared the man down. He was dressed in a dark short-sleeve shirt, dark pants, and not suited as Fiore and Bartolo had been. Jack lifted the bottom of his shirt up, revealing the confiscated pistol. It didn't register with him until Jack moved his hand to the grip. The goon froze, getting the message. Jack turned and looked back up the street from the direction he'd come. He saw Bartolo emerge around a street corner up the hill.

Jack turned and ran across Hermosa, not even bothering to check for traffic.

Tires screeched and horns blared, someone in an open-topped Wrangler called him a stupid motherfucker. Jack ran to the sidewalk, again slipping into the gap between buildings. There was a single-story house to his right and a two-story house on the left. Because the houses were so close together, at least the curtains were drawn on ground-floor windows of both homes. Jack walked through to the other street. He just needed to run another couple of blocks, and then he should be safe enough to call Rusty and Enzo. Then he'd—

The sharp crack of a gunshot split the air, and Jack fell backward to the ground.

He landed on his ass and immediately went for the pistol. It took him a second to realize he hadn't been shot, it was just a reflex.

"I've been waiting a long time for this, Jack," Niccoló Bartolo shouted from up the street.

Police sirens were getting louder.

Jack was downhill from Bartolo, but since he'd fallen back, he was at least blocked by a building that extended out slightly farther than the one he was next to. Jack pulled the pistol out and then drew his legs in so that he was in a kind of runner's stance. *Just keep moving*, he told himself. For his safety and the innocent people all around them. Jack scanned the houses across the street. Several had fences blocking the narrow gap between them, but he saw one that was two downhill from him, a white mission style, that did not. Jack didn't bother looking; he just sprinted across the street for the opposite yard, and another shot pierced the air.

The house in front of him had a long, narrow stairway leading up to the front door, which was a bit off street level. Jack bounded up the steps. The house next to it had some privacy landscaping, making the most of the little land they had to work with, and a tall, bushy tree obstructed the view from the street. When he reached the top, next to the front door, he saw that a concrete path continued straight to the backyard. Jack looked back over his shoulder as he mounted the steps and saw Bartolo running for him at full speed. Jack thought about evading by jumping from the stairs down to the neighboring yard, but Bartolo was too close. He'd also have the high ground by the time Jack recovered from the fall. Looking at it, Jack realized he'd be boxed in.

But Bartolo was a clean shot.

Bartolo was running up the stairs, and Jack was at the top of them. Bartolo had no cover but to dive for the yard next door, quite a distance down and dangerous.

A thousand images flashed through his mind, but the one that froze, as if it were burned into the back of his retinas, was Bartolo holding a gun on him that night in Turin, 1997. The night he learned Giovanni Castro was an undercover cop and was going to bust the School of Turin. The night he mistakenly told Giulia and the night he learned she'd been two-timing him with his "friend" and "mentor," Niccoló Bartolo. Nico almost killed him then, and there were a lot of long, dark nights when a young Jack Burdette wished he had.

Jack's hand went to his pistol and, in the next motion, drew it and leveled it at Bartolo.

Nico froze, and Jack could see in Bartolo's eyes everything that had passed between the two of them.

No one moved.

Jack couldn't pull the trigger.

"Shit," Jack growled, and he turned and ran down the concrete path, hoping to reach the backyard and the cross street beyond.

He couldn't bring himself to do it. Jack knew that there were a lot of long nights ahead of him dealing with what happened in Rome, but he wasn't going to compound that grief by adding another body to the tally. There was another, more practical reason, which was if Bartolo died here, it would be obvious who did it. Fiore could just call the Hermosa police on an anonymous tip, and then the manhunt would begin.

Footsteps behind him.

"You always were a fucking coward," Bartolo shouted, not far behind him.

Jack accelerated as fast as he could down the flagstone pathway between the houses. Jack reached the end and realized that this was actually the front of the house. The path ended abruptly, hooking in to the front porch. Jack had too much momentum to stop, so he let it carry him over the low ledge and he leapt into the air. He crashed down on the lawn in the middle of a bunch of what looked like waist-high palm trees. Jack stood and was about to run when a crushing weight slammed into him.

Jack and Bartolo landed in a tangled heap on the lawn, in the middle of that cluster of palms. Fists were flying before either of them slid to a stop. Jack landed one good hit on the side of Bartolo's face. Jack realized instantly that his gun had come out of his pocket when he landed. He grabbed Bartolo's right hand with his left and tried to keep the gun at arm's length and aimed somewhere else. The two struggled with each other, grunting and thrashing.

Bartolo had always been a large man, muscular, and sixteen years in a Belgian prison did little to diminish that. Jack used all his strength to slam Bartolo's hand repeatedly against the trunk of one of those low palm trees. On the third or fourth hit, Bartolo's gun knocked loose and fell into the thick underbrush. Jack brought his leg in and kicked, driving it into Bartolo's abdomen. The old thief grunted and crumpled. Jack pulled both legs in and kicked out, driving Bartolo off him. Jack reached for his gun and Bartolo's fist connected with his face, hard. Jack's head bounced off the ground. But Bartolo was no longer on top of him. Jack rolled over onto his hands and knees, grabbed his gun, and staggered to his feet. The fronds of those stubby palms scratched him. Bartolo was getting to his feet too, and he'd found his gun.

Jack took off again at a run, pushing through that last cluster of fronds like it was a green turnstile. He ran to the edge of the lawn, which was above street level, so he easily vaulted the low wall that ran along the sidewalk. Jack ran across the street. His chest heaved and his limbs felt like rubber. He looked back and saw Bartolo had gotten to his feet. Jack held his pistol up. "Back off, Nico," Jack said, huffing.

Something caught Jack's attention out of the corner of his eye, and Jack turned his head to the left, looking downhill. About a block down, maybe a little more, he saw a police car race by, heading in the direction of the beach. Jack turned his attention back to Bartolo, but he was running back up the stairs the way they'd come.

Jack lowered his pistol and then jammed it in the small of his back.

Jack turned and ran in the opposite direction, cutting through another three or four blocks of residential neighborhoods and dashing between homes before he came to a commercial district. The dividing line between the two was a long strip of trees with a dirt running path in the center. It looked like it might be a municipal park. Jack saw several people jogging, walking pets. His clothes were dirty from the scuffle on the ground, and he had a myriad of small cuts on his forearms. He felt like his face was probably the same. But he stepped beneath the leafy trees for some shade, and when no one was looking, Jack dumped the pistol into a city garbage can. He continued walking and finally removed the remnants of the latex gloves, now ripped and dirty. He balled them up, carrying them in a clenched fist for another block before he found a trash can to get rid of them as well.

Jack needed to get out of here and fast. Rusty and Enzo had the car. He couldn't use a ride share service, though, because they tracked riders and that was the last thing Jack needed. The police would probably contact the services and see if there were pickups around the time of the shooting within a certain radius. To say nothing of the fact that Jack looked like he'd gotten in a fight. Jack turned north, walking along a main road. He pulled his phone out and dialed Enzo, checking around to see if there was any police activity near him.

"How'd it go?" Enzo asked when he answered. "We're sitting in this fucking traffic. This place—"

"Enzo," Jack broke in, "Bartolo is here."

"*What?* How do you know? Are you sure?"

"Pretty sure. We just mixed it up in somebody's lawn. And he took a couple shots at me."

"Shots, like gunshots?"

"Yes. He's here with people too. Cannizzaro's people. I recognize one of them from the bank. Constantino Fiore. He was the one who killed Gio," Jack said, using their nickname for Giovanni Castro.

"Holy fuck," Enzo said in a vacant voice, and Jack knew that meant he was thinking. When Enzo wasn't sure what to do, he just peppered the landscape with curses. "Okay, we're turning around. Tell us where you are."

"Do *not* do that," Jack said. "You guys have to keep following Reginald and see if you can find out where they're hiding the diamonds. I don't know if Fiore would have found the bug or not, but that place is a fucking crime scene now. Reginald and Vito aren't going back there anytime soon. I'm trying to find a cab. I'll call you when I get somewhere safe."

"Are you sure?"

"Yeah. This is our only chance to figure out what's going on. But, Enzo, we've got to figure out how Cannizzaro knew about Vito and where he would be. They obviously followed him here."

"I don't know, Jack," Enzo said in a defensive tone.

"I know, but we have to figure that out fast." Jack saw what looked like a white Prius with "Beach Taxi" stenciled on its side on the other side of the street. Jack flagged him. The driver caught his eye and began to make a U-turn. Jack had lived in Los Angeles when he and Reginald were running together in the early nineties, so he was familiar with the area, though he didn't spend much time down here anymore. Occasionally, Jack would fly down if Frank Fischer had a meeting with a wine distributor or a maybe a restaurant that was going to carry Kingfisher. So, when the cab picked him up, Jack just told the guy to take him to El Segundo. It was two towns north of Hermosa Beach and was far enough away that it would be outside of any dragnet the police would throw.

The cab driver was mercifully silent. The entire trip, Jack was scrolling local news sites, looking for updates on the reports of "shots fired" in Hermosa Beach. As the cab took him away, Jack was confronted with the thoughts of how an Italian mafia boss knew about these diamonds and could dispatch his people to come get them. Had they followed Vito here? Or worse, had they followed Enzo?

THIRTEEN

Rusty hid his nerves well, but he hadn't been on this sharp of an edge in fifteen years.

Not since Berlin.

Rusty also never intended to get involved with the scores his clients planned. The scores, the schemes, the revenge-for-hire bits, the industrial espionage and yes, occasionally working with intelligence agencies. Even his own. On the street, he was known as a fixer. If you had a problem, Rusty made it go away. Maybe that problem was needing dirt on a public official, access to an untraceable weapon, or maybe that problem was a dead body and bloodstains. From his time as a counterintelligence officer, he knew how to craft fake identities, travel documents, even passports. He knew where to find weapons of all calibers without serial numbers, clean cash, and clean cars. By the time he first started working with a young jewel thief named Gentleman Jack Burdette, Rusty had established himself as one of the premier illicit logisticians in Europe. He only took clients that were vouched for by people he trusted. Jack came recommended to him, and he immediately liked his style.

The fact that he had any at all.

Rusty also liked that Jack wasn't trying to hurt anyone. For as much as he hated the United States government for what they did to him, Rusty wasn't a sociopath and didn't want anything bad to happen to civilians. So, he appreciated that Jack only took small scores, worked mostly at night and never with a gun. They'd been working together two or three years before Jack even asked him for one. Then there were the cars. That proved a unique challenge that he truly enjoyed. A Ferrari or a Maserati, as fast as they were, weren't ideal for a car chase, but Jack would tell you that if you'd gotten into a chase, your plan had failed. No, he requested those cars because the police never looked twice at guy in a Maserati GTO or an Aston Martin DB-9, except maybe in envy. It never occurred to them there might be two million in stolen jewels in the trunk.

Rusty had a home in Switzerland and another in Mallorca.

Rusty lived a good life.

At least, as good of a life as he could come to expect.

He made it a habit, a survival mechanism, to stay out of his clients' business. It wasn't so much the deniability with law enforcement, should he ever be caught. If he ever found himself explaining to a cop how and why he came to be in possession of a stolen car, stolen plates from a different car, ten thousand in cash, and a Beretta with no serial number, the intents wouldn't much matter.

No, Rusty didn't want to know what his clients did because he didn't want any part of it. He could put enough together from the news. Rusty first edged over his red line eight years previous when Jack, having just pulled one of the largest, most daring, and certainly most out-of-type scores in history, the Carlton InterContinental job in Cannes, was in a bind and needed help evading a particularly violent crew of the international thievery syndicate known as the Pink Panthers. Rusty took the job and made several million for it. After that, he continued to work as Jack's fixer, but they'd developed a friendship.

But Rome changed all that for good.

After Cannes, FBI Special Agent Katrina Danzig figured out

who he was, and Rusty never really learned how. He still had Bureau contracts, people that fed him information, people that knew he got a raw deal. It was possible one of them flipped. It was also possible that one of his Agency contacts dimed him out. He'd created a nearly flawless series of false identities that he lived under, but the people in the CIA who knew he'd been burned (probably *by* them) knew how to find him once he'd set up his new occupation. They used his services constantly, but that didn't mean they were loyal.

But Danzig had a hard-on for him because he was one of their own and was now playing for the other side. She went after Rusty hard when Jack was exposed on the Paris job that went south two years ago. The job that landed him in Aleksander Andelić's web. Danzig engaged the State Department's law enforcement agency, the Diplomatic Security Service, to go after Rusty for his passport forgery. That got him on the run. That also made him a player in Jack's scheme to liberate a hundred million in stolen diamonds from a mob-controlled bank in Rome.

Sounded kind of crazy when you said it aloud.

Rusty became a member of a crew then, something he said he would never do.

Instead of making him twenty-five mil and the ability to disappear forever, he got a .22-caliber round in the leg and another in the lung.

He limped for six months and couldn't move without a cane.

Physical therapy wasn't the easiest thing to get for a thief on the lam.

He recovered and was, more or less, back to full health.

So now he was a member of a crew. If he was going to break that rule, if he was really going to work with someone, it would only have been Jack. But crossing that line wasn't the thing that set him on edge. It was just the fact of being back in the United States as a former FBI counterintelligence officer, framed by his own government because that was the easy way out, the *deniable* way out. Rusty, whose real name was Scott Donners, was on every watchlist there was—FBI

Most Wanted, INTERPOL Red Notice, and a score of others. You could hide in Europe and do it easily. There were former KGB officers in Austria, Rusty knew three of them, he had drinks with one of them on occasion.

Rusty knew the FBI hung him out because it was the expedient thing to do and would avoid an international incident. He learned from one of his friends inside that they were basically letting him run, that it was their fucked-up way of paying him back for ruining his name and wrecking his life. So long as he didn't ply his trade helping out terrorists or Russians or any other of America's bêtes noires at the time, they were fine to let bygones. All of that was fine so long as he stayed outside the United States. Because once he reentered the US, they'd believe he was forcing someone's hand to reckon with what happened, and America's leadership was not particularly well disposed to affirming publicly the nasty things they did in the interest of "national security."

So, Rusty was giving a command performance in hiding his nerves.

Having something to concentrate on helped. He followed Reginald's Range Rover from Hermosa Beach to Hawthorne, where he picked up the 105 just outside LAX. You could practically trip over a black Range Rover walking into any parking lot north of downtown, but so far he'd been able to keep them sighted. A Malibu wasn't the ideal chase vehicle, but it did blend in. From there, they picked up the 110 northbound and rode that, gradually, to downtown.

Running a tail with one car was incredibly hard. Normally, it required two or three cars, all coordinated by radio, with the lead chase cars swapping out periodically so that the target never got wind of the pursuit. Or, more importantly, you had backup if the chase car was stuck in traffic, was sideswiped by some asshole looking at his phone, or the chase got made. They could have done it with Jack driving a second car, but they'd all agreed that it was best for Jack to stay as far from Reginald and Vito as he could, as they could both make him. Enzo had never been to Los Angeles before and didn't know the roads. It would be hard enough for him to navigate, paying attention to the sludgy sluice of LA traffic, without having to run a tail. So they decided to take their chances with one car. Rusty focused on the road and was careful to stay several cars back from the Range Rover while Enzo kept eyes solely on the target.

Rusty made sure that they never got close enough to the Range Rover for visual recognition.

Vito obviously knew Rusty by sight, but Reginald had never met Rusty in person, so if LeGrande happened to catch him in the rearview, it would be just another face. Reginald had met Enzo before, but it'd been at least ten years. He wouldn't recognize Enzo. Vito would, of course, but he'd only have a side mirror and they were both wearing sunglasses.

Besides, they had the cell phone tracker. If they lost him, Rusty expected that Reginald would make a call when he got to his destination, lighting up his location on their tracker. Sure enough, the Range Rover pulled into the exit lane at the Sixth Street off-ramp, and Rusty knew almost immediately where they were going. He waited until the Range Rover was on the off-ramp and then accelerated.

"What are you doing?" Enzo asked, confused, as Rusty jerked the Malibu around one car and barely missed the front end of another. "Hey, that was fucking close. We get in an accident and—"

Rusty turned his head ever so slightly, and Enzo didn't say anything else. He'd been well trained for situations like this.

"They're going to the Jewelry District," Rusty said. He weaved through the midday traffic, lighter than rush hour but still thick, to the next exit, which was Third Street, three blocks up from where Reginald exited. At the bottom of the off-ramp, Rusty turned south on Figueroa, then to Fifth, and then back east, in the direction of the Historic Core. That's what they called the buildings that they didn't demolish and couldn't renovate. Rusty rolled through the Hill Street intersection and pointed out Enzo's window. "Check it out."

There was the Range Rover, parked in front of the International Jewelry Center.

Rusty pulled around the block so that he'd approach them from behind. The Range Rover was parked halfway down the block. Rusty rolled past the Rover and spotted the two heavies they'd seen with Reginald and Vito earlier sitting in the front seat. As he passed the SUV, Rusty spotted a sign on the first floor of the Jewelry Center. The sign said "WorldSecure" beneath a stylized outline of a globe with a key at the center. "Get your phone out and look up 'WorldSecure,' 550 South Hill Street."

"On it," Enzo said and typed the name into his search engine. "'WorldSecure is the premier secure global storage and logistics firm of choice for collectors, investors, and high net worth individuals.' Says they store and transport precious gems, metals, and fine art for their clients."

"Son of a bitch," Rusty said. "That's where they're hiding them. Reginald must have had enough front money to get himself an account."

"Wouldn't they do background checks, though? Income verification or something?"

"Oh, of course they would. But all of that can be falsified if you know how, and Reginald does."

Rusty drove up a block and pulled a U-turn, then parked a half a block up next to Los Angeles's historic Pershing Square park. They were across the street from the Range Rover. Reginald and Vito left the building about ten minutes later. Rusty watched the SUV fall in behind an armored car that emerged from a parking lot next to the Jewelry Center. The armored car wasn't parked there before, so there must have been a covered access point on the other side of the building. Rusty could see an alley behind it. The armored car pulled out onto Hill, almost directly across from the Malibu, and turned right. The Range Rover followed the truck through a left turn onto Fifth Street. Rusty pulled out and U-turned, earning a long honk and a middle finger from the driver he'd just cut off. Rusty hit the corner just in time to see Reginald turning right onto Olive and then pulling into a metered space (and taking up two) across the street from an immensely tall, needle-shaped building of blue glass that must have been sixty floors or more. Part of that building stretched across Olive, creating a kind of tunnel. The Range Rover parked there, out of the sun.

"Jesus, all that for a block?"

Rusty had lost the armored car. By the time he'd turned the car around, it was gone. He'd lost sight of it after the left onto Fifth. Rusty didn't want to chance looking for it, so he had to assume that there might be an entrance to a parking garage underneath the part of the building that went over Olive or perhaps a delivery entrance on the other side of the building. All he knew were that the traffic patterns in this part of the city were a very confusing mix of one-way streets that he had yet to figure out.

Rusty paused a moment in the intersection, waiting to see if Reginald and Vito got out. This drew another angry response from another impatient driver. Rusty slowly turned right, eyes on the tunnel. He thought he saw two figures walking across the street in the shadow of the tunnel. The car behind him whipped around him, his patience exhausted, and the last thing Rusty saw before he completed his turn was its brake lights. He'd blasted his way up half a block only to have to stop for Reginald and Vito crossing Olive beneath the tunnel.

Olive, in this direction, was moving uphill, so when Rusty turned right onto Fourth Street, just before the block where Reginald parked the Range Rover, he was now facing downhill. Rusty drove halfway down, almost to Hill, before he found a parking spot to squeeze the Malibu into. There was a park on the left side of the street and, he realized too late, a parking garage on the right. Rusty had to parallel park aiming downhill, and it took him a few tries before he got it right. Every second he wasted was another step Reginald and Vito got farther from his sight.

"I'm going to go have a look around, see if I can figure out where they went," Rusty said, getting out. Enzo said nothing, likely knowing that Rusty would already be aware of anything Enzo would admonish him to do. Rusty stepped out into the heat of midday. There was a park on the block he'd parked on with several leafy trees that hung over the tall chain link fence separating the sidewalk from the park. The ground on the other side of it was brown and scorched. The trees themselves were a mixture of green and brown, as though they'd given up to the inevitable. Rusty walked uphill quickly to the corner of Olive and Fourth; it was steep, and he'd broken out into a sweat. He glanced up the block and saw the Range Rover. The rear window was tinted, so he couldn't tell if the heavies had gotten out with Reginald and Vito or if they stayed in the car.

Rusty crossed the street with the walk signal and found a set of stairs adjacent to the building that likely led up to the entry plaza. Rusty wore a tan suit, dark blue shirt and no tie, and sunglasses. He'd also grown his hair out over the last year. His style, for years, had been a thin layer of stubble on top of his head. Rusty liked the look, but it was also practical. He often disguised his appearance with wigs, facial appliances, and makeup when meeting with prospective customers he didn't know. Someone needed an introduction to talk to him, but that didn't necessarily mean they were trustworthy. Rusty hadn't taken any clients during the time he was recuperating and had just let his hair grow. His look was different enough that Vito probably wouldn't recognize him at first glance, particularly if he saw Rusty from afar and he had his sunglasses on. Still, he needed to be careful.

There was a long line of steps with an outdoor escalator next to them, and Rusty opted for the latter, taking the escalator steps two at a time. He exited in a covered entry indicating that he'd arrived at One California Plaza. Rusty saw signs for Los Angeles's famous Angels Flight and a large food court. He made a quick scan for Reginald and Vito but didn't find them in the crowd. Rusty climbed another set of steps that took him to the outdoor plaza between One California and Two California buildings. They looked like immense spires of blue crystal, reflecting back an angry and hateful sun. The outdoor plaza between the two buildings was three levels and reminded him of an inverted ziggurat, with reflecting pools and fountains at the center and surrounded by trees, modern art sculptures, and benches.

Rusty skirted the edge of the plaza to One California and entered. The building was immense, so was its atrium, and crowded with people, but Rusty found what he was looking for easily. A building directory. It took several minutes of searching the touch-screen interface, but he eventually found it.

A.G. Barret Diamond Brokerage.

FOURTEEN

Carter LeMothe looked like California.

LeMothe was deeply tanned, tall, and lean in the way that came from a five-hundred-dollar-a-month health club membership, and he filled in his twelve-hundred-dollar suit perfectly. The suit was navy, with a pink shirt and a dark-colored tie that looked like it had a subtle pattern that only got more complex the closer one got to him. Carter's blond hair was over-styled but still perfectly in place and was done in such a way that it looked sun bleached and weathered, though if Reginald were to guess, that was the result of another expensive treatment. Carter's jawline could have been cut by an expert jeweler (or surgeon). He had pale blue eyes that always seemed intently focused on something, just not the person he was talking to.

Carter looked like exactly the kind of person who would have a last name for a first name, which is to say, an asshole.

They weren't kept waiting long. A pair of armed guards hefting a strongbox had a way of opening doors.

The two men from WorldSecure would stand by in A.G. Barret's lobby until it was clear that the transaction was made and they wouldn't be carrying the diamonds back to the vault. They were paid to wait, it was part of the fee.

Reginald and Vito stood in the center of Carter LeMothe's office, white porcelain espresso cups and saucers in their hands. Carter moved about his office, usually gesturing grandly with his right hand. He was telling them about A.G. Barret, though mostly that was the story of Carter LeMothe and his role as vice president of acquisition, which meant he was responsible for negotiating deals for precious gems and metals throughout the world. Emeralds were very big right now, were they aware? Reginald said he'd read that as well, though he hadn't actually. This was Carter LeMothe's way of starting to lowball them. *Emeralds are in, diamonds are out, I'll do you guys a favor, but I'm totally taking a bath on this one.*

Carter had a commanding thirty-seventh-floor view of Bunker Hill.

Carter had an Aston Martin DB11 Volante the color of liquid metal.

He lived in Palos Verdes with a wife he couldn't afford and a mistress that knew what he was worth.

Carter had a boat that he liked to take to Catalina with either of the women in his life when the mood struck him.

Carter was leveraged to the gills and he would deal, so Reginald listened to how emeralds were up, sapphire was on the rise, and diamonds were down because Gen Z wasn't into material wealth. Reginald listened to how Carter LeMothe put together several multi-million dollar acquisitions a month and how these things took time and he'd like to work them in. If he could, of course.

Reginald listened to this for a solid fifteen minutes, until he decided it was time to cut the shit.

"How much commission do you make on thirty million?"

And Carter LeMothe smiled.

They hadn't brought that much with them, not even close. There was approximately five million in diamonds in the small steel carrying case, which looked like a metal briefcase. It was sitting on

LeMothe's coffee table. This was carried by the guards in the strongbox, which they had presented to Reginald when they first entered the room. He'd thanked them, and they'd disappeared from the office to await further instructions. Carter LeMothe had yet to look at the contents of the case.

Reginald walked over to it and unlocked the case with the key the business manager at WorldSecure gave him when he signed his property out. Reginald opened the case with minimal flourish. The interior of the case was lined with padded velvet, and two small velvet pouches were secured to the lining with padded straps. The side of the case without the straps doubled as a presentation tray. Reginald opened the first bag and gently placed the contents on the tray and then did the same with the other. The diamonds glittered, tiny fireballs, as they rolled to a stop on the tray.

"Our mutual friend said to look you up and, looking around here, Carter, I'm glad he did. I think you're a man with some vision, a man who can recognize an opportunity when he sees one." Their "mutual friend" was F. Norris Tillet, who was an acquaintance of Reginald's during the end of his sentence. F. Norris did three years for tax evasion and money laundering, and though the original sentence was much longer, it was knocked down considerably due to updated guidelines for nonviolent crime, good behavior, and ratting out a whole lot of customers. F. Norris said that his old friend, Carter, traded under the table and had bragged to him about skimming. He was the one who tipped Reginald to Carter's financial problems. When F. Norris made the introduction, he neglected to mention that they'd met in prison. Reginald would take care of him once they had the money.

"Same, yeah," Carter said, his mind already on something else. "Norris got a raw deal. He's not doing anything any other banker isn't doing already. Bunch a bullshit, you ask me."

"Carter, I'll level with you because I trust Norris and he said you were someone I could trust. My associate, Vito, and I are sitting on a lot of diamonds. What you see here is about seven million worth.

About two years ago, we put a very large deal together. Wholesaler in Israel was about to get indicted for smuggling—much like with our friend F. Norris, a bunch of bullshit. Vito and I put a company together and bought his supply. Everything is perfectly legal, and the deal closed before he was arrested."

"His problems are not our problems, right? And I bet you got a hell of a discount."

"Carter, I'm sitting on one hundred and thirteen million in diamonds."

That got Carter LeMothe's attention.

"Vito and I made the purchase for eighty-five. That's how desperate this guy was."

"Jesus, how'd you raise that much money?"

"We owned a company that did rare earth element and mineral speculation in the developing world. Really dangerous shit. I've been shot at more times than the Marines. We sold that off to put this deal together, as well as some financing from a few investors. They're anxious to be paid back."

"I bet. Well, look, Norris speaks really highly of you, and I'd love to help you out, but like I said, there isn't much market for diamonds right now."

"Carter, we both know that's not true. It's a banner year for stones. People have been stuck at home for year with nothing to do, and they're impulse-buying jewelry."

LeMothe shrugged, and he half turned to look out the window. "Reginald, while it is true that trends have been on the upswing, my firm is not in a position to give you one hundred and thirteen million. That's half of what we'd do in a year."

"Of course," Reginald said. "Vito and I understand that we're not moving all of these at once. And frankly, if we did, our investors would be very skeptical."

Vito, who'd been silent to this point, said, "That's right."

"No, we are looking to establish partnerships with some trusted buyers. We don't need to sell the entire stock at once, but a portion of it will go a long way to mollifying our investors and giving us a little breathing room."

Carter walked over to the table and inspected the diamonds on the tray. Reginald figured this was probably as close to a loose stone as he'd been in years. "So, let's do this," Carter LeMothe said. "I'm going to have our guys check it out and appraise them. If everything comes back okay, I'll purchase this lot from you at five five. Give it a couple of months, and I can probably take more."

"Carter, International Gems offered me six million eight for these. Now, they want a ten-day escrow, like I'm buying a fucking condo. If you can close it today, tomorrow at the latest, I'll meet you at five nine." Reginald looked over at his partner. "How do we even know you can deliver?"

"Ha. I do million-dollar deals for breakfast."

Without missing a beat, Vito said, "I prefer a nice croissant and an espresso myself. Plate of eggs."

Reginald had to suppress a snort. That was how you dealt with people like Carter LeMothe. You took the wind out.

"Carter," Vito said, and the way he annunciated the name, it sounded like the word went over a hill between the *a* and the *r*. "Reginald said we didn't expect to sell these in one sitting, and that is mostly true. What's also true is that we have other potential buyers that we'll be meeting with. Some are looking for large amounts, others small. But they are all willing, and they come with cash."

Reginald leaned forward to speak and Vito held out a steadying hand, just like they'd practiced.

"Now, my partner wants to work with you because a friend of his vouched for you. Reginald would like to see his friend taken care of. I'm fifty percent of this deal, and I am less interested in who buys my diamonds. I'm much more interested in the boat I'm going to buy with that money. Do you understand me? As we say in my country, *Batti il ferro finché è caldo.*"

Carter looked at him with a blank and stupid expression on his face.

Vito sighed, just slightly, as though he were both tired and annoyed. "Beat the iron while it's hot."

Carter stared at them both for several beats, and while his face was expressionless, it was clear the mind was at work. Reginald had stared down many a man in his career, thief and cop alike. He could always tell when someone was calculating the odds in their head.

"I've got an idea," Carter LeMothe said. "I'll be honest with you both, because I like you. A.G. Barret isn't the right place for you *or* your diamonds. To be honest, I'm not sure how much longer I'm going to be here. I can't tell you how many times I've had a phenomenal deal," Carter cupped his hand and held it up, like he was protecting something in the palm of it, "and these idiots refused to jump on it. I've lost more than a little money on account of it. I'd feel badly if I put something together for us and then I wasn't here to see it through." Carter LeMothe leaned forward in his chair. "So look, I've got a broker that I deal with a lot in Hong Kong, high-volume dealer. This is someone I trust. When I've got trades that A.G. won't make, I call my friends at LGK. I think A.G. might be good for ten million, and LGK can likely buy the rest. Unless they want the whole lot right away, and I'll step aside."

"And I suppose you get a nice finder's fee on top of that."

"A nice, quiet one," Carter LeMothe said.

He was in.

FIFTEEN

Jack changed cabs twice and used a ride share service on his trip back downtown to make sure he wasn't followed. There were many techniques he'd developed over the years of being a thief that helped him calm frayed nerves before a job and that odd combination of exhilaration and panic after one. He likened it to skydiving with an untrustworthy chute packer. You didn't know if it worked until it did. But none of those things he used to calm his mind, steady his breath, and project calm and certainty to his crews was working right now.

Niccoló Bartolo was in Los Angeles.

Constantino Fiore was in Los Angeles.

They knew the diamonds were here, somehow, and staked out Reginald's place. Two possibilities came to mind. Either they'd followed Vito from Rome to LA or they'd followed Enzo. Both of those seemed like stretches to Jack. There was just no way that he could reason out that the Cannizzaros could pull that off. Sure, he believed Danzig and Castro before her, when he'd heard they were now a highly sophisticated smuggling operation, they'd had judges and politicians in their pocket. Whatever. They were still a mafia. Their soldiers were barely literate thugs, career criminals, and most of them heavies. This was not an organization capable of pulling off surveillance and sure as shit not capable of tracking someone across continents.

Jack hit refresh again on the local news sites he'd opened on his phone for an update. But there was nothing substantive. One TV station was reporting that there was a shootout in Hermosa Beach but offered no other details. No one else had picked up the story yet. It wasn't even a mass shooting, Jack noted sardonically. People shot guns in LA all the time. The car crawled up the 110 toward downtown, and Jack had to restrain himself from asking the driver if this was as fast as he could go. Eventually, *gradually*, Jack thought sourly, the car pulled off on the freeway and Jack's view shifted from a green-and-brown ribbon of crumpled mountains in the distance to the concrete and glass canyons of downtown. The driver turned south on Figueroa and headed two blocks to the Ritz.

Jack refrained from texting Enzo and Rusty during the trip, fighting the impulse to update his team immediately on these events because he couldn't take their inevitable call while he was in the car with someone and also didn't want to take their focus away from following Reginald. Though he wondered how much that mattered now. This job was compromised. He stepped into the hotel, feeling the sharp slap in temperature change from the raw and dirty heat of the streets to the cool comfort and traces of eucalyptus of the lobby.

Jack gratefully accepted a bottle of water from an attendant in the lobby and went to his room.

That Bartolo was here was unquestionably bad. It would actually have been the worst possible thing but for one small fact that was actually something much, much worse.

Jack learned about Cannizzaro's involvement in this from the FBI. The Italian antimafia police had someone, an informant or an undercover, in Cannizzaro's organization. If Cannizzaro knew the diamonds were in Los Angeles, the FBI might now know that too.

As soon as Bartolo reported back to his boss that Jack was here... the FBI would know that as well.

"FUCK," Enzo said.

Jack called the other two and said they needed to get back to the hotel as soon as possible. Enzo told him they were already on their way back. Jack filled them in on what happened at Reginald's place as soon as they walked in the door. He had the TV on to local news, desperate for coverage. It wasn't just that he was worried about himself being identified, it was more that if Fiore or Bartolo were arrested, "Jack Burdette" would be the name they had. Jack's nerves calmed slightly the farther he got from the events of that morning, moving to the adrenaline crash following fight or flight.

Getting caught was a new experience for him.

"We know the Cannizzaros figured out Vito had the diamonds, because they were in the house at the same time as Enzo," Jack said, forcing a steadiness into his voice that he didn't feel. He'd already chastised Enzo for that, and picking at old wounds wasn't going to help their situation. The one part of that night that never sat well with Jack was the coincidence of it all. That Enzo would be in Vito's house at the same time as Cannizzaro's people. Jack had pushed those thoughts to the side before, but they sure seemed relevant now. "But that doesn't explain how they figured out Vito brought them here."

"I was fucking careful, Jack," Enzo said. He was pacing now. Enzo's stress response mechanism was swearing. When he was under pressure, the floodgates lifted and Enzo spoke almost exclusively in expletives. "I fucking lost them in Stresa and made sure I wasn't followed on the Autostrada." Enzo had driven to Rome, where he hid out for a day, until he was able to get a flight to Los Angeles. Tailing someone at night was difficult, but spotting one was equally difficult. And to be fair to Enzo, this wasn't something that he necessarily knew how to do. Enzo had never been a wheelman like Jack had and certainly didn't have Rusty's law enforcement training. The chances of him being able to spot a tail, particularly at night, were no better than the average person's.

"How they got here," Rusty said, "makes *some* difference, but ultimately not that much. The thing is, they are here. That's the part we have to contend with. The question is, what do we do about it?"

"Well, we don't know who they were tailing. Meaning, we don't know if they were staking out Reginald's place and happened to be there at the same time we were." Jack paused his train of thought. Again with the coincidence. He knew that a stressed mind had a way of jumping at shadows, at believing wild conspiracies, but this was now two times. That was a pattern. "If they were following us, then they were trying to jump me when I was in Reginald's place."

"But why would they do that?" Rusty asked. "That wouldn't get them the diamonds."

"They could probably guess why I was breaking into an apartment," Jack said dryly. "If they were following Vito, likely they were doing the same thing we were."

"Trying to figure out where they were hiding them," Rusty said.

Jack nodded. "Exactly. It bothers me that it happened at the same time. That both of us were there at the exact same time. That seems to me like they're acting on information."

"Let's not speculate, Jack," Rusty said in an even tone. "Stick to the facts." In that moment, he could see the glimpses of the man Rusty used to be coming out.

Jack replayed the events in his mind, from the moment that he picked the lock on Reginald's door. Jack snapped his fingers.

"What?" Enzo said.

"The first thing Bartolo said to me was, 'What the fuck are you doing here?' I mean, all it tells us is that they didn't expect to find me in Reginald's apartment, but that's something in and of itself."

"Like they weren't there to ambush you," Enzo offered.

"Or I wasn't the one they were expecting to find there. Either way, we need to be more careful now," Jack said. "Watch for tails and make sure that we don't have any communication outside of the encryptor. So now we've got another group to contend with, and we'll have lost anything we were going to have gained by planting a bug in Reginald's place. It'll be a few days before the police turn it back over to him."

"Okay, so we've got a shootout in Hermosa Beach," Rusty said. "Jack was made by Bartolo and this Fiore guy, but not by the police. And as far as we know, they all escaped, so maybe we're good there. To your point, Jack, knowing how *they* knew to find Reginald is important because that informs our decisions going forward." Rusty paused a moment, and when no one said anything further on that situation, he continued. "We followed Reginald to a place called WorldSecure. It was in that diamond center building where we tailed him the first time."

"I know it," Jack said. Every jewel thief worth a shit should. "They're a high-end storage and transportation company. They specialize in storing private collections of precious gems, metals, and art. They also have a global transportation service, armored cars, armed guards, the whole nine."

"Could we break into it?" Rusty asked.

"No vault is impregnable, but this one is close, from what I hear. I've never been inside one. Without inside information, I think we consider that impossible." The other two nodded, and Jack could tell they were thinking the same thing. "What we *can* do is flush Reginald out. We might be able to convince them that Reginald is a criminal."

"Wouldn't they just turn the diamonds over to the police?" Enzo asked.

Jack shrugged. "These have been in the wind so long, the only people that know they're stolen is us. I mean, it's possible that WorldSecure would contact the authorities, but they'd have no real evidence that those diamonds were stolen, only that Reginald opened the account fraudulently."

"That'd be enough," Rusty said. "That's all the FBI or LAPD would need to seize them."

"What if *we* seized them? We've got the badges."

"They'll never give them up without a warrant," Rusty said.

"Could you forge one?"

"Easily. They're just a form letter with stamp and a signature. That's not the point." Rusty's mouth broke into that smirking, half-cracked smile of his. "I mean, in light of all the other laws we're breaking on this thing, forging a search warrant probably isn't all that bad. The problem is we don't have a way to hand it to them without getting our fingerprints on it. It's not like we can roll into that place with gloves on. Eventually, they'll figure out it's bogus and call the actual police. Both our prints are in the system." Rusty walked over to the suite's mini fridge and got them all bottles of water. He opened his, drank, and then continued. "Enzo and I followed Reginald and a WorldSecure armored car to One California. It's this huge plaza between two big buildings. The Angels Flight is there. This place is huge, and it would've been impossible to see exactly where Reginald and Vito went without being in the elevator with them, but I scanned the building's directory and I'm pretty sure they went to a place called A.G. Barret. They're a gem and metals broker."

"The kind of place that could do a bulk buy," Jack said.

"Exactly. So, they've been at this, two, three days, right? There's no way that they're making a sale for the whole load. But they might be setting that up. You'd know this better than I would, Jack, but I'd imagine that even in the legitimate world, they aren't buying diamonds sight unseen. We've got no way of knowing, though."

"Sure we do." Jack opened his phone, tapped through a few screens, and dialed a number. He set his phone to speaker and put it on the counter near where they were standing.

"Good afternoon, WorldSecure Los Angeles, how can I help you today?"

"Hi, my name is Kurt Garland, I'm the senior director of security for A.G. Barret. Could I speak to your operations manager, please?" It took a few bounces to get the right person, which had Jack repeating the line a few times. But on the second hop he landed at the dispatch supervisor. "Mr. Wakefield, was it? I'm just calling to follow up on a delivery from your location to ours earlier today. We've got to audit these things now."

"I understand, sir, how can I help?"

"Could you just verify the declared value of the transport? I believe it was under a Mr. Reginald Burton's account."

"Oh, of course." They heard some typing on the other end of the line and a muffled conversation as Wakefield issued instructions to someone on his end. "I've got it right here. We've got a declared value of seven point five million."

"Perfect," Jack said with a broad smile. "And what was the declared value on the return trip?"

There was a pause. "Well, the car came back empty. I figured you'd know."

"I know, I know," Jack said in a mock-weary voice, one wage slave to another. "We gotta ask now. It's this new process."

"Yeah, I got that," Wakefield said and chuckled.

"You've been a great help."

Jack closed the call. "Well, looks like that son of a bitch has some walking-around money."

"Is your guess that he's still going to sell these piecemeal?" Enzo asked.

"That's what I think he's going to, yeah. He makes one significant deal, say ten to fifteen million, and now he's set for a long time. That buys him stability, gets him out of a shit-box apartment over a convenience store. He and Vito can sell them over the period of a few years. Now, thanks to Bartolo, he knows that *someone* is onto him, so I suspect that'll move their timeline up some."

"What's our next move?" Enzo asked.

"We might be able to pull a version of what I just did with World-Secure to figure out when the next deal is going to go down. Now that we've lost our bug, I think that's the only real option we have. We're not really set up to do a long stakeout of WorldSecure. I'm open to ideas." Jack popped open his water bottle and drank.

He and Reginald LeGrande went back as far as it went. Jack was a dumb kid boosting cars when Reginald discovered him in the early nineties. Reginald got him driving on crews, mentored him, showed Jack how to hide money. After a few years, when Jack had established himself as one of the best wheelmen in the game, Reginald brought him on the inside as part of a crew. That job went south, and Jack fled to Europe for a few years to let things cool off. When he returned, Reginald took a risky job that he wanted Jack in on, and Jack refused. Reginald was busted and did five years. Jack didn't know it at the time, but Reginald became an informant then as a way of reducing his prison sentence. Over the next decade, Reginald put jobs and crews together and set up rivals for the police to take down.

Jack always believed they were tight, close to being family. Turned out, Reginald had other ideas. He was playing a very long con. Reginald figured out that Jack, under an alias, bought Kingfisher and was using the winery to legitimize his money. Reginald got an associate of his, the guy who laundered Reginald's money, to apply for a job as the winery's accountant. They were successful, and over time, Paul Sharpe skimmed millions. The idea was to keep Jack hungry and working for Reginald. Wineries bled money, so it wasn't hard to pull off, and no one noticed. Jack discovered the deception after Reginald tried to force him into the Carlton job.

Jack didn't turn the tables on Reginald so much as he flipped the table over and spilled the contents all over the floor. He set Reginald up for passport fraud, which he was absolutely doing, and then burned his house to the ground. In hindsight, arson was probably unnecessary and dangerous, but Jack was rightly furious at the betrayal and needed to exact some measure of revenge. The police were never able to connect Jack with the crime, and Reginald's claims that Frank Fischer, a respected Sonoma winemaker and legitimate businessman, was actually notorious jewel thief Gentleman Jack Burdette went unheeded.

Jack made sure anything connecting the two of them burned up in the fire. Arson can be an effective tool when judiciously used.

In the back of his mind, Jack always knew this day would come.

The reckoning between him and Reginald.

Admittedly, Jack hadn't seen this coming, Reginald and Vito teaming back up. When Vito approached him about Bartolo's diamonds, Jack believed that he was just an old thief that saw an opportunity. He didn't see this, but he should have.

Reginald blamed Jack for both of his stints in prison. The first one, because Jack wasn't on the job, and the second, rightly, because Jack served him up to the police. Jack knew Reginald wasn't going to stop this time until one of them was ruined, in jail for the rest of their lives or dead.

Niccoló Bartolo was an equal problem and a very dangerous threat. Nico lived in a world without morals. He simply didn't acknowledge that they existed. He would kill or steal without compunction or equivocation; it was simply an "act," a thing that he did. Murder wasn't something Bartolo did wantonly but rather as a way of sidestepping an obstacle. In Jack's mind, that coolness made it somehow worse.

Reginald would ruin Jack to get what he wanted. Bartolo would burn down the entire world to get what he was after, and he wouldn't waste a breath doing it.

"You're quiet," Rusty said in a thoughtful tone. "What's on your mind?"

"Bartolo may know where I live," Jack said slowly and quietly. This, on top of everything else. Not only was it highly likely that the FBI would find out Jack was involved as soon as Bartolo reported back home, he might also know where Jack's home was. "When we were in Rome, Giulia Montalto also tried to get me to steal Nico's diamonds." Enzo and Rusty knew the story. Giulia had been Jack's lover when they were together in Turin all those years ago, but her survival instinct outpaced any feelings she might have had for him. She told Nico that Jack's friend Castro was actually an undercover cop. Nico tried to kill him, and Jack escaped. Then, when Nico pulled the Antwerp diamond heist, he used Giulia to hide the diamonds in the last place anyone would look, the Commerce Bank of Rome. Giulia was supposed to wait for Bartolo, and he likely promised her the stars—he certainly had the money to deliver it. But he ended up serving ten years longer than he planned, and Giulia got tired of waiting. By then, she was tied up with the Serbian gangster and Pink Panther, Aleksander Anđelić. Anđelić and Reginald were connected, and Anđelić got much of the material he had on Jack from Reginald.

Which meant Giulia likely knew it as well.

Jack used her to find out the name Bartolo used to open the safe-deposit box in the Commerce Bank vault, on the pretense that they'd go away together. Jack had no intention of doing that. Giulia served him up to Bartolo to be killed once, and that wasn't the kind of thing he would just forgive and forget. Spurned and angry, Giulia would have gone to Bartolo for some good old-fashioned get-back. If she knew where Jack lived and the name he lived under...then it was a good bet that Niccoló Bartolo did too.

"But Nico kind of shot himself in the foot, though, right?" Enzo asked. "With that shit this morning. They had to have lost any chance they had of following Reginald."

"If what I said is true, they may not need to. Their backup plan can be to just let us do it, go to my home, and force me to hand them over."

Enzo did have a point, though. Nico was incredibly resourceful, but he was also sixteen years out of the game and he'd never played it over here. There were generations of techniques and technologies that were born and died in the time he was away. Fiore and the rest of Cannizzaro's thugs? They were not detectives. "I agree with you about their following Reginald. But they also wouldn't have come all this way with no leads. LA is a really big haystack to start looking for needles. I think we need to be on the safe side, and let's assume that Nico and his crew have some way into this. We need to plan on them making a play. But I think we can also assume that we're a step ahead."

"I agree with that, so what's *our* play?" Rusty asked.

"The trick we tried just now with WorldSecure can work. We find out where Reginald is going to make the sale and then intercept them when they are en route to the destination. We've got badges. Let's pretend we're cops."

"We'll need to separate Reginald and Vito from the armored car, though," Rusty said.

"I'm open to ideas." Jack's phone rang. It was Megan. He tapped it and sent it to voicemail. A text appeared immediately asking him to call her. "Guys, I need to take this." Jack stepped into his bedroom and closed the door. Then he called Megan. "Hey," he said. When she said, "Hey" back, he could hear the concern in her voice, and he immediately asked what's wrong.

"We've got several fires in the county now," she said. "The Big Ridge fire isn't close enough that I'm losing sleep, but you can see smoke in the hills." Big Ridge was on the other side of Sonoma from the Alexander Valley, where Kingfisher was located. But what had happened the year before was lightning strikes had started blazes near the city of Healdsburg, and that turned into one of the largest fires the state had ever seen. They'd been able to see flames from the property. One of the biggest dangers with these fires was when individual wildfires combined. "But there's one in Foothill, and that one does have me worried," she said. Foothill Regional Park wasn't far from Kingfisher. "Jack, everyone here is pretty tense. I know you've got things that you need to take care of, but we need you here."

Jack closed his eyes and felt pressure building behind them. They'd come close to losing the winery the year before. That fire that ravaged the city of Healdsburg was close enough to them that they'd had to shut operations down and evacuate their people. Amazingly, they didn't lose any of their crop, but looking at the wildfire trend over the last several years, it only seemed like a matter of time.

He knew that he needed to be there for his people. Jack couldn't stop the fires, couldn't prevent them from striking their vineyard if it came to that, but he was the leader and they looked to him in a time of crisis. Jack needed to be there for them. But if he lost the winery, he lost *everything*.

"Jack, I know I promised that I wouldn't ask any questions about...about any of that." Megan was being cagey because they were talking on an unencrypted line, but he knew what she meant. Jack could also hear not just the worry but the burden of carrying this weight by herself. "But the team is concerned and getting closer to scared. I have to know that what you're doing, whatever it is, is worth it. You don't have to tell me what, just tell me that it is."

"Reginald LeGrande is out of prison. I'm trying to make sure he can't ever hurt us again."

Megan had learned the full measure of Reginald's scheming in Paul Sharpe's embezzlement trial. They only got back a fraction of what he stole. The fact that Reginald set that up just to keep Jack in a position of needing to keep working as a thief...Megan hated Reginald almost as much as Jack did.

"I understand," she said. "Please be careful."

"I will."

"Jack, I love you."

"I love you too, Megs."

"When will you be home?"

SIXTEEN

So, his old protégé was here after all.

Nico expected to find Jack on this trip; in fact, he was counting on it. He was planning an excursion to this winery that Jack apparently ran where they would finally settle accounts. But he hadn't expected to find Jack in LeGrande's apartment this morning. Nor had he expected that idiot Fiore to open fire in the middle of the city. He tried to explain that this was America and not only did the police actually respond to shootings, they tended to do so quickly. You also couldn't just pay them off and make them disappear. Fiore just shrugged it off. That's the problem with soldiers, you can't tell them anything.

Of course, Jack would know about the LeGrande-Verrazano connection; that's how Jack came to know Nico, after all. But his knowing where LeGrande lived, that was something that Nico hadn't counted on. The don's people hadn't known either. Nico had to assume that Jack had a plan and that it was well underway. That meant Nico had less time than they'd planned.

And they were lucky to escape the beach with none of them arrested.

Though they'd tracked Bachetti to the US and that was how they knew Vito was here, they'd used Reginald LeGrande to find Vito.

Nico stood in his hotel room at the Westin in downtown Los Angeles, staring out at the city. There was a glassy gray line on the horizon, which he believed was the ocean. Their American "hosts" admonished him to keep the shades drawn in case the police had surveillance up, but Nico didn't find that likely, and anyway, it was an impressive view. He'd never been to Los Angeles before.

Nico wasn't very impressed with the American mafia, but then, the Sicilian mafia never impressed him much and they started the goddamn thing. Still, their American "cousins" had delivered for them, and that was to be commended. They had cars, money, and guns. They also had people who knew the layout of the city, and that was helpful as well. Nico didn't know what Salvatore told these guys or promised them, but they were strangely cooperative. That alone made Nico cautious.

Crooks didn't cooperate for free.

Nico knew about Vito's history with the American, Reginald LeGrande. He talked about it enough when they worked together in Turin. Vito was tight-lipped about the jobs he pulled before he joined the School of Turin, which Nico always appreciated. He didn't trust thieves who ran their mouths. Usually, the bravado wasn't backed up and they folded under pressure. Vito never cracked. Nico eventually learned about Knightsbridge and admired Vito's patience, his vision. That spoke well of him. So when Nico learned that the rat stole from him, Nico's first thought was that he was working with LeGrande. It didn't take long to figure out that LeGrande had just recently been released from prison and, from there, that he was living at that apartment on the beach. Once they knew where LeGrande lived and what he drove, it was a simple matter of hiding a tracker on his car. Fifty dollars on Amazon got them a GPS tracker with a magnetic case that they clamped to the underside of LeGrande's Range Rover. They could track him anywhere in the city until he found it.

They followed LeGrande and Vito to a place called WorldSecure, which a quick Google search showed them was a high-end vault for wealthy customers to stash their valuables. This proved Nico's theory that Vito and LeGrande were trying to sell the diamonds legally in order to realize their full value. That was greedy and stupid. Fifty million each? They couldn't spend that, not with the years they had left.

Nico smiled, remembering that he was just a few years younger than Vito. *He* could spend that kind of money in the years he had left...but it was going to be a big fucking boat.

Except for the incident this morning, Nico was happy with their progress. They knew where LeGrande was keeping the diamonds, and they knew how and where he moved. The idea for the GPS tracker came from their American counterparts. Apparently, they used that technique to keep an eye on their rivals. A lot had changed in this game. Nico walked over to the ice bucket in his room and drew out the half-consumed bottle of Sauvignon Blanc, then refilled his glass. He'd gotten the bottle along with his room service lunch. Though he was working, Nico saw no reason not to enjoy himself, and his cousin was picking up the tab. Or whoever owned the credit card they'd stolen was. Either way, it wasn't Nico, and creature comforts weren't something he'd had much of over the last sixteen years. The Belgian prison system was known to be one of the worst in the modern world.

Nico was returning to his view and planning out their next move when a sharp knock interrupted his thoughts. Nico set the wineglass down and went to the door, checking the peephole first. Seeing it was Fiore, he opened the door, and the other walked in without being invited.

Constantino Fiore was relatively new to his cousin's organization. He was Roman, rather than Sicilian, and while Nico had yet to discover any special qualities about the man, he certainly had Salvatore's confidences. Fiore was in his early thirties, was well muscled and lean like a predator that relied on speed. Fiore kept his hair short; there was barely enough to part. His eyes, that was the one thing that

Nico thought they had in common. Fiore's eyes were cold and dark. They were the eyes of a man who killed without hesitation. Fiore had changed clothes since their misadventure at LeGrande's apartment. He was wearing a dark gray suit, a dusty rose shirt that reminded Nico of sandalwood, and black tie that had a sharkskin sheen to it.

"What," Nico said and returned to his wine.

"The don isn't happy. It's taking too long."

"Well, I hope in your report, you mentioned that you were the one who opened fire." Nico turned to see if the shot landed and saw a kind of vacancy in those eyes, but as they narrowed slightly, the expression turned to one of seething. "We know where LeGrande is and where he's going. We know where the diamonds are. We—"

"But you can't get them," Fiore snapped.

"Not in the vault, no." Nico had to remind himself that Fiore was a soldier and not a thief. He would have to explain himself as he would to a child. He knew that Fiore's job had been to be Salvatore's man inside the Commerce Bank, ostensibly a security guard, a "soft" presence to ensure that the don's reach was not just understood but felt. Nico also learned that during the attempted robbery, Jack had disarmed Fiore with a bluff.

"Didn't you break into the vault in Antwerp? Why don't you just do that now?"

Nico restrained a sigh and concealed his expression by taking a drink.

Fucking amateur.

The Antwerp Diamond Centre had been a masterclass in thievery. Nico had his sights on that job for years, and that was largely why he'd assembled the School of Turin. It wasn't just that Jack allowed himself to get turned by that undercover cop, Castro, it was that the arrests that resulted from that broke up the School of Turin and robbed Nico of some of his best pupils. Including Burdette. Nevertheless, Nico proceeded with it. He was forced to push the job back several years, but in 2003, he and his crew executed it flawlessly. They rented space in the diamond center and Nico himself became a frequent face, under the guise of being a diamond merchant, which not only established trust but helped him fade into the background. They secretly installed cameras over the vault door so they could record both the patterns of the security guards and the code to enter it. Once inside the vault, they located the nearly twelve-inch interior vault key. This was supposed to be stored in a secured locker elsewhere, but it was large and heavy and the guards were complacent. After all…who was going to break into an impregnable vault?

Before the job, Nico convinced the building manager that he was looking to construct his own vault, which would have netted that company millions, and the manager was only too happy to lend his assistance. He gave Nico access to a full-scale mockup of the vault they used for tours with high-profile potential clients. It never occurred to the man that Nico and his crew would use this for practice. So, once they were inside, the crew could work in almost total darkness because they knew the layout. They worked all night, drilling in the darkness, but they netted close to one hundred million dollars' worth of loose, finished diamonds.

The job took years of planning, months of execution, and Nico had a crew that he'd worked with and trusted implicitly.

The fact that this imbecile thought he could just "do" that by walking into a place didn't just prove his stupidity, it placed an embossed stamp of authenticity on it.

"No," Nico said flatly. "That job took years to plan and months to execute. I had a crew, highly specialized, that I'd been training for a long time. We knew the layout of the vault, we knew the security procedures and the technology they used. Besides, that was nearly twenty years ago. The kinds of systems they have on these vaults now would make a job like that impossible." Nico actually had no idea, though he felt it was a safe assumption. Honestly, he just wanted Fiore to shut up and leave him alone so he could think. However, Fiore was the don's eyes, ears, and, unfortunately, mouth. Nico had to tread carefully. "Constantino, we are not going to break into that vault. But I did notice a slight flaw in their security."

"Oh, and what's that?" Fiore said, his voice dripping with skepticism.

"The way we got into the Antwerp Diamond Centre was by analyzing their security practices and finding the flaws that we could exploit. We don't have the time to figure out what the flaws are inside WorldSecure and, I suspect, LeGrande and Verrazano won't give us that time either. However, I have noticed one thing that I think we can use." Nico took a drink of wine and studied the reaction on Fiore's face. Nico had to hand it to the man, he was very hard to read. "They have three men in the armored car. There's one driver and two guards. The guards are armed, but they just have pistols and no body armor. That will only deter someone seeing this as a target of opportunity. We have four of us, plus any of the Americans we care to leverage."

"To do what?" Fiore asked.

"Outnumber them, Constantino. Now, what kind of weapons can our friends get for us?"

Fiore shrugged. "I think they can get whatever we want."

"Okay, good. I want pistols, shotguns, and automatics. UZI or MP-5, something like that. Let's also get body armor if they can do it that quickly. It shouldn't be too hard in a city this size."

"How quickly do you want them?"

"Right away. I think this is going to happen fast."

"I'll see what they can do." Fiore walked to the door. He turned and glared back at Nico. "Close your fucking shades. The police here have cameras." Fiore walked out.

Nico exhaled and took his wineglass back over to the window. If the police didn't know they were here, they wouldn't know to surveil them. If the police did know they were here, they were busted anyway and it wouldn't matter. Why not enjoy the view?

You can't tell soldiers anything.

SEVENTEEN

Carter LeMothe didn't have time for fucking Janelle and her fucking conference room.

He needed to be on the links in two hours, and it was at least an hour to get there this time of day. She didn't really get this business, didn't understand that it was entirely relationship driven. No one was going to enter into a multimillion dollar deal with someone they didn't know, someone they didn't have a rapport with. Especially now that the markets were turning around so rapidly and people were spending money hand over fist. Carter figured his golf game alone brought them an extra fifteen percent each year.

Carter straightened his tie and walked into the conference room, which was in between his office and Janelle's. The interior wall was glass, though it was soundproofed, and the other side faced the street, like Carter's office did. Janelle was seated at the head, as she always was, wanting to make sure everyone knew she was the COO. Carter wasn't racist, but he couldn't help but wonder if that was a Black thing. Or maybe it was because she was a woman, that constant need to assert her authority to the men in the room. Carter LeMothe could read a business card, he knew what her title was.

Then there was Don Levitt, their chief legal officer. Levitt was a good enough guy and was clearly on his last job before an early enough retirement. He stuck it out an extra few years because he had two kids in expensive colleges; also he and his wife traveled a lot and preferred to go first class. They went "on safari," apparently, like they were English. Levitt was a scratch golfer and they used to play Fridays, but now that Carter thought about it, it'd been about a year. Not since Janelle showed up.

God, was this another one of those bullshit sensitivity seminars? If Carter was going to be asked to do another virtual trust fall, he was going to lose his mind. He looked down at his Rolex. He had exactly fifteen minutes to wrap this up or he was going to be late for his tee time.

There were two other men at the table, one Black and one white, both in suits, though they weren't very well cut. If these were prospective clients, Carter wasn't sure they could afford to do business here by the look of them. Levitt was seated next to Janelle, with his back to the door, though he half-turned in his chair when Carter entered. Now he understood. This was some bullshit audit that they, IRS, or Customs, or whoever the fuck made them go through every so often. Well, they'd have to reschedule. Carter had places to be, and those places made him money, and why the hell couldn't Janelle ever read a calendar. That's why they had the goddamn things.

Carter shot his wrist out so the watch was exposed and then made a show of flashing the watch as he looked at it again, just to make sure everyone in the room knew that time was a factor. Like they said at the draft, *You're on the clock, Janelle.*

Carter sat down at the other head of the table.

"What's this about," Carter said. "I've got places to be." Negotiations were won and lost by taking the initiative, and that was something Carter LeMothe never ceded.

"Carter, this is Special Agent Fuery and Special Agent Reaves of the FBI," Janelle said.

She motioned to each of them, but Carter wasn't paying attention. He couldn't get that line from *Die Hard* out of his head. The one about the two "Agent Johnsons."

"Mr. LeMothe," the Black one said. "Can I call you Carter?"

"That depends. If you're selling me something, I prefer Mr. LeMothe."

"Carter, I'll cut to the chase. You're in deep shit." The agent opened a folder that Carter now noticed was sitting in front of him next to a yellow legal pad. "We have transcripts of your phone calls going back six months."

"Wait, you're tapping my phone? That's fucking illegal."

"No, Carter, it isn't." And he produced three pages that were stapled together and handed it to his partner, who slid it halfway down the table. Carter didn't touch it, wasn't going to give them the satisfaction, but he saw the word WARRANT across the top in big, bold type. "We've had a wire up on you for some time, and I have to say, Carter, for someone with as much to lose as you do, you don't cover your tracks very well."

A cold and sick feeling washed over Carter. If Ashton Kutcher or Pauly Shore or some other washed-up asshole with a microphone was going to jump out and yell, "Surprise!" now would be the time.

The Black agent continued, and Carter now wished he'd taken time to learn the guy's name.

"You've been defrauding the government for some time with this scheme of yours, but the 'consulting fees' that you've been taking have been unreported income. By our estimation, you owe the federal government at least two million dollars in taxes."

"So, I'll write a check to the IRS. Are we done here?"

"Not by a long shot, pal."

"Carter," the other agent, the white guy, said. His voice was still stern but slightly softer than his partner's. If Carter hadn't been scared shitless, he'd have eye-rolled the "good cop" routine. "We believe the diamonds that you arranged to sell to your contact in Hong Kong, LGK, are stolen."

"No one just shows up at your doorstep, Carter," the other one broke in, "and offers to sell you clean diamonds sight unseen."

"We don't have any record of a Mr. Reginald Burton or a Mr. Vito De Angeles being registered diamond brokers, and their company," the agent paused for effect and then looked down at a paper in front of him, "Endeavor Diamonds and Metals appears to be owned by a holding company registered in the Caymans. That's just what we've been able to dig up over the last twenty-four hours."

Carter didn't see what the big deal was and didn't understand why these guys were wasting his time. Burton and De Angeles ran a small operation and Carter didn't care if the company was a shell, and he didn't particularly care if the diamonds were bought on the gray market—he was getting an incredible deal on them. He realized his mistake now. Janelle was pissed that he was selling on the side to LGK rather than through A.G. Barret.

"Gentlemen," Carter said and put his hands on the table. It was time to end this. He was going to have Janelle's job over this and probably these two agents too. "This has been really interesting, and my attorney is certainly going to have some words with you about tapping my phone. I'm guessing you don't have any understanding of this business or you'd know that half of these companies are registered in the Caymans or the Bahamas or Ireland or wherever the hell to avoid paying taxes in the US because you guys are so insistent on killing businesses. Janelle, I apologize for teeing this up for a colleague instead of buying them here, but I knew you wouldn't authorize it." Carter's blood was flowing now. He just needed to retake the initiative. "And Janelle, you can believe we're going to have a conversation with Masterson about this." Carter stood.

"Carter, please sit down. You're in a lot of trouble," Janelle said and tried to sound concerned.

"I don't think so," Carter said. "You want a tax check. Fine. I'll write that."

"Carter, trafficking in stolen diamonds is a felony. Based on what you purchased from Burton and De Angeles alone, a judge can give you fifteen years. You're looking at another five for the tax evasion. And that's just this week." He slid a piece of paper across the table, and a fast glance told Carter it was a transcript of his conversation with Lau. "But eighty million dollars, Carter, that puts you in jail for the rest of your goddamn life. Now, sit down and stop playing hard-ass. The only reason I don't arrest you now is I want to catch Burton and De Angeles."

The blood drained out of Carter's face, felt as though it drained out of his entire body, and he did sit back down.

"What Special Agent Fuery is trying to tell you," that was the white guy talking, which made him Reaves, "is that you have an opportunity to help yourself. To help your family. We're going to give you a chance to stay out of prison by helping us apprehend these two."

Carter looked out the window. The building faced west, and he saw Fourth Street and beyond that the 110. There was too much smog and haze today, but on a clear one you could sometimes see the ocean from here.

"All right," Carter said in a voice that had lost all of its verve. "Let me hear it."

Fuery walked him through it.

These feds were like goddamn pushers the moment they realized you were a full-on junkie. He could already tell. You do a thing for them and it's never enough.

Carter was going to call Burton and tell him that he'd spoken to his contact in Hong Kong and they wanted in. The FBI was going to set up a fake office in a building somewhere that they would have wired up, and that's where the meeting would take place. Carter would tell Burton that his Chinese buyer had a US office and that's where the buy would be. He'd facilitate the sale. The buyer would be an undercover FBI agent. They would arrest Burton and De Angeles and Carter would be free to go. Well, not exactly "free"—they were still serving him up to the IRS for tax evasion. That wasn't part of their deal, and Janelle said he was terminated immediately.

What was he going to tell Amanda?

She didn't have to know that they'd threatened him with jail time. All she needed to know was he was helping the FBI with a case and he was leaving A.G. Barret because fuck Janelle, right?

He'd figure the IRS thing out later. He'd make something up. His fraternity brother Todd Weyland was an attorney, Stanford JD, he'd help with that end.

Carter had met with Burton and De Angeles two days ago and the FBI already had this sting set up. That seemed pretty fast to him. Maybe this *was* bullshit after all? "How did you get this together so quickly?" Carter asked. "I just met with them two days ago."

Reaves spoke first this time. "Like we said, we've been monitoring your phones for some time. But we have playbooks for this sort of thing. Not our first rodeo, pal."

Carter hated that phrase.

"Something funny?" Fuery asked. Carter realized he was smirking and dropped it. He was imagining what Fuery and Reaves would look like in their first rodeo.

"No, sorry. It's just strange to me that you'd be able to put this together so fast."

"I'm not sure what you're implying, Carter," Reaves said, "but generally, yes, these things do take time. As I said, we have playbooks for operations like this, and we have an asset from another investigation that we can divert for this. The Bureau can move quickly when it needs to."

"Whatever you're trying here, Carter, do yourself a favor and knock it off. Playing the hard-ass is not what you want to do in this situation," Fuery said. "You're going to want to make that phone call to Burton, and you're going to be convincing. Now, I've been listening in on your phone calls for the last year, so I know you know how to bullshit. So you're going to do that now and you're going to bring your A-game. If you tip Burton off in any way, if I think for a *second* that you aren't pitch perfect on this, the deal is off. We will arrest you, you will get at least ten years, and your kid will get to watch her daddy get shipped off to prison." Fuery paused a moment and then leveled a hard stare at Carter. "You know what the conviction rate is at federal trials? It's ninety-nine percent. Think on that as you're weighing your options. Because I've dug deep on you over the last year and, Carter LeMothe, I'm here to tell you that you are not a one percenter."

"Should we get this over with," Carter said. He'd make the call just to end Fuery's speech. Reaves pushed another piece of paper down the table.

"This has all of the details of your contact, his name, where his office is, company, everything. I doubt that Burton is going to do a check on them, but if he does, it'll appear as a perfectly legitimate company."

Carter reached into his pants pocket and pulled out his iPhone. He opened it and scrolled through the contacts until he found Burton's number.

"Put it on speaker," Fuery said.

"Then it'll sound like someone's in the room," Carter said.

"I don't care. Tell him it's your secretary."

Reaves took Janelle and Levitt out of the conference room. Carter tapped the speaker feature and dialed.

Carter flipped the switch.

"Reg, hey. I've got good news, buddy."

"I could use some good news," Reginald said. Carter didn't know the man, but his voice sounded stressed. "How about I come to your office and you tell me?"

"No need for all that." Carter had a flash of panic. Burton was cagey and probably these diamonds weren't totally legal, so there was a good chance he was too smart to do this over the phone. If he insisted on doing this in person, Carter had to imagine that would fuck things up. He talked fast. "So, I spoke to my friend in Hong Kong, and he's in. I actually caught him while he was here in LA. They've got an office in Inglewood near LAX."

"That's convenient," Reginald said.

"Yeah. Anyway, they're interested."

"For how much?"

Carter felt an intense relief wash over him. *Sorry, pal, but better you than me.*

"Originally, he only said he'd go forty-five, but I told him we had other buyers lined up. I knew he was just trying to hardball me. I got him to go for the full amount."

"You serious?"

"Right? So, minus the seven million that I bought from you directly, you'll get about seventy-three from him."

"How is it paid?"

"They'll do a bank wire to any account you name."

"Okay, sounds good. When do we meet?"

"I need about three days to get everything together. That work for you?"

"That works."

"Great. Listen, I'll be in touch with the exact time."

EIGHTEEN

Jack watched the sun fall off the edge of the world.

This was a bad idea.

He was in Santa Monica, on the beach about a block up from where the meeting was supposed to take place.

Vito had called him earlier that day, said he wanted to talk things out. He wouldn't say much on the phone; as it was, Vito spoke in rushed tones and hasty words. Like he was a man without much time to talk. And scared.

Jack rolled that thought over in his mind.

The sky was turning dark. It looked like a day-old bruise but for the ribbons of fire on the horizon and the carnival lights of the pier that lit up the evening sky. Jack was supposed to be in position now, but he'd already decided that he was going to be late. Give the son of a bitch a few minutes to twist, wonder if he'd been set up. Wonder if the script had finally been flipped.

Jack wanted nothing more than to run. To go back to Sonoma and forget about all of this, to deal with the very real threat to his livelihood and the people he cared about, but he knew his enemies would never let him. This was in motion now. Even if he walked away tonight, Reginald would still come for him to make sure that Jack could never threaten him again. There were no assurances Jack could give that Reginald would believe. There was also the spite.

And Bartolo would do the same.

So, instead of running, Jack was here in the growing darkness creeping just above the Santa Monica Pier, walking into what was certainly a trap.

"I'm in position," Enzo said in Jack's ear. They hadn't had much time to prep, that was probably the point to the last-minute call, but they'd purchased two-way radios for this job. The thick, rubber-covered antenna were difficult to hide, but at least the thing fit in his pocket. There was a clear earpiece that wrapped around the back of his ear. Anyone looking at him closely would probably think Jack was an undercover cop.

He had debated telling the others that he'd gotten the call today. Not because Jack didn't trust them but because he was afraid of what Rusty might do when he found out that Vito called asking for a meet.

"I'm in position," Rusty said. "No sign yet."

Rusty's voice was calm, though admittedly it was hard to discern stress on a radio.

They were both positioned within visual distance of where Vito asked to meet.

Vito had called Jack that evening, maybe two hours ago, and said he wanted to talk. Jack told him to go to hell, but Vito persisted. He said that he had information Jack wanted, would make it worth his time. Of course it was bullshit and almost certainly a setup, but Jack agreed. If nothing else, he wanted to look Vito in the eyes after these long months and tell him with absolute certainty that they would be stealing their diamonds back.

That Vito could call him at all was a sign that Jack's tradecraft was slipping. He should have dropped that phone after Rome, but he didn't.

Rusty was calm when Jack told him.

Jack didn't know what he expected from the exchange. He realized that he'd only ever seen Rusty under strain twice in all the years they'd worked together. The first he didn't even "see" because it was over the phone and Rusty was telling Jack that he was running, that Jack should do the same because Special Agent Danzig had figured out who he was and had loosed the Diplomatic Security Service on him. The second time was after Vito shot him in Rome.

So, Jack didn't quite know how Rusty was going to react.

Getting shot was a funny thing. He knew plenty of thieves that just accepted that as an occupational hazard, took their stitches and moved on with it. There were others, though, that reacted poorly. They internalized it, personalized it, and they thought of little more than the get-back. But Rusty wasn't a thief. Sure, he was a criminal in the classic sense in that he made a living doing illegal things, but he wasn't a *thief*. He was brought up with a different code.

He'd been a cop once, and they tended to be a little less forgiving.

"Vito wants a meet," Jack said when he'd hung up the phone. "Says this thing has gotten out of control and he wants to talk it out."

"Vito and Reginald?" Enzo asked.

"Just Vito," Jack said.

"It's probably bullshit," Rusty said.

"It's almost certainly bullshit," Jack countered, "but I want to hear him out."

"I agree with Rusty," Enzo said. "Vito wants to talk, he can do it on the phone."

"I said it was bullshit. I didn't say we shouldn't go," Rusty said with an anger in his voice that, while subtle, was definitely there.

Vito was lean on the details, said he couldn't talk long. Told Jack he'd meet him at the Santa Monica Pier. He'd be sitting in a gazebo in the parking lot, the second one in on the shore, facing the pier. Vito said he'd be alone and asked Jack to do the same. "If I see the others, I walk. I'll only talk to you. I know you're reasonable." In other words, *I'm afraid of Rusty*.

So, Vito wanted to deal. Or at least he wanted Jack to think he did.

Jack dressed, uncharacteristically, like a tourist.

He wore a loose fitting, off-white camp shirt over light gray golf pants and canvas sneakers. He could run in these clothes if he had to, and the shirt covered up most of the radio's bulk. It also hid the pistol Jack had in the concealed holster on his waist.

"I'm approaching," Jack said into the mic. He walked south toward the pier along the concrete footpath parallel with PCH. The pier was lit up like a circus, and the sound washed over him, as did the smell of confections mixing with the pungency of the ocean. Jack hit a large square parking lot that was now about half-full. Wispy tendrils of sand washed across it in random places. Traffic was heavy on PCH, which ran immediately along the beach, as well as on Ocean Avenue beyond it. In Vito's mind, this would be his version of a locked room meeting. If Jack couldn't escape easily, Vito would reason, it would make it much less likely that Jack would try to double-cross him.

Jack walked across the parking lot, and the sounds of the pier intensified. It was a nice night, warm, and the rains hadn't started yet. People were out enjoying the night. That was a good sign. Santa Monica also was one of the few parts of California that wasn't on fire, it seemed. Jack spotted the first building in the row on the pier, the aquarium. It was a large pink building with gray trim and the circus-tent roof. There was a small space, no bigger than an alley, between that building and the long, low one next to it that held smaller shops and a few restaurants. Jack walked through that space. It was lit, but both buildings cast long shadows. Jack entered the parking lot on the other side and spotted the Victorian-style gazebo on the far side.

When Jack had gotten the call, Rusty's first instinct was that Reginald and Vito somehow figured out where they were staying. Wanted to get them out of there so that they could plant bugs in the room. Rusty suggested that one of them stay in the room, just to make sure. But Jack told him that Reginald would have no way of knowing they were staying downtown, and they were always careful to check for tails when they went back to the hotel. But they hung a "do not disturb" sign on the door and set a full water glass just inside the entry way. If someone opened that door, it would tip the glass over and they'd know someone had been in the room.

"I see him," Jack said. Enzo and Rusty both copied.

Rusty was in a different car, a black BMW X6 M, that was parked in a small lot along Appian Way, maybe two hundred yards from where Jack was to meet Enzo. Even though Rusty had never worked in the US as a fixer, he still knew people here, and it didn't take him long to set a network up. Within a few days, he was able to get them nearly anything they needed, clean cars, weapons, whatever.

"I've got him too," Rusty said in Jack's ear.

Enzo was positioned at the lifeguard building located on the beach on the far side of a row of volleyball nets, about a hundred yards from the gazebo. Jack couldn't see him from his position but knew that Enzo was in the lifeguard parking lot adjacent to the building, in the shadows beneath the palm trees. They had Vito's exits covered. If he decided to make a run for it, his only escape route would be the roller coaster at the end of the pier or jumping into the water.

Jack walked purposefully across the half-empty parking lot. There were still a few straggling beachcombers, tourists packing up the last of their belongings and dragging their kids to the cars. A few cars were pulling into the lot, looking for an evening's entertainment on the pier, but it was generally light, as it was a weeknight. Jack maneuvered between two cars slightly up from the gazebo, but the last fifty or so feet across the blacktop was open air and no possibility for cover. "Moving in," Jack said.

The gazebos were large and circular, fashioned from iron, and during the summer, Jack thought they might have had canvas tarps over the top to shield them from the sun. There was a circular table in the center, which was well lit from the pair of bright lights atop the gazebo that shone down on the interior. They were located on the southern edge of the parking lot, on a small ledge that was about twelve feet over the beach. The area was well lit on two sides, with rows of tall lights along the edge of the parking lot and another in between the volleyball nets on the beach. All four of the beach volleyball courts had games going. Because of the glare from those lights, Jack couldn't see exactly where Enzo was positioned. Jack saw Vito sitting at a table with a cup of coffee in front of him. Jack held his hands out to his side to show that he was (visibly) unarmed.

"Can I come in?" Jack asked.

Vito nodded, and Jack entered. Apart from jumping through the space between the bars—what passed for a window in the gazebo—and the resultant twelve-foot drop, there was nowhere to run to.

Vito looked like a hunted man.

His face was drawn and haggard, and even now Jack could see his eyes looking for the corners of the room. A space Jack noted ruefully that had no corners to speak of. Vito always had a slight build, but he looked diminished now. He was too old to be on the run, and every step he took probably reminded him of it.

"I've never liked the coffee here," Vito said.

"I wasn't aware you'd been to the States before."

Vito only shrugged.

"The earpiece? What the fuck," Vito said, now glaring at Jack with hard, dark, and unforgiving eyes.

"Relax, Vito. I didn't come alone. As I suspect you didn't either. My friends are just nearby to make sure this little chat stays civil. Nothing more." Vito didn't appear convinced and moved to stand. "Sit down," Jack snarled. "If I was going to kill you, I'd have shot you when I walked in and been done with it." Jack's temper flared like a rogue wave, and he stopped himself before he said anything else. He could already feel his control slipping away. "You wanted to talk. What about?"

Vito let his breath out slowly, and Jack could smell the bad coffee on it. Vito looked away, not to the sea but inland to the buildings on the far side of the sand and the line of slowly moving cars in beachfront traffic.

"Vito, I don't have a lot of patience for you, and what I have is running out fast."

"Reginald is crazy," Vito said, still looking away. "I think something happened to him in prison."

"I don't care. Why are you wasting my time?"

"The thing at his apartment, we figured it was you. The police from that town called him and wanted to know if he knew why someone would try to break in and how that would turn into a shootout. It spooked him."

"Vito, look at me."

Vito turned his head back to face Jack.

"Nico was there. He showed up right after I did."

Vito tried to hide it, but the look of shock was unmistakable. Jack saw something else as Vito's expression darkened. Mortality. Niccoló Bartolo was the only person on this earth Vito was well and truly afraid of.

"Constantino Fiore was with him. Why is Salvatore Cannizzaro involved in this?"

"Because I tried to sell him the diamonds once. Reginald and I were planning this from the beginning. Before I even contacted you. But when Europe locked down and it was impossible to travel, I got worried. I called Cannizzaro and told him what I had and could I sell them to him, since I knew he had a smuggling operation going. He offered me pennies, but what choice did I have?" Vito shrugged. "Then things turned around, and Reginald told me he had everything taken care of. I figured I could disappear."

"Cannizzaro sent his people looking for you. Enzo broke into your house in Stresa to get the diamonds. Instead he found Cannizzaro's men. Apparently, the don made up with his cousin and hired him to find you. But that just explains the what, not the why. What aren't you telling me?"

Vito looked genuinely uncomfortable, like a bug under a magnifying glass. He shifted his focus to look over Jack's shoulder at the beach volleyball game behind him, or possibly just staring off into space. Vito did that when he wanted to avoid answering direct questions.

"The Russians. Cannizzaro is in bed with some Russian gangster. Well, I guess he's a businessman, but in that country there isn't much difference between the two. I only know about this because I still have some contacts in his outfit. The story is that Cannizzaro found this Russian, Gennady Sokolov, who was a major smuggler. Sokolov really needed the diamonds for something. I don't know what, so don't ask. That's why Cannizzaro is so hot to get them. He's in deep shit with the Russian if he doesn't."

A cold laugh oozed out of Jack's mouth, and Vito sneered at the sound. "I wouldn't want to be you," Jack said.

While Jack didn't exactly confirm that it was him in Reginald's apartment, he didn't deny it either, and at this point, there was no way to hide it. The event might cause Reginald to change his patterns, drop his phone. Seeing Vito's reaction when he learned Bartolo was involved was worthwhile. Jack surmised that Vito assumed the same thing about Cannizzaro, that there was no possible way his reach could extend all the way to the United States. Frankly, Jack wouldn't have thought the man could push much farther beyond the boundaries of Rome. Vito knowing that it could was one thing, knowing that Bartolo was now involved would also put him on edge. This was the point where Vito and Reginald would start making mistakes because they were scared.

"Why am I here, Vito?"

"I told you Reginald is spooked. He's erratic. After that thing at his place and the gunfight, like you're fucking cowboys—"

"For the record, I was unarmed." Mostly.

"Reginald is moving the diamonds to Singapore. He thinks he can sell them there to some of the Asian crime syndicates. He's got them in this vault downtown called WorldSecure. The company can move them anywhere in the world, armored cars, guards, everything. They're flying out the day after tomorrow."

"You said 'they.'"

"Because I think he's going to cut me out. I'm the link to you *and* Cannizzaro. Plus, Reginald doesn't need me anymore. I already delivered the stones to him like it was fucking Christmas."

"Killing you only severs the link to Cannizzaro. It doesn't cut him off from me. Does Cannizzaro know anything about Reginald?"

"No," Vito said and shook his head slowly.

"What's his plan for me? He goes to Singapore and then what?"

Vito wasn't the only one looking for exits here. If Reginald wanted to disappear to Asia, Jack might actually let him do it. If he left right now, even if Bartolo told Cannizzaro he was in Los Angeles and Danzig's informant found out, Jack hadn't done anything that Danzig could arrest him for. Well, impersonating a federal officer was unquestionably a felony, but Bartolo didn't know anything about that.

Vito didn't answer at first. When he spoke, his voice was low and measured, perfectly timed.

"When this is all over, he's coming for you. He still blames you for going to prison."

"Which time?" Jack said snidely.

"I'm serious, Jack. He said he's going to burn your winery to the ground."

Maybe it was the very real fire threat they were facing, but Vito's words struck home. Vito couldn't know about the wildfires, so it was just his phrasing and unfortunate coincidence, but the result was the same.

"Why are you telling me this?"

"I never wanted to hurt you, Jack. We were close once. But this was a lot of money. And Reginald was my friend, or at least I thought he was. He said you betrayed him, gave him up to the police. I thought that was wrong."

"He probably left out the part where he got someone to embezzle ten million dollars from my winery."

Vito didn't say anything.

"I thought so. So, you traded a four-way split of eighty million for a two-way split, and you expect me to believe that it was over some code of ethics you have?" Jack gave him a sharp, bitter laugh. "There's no way in hell that you decided on a whim to shoot Rusty that night. You'd never have run with that amount of money without a plan. I've had a lot of time to think about this over the last two years, and I always believed you had a partner, I just didn't think it would be *him*. For all I know, this is something you two have been planning for years and Reginald just had the bad luck of landing himself in prison again." Jack held up a hand. "Don't bother, I don't care. Now he's fucking *you* over because that's what he does, and you're coming to me for what, sympathy? Fuck you, Vito. That's what you get for getting into bed with him. I wish you luck."

"What happened in Rome...I'm sorry for that. That was business, but Reginald doesn't have any right to go after your life like that. Like I said. I think he's crazy."

"I don't believe for a second you feel an ounce of remorse over anything you've done. And it's not clear to me why I needed to waste my night talking to you."

"What if we got the diamonds instead?"

Jack laughed again in that same acidic tone, but his eyes narrowed. *This* was what he came here for tonight.

"So, what exactly do you propose? These guys have armored cars and guns. They control the diamonds end to end. I'm sure you can't get them out of the vault without Reginald's authorization. How exactly do you think I can help you? And are your two goons in on this, or are they siding with Reginald?"

"The plan is to fly out of that small airport north of here, Van Nuys, I think it's called. WorldSecure will deliver the diamonds right to the airplane and manage the export paperwork. You and Enzo can easily sneak in and pretend to be ground crew. You just take the box from the guards. Make a switch. As for my men, I think Reginald got to them. I offered to pay them a million each for the week, then they go home. I suspect Reginald is offering much more."

It was a plan, Jack could say that much for it, but there were holes you could drive through. Not the least of which was that the World-

Secure guards would maintain a chain of custody that didn't end until that box was in the cargo hold. Though it might be possible to fake a ground emergency before takeoff or even fake a maintenance issue that forces them to unload the plane.

"You think Reginald is going to cut you out. Any idea when that happens?"

"Once we're in Singapore. If this was his plan all along, then he's got support there. Tommaso and Lucio have to check their weapons before they get on the plane, so I assume he does something once we get on the ground before they can re-arm. Or if they are working with him..." Vito shrugged.

Jack nodded in agreement. There were lots of ways this could be handled.

"I appreciate the warning about my place."

Vito only nodded in response.

"About the other thing, I need to talk to my partners. You have to appreciate that we don't trust you. Particularly Rusty."

Vito blanched at that.

"Are you going to be in a place that I can call you later?"

"Yes. We're renting a house now. Not far from here."

"Okay," Jack said, and he stood to leave. "I'll let you know tonight if we're in."

THIRTY MINUTES LATER, Jack met Enzo and Rusty at a beachfront diner called Patrick's Roadhouse a few miles north of the pier on PCH. Enzo and Rusty rode together, Jack took a couple of cabs to make sure he wasn't followed. They had a booth near the back, and both of them had glasses of beer when Jack arrived and one for him. Enzo had the side of the booth that would allow him to see the entire restaurant, since he could identify both Bartolo and Vito by sight. Jack slid into the spot next to him. The place had a gaudy Irish theme. The booths were bright green with a big shamrock right in the center of them. The music was loud and it was mostly full, which was what they wanted.

Jack shook his head and took a sip.

"What's your read," Rusty said.

"Oh, he's so full of shit his eyes are brown," Jack said. "But that doesn't mean that he isn't willing to double-cross Reginald. He said Reg is scared after that thing with Bartolo at his apartment." Jack shifted his gaze to Enzo. "He looked genuinely freaked out when I told him Nico was involved. I think that was news to him."

Enzo nodded and said darkly, "To all of us."

Jack continued, "Vito said Reginald is going to move the diamonds to the WorldSecure vault in Singapore day after tomorrow. Feels safer there. He's going to try selling them to the Asian crime syndicates. That was the phrase he used."

"Singapore has some of the toughest organized crime laws in the world," Rusty said.

"Which any thief worth his salt would know."

"You think he's on the level?"

"I did until the Singapore thing. Now I'm not so sure."

"What if he's telling the truth?" Rusty asked. "Could it be possible that Reginald really is wigged out? It's not an uncommon pattern with people like him. He's been in the system twice now. Three strikes and he dies in prison. We've got an Italian organized crime outfit having a shootout at his apartment. The police are now involved. His parole officer is going to ask questions Reginald won't have good answers for. With Reginald's track record, playing dumb isn't going to cut it." Rusty paused to take a sip from his beer. "He is probably more scared of going back to prison than anything. I think Vito *could* be on the level."

"Yeah, and it's been at least a week since he's sold someone out," Enzo said dryly.

"We've basically got the ride home to think this through. If we believe Vito enough to side with him, we need to tell him tonight."

"The other option," Enzo said, "is we could say nothing and just go do it."

"If we don't tell him, though, does that risk him saying something to Reginald?" Rusty asked. "He wouldn't tell LeGrande that he came here tonight, but there are ways to drop hints that he thinks we may be onto them."

Jack signaled for the check.

"If we're in, we need to tell him. Take the ride home to think it through."

They drove back to downtown mostly in silence, a classic rock station played on the radio. They valeted the X6 and walked up to the room.

Jack was the first into the room and noticed the dark splotch of spilled liquid on the carpet. He held up a hand and then brought one finger to his mouth, indicating silence.

The cup of water behind the door was tipped over.

NINETEEN

Danzig was in this room because of the memory of a dead cop.

And that welcome was almost worn out.

Giovanni Castro had been running an informant in the Cannizzaro mafia for years. True, this was while Castro was himself on Cannizzaro's payroll…but organized crime in Italy was a complicated affair. When Castro turned up dead of an apparent suicide, his informant called the phone number on the card Castro gave him. The thing he was supposed to do if what happened actually did.

That was Special Agent Katrina Danzig's cell phone number.

This was a serpentine investigation, and the FBI's presence here was tenuous. The Bureau didn't have jurisdiction outside the US over crimes that didn't involve American citizens, but they did provide bilateral support in law enforcement, intelligence sharing, and counterterrorism. Though on that last score they'd stretched their mandate to the absolute limit. These activities were coordinated through the FBI's senior officer in a given country, the legal attaché, or LEGAT. This situation was different, though. Not only did Danzig have the informant, but he abjectly refused to talk to Italian law enforcement. Maybe it had something to do with the fact that he was run by a dirty cop. On top of that, everything they knew about the massive money laundering and public corruption scheme that Salvatore Cannizzaro was running out of his bank in central Rome came to the FBI courtesy of a different informant, one Gentleman Jack Burdette. The Italians didn't think they had enough to prosecute Cannizzaro at the time; Danzig believed it was because he had a judge in his pocket. This was the reason that the investigation shifted to their DIA.

That's where it got complicated.

The Italian government was only too happy to accept the help (and resource support) that came with running a joint operation with the Americans. But that feeling of cooperation did not permeate to the operational level. This might indeed be a different kind of operation, but Tenente Colonnello Mauricio Bruni didn't see it that way. Bruni was an officer in Italy's Guardia di Finanza, which had the lead for investigating crimes involving the mafia. His unit was attached to a joint organization, the Direzione Investigativa Antimafia, or antimafia police, which was comprised of Italy's three police forces: Guardia, the Polizia di Stato, and the Carabinieri.

Danzig had given up trying to puzzle out Italian law enforcement.

Bruni was an asshole and a chauvinist. In Danzig's experience, one tended to follow the other, but Bruni seemed especially adept at both. He resented that their informant wouldn't talk to any of his people, resented that he had to let the Americans play along, and really resented the fact that he had to involve them in his decision-making. Max Silva, the LEGAT, warned her this morning that Bruni was starting to make waves with the command element at DIA, complaining about having to cooperate with the FBI and that they were withholding critical information.

Namely, Sergio Mazza's identity.

Mazza was Cannizzaro's bank manager and chief accountant, but interestingly he was Roman, as opposed to Sicilian. Perhaps that wasn't novel; the Cannizzaros moved their operation to Rome in the nineties and cut ties with the Sicilian mafia afterward. Even though he'd been in the organization for close to twenty years, Mazza told her that he always felt like an outsider. Still, he had managed to work his way up and into if not Cannizzaro's inner circle, certainly a position of trust. After all, Mazza was the banker. The Commerce Bank of Rome was already bent like a U-turn when Salvatore's father, Vincenzu Cannizzaro, took it over in the late nineties. The fact that he even could was still mind-boggling to Danzig and her team, but from what they understood of Rome at the time, governmental oversight wasn't exactly a core competency. Now, Mazza ran all of the money-laundering operations and managed the books for Cannizzaro. That was how Mazza came to be an asset of Giovanni Castro's. Castro was paid to keep the Italian financial police away from the bank. It was only natural they'd cross paths.

It was with that on her mind that she and Choi walked into the DIA's headquarters in the Department of Public Security building, a long, tiered structure that was laid out like a stretched-out S. The grounds were located about fifteen miles to the southeast of Rome proper. They arrived at nine thirty for their ten o'clock morning briefing with Bruni and his team. Danzig had a squad of four here TDY and they'd been detailed here for months. While everyone at home understood that investigations took time to put together and each had their own unique rhythm to play out, Danzig knew that she was under pressure to show tangible results soon in order to justify the continued investment in time and resources. Bruni causing problems didn't help. She knew there was mounting pressure to just hand Mazza over to the Italian officials and let them deal with it. The only thing keeping them in the game was the Russian.

The Bureau was shifting its focus away from counterterrorism and was now concentrating on the highly complex, hydra-like threats posed by China and Russia. If Salvatore Cannizzaro could lead them to Gennady Sokolov, the US government was still very interested. If he couldn't, they couldn't continue to justify this operation. Sokolov had emerged as one of the major players in Russian transnational crime in recent years. The word was that Sokolov and Putin were rivals in the KGB. The former left the service in the nineties and established himself as a businessman, making a literal and figurative killing. Putin despised him because he believed that Sokolov represented everything that Putin hated about the post-Soviet era. That embodiment of overt criminality made them appear weak in front of their rivals in the West.

Danzig was read in on Operation Flipside, at least the parts she needed to know. Flipside was the Bureau's idea that they could capitalize on the rift between Putin and Sokolov. Sokolov owned a shipping business and, more importantly, a large digital media company. Officially. Unofficially, it was a cybercrime outfit that targeted the West, but in Russia that was largely a matter of semantics. Sokolov was currently too dangerous a rival to dispatch, even for someone like the Russian president, but the intel was also that Sokolov believed his days of operating safely within Russia's borders were limited.

That's where the diamonds came into play.

The intel assessment on Sokolov was that he believed Putin's days were numbered and that the president was going to force a disastrous confrontation with the West. One that Russia couldn't possibly win and would result in Russia being reset to basically 1994. Sokolov wanted to insulate himself for when that happened. While Sokolov had hundreds of millions in business assets, very little of it was liquid and almost all of it tied up inside Russia. If Putin decided to shut him down, he could (however disastrous that might be for him), or if this confrontation with the Americans actually happened, Sokolov was looking for a safety net. The gem trade was attractive to him for all of these reasons. The Bureau hoped to snare him in a joint sting with the Italians, the latter getting the Cannizzaro mafia and all of the public corruption, money laundering, and smuggling that entailed. The Americans got a chance at turning a Russian crime boss into an asset that might just give them the best source of intelligence on the Russian president they'd ever had.

The only thing currently standing in their way was a self-righteous Italian police officer who didn't want to deal with a woman.

The FBI wouldn't share those details with their Italian counterparts at any level, so it fell on Danzig to navigate those waters herself. When Danzig spoke with her section chief back in New York, she was advised to just grind it out. There was too much riding on them getting access to Sokolov.

"How much are we going to tell them?" Choi asked.

"No more than we have to for now," Danzig said. "If Bruni is going to keep this shit up, we'll do the same."

"That's not going to get us far."

"No, but until he earns some trust...," Danzig said and let her voice trail off. They'd learned information last night that was throwing the entire operation at risk, and she didn't feel comfortable enough with Bruni to share it.

"So, we're going to share information with a thief but not a cop?" Choi asked.

They'd been through this, a lot, over the last two or three days, but Choi still wasn't comfortable with how much they'd shared with Burdette. While he certainly understood that they weren't going to share top secret, code word–level operational details with Bruni, he was completely uncomfortable with the level of information they'd given Burdette. Choi didn't agree with them flying all the way to see him themselves and didn't understand why they couldn't have tapped someone from the San Francisco or Sacramento offices to do it. In his eyes, it was a waste of time, energy, and money. Now they were jet-lagged in both directions, if such a thing was even possible.

Danzig left the bait where it was and decided not to carry the argument further. It wasn't going to get either of them anything, and both of their positions were entrenched at this point. Danzig could justify the action in her own mind, and that's all that mattered to her.

Back to the topic at hand, Cannizzaro had lost the diamonds and apparently only had a few days to get them back.

Danzig had spoken to Sergio Mazza last night. He was edgy and scared and nearing the point of doing something stupid. Mazza told her that the diamonds were in America. Cannizzaro sent his people to get them from Vito Verrazano and found that he was gone. They found someone else in his house, Mazza didn't get the name, in fact these were all things he'd overheard or had eavesdropped to find out. That was why he was on the edge of panic now. Cannizzaro sent men to America to retrieve them. Her team was putting the word out now in the Bureau for any information on large diamond buys. The other name Mazza gave her was Niccoló Bartolo, Cannizzaro's cousin and the thief who originally stole those diamonds in Antwerp in 2003. Apparently, the cousins had kissed and made up, and Cannizzaro enlisted Bartolo to lead the search.

Verrazano was a onetime accomplice of Reginald LeGrande, whom Danzig confirmed was now out of prison. Her squad had calls into his parole officer. LeGrande was based out of Long Beach, so if Verrazano had taken the stones to America, it seemed logical that it was to team back up with LeGrande. That didn't mean they'd attempt to sell the stones there, but LA did have a jewelry district and did a fair amount of diamond trade for the West Coast. It was equally likely they intended to hold them for the trade shows in Tucson or Vegas.

If Verrazano and LeGrande were successful, and Cannizzaro's people couldn't get the diamonds back, he wouldn't have anything to sell Sokolov and Operation Flipside was over.

Danzig couldn't believe she was in a position to actually have to root for the bad guys.

Mazza told her that Cannizzaro seemed scared. He was starting to act erratic, was having Mazza move money around and set up accounts in other places to make sure he could access it. He told Mazza to "have a fucking bag with him," which meant, be ready to travel. Cannizzaro was getting ready to run.

Danzig could guess why.

Cannizzaro had an impressive operation in Rome. He had judges, cops, and politicians on his payroll. He controlled a bank.

He'd somehow gotten control of a small shipping company that serviced routes between Italy, Greece, Turkey, and North Africa. Using that, he'd set up a small but growing smuggling operation. Cannizzaro could've stayed at this level for the rest of his life and was likely insulated enough that he'd never face prosecution. But he tried to put himself into a different orbit by making a deal with Gennady Sokolov, and that had consequences that the mafia boss was only now becoming cognizant of. Sokolov himself, a man increasingly facing existential pressures, was not a man who was going to accept that Cannizzaro couldn't deliver.

Danzig and Choi waited in silence to be let into the briefing room.

These were held daily now and were intended to coordinate activities between the DIA's part of the operation and the FBI's. Danzig felt distinctly that they were made to feel like their presence was a tolerable inconvenience. She stopped bringing the rest of her squad. They knew how she was being treated, but Danzig didn't particularly feel like they needed to see it firsthand anymore.

One of Bruni's men opened the door about five minutes prior, and people started filing in for the ten o'clock briefing around 10:01. The room was laid out like a classroom, with rows of tables that faced the front. This was not where Bruni's squad operated from, however, and there were none of the elements of a large investigation in this room. There were no mugshots with names and KAs beneath them, taped to a wall, organized by their relationship to the target. There were no maps. There weren't even the signs that dedicated people were working furiously against a clock—Styrofoam cups, leftover foot wrappers, torn sheets of paper with scribbled notes. The room was empty because the DIA squad worked elsewhere and Danzig and her team weren't permitted to see it.

Danzig and Choi sat at a table up front and kept to themselves. They were largely ignored by their DIA counterparts who milled about and talked while they waited. They were in the Guardia di Finanza's duty uniform, which was a dark gray jumpsuit, sleeves rolled up to the elbows, and a bright yellow ascot. Green berets were left on tabletops. Some of them acknowledged her and Choi eventually.

"We have to tell them *something*," Choi said.

She knew he was right, as much as it galled her to admit it. If word got back that she was intentionally withholding relevant information that the DIA was cleared to have, there would be serious repercussions.

Bruni walked in at ten after. He wore his service uniform today, a dark gray jacket with his rank outlined in gold on the epaulettes, the Italian equivalent of an American lieutenant colonel. The uniform also sported a bright yellow design on the lapel that nearly ran to the collar. The jacket was over a white shirt and crisply knotted black tie. There were badges and pins throughout the uniform that no one bothered to explain the meaning of. Bruni had a wheel cap with a thick gold braid across the brim tucked under one arm.

Bruni carried a smug expression on his face, a teacher that knew the answers to the tests because he had the book in front of him. He wore a thin beard and had dark brown hair, cut short, though he was starting to bald. His eyes were wide set on his face. He greeted his men in Italian and then offered a perfunctory, "Good morning" to Danzig and Choi in choppy English. Bruni began the briefing by sharing what his surveillance teams had picked up the previous day, which was not much. They had teams watching the bank and Cannizzaro's villa outside Rome. The FBI provided them with a small surveillance drone that you could control with a laptop. It was about the size of a smartphone and from a distance would look like a bird to human eyes. This gave the DIA the ability to look into Cannizzaro's backyard, where he took most of his meetings. They couldn't record the conversations but could at least see who he was meeting with.

"Cannizzaro appears to be staying put," Bruni said, addressing the room. He stood behind a podium at the front with the Department of Public Security seal on it. Bruni gripped the sides of the podium as though he were delivering a lecture on policing. "He hasn't left his compound in four days. We're not picking up anything useful on the taps that we have on the mobiles or on the house line. Unfortunately, he's being very selective about what they discuss on the phone. Cannizzaro himself hasn't been to the Commerce Bank in two years."

That didn't surprise Danzig much. These days, most criminals knew to use encryption apps or messaging via the dark web. Wiretaps could certainly be effective, but normally for people who didn't think they were under surveillance yet.

Bruni leered over the podium. "Agent Choi, what do you have for us?"

Daniel cleared his throat.

Danzig's cheeks and the back of her neck felt hot. Fury roiled up inside her, but Danzig wouldn't give the bastard the satisfaction of seeing her react to it.

"I believe *Supervisory* Special Agent Danzig has the Bureau's update prepared," Choi responded icily. He muttered something under his breath, but Danzig didn't catch it. Choi was fluent in Korean and often swore in it when he wanted credit for saying something aloud that no one else could understand.

"I spoke with our informant last night," Danzig said, pushing out her chair and standing. She wasn't going to address Bruni sitting down. Instead, she walked to the side of the room and turned slightly so she could also see the other DIA men. This was stupid and petty and it was getting in the way of their mission. "The diamonds are in America," she said. Danzig hadn't intended to tell them, but she realized that was a mistake. She was letting herself get caught up in Bruni's pettiness.

Their reaction was worth it.

"Maybe if you'd shared your information with us, we could have set up a sting," Bruni said, trying to recover his own embarrassment at not knowing.

"No," Danzig said flatly. "He just found out. And as far as information sharing, you and I both know that's bullshit. We've been nothing but transparent with you. The only thing, the *only* thing I've held back is the name of my informant, which you don't need."

"How can I trust the source if I can't prove who he says he is?" Bruni countered snidely.

"Because you can trust that we wouldn't bring it forward if we didn't think it was credible. You have obstructed us every step of the way, and because of that, these stones slipped right out of your grasp. Your agency polices smuggling in this country, not mine. Now, we can keep bickering with each other, you can keep up your petty bullshit, or we can try to cooperate." Danzig looked down at her watch. "I have somewhere to be, and I'm running out of patience."

"Well, if the diamonds are in America, the investigation is over. Congratulations. I hope you get him."

"Cannizzaro sent a group of people to the States to get them back, including Niccoló Bartolo." Her initial outburst subsided, Danzig made sure to address the entire team so it didn't look like she was just parrying with Bruni. "We think that Vito Verrazano went to America to meet with a thief and con man named Reginald LeGrande. They've been working together, on and off, since the late 1980s, with the exception of two stints LeGrande has spent in prison. One of those courtesy of me. We rolled up LeGrande's passport forging operation and he's on a watch list, so we don't think he's going to risk leaving the US."

"Can they sell the diamonds in the United States?"

"They wouldn't do it if they didn't think they could, so this has likely been in the works for some time. That said, I think it's unlikely that they could find a buyer. Certainly not before Cannizzaro's men find them."

Bruni narrowed his eyes, but she couldn't tell if it meant he was concentrating or was getting angry. "So, you think that Cannizzaro's men will find the diamonds and bring them back here?"

"We do," she said, nodding slightly. "Cannizzaro knows what happens if he doesn't deliver for Sokolov. He won't stop just because he thinks LeGrande and Verrazano gave him the slip here." She paused and directed her comments to the room. Bruni and the DIA knew about Cannizzaro's intention to make a deal with Sokolov, they just didn't know about the FBI's larger operation surrounding it. "Gentlemen, neither of our country's interests are served if those diamonds are sold in the States. The FBI is committed to helping you arrest Salvatore Cannizzaro, and these diamonds are our best chance. That also gives the FBI the opportunity to target another international gem pipeline, which is a priority for us, as you know. We can't question Cannizzaro if you don't have him in custody."

"What happens if Verrazano is successful?" Bruni asked. None of his officers had spoken yet, not even to ask a question. Danzig figured they knew this little banter was about a lot more than sharing an informant's name, and they weren't about to get in the middle of it.

"On the off chance that LeGrande and Verrazano actually manage to sell the diamonds, in their entirety, and escape, the answer is obvious. If they are arrested during the commission, it will most likely be the FBI or US Customs that makes the collar. In that case, we have ways of getting those diamonds released here for this operation."

"You can do that?"

"LeGrande is an American citizen, and he doesn't have enough years left in his life to take a third stint in prison. I can get him to cooperate. In short, I can do any goddamned thing I want."

Bruni studied her for a string of long, silent breaths. Then he nodded slowly.

"I don't know," he said heavily. "It seems we're putting our hopes on whether one group of smugglers is good enough to sell the diamonds on the black market. Or on another set of hopes that we could set up an elaborate sting operation that still requires you to catch the smugglers in your country," he made an elaborate motion with his hand, "and then bring them back to our country." He mimicked that sweeping gesture with his other hand. "I think maybe it's time to fold this up. As you say, the diamonds are no longer in this country. I think, perhaps, our partnership has come to an end. We can focus on the bank. I think we've got more than enough there for an arrest."

"But can you get a conviction?" Danzig challenged.

"That's my problem," Bruni said dismissively.

The meeting concluded quickly after that. Bruni dismissed his men and then bid good day to Choi and Danzig, in that order. Danzig stopped him in the hallway.

"You're making a big gamble," she said. "You'd better hope you're right."

"I'm sorry?"

"I doubt that, actually," she said. "Your government asked the FBI to step in and my team specifically, because of the experience we had with Salvatore Cannizzaro and his operations at the Commerce Bank. You're months away from being able to make an arrest there without our help. There was also the matter of some fairly widespread corruption among Italy's law enforcement and *your* branch specifically." Danzig knew on a level that she should proceed with caution, Bruni had a fragile ego, wasn't used to being challenged by a woman, and was under a lot of pressure from his superiors. But he'd also obstructed her at every turn, and playing politics so far hadn't netted them any better results. "The FBI is here because the Italian government doesn't want to be embarrassed by Cannizzaro. Again. So, you can push back here and make a good show for your troops, but you know damn well you can't push that shit uphill. And until I am confident that the identity of my informant is going to stay safe, I'm not handing him over to you."

"I hope you're right about Verrazano and LeGrande. It would be unfortunate if a thief outmaneuvered you again."

Bruni turned crisply on his heels and stalked off. Danzig said nothing, just listened to the sounds of Bruni's heels clacking on the tile.

"Well, *that* was fun," Choi quipped.

"Prick," Danzig said to the empty hall.

They turned and started walking in the opposite direction, making for the exit. This was a massive building, and it was about a ten-minute walk to their car, all told.

"I don't want to be forced to give them Mazza, because that would be everything they need to move on the bank and forget about the diamonds," she said, keeping her voice low. "Regardless of what Bruni said back there, it'd be hard for them to roll that up with him."

"I'm not sure how much longer we can keep this up, though," Choi said. Choi came to the Bureau after serving six years as an Army special forces officer. His next six years in the Bureau was with their elite Hostage Rescue Team, the FBI's equivalent to the Army's Delta Force. He was two years off of that when Danzig met him here in Rome, was immediately impressed, and when she learned that the Bureau was giving her a squad to catch gem smugglers, Choi was her first call. "We haven't really had a chance to talk about the LeGrande-Verrazano angle yet," he said. They'd only learned about it the night before. "You don't really think that play with arresting LeGrande and then using that as a sting to get Cannizzaro is an option, though, do you?"

"I think it's *an* option, Dan. I never claimed it was an ideal one." She stopped walking, turned, and faced him. They were in a long, wide hallway. The wall behind her was a row of windows above shoulder height on the building's western side. "Bruni isn't going to pull the plug on this thing, and he'd have a fun time explaining to his superiors here that they let Verrazano slip out of the country with six pounds of diamonds."

"I know," Choi said, "but scoring points in an argument doesn't give us Cannizzaro, and it doesn't get us Sokolov."

Danzig nodded. They made their way out of the building and into the late morning air, warm, dry, and bright. A seven-foot concrete wall surrounded the building with another seven feet of metal mesh fencing above that. Their car was on the other side. They were quiet as they made their way through the security checkpoint and to the car. "Job one is to figure out whether anyone at the Bureau is working a smuggling case." Those were long odds. Unless this serendipitously fell into someone's lap, because of how quickly this came together, those diamonds could be sold long before anyone in law enforcement even knew about it.

"I think we need to press Mazza a little harder," Choi said. "He's got to kick us something or we kick him loose. Let him think that, at any rate. He needs to figure out what's going on back home. There's still the problem of even if they're successful..." Choi let his voice trail off; nothing more needed to be said. These were mafia heavies, not skilled smugglers. Getting stones was one thing, but sneaking them across international borders was another. That explained why Cannizzaro made up with his cousin. His shipping operation didn't extend to the United States, and anyway, that would take too long. Bartolo was his only real hope of getting those diamonds back.

A plan was starting to form in Danzig's mind, but she wasn't ready to put it to words yet. It was either an incredibly bold move that would nab them a Russian crime lord or the kind of thing Wile E. Coyote would concoct to snare the Road Runner, and she wasn't sure on what side of that line it fell yet. All she knew was that if those diamonds didn't get back to Italy and into Salvatore Cannizzaro's possession by the date that he'd promised them, Sokolov would slip right through their fingers.

TWENTY

They silently packed their things, giving each item and each article of clothing a once-over. The computers were password locked, but Rusty would check them later. Toiletries, anything that would come into contact with the body were disposed off. They were out of the room in under ten minutes. Jack checked out of the suite, explaining to the front desk manager that their plans had changed. The manager needlessly apologized that the universe had placed an imposition on his guest but thanked them for their stay. By the time the valet brought the BMW around, Rusty already booked them an executive suite at the InterContinental a few blocks away.

"The InterContinental?" Jack asked as he accepted the keys from the valet and climbed into the vehicle.

"Seemed appropriate," Rusty noted wryly.

Jack pulled away from the Ritz and headed toward Wilshire. Jack had never gotten the appeal of Sports Activity Coupes. They always seemed to him to be a weird hybrid of an SUV and a sports car, but he had to admit that the M-series X6 was a hell of a lot of fun to drive. Even in LA traffic.

They checked in to their suite and set about getting reorganized.

Rusty checked the computers first and found no evidence of tampering. They thought the probability that the computers could be tampered with was low, but they would take no chances.

If they'd been on the fence about believing Vito before, they all believed that he'd been setting them up now. Vito probably wanted them to think and therefore plan on his and Reginald's departure from Los Angeles as much as he wanted them out of the room so Reginald could do whatever it was he intended there. Planting a listening device most likely, but they hadn't ruled out something more dangerous, which was why they offloaded anything that would come in contact with their bodies. Now they had a game of bluff to play.

If Reginald had planted a bug, or worse, a camera, in their room at the Ritz, he'd know they'd checked out. But Jack still had to tell Vito that they were in on his plan to double-cross Reginald and steal the diamonds from him. Vito would know they were bluffing.

It was always possible that the glass was tipped over by some other means, but they wouldn't chance that.

Jack called Vito and said they were in. Difficult to gauge reactions over the phone, but Jack couldn't tell one way or the other if Vito bought it. He just said that he'd call Jack as soon as he had the flight information.

The next morning, Jack called WorldSecure.

"Good morning, this is Agent Hoskins with US Customs. I'm the aviation liaison officer at Van Nuys Airport."

"Hello, sir. How can we help you today?"

Jack gave the practiced, perfunctory laugh of bureaucrats the world over. "Paperwork, man. You know how it is."

"You bet I do. Shoot."

"We tracking a shipment from one of your clients, and I have to reconfirm it. It's been confirmed once already, but there's this new process says we gotta do it twice. It's supposed to be moving out of here tomorrow. I'm showing a declared value of," Jack flipped a few pages in his notebook as if he were looking it up, "of seventy-three million."

"Okay, what's the name on the shipment, sir? Who is the account holder?"

"Reginald Burton."

Jack heard typing on the other end of the line. "I'm sorry, Agent Hoskins, was it? I am showing a dispatch order and the declared value of seventy-three million, which we have to disclose for insurance purposes. But this is showing a local delivery. It's an address in Inglewood. Says here, 'Pan Pacific Metallurgy and Minerals.' Business type is listed as an importer-exporter."

Jack copied down the address onto his notepad and then looked it up on his laptop. The location was an office park at the southwest corner of the 105 and 405 interchange, just outside LAX. If they were an importer-exporter, that would be a perfect location for their offices.

"Hmm," Jack said, "maybe they've changed plans and have decided to move from LAX instead of Van Nuys."

"Looks like it, sir."

Jack sighed into the phone, the tired and overlooked cog in the wheel. "Obviously, I'm always the last to know. Thanks a lot for your time."

Jack hung up. He got up and refilled his coffee cup from the pot room service had brought up. "So, Vito was lying."

Enzo said, "That guy needs one of those 'days since safety incident' signs, only for bullshit." No one laughed, because they were all thinking the same thing.

Jack filled them in on the details of the phone call. "Looks like the Singapore thing was a red herring. Assuming they don't know that we checked out of the Ritz, they probably believe that we're planning on that and therefore are focusing our efforts on getting in as ground crew at Van Nuys. They'll believe we're sidelined and will only be planning on Bartolo's crew."

"Who will not be as organized," Enzo said.

"Exactly. So, first up, Rusty, we need to get everything we can on this Pan Pacific Metallurgy."

"Already on it," he said.

"Next up, let's go do some recon. Enzo, you can roll with me. Grab some notebooks, your computer, and a Wi-Fi brick."

"Take this one," Rusty said and held up a small hot spot. "I had this one with me in the Beemer last night in Santa Monica, so it wasn't in the room." That was smart. If Reginald had been in the room, he could have copied down the IP information for any of their Wi-Fi devices left there.

Jack and Enzo had done an armored car job before, but it had been about twenty-five years ago, and it wasn't as though Turin in the nineties was doing state-of-the-art security. The Fiat payroll job was one for the record books, though, and that's what got him in solid with Niccoló Bartolo and the School of Turin. While they weren't planning to intercept the car en route from WorldSecure to Pan Pacific, knowing how long that drive would take was important. They also needed to know the possible alternate routes, in case of an accident or construction. Jack guessed the sale would be between the core business hours of ten and two, so they timed the route to start by rolling past WorldSecure just before ten thirty that morning. Jack took Hill Street to the 110 southbound, just south of the USC campus, and followed that crawl to the 105, which he followed practically to LAX, exiting at Imperial and going through a rather involved turnaround to head into the office park. Enzo timed it at forty-two minutes, fifty seconds. Jack kept his speed at a conservative rate, going slightly slower than the flow of traffic, trying to match what he thought the armored car's pace would be.

Pan Pacific's proximity to the 405 and 105 freeways was nearly a perfect setup. While the plan didn't call for a rapid getaway, the need for one was always a possibility. Being so close to not one but two freeways as well as one of Los Angeles's major north-south arteries, La Cienega Boulevard, gave them multiple potential escape routes and would force any pursuers to either split up or guess correctly if they didn't have eyes on them at all times.

The office park was three buildings arranged in a circle around a roundabout and water fountain. The buildings were all four stories of white exterior and square-shaped blue-green windows arranged in a grid. The buildings were slightly curved so as to follow the contours of the circle, as though they were forming the outer rings of a larger one.

Jack rolled down the long entry road. It was lined with palms on either side, sidewalks and then raised berms with low hedges between the trees. This created a chokepoint; it was the only road in or out of the complex, and the landscaping would prohibit someone from jumping the curb and escaping. Enzo noted that as they drove down it, and Jack confirmed that he was thinking the same thing. He took one pass around the roundabout.

"It's that middle one," Enzo said, referring to the building.

There was an access road between each of the buildings and a small number of reserved parking spaces.

"The armored car is going to stop right here," Jack said, rolling slowly past the building. Normally, they'd have gotten out and done recon on foot, but these were relatively new constructions and would almost certainly have security cameras. That footage would be turned over to law enforcement as soon as WorldSecure realized the diamonds were stolen. The police or, more likely, the FBI would review the footage from the previous days to see if anyone was casing the location, just as Jack and Enzo were doing now. They'd sprayed the license plates with a camera blocker so that wouldn't show up either, but they weren't getting out of the vehicle.

Jack did one more turn around the traffic circle with Enzo filming on his camera. As he completed his second pass, instead of turning back down the main road, Jack turned right onto the access road between the target building and the one next to it. The access roads all led to a series of parking lots that ringed the buildings. The lots were separated by a similar landscaping scheme as the entry road, palm trees and hedges atop raised sidewalks. Jack drove the length of the lot's outer perimeter, confirming what he'd thought on the way in. That main road was the only way in or out. The BMW did have the ground clearance to hop over the curb, but there looked to be a low concrete wall on the far side of it, which separated the parking lot from the residential neighborhood on the other side.

"It's not long from the building to La Cienega, maybe forty-five seconds at full speed," Jack said. "But it's a half mile in either direction to get onto the freeway, if it comes to that. Look closer on the map."

"Your cops aren't lazy like ours are, so I don't know how quickly they'd respond," Enzo said.

"The real hole in this is if the guards don't turn over the diamonds until they call the warrant in. Then we're stuck and in a position to take it by force, which is where the egress calculation comes in. The other variable is whether Reginald and Vito are with them."

"In the car?"

"No, they won't be allowed to ride in the armored car, but it's very likely that they would be arriving at the same time or close to it. You can even imagine a scenario where Reginald is waiting out front and wants to walk it in."

"Yeah," Enzo agreed. "That feels like him. Since either of them can identify at least two of us, we can't use someone to run a distraction. Not without a disguise."

"We've done that before. Rusty has too, I think."

It was a flaw and a very real one. No plan was perfect, but they planned jobs months in advance, rehearsed every detail, every contingency. This was being done with just days to plan and almost no logistical support. If Reginald and Vito rolled with the armored car, the bluff they planned wouldn't work, and there would only be one recourse. And that was an option Jack wasn't willing to take. He wouldn't, but could he say the same about both of his partners? Jack had only shot another person once before. It was in self-defense. And his friend, a bent Italian cop, covered it up.

There was a time Jack never would have put himself in this position.

Jack had developed a set of rules that he used to test whether he should take a job, and in many ways, they were based on the mistakes he'd seen other thieves make. Including Reginald. The first was never to take a score large enough to chase. Eventually, law enforcement and insurance companies forget about the jewelry store thefts of the world; the Antwerp Diamond Centres, they never do. Never steal out of hunger. Jobs born out of necessity are often hastily planned and the thief might not be thinking clearly about the risk because they are too blinded by the need. Finally, and perhaps most importantly, never steal from someone with the will or the means to get it back. This job would have violated all three of those principles.

"You'll be outside WorldSecure when the armored car leaves," Jack said. "So you can notify us if Reginald and Vito are driving with them."

"We don't have enough cars to do a tail. Not unless you're willing to leave Rusty alone or be alone yourself." The plan was for Jack and Rusty to wait here in the parking lot and intercept the guards outside the building. WorldSecure's guards would be trained in anti-thievery tactics and would know how to spot when they were being followed. Enzo's suggestion would mean that they'd need a second car on the road that could switch off following the armored car.

"No, I think we stick with the plan. You follow them, but at a distance. It won't be hard to keep that thing in line of sight on the road, and I doubt they'll ever get over sixty. The thing we have to decide on is what do we do if Reginald and Vito are driving with them."

"You're not going to get into a shootout with them in the street," Enzo said flatly.

"No, I am not. Get some pics of the parking lot," Jack said.

Enzo took several from his side and Jack got a few more. He then drove to another part of the lot so he could capture the access road between the buildings and show Rusty where they'd need to come in from. "On our way out, let's also get video of the entry road."

"Got it." After a beat, Enzo said, "How much longer are you

going to avoid the question by asking me to take pictures? What happens if this comes down to us having to force Reginald to give them up?"

Jack laughed, but there was no humor behind it.

"Reginald deserves to die facedown in a gutter, but I'm not going to be the one to put him there. If he and Vito are following the armored car, I think we waive off. Even if I was willing to shoot them both, and I am not, there are still the security guards to think about. They're civilians. Besides, a double homicide turns this into a freeway chase, and that only ends well for the cops."

Enzo nodded.

"If it comes to that, I'll tip Reginald and Vito to the authorities, and we can hope that they at least get arrested eventually."

"What do you think about what Vito told you—about Reginald settling his score?"

"Oh, I think that's the only honest thing Vito said last night," Jack said and started to drive forward and leave the complex. "I think Nico will too." Jack paused so that Enzo could film their path down the main drive. He continued as they pulled onto La Cienega and headed for the freeway. "I created Frank Fischer so that I'd have a place to hide that didn't feel like hiding. Before I did the Carlton job, I was already on my way out of the life. Maybe another three, four years. But the idea was I had a secure identity that I could live under, a source of legitimate income and a way to clean my money. It was a place that the Bartolos of the world could never find me. Reginald robbed me of that. Thanks to him, now that lunatic Aleksander Anđelić found out and now Bartolo too. I don't want to abandon that life, or those people, but even if we succeed here, I don't see how Reginald and Bartolo let me walk away. And one or both of them can come find me."

"Not until all your enemies are dead," Enzo deadpanned.

Jack half laughed again.

That was a toast they used to say when they were running together in Turin. There was this eccentric thief they worked with on occasion, and he used to say that's when he'd retire, when all his enemies were dead. Then he was gunned down by some mafia heavies after he took down the wrong score. The School of Turin used to toast themselves with that after a job: "When all my enemies are dead." It was the kind of black humor that one needed to insulate themselves against the darker parts of the life they'd chosen.

They drove for a time in silence.

Jack continued to think of ways that they could separate Reginald and Vito from the armored car. He and Enzo lobbed ideas between them, but all of them required either a level of additional support they didn't have, were too complex for the size of their team, or relied on a face that their enemies didn't know. Jack hadn't worked as a thief in the United States since 1995, Rusty and Enzo never had, so they didn't have a network of people they could tap for assistance. There was no one they could sub in.

There was a reason that armored car jobs had essentially been wiped out from the criminal ecosystem.

"If Reginald and Vito are with the WorldSecure car, we have to call it off. With what we've got available to us, we can't separate them, and I'm not willing to risk innocent people getting hurt."

Enzo said nothing. He just stared out the window as they merged on the freeway, heading back for downtown.

Jack knew what was going through his head.

Enzo bought an olive farm in Calabria a few years ago and semi-retired. He basically only worked when Jack called. His place was on Italy's southern edge, the sole of the boot, as it were, overlooking the Ionian Sea. Enzo wasn't a particularly good farmer, but he hired that out mostly. He grew olives and peppers and sold his stuff locally. He'd been with a woman for several years now; she knew about his past and didn't care. Enzo wasn't in the mafia, and that's all that mattered to her. But now Cannizzaro knew that he was involved, and Enzo couldn't be certain that win or lose, there wouldn't be repercussions for him. His share of that take would help him disappear if he needed to. Or buy the kind of security that would make him not worth the while.

Rusty had a similar decision.

He was actively on the run now from the US government. That cost money. There was also the expenses they'd put into this operation so far. They'd chartered jets in Italy, plus the clean cars, the untraceable guns, the hotels, and the forged passports that would stand up to a CBP officer's inspection. They'd spent a small fortune on this job already.

Maybe that's why Jack landed in winemaking.

It took a large fortune to make a small one. Seemed like it was the same with thieving.

They returned to the hotel and debriefed.

Their suite had floor-to-ceiling windows that ran the entire length of the room, affording them an unparalleled thirty-eighth-floor view of downtown. Even the smog was breathtaking from up here. Their room faced north, and they could see the long gray ribbons of freeway eventually disappear into the mountains.

"Pan Pacific is a registered business," Rusty said. "The address checks out, and I called the management company to confirm that they are leasing that space to Pan Pacific."

"They say how long they've been there?" Jack asked.

"He told me a few months. They've got a corporate website, but it's pretty generic. I called the number listed and got an answering service. They didn't say they were an answering service, but I could tell. It felt like a front. It's the kind of presence you have when you want someone to think you have a presence. We used to do stuff like this in Bureau all the time, set up fake businesses for stings. Honestly, this felt a lot like that."

"Yeah. Once we found out that they were going to sell the entire load in one go, I knew it couldn't be a legitimate business. No one could put this amount of honest money together that fast. Plus, with that shit Vito pulled last night, trying to throw us off."

Enzo walked over to the window and studied the view. When he spoke, he was still facing the window. "So, Reginald found a crooked diamond broker, and they've set up a bogus shop in this office park?"

"Looks that way," Rusty said.

"And they have just enough polish to make it look like a real business at a fast glance, which is all someone looking to sell eighty million in diamonds is going to do." The other two nodded. "Reginald would have sold them some story about how he got the stones, maybe they believe him and maybe they don't, but the buyers probably don't think they're stolen."

"Pan Pacific are probably crooks," Rusty said.

Jack laughed genuinely for the first time in what felt like forever. The pair that stole from them was about to get taken themselves. "That's our backup plan, Enzo," Jack said.

Rusty looked confused. "I don't get it," he said.

"On the way back, Enzo and I were trying to think of what our backup plan was. What we would do if Reginald and Vito followed the armored car to the sale. Do we still try to pull the con and risk getting into a standoff with them and the guards? We were trying to figure out what the Plan B was in that situation, and there were no good options. But now…" Jack smiled and spread his hands.

Rusty finished the thought for him. "If we can't do the intercept before the sale, we'll just do it on the back end when the Pan Pacific crew is trying to clear out."

"Exactly. Think about it. This place is what, three miles from LAX?"

"If that. Less if they have access to the cargo terminal."

"That might actually be safer, honestly," Jack said. "How quickly can we get a layout of the building?"

"I've got it right here," Rusty said and turned his laptop around to show him. "Pan Pacific is in 208. Most of that building is one of those continuing education schools."

"Perfect. Okay, you and I will still be together for Plan A. If that falls through, we enter the building here." Jack grabbed a pen and pointed at a rear entrance. "That's right near the stairs. Enzo will arrive shortly after the armored car and can watch the front of the building to tell us when Reginald and Vito leave. That'll be our cue to move in."

Rusty nodded in agreement. "The other crew won't leave right away because it'll look suspicious. We should assume that they'll be armed, but the weapons won't be out. Enzo can come in once Reginald and Vito have left. Backup if we need it."

"Speaking of backup," Jack said. "We haven't really talked about Bartolo. He's here, and he's not alone. They at least know where Reginald lives, so they've got some kind of lead. Do we think they make a play? Any chance they know about this Pan Pacific thing?"

"Doubtful," Rusty said. "Unless they've got really good surveillance or a mole, I don't see how they'd know."

"A mole isn't out of the question," Enzo said. "Cannizzaro is everywhere, seems like."

"Listen," Rusty said in a tone that sounded like a hand wave. "I've squared off against the mafia on both sides of the street. I've gone up against them as a cop, and I've worked with and against them after, and I'm not impressed."

"They found out where Reginald lived," Jack said.

"He's a felon, Jack. A public records search can get you that. These guys aren't that sophisticated."

"You don't know Nico like I do," Jack said. "But I don't know that it changes much. If they show up, it's going to be a firefight. The part I do agree with Rusty on is that they aren't subtle. If they roll in, I think we have to abort."

Enzo nodded in agreement.

Jack grabbed a piece of drafting paper and a ruler from their supplies. He sketched out a scale rendering of the building's second floor, the rear stairwell and rear parking lot.

"What's our exit strategy?" Rusty asked.

That was a good question and one Jack hadn't given much thought to since the game had changed. He'd been so focused on how they were going to adapt to the new situation, he hadn't had the time to consider what they would do when they left. Reginald and Bartolo wouldn't go away just because Jack had won.

"Cannizzaro," Jack said.

"What?" Enzo asked, astonished.

"Once we steal these things, that only takes Reginald and Vito off the table. Bartolo knows we're involved, which means Cannizzaro does too. What if we offer to sell the diamonds to him? At least that way, he's not also coming after us when this is over."

"Us, or you?" Enzo asked, challenge rising in his voice.

"I'm going to have to deal with Reginald," Jack said. "I would much rather also not have to worry about a mafia boss with it. Normally, I wouldn't have thought much of it, but they're here. I'm not saying it isn't risky. We know that the Italian antimafia police have infiltrated Cannizzaro's organization and are working with the FBI. Danzig knew about Vito and the diamonds, so we can assume the source is pretty well placed. But I also don't want to spend the rest of my life looking over my shoulder for Nico Bartolo. I don't think you do either, Enzo."

"No, but I didn't steal his woman."

"It was the other way around." Jack's dour expression broke into a grin. "Asshole." There was a laugh that sliced the tension, which they all needed. "Guys, it's really risky, I admit. But it takes bad guys off the board."

"Why do you think Cannizzaro will sell to us? Why wouldn't he just kill us and be done with it?" Rusty asked. It was a fair question.

"Vito told me that Cannizzaro made some kind of a deal with a Russian gangster." Jack opened up his phone and flipped to the notes app. He'd made a note of it as soon as he got in the car. "Gennady Sokolov. I looked him up on the ride here. Officially, he's a businessman, shipping, looks like. According to Western media, particularly the British, he's the next boogeyman. Smuggling, arms dealing, human trafficking. If it makes dirty money, he does it."

"Why's he so interested in diamonds?" Rusty asked.

Jack shrugged. "Vito didn't know. He only knew that Cannizzaro seemed genuinely afraid of him."

"Holy shit," Enzo said, looking down at his phone. "Jesus, if half of this stuff is true."

"It's kind of funny," Rusty said. "From what you've told me, Jack, Cannizzaro has been the apex predator of his ecosystem for the last twenty-five years or so. This guy isn't even afraid of his government. Now, all of a sudden, he's swimming in the ocean and there are sharks."

"Globalization is a bitch," Jack said. "So, guys, I know this one carries with it some risk. But it's an option to make our money fast and reduces the number of people coming after us. We probably make less than we would selling on the gray market, but we get it faster."

"And we're still talking about a fucking lot of money," Enzo said.

"Let's estimate he just gives us half, for the sake of easy math. Minus what Reginald already moved, that's still twelve million to each of us. I can live with that."

"Twelve million and a threat off the board," Rusty agreed. He nodded as he spoke. They both looked to Enzo.

"Hey, I'm just a simple olive farmer that you two brought into your," Enzo rolled his hand, "so-called web of crime."

Jack laughed again and the others joined in. This one lasted for a while. One of the things that he'd always loved about Enzo over the years was his friend's singular, if not slightly offbeat, wit and his ability to weave that into the tensest of situations. The chuckling receded to a manageable level.

"I think there's ways to manage Cannizzaro," Enzo said. "We can point out that while he may have bought police off, that door can swing both ways." Enzo didn't mention Giovanni Castro by name, because that was still very real for both him and Jack. "Cannizzaro will deny it, of course, believe he's too smart for it, but the message might get through. How do you propose getting the diamonds to Rome?"

All of this just to get the diamonds back to the place where they came from.

"I'd always figured that we'd have to move these back to Europe, so I've already placed some phone calls. We're going to do a version of the cameraman."

Enzo nodded and smiled. One of the biggest challenges in dealing in stolen gems and jewelry was that a thief had to be able to move them securely to a fence. In Europe, that invariably meant *someone* had to move them across national borders. One of the tools they used in the past was having hardshell transit cases that had small compartments built into them. These spaces would be along the edges of the case, usually running along the hinges. They would be lead lined, but thinly, so that it would appear on an X-ray to be just part of the case's hardening. The main part of the case would be packed with something fragile and expensive, like camera equipment, something that most airport or border security guards wouldn't want to handle for fear of breaking it. One of the things you could count on the world over was the cogs in a bureaucratic machine playing their parts. Those that were on the lowest part of that machine would go to great lengths to avoid getting in trouble with management, because that meant extra work, reprimand, or worse. They wouldn't overlook something obviously illegal but would absolutely give the lightest of touches to something like a five-thousand-dollar camera, because that wasn't coming out of *their* pay.

"I had the cases made up about a year ago. We'll spread them out over two cases. I brought them with." Jack walked into his room and returned with a black rolling suitcase. It looked like any piece of carry-on luggage, just that it was made of hardshell plastic. He set the case down on the floor between them and opened it. Inside was a camera and its associated equipment. Jack lifted that tray out and set it on the ground next to him. He pressed in a rounded section above one of the wheels, and it detached. There was no visible seam other than the contour of the case from the injection molding. Jack removed that panel and showed the interior. "This piece and everything around the compartment is lined so that on a scanner, it'll look like reinforcement for the wheels. The diamonds will be packed in padded felt bags, which I also had made to spec."

"That's what those were?" Enzo said. "Honestly, I just assumed that was your luggage. You have so many fucking clothes, even for a heist."

"Rusty, what does a charter plane run us from here to Rome?"

"If we have the whole plane to ourselves? Hundred k."

"How much is left in our budget?"

"We've burned through almost everything. I can book the plane on a dummy corporate card. But assuming that we'll want a clean car in Italy, place to stay, and weapons, we'll need cash for that. Call it twenty to be safe."

"Make it happen," he said.

When that was done, they went back over day-of plans and their backups, should something go off. Jack studied the drawing he'd made of the building's interior where the Pan Pacific offices were located and committed it to memory.

Jack smiled. He was feeling a lot better about their chances.

TWENTY-ONE

Reginald paced in the front room of their rented house, unable to sleep.

He hadn't been on a job in over twenty years, and that one ended with him getting five years at San Quentin. This wasn't exactly a "job," but his nerves were still up. There were any number of ways this thing could fall apart on them today. In the past, he would never have done business with a fence he didn't know and certainly wouldn't do it with a take like this. But Pan Pacific wasn't a fence, they were a real business, they were just looking to undercut their competition in a highly competitive industry and probably the government too. Reginald wouldn't fault them for that. He had to play this carefully and make sure that he and Vito had their backstory rehearsed, their roles down. They probably knew that Reginald Burton and Vito De Angeles had done some undercutting of their own to get this many diamonds, which they'd be fine with, but if these guys found out they were really thieves, this thing was over.

Business like this was like being in a relationship with an unfaithful woman. People needed just enough to convince themselves that it was on the level.

Reginald looked into Pan Pacific and everything checked out. Website looked good, had sales figures and everything, had all the numbers and codes that the government requires and whatnot. He even called around, checked with the building owner, couple of other places. No one at WorldSecure had heard of them, but Reginald actually would have been surprised if they had. WorldSecure's clients were private investors; there wasn't anyone there that was doing institutional-level investing in diamonds.

Reginald pulled the curtain back on the front window. The sky was pre-dawn gray. Santa Anas had been bad last night. He hadn't slept well to begin with but had dreams about the skin being stripped from his bones by that wind. Must've been able to hear it in his sleep. Reginald decided that he needed to get out and move, calm his nerves, so he decided to walk a couple of blocks and get some breakfast. When he'd rented this place two days before, he chose Westlake because of its proximity to downtown, just a couple of miles as the crow flies on the other side of the 110. Reginald had lived most of his adult life down in Long Beach, but he knew LA pretty well still. Before he'd gone up, Westlake was a hellhole. El Salvadoran immigrants took the place over in the nineties and brought MS-13 with them. Lots of drugs, lots of gangs. Sure as shit not the kind of place he'd park a hundred-thousand-dollar Range Rover on the street (stolen or not), but the rental place assured him that Westlake had solidly gentrified.

He found a place a few blocks away where he could get breakfast burritos and a coffee. He bought half a dozen and one coffee. He didn't want to listen to Vito bitch any more about how Americans didn't know how to make it, so he could do without.

On the way back to the house, walking under the yellow-orange streetlights, now with his blood flowing and the caffeine hitting his system, Reginald could feel the cogs starting to move. Looked like the day would be overcast. He thought through their risks and their backup plans. Vito said he had Jack and his crew handled. They believed that Vito was switching sides, not an injudicious conclusion, he noted, and that Vito would be teeing the diamonds up for them to take. He'd be calling them in a few hours to let them know he and Reginald would be leaving out of Van Nuys at noon. They'd also have spent the entire time from when Vito talked to them figuring out how they'd get into the Van Nuys airport under the guise of being ground crew and *not* following Reginald and Vito around. Reginald would have been disappointed in Jack if he hadn't been able to pull off something like impersonating a customs officer. Yeah, he'd thought it was legit when it first happened and two of their earlier meetings got cancelled. Those were mostly backups, anyway. So, Gentleman Jack Burdette was handled, but they didn't have a solid plan for the Italians.

Fucking Vito.

He couldn't just have been patient. That was the problem with the guy and why Reginald had stopped working with him in the first place. He was a good enough thief, but his nerves didn't hold. He wasn't the kind of guy that could sit on a take for a long time. Reginald always thought it was Knightsbridge that broke him, made him paranoid. Guy was steel threaded before then. Admittedly, Vito had been sitting on this knowledge of where Niccoló Bartolo hid the take from the Antwerp Diamond Centre for some time, but he didn't have the ability to go get it. Or a crew he trusted enough to pull it off. Reginald told him a hard "oh, hell no," when Vito came up with the idea of letting Jack do it, but he eventually came around to the idea. Especially when he heard about how Vito would pull off the rest of it. That worked out okay. Reginald would have preferred that it was Jack in the car and *he* be the one Vito shot twice, left for dead, but you can't always control these things. No, it was the crumbling of nerves over the last year where Vito panicked and went to his old friend the mafia don and casually said, "Hey, I have six pounds of diamonds that were stolen out of a bank you own and would you like to buy them?"

Whenever Reginald thought about that, he couldn't believe that even Vito would be that stupid.

You can't even have that conversation in your head and have it make any logical sense.

About the only helpful lesson Reginald picked up in prison was this bit he got from a lifer who told him that everybody in here goes crazy their first year as they get used to the bars. But you can learn to accept the world as it is or only as you'd like it to be.

Reginald found that philosophy exceedingly helpful in dealing with Vito Verrazano.

So, this angry mafia don sends his cousin all the way here to LA after Vito and the diamonds and because God likes fucking with Reginald LeGrande, and it's the same guy who stole the goddamn diamonds in the first place all those years ago. Jack was handled. But this Niccoló Bartolo was an unknown. Of course, Reginald knew all about him by reputation. For the first couple of months after Jack returned from Italy in '97, Bartolo was all he talked about. Whined was more like it. Kid was jumping at shadows for months. Bartolo also spent sixteen years in a Belgian prison, so he'd be angry, impatient, and rusty. That made him both unpredictable and much more prone to a smash-and-grab type operation than a solid con.

Reginald figured that much from the O.K. Corral shit Bartolo started outside his apartment.

Reginald didn't know how Bartolo and his crew determined where Reginald lived or that they'd piece together that he and Vito were working on this in the first place. The only thing Reginald could gather was that they'd somehow tailed Vito here to the US and from there followed them both to Reginald's apartment. But he couldn't fathom what would possess them to open fire multiple times in a quiet beach town.

It was hard to predict the moves of a desperate man. Reginald had to assume that Bartolo somehow had insight into their moves and would try something today. Whatever he did would likely be fast and violent. Smash and grab.

However things went down, it wouldn't be over today.

Now, Reginald had the police to deal with.

The Hermosa cops were kind of understanding. But they wanted to know why someone would try to break into an ex-con's apartment in broad daylight, shoot at someone, then start a foot chase with him and shoot at him some more. What was in your apartment that someone would want to steal, Mr. LeGrande? Why would armed men be looking for you, Mr. LeGrande? There are a lot of expensive properties in Hermosa Beach, Mr. LeGrande, why would someone break into yours? His parole officer started in on him shortly after that. You, having been arrested previously for armed burglary, forgery, identity theft, and fraud, and now someone is breaking into your house looking for something, what could that be?

Reginald deflected and told both his PO and the police that he had no idea why someone would want to break into his apartment and that he didn't have anything worth stealing. He was just looking for a quiet life where he could start over, stay out of trouble. PO actually had the nerve to say, "Well, it looks like trouble found you." Like he's in a fucking movie. And a bad one at that.

The police said they'd be in touch, that the investigation was ongoing. His apartment wasn't a crime scene anymore and he could return whenever he liked. His PO was less understanding. He said that obviously he needed to keep a closer eye on Reginald to make sure that he wasn't slipping back into his old habits and increased their monthly check-ins to every other week. Probably some unannounced visits to Reginald's residence, too, chats with his landlord, his employer. And it wasn't going to be that over-the-phone shit either.

This would complicate his life for a while. Reginald had another five years of parole. The original plan was that he'd pull the same scam he'd used the first time he was on parole, which was to maintain a shit-box apartment to show his PO that he could hold down a place. He still knew guys that would vouch that he worked for them for a fee. Meanwhile, Reginald would live in accommodations that were a little more fitting of his accomplishment. He needed this Bartolo break-in thing to go away quickly so that he could slide into a new life once he had the money. Reginald thought about just running, leaving the country. The US government wasn't going to send a marshal halfway across the world chasing someone like him for skipping parole. But if the dots were ever connected and some enterprising son of a bitch figured out that the diamonds he was going to sell today were stolen, that changed things some. It was better to play the game, serve out his time, and maybe petition the court to end his parole early. The risk, of course, was that as long as there was someone around who could tip Reginald and this job to the police, he was in danger.

Reginald took another long drag of coffee, the cup much cooler and lighter than when he'd started. He didn't know how long he'd been standing out in front of the house, thinking things through. The sky was brighter now, and there were more lights on in the houses on the street. The place was waking up. Westlake was one of LA's older neighborhoods, most of the houses dating back to the twenties and thirties. Reginald walked up to the house's front porch and grabbed one of the metal chairs, pulling it around to where he could view the street. He unwrapped one of the burritos from the foil and started eating.

Jack and his crew would be sidelined today, but not forever. Reginald couldn't just slide into a new life and alias while keeping his front with his PO, not while Jack was still out there with knowledge. Before this would be over, Reginald had to tie up the loose ends. And the way you did that was by taking a match to them, burning the frayed ends so that they could never unravel again.

Reginald shook his head at the shame of it all. He and Jack could have been fucking *legends*.

But his protégé had made his choice, unfortunately. At every conceivable turn, Jack seemed not to take the logical, sensible path. Reginald truly thought he'd taught him better than this. He had, actually. He'd brought Jack up in this life. Showed him the *way*. Reginald knew that it was impossible to pinpoint the exact moment it happened, because this was more like erosion than a crash. Over time, Jack lost his nerve, he became a civilian and still wanted to have his life. He wanted a foot in both worlds and pretended there were no consequences to that.

We can choose to accept life as we want it to be, or as life is.

It should make Reginald sad that it would come to this, but these choices had been made long ago. In fact, if Jack hadn't gotten involved now, Reginald would have let the past be the past. Reginald would've gotten his share of the eighty mil, and that was more than enough to make a man content. But Jack couldn't leave it well enough alone, couldn't accept defeat. Now, the only way out of this was that Gentleman Jack Burdette was going to have to fill a hole in the desert.

Reginald balled up the foil wrapper and dropped it in the bag.

Reginald learned a long time ago that when planning and executing a job, you had to separate your problems into the things you could solve today and the things you couldn't. A thief who worried too much about how they were going to move the goods, for example, before they even stole them usually didn't have the focus they needed to carry the job out.

Jack Burdette was a "tomorrow" problem. By the time Jack realized that he'd been had, it would be too late to do anything about it.

Bartolo was the variable. Reginald didn't know how *he* knew how to find them, and that meant he couldn't predict what the man would do today. Bartolo had help, that much was clear. The question was, from where and by whom? Without even thinking about it, Reginald turned his head to look back over his shoulder, back into the house.

Where indeed.

TWENTY-TWO

Jack got little sleep.

By four, he realized that he was up for good and walked out to the main part of the suite and fixed a coffee. Enzo had the other room, and Rusty was in a different one on that floor. The suites only had two bedrooms. Jack took his coffee and padded softly across to the window. The city was dark and even thirty-eight floors removed from the streets, he could tell, hauntingly quiet. There was a low layer of clouds hanging in the sky. Some of that, Jack knew, was ash. But hopefully it also meant that the Santa Anas were over and rains would be coming soon. He'd tried to stay off the news, but he couldn't help it. He'd watched until the low hours when he finally dropped into a fitful sleep. Then Jack dreamed of fire.

After the coffee and a shower, he dressed in a conservative light gray suit that he'd had made in London once. He wore a white shirt with the slightest light gray pencil stripes that one had to be close enough to see and a dark blue tie. While this con required him to convince people that he was a US Customs agent, Gentleman Jack Burdette was going to be damned if he was stealing eighty million in diamonds wearing the kind of suit a fed could afford.

Seventy-three million, he corrected himself.

Rusty arrived at seven thirty, and they had a quiet breakfast in the room. No one spoke much. Day of, you didn't rehearse, you didn't go back over it "one last time" to see if there was anything you missed. That's when the details of the plan started getting crowded in your mind. Maybe you practiced it slightly different that time because your nerves were up, misremembered a move or a line. If it was a night job, you might, but on a daylight score like this one, by now the plan was set and practice done.

Jack stepped into his room and called Megan to tell her he planned to be home sometime tomorrow.

Enzo took the Malibu at eight that morning. He'd park down the block from WorldSecure and watch. While they believed that Reginald would move the diamonds during the hours of ten and two, because that was offset from rush hour, they couldn't know for certain. Enzo posted early, making sure that they didn't miss the departure. He called them to say that he was in position.

They were both armed with their weapons in shoulder holsters. Rusty would be reprising his role as an FBI agent. He dressed in a black suit, white shirt, dark red sateen tie that Jack knew he recently bought off a department store rack, and an American flag lapel.

Jack looked over at Rusty and said, "Let's roll."

A bellman brought their bags down and loaded them into the X6's hatch, including the two hardshell Pelican cases. Jack tipped him and then the valet. Rusty emerged from the hotel, wearing sunglasses and buttoning his jacket as he walked. "We're all set," he said as he climbed in. Jack pulled away from the InterContinental. The hotel was so close to the 110, it seemed to lord over it. Jack grabbed the 110 south and picked up the 10 westbound in order to cut over to the 405 south. He hoped he'd be able to avoid most of the traffic, but it was LA in the morning and there was no concept of counter-commuting. It took them forty-five minutes to get to the vicinity of the airport. They agreed the day before that they'd post at a Denny's about a mile south of Pan Pacific's office so that they didn't arouse suspicion by camping out in the parking lot for a few hours.

They both ordered coffees with low expectations and were summarily disappointed.

"How are you feeling?" Jack asked after the server, a kid named Brad, brought their coffees and they told him they wouldn't need anything else for a bit. Maybe it was an unwritten rule, a tradition, or a courtesy, Jack didn't exactly know, but you never asked someone how they were doing before a job. You worked with a professional and you *knew* how they were doing. If they showed up, they were ready. If they didn't show, they weren't.

However, this was Rusty's first time on a job, and Jack could tell he was off.

"How are you supposed to feel?" Rusty said. He ran a hand through his wavy, dark blond hair. He was still getting used to it.

"Lot like going on stage, I suppose. You've always got *nerves*. The difference is whether you're *nervous*."

"I'm probably nervous."

They passed the time in silence for a while. Brad came by to refill their coffees once and asked if they were ready to order. Jack said they were good for now. Brad sucked his teeth loudly as he stalked off, probably thinking about the tip he wasn't getting. Brad was sloppy, but not in a trendy way, skinny and probably wanted to be an actor or a rock star. Jack checked his phone; there was nothing from Enzo.

The restaurant was packed with the morning rush, and there were some people orbiting the hostess station, which was probably why Brad kept bothering them about ordering. The place had an interesting mix for a Denny's. El Segundo had a blend of high-end technology companies, aircraft manufacturers and government contractors, think tanks, and blue-collar workers. It was also just down the street from a small Air Force base, which apparently didn't have any airplanes. A steady crush of traffic rolled down El Segundo Boulevard in both directions.

There was a lot of ambient noise, and the conversations happening on either side of their booth were fairly loud, but when Jack spoke he kept his voice low. "Rusty, this isn't something you have to do. If you don't feel one hundred percent, Enzo and I can manage the job today."

Doing this with a crew of three was already stretching it to the limit of what Jack thought was feasible, let alone wise. Jack needed Rusty to make the con work. It was probably thanks to TV, but when people saw federal agents they expected to see them in pairs. Seeing a solo agent might just make someone subconsciously pause long enough to ask the question, *Is this real?* Still, it was better to go a man down than roll with someone who wasn't fully prepared, who was not solely focused.

"I'm good," Rusty said quietly. "This is just new."

There was a psychology at play that, in other circumstances, Jack might have found interesting to explore. Rusty spent the last fifteen years or so acquiring stolen vehicles and guns, forging passports, laundering money, and arranging transport for the people who did what he was going to do today. It wasn't breaking the law, Rusty did that by waking up in the morning, it was the way he'd be doing it today that was different for him.

"My first time on a crew, I mean inside, not driving, I screwed up really bad. Place was downtown, maybe a block from WorldSecure. Was an armored car depot at the time. We had a guy on the inside, he's the one who brought the job to Reginald. Safety inspector, found out he was going to get canned, so he decided to take out a new pension plan. Anyway, we go in on a Friday night. They're about to start loading up all the ATM cash for the weekend. Subdue the guards. There was one guy on shift who wasn't supposed to be there, regular guy called in sick. We think he was in on it and chickened out at the last minute. The guard who replaced him was, of all things, a Marine from Desert Storm and an MP."

Rusty issued out a short laugh.

"We got him down, though, bound his legs and wrists with duct tape. Reginald told me to get his weapon, so I did. Grabbed his pistol and put it in the bag. What I didn't do was check him, which is what Reginald meant. Turned out he had an ankle piece, little snub nose. The guard pretended to be unconscious, and because I didn't think to bind his hands behind his back, when we weren't looking, he was able to grab his ankle piece." Jack paused to take a drink of the burnt, bitter coffee. He was convinced that Brad was holding this one special for the assholes of the world who didn't order a greasy plate of whatever and a side of pancakes.

"Shot one of our guys in the back of the head. Everything kind of fell apart after that. It wasn't just that. We'd taken longer in the vault than we'd planned. Once they heard the shot, the other guards were coming to, made an effort to rally. Reginald took a round. I made it out okay, helped him get to the van. Inside guy, the one who planned it, took off with his money." Jack shook his head. "He didn't even stick around to make sure anyone else got out of there. He was arrested about two weeks later. Anyway, Reginald and me and a third guy, Lenkowitz was his name, made it to the van. Guard shot Lenk in the head." Jack looked out at the cars slowly creeping by on El Segundo Boulevard. "Got him right through the van's back window. One-in-a-million shot. Reginald and I got away, took the van to a chop shop I knew in Long Beach that would dispose of the van and whatever was in it, no questions asked." Jack brought his eyes back to the table, to Rusty. "The reason I'm telling you this is that one small mistake on a job can send things out of control really fast. When a job goes south, it tends to do so like a car crash at high speed. There comes a point when you lose control and you cannot get it back. After that, it's up to forces that you do not control."

"Gravity and inertia?" Rusty asked. His voice wobbled on the line between sarcasm and flat bitterness. Maybe he didn't appreciate the lesson for what it was, a way out.

"We have a good plan, at least as good of a plan as we're able to put together given the situation we're in. If we're going to pull this off, we've got to be able to call audibles in the moment and go with it, do so as though that were 'the plan.'"

"Jack, I got it."

"All I'm saying is that if you're not one hundred percent sure, you can walk. I would rather you do that than you live with knowing you got a man killed."

An expression passed over Rusty's face, as fleeting as clouds moving quickly across the sky, but it was there. Concern, consternation, pain? It was hard to read exactly what it was, but the evidence of emotion was there. There was something buried deep, and it was clearly troubling him. Rusty refocused himself, narrowed his eyes once, and took a drink of his coffee. When the mug touched down on the table, his face was blank. "Jack, I used to run counterintel operations against the successor to the KGB. I can handle a couple rent-a-cops in a van."

Jack thought about calling the job right there, because Rusty wasn't ready.

Jack knew from his own experience that he'd once made the mistake of believing that because he was an expert at one kind of hard thing, he could do all hard things. It turned out that just because he was one of the world's most skilled jewelry thieves, he didn't know shit about running a business and damn near ran Kingfisher into the ground. He would have if it weren't for a hard intervention by Megan and Hugh Coughlin.

Rusty was making the same mistake that Jack had.

There was a certain element to most of the heists Jack pulled that required some sort of con. Perhaps it was the setup, maybe it was the recon, maybe it was the getaway, there was typically an element of deception. Not since the Carlton job had he relied so heavily on a con, and even that one ultimately amounted to a hundred-and-forty-five-million-dollar stickup. Jack knew Rusty's mindset. From what little Rusty told him, counterintelligence was a lot like running a long con. But this was different in ways that the ex-FBI man didn't yet appreciate or even know about. That was dangerous ignorance.

Jack could walk away now. He'd sunk everything he had into the winery and there was very little left for a safety net. Still, he was in the clear now. Apart from driving a stolen car and passing himself off as a customs agent, Jack hadn't done anything yet that he couldn't back out of. Losing this money would definitely hurt, and there was no guarantee that his winery would survive. It was a hard business, but he was free and clear as far as the law was concerned. Before he'd run into Nico and Constantino Fiore in Reginald's apartment, Jack's partners convinced him to walk away for all of those reasons. He stayed because he believed that win or lose, this wasn't over until all his enemies were dead.

But what if he called Danzig right now?

He could give her Reginald, Vito, and Bartolo. That would knot up Cannizzaro too. She'd also be able to claim credit for solving a nearly twenty-year-old unsolved crime, the Antwerp Diamond Centre heist. A job that...

A crime that she'd already technically closed.

When they'd stolen the diamonds out of Cannizzaro's bank, they left about twenty million worth behind, because that's what Bartolo claimed he'd stolen while he was in prison in an attempt to disguise the actual amount. Jack had told her that's what the Pink Panthers were after when they tried to force him to break into that bank. Danzig and the FBI got credit for closing that one, and to the world's eyes, it was solved.

Vito and Bartolo could both positively identify Jack as being here in Los Angeles, as being involved. Bartolo could confirm Jack committed a B&E (which he'd forgotten about in the list of minor crimes committed so far).

That old Turin toast rang in his ears.

When all my enemies are dead.

Jack's phone buzzed. It was Enzo.

Rusty was not ready for this. Rusty also wouldn't give up. Thanks to his partnership with Jack, the FBI was actively hunting for him, as was the State Department's Diplomatic Security Service for his passport forgery. Jack had a sense that the Russian government might be as well. Rusty needed this money to disappear for good. Something he wouldn't have needed to have done but for his association with Gentleman Jack Burdette.

Jack could walk away, but he couldn't do it clean.

He picked up the phone.

"They're moving," Enzo said.

Jack looked at his watch. It was 10:37.

Jack put a five on the table and stood. "It's go time," he said. Whatever Rusty did now was on him.

Jack walked out to the sidewalk, pulled the squared-off aviators from his inside pocket, and put them on. Rusty fell in step beside him. The parking lot was on the far side of the restaurant. The sky remained overcast, and it kept the heat lower than the previous few days, which would make it easier to sit in a car for a while. But the air was still thick with the smell of smoke, a very visceral reminder that he had problems ahead of him that diamonds couldn't solve. Not to mention real people who needed him more than a pair of thieves did.

They drove the last mile in silence.

Jack parked the X6 in a spot that was in a row of spaces in front of the third building, facing the traffic circle and the other two. From here, they would be able to see the armored car entering the complex and follow its path down the palm-lined road all the way to its ultimate destination. It was a short walk from the parking spot to the rear of the center building, if Jack needed to execute the backup plan.

Jack dialed Enzo, asking for an update.

"Reginald has been with the armored car ever since they left WorldSecure," Enzo said.

"Thanks," Jack said and closed the phone. He looked over at Rusty. "On to Plan B."

IT WAS AN OBVIOUS POINT, but Reginald would feel a whole lot better when he had seventy million in his bank account.

Lucio drove, following the WorldSecure car. Tommaso was in the front seat next to him. They both wore black suits, white shirts, sunglasses, and had earpieces in their left ears. They weren't attached to any radios, but an observer wouldn't know that. Both were armed and knew to identify themselves as private security contractors who'd followed the diamonds here from Italy, should anyone ask. Reginald had called Carter LeMothe when they'd left WorldSecure and given him their ETA according to the navigation system. The idiot actually said, "Roger that" like he was in the fucking army.

Reginald sat in the Range Rover's expansive back and tried to relax with his coffee. Lucio was a pretty good driver, as it turned out. Reginald had only been nervous about him doing it because he wouldn't know the signage, and God knows most Americans couldn't decipher the parking/no-parking calculus on most city streets. "I'd like to get there a little ahead of the armored car," Reginald said, leaning forward in his seat.

He saw Lucio's eyes flick from the road ahead to him in the rearview. "You want me to pass them?"

"Yeah," Reginald said.

Vito looked over, a questioning expression on his face.

"Optics," was all Reginald said.

The Range Rover accelerated past the armored car. Reginald called WorldSecure's dispatch to tell them he planned to arrive just a little ahead of the car. They confirmed the change in plan.

Reginald and Vito planned to split up as soon as the money was divided. Reginald and Vito agreed that whatever they were going to cut Lucio and Tommaso, they'd do jointly. Reginald wanted to get away for a bit, let things cool down around here, but also to just have a goddamn break. He wasn't sure exactly what he could get away with if his parole officer was going to be a prick about it, but maybe Miami or the Virgin Islands. One of the first things he was going to do with that money was hire a better lawyer. Reginald had been thinking about leaving California anyway, but had made his mind up in the last few days. Traffic had somehow gotten *worse* while he was in prison, and he just didn't want to deal with it. That, and he just couldn't recognize the place anymore. Or maybe it was that everything was *too* familiar. Every time they'd gone to WorldSecure, he was reminded of that armored car depot job he and Jack did in '95. You always puckered a little walking past a place you hit once. Twenty-five years later and there, on the street, was the *one* person in this whole world who got a clean look at you that night and somehow they knew it was you. Because that's how this fucked-up world worked.

And Reginald had a dozen places like that throughout LA.

So, yeah, it was time to leave.

He couldn't leave the country, not legally at least, ever again. He'd been convicted of passport forgery, and now he didn't have the network to have a new one made. Reginald also wasn't willing to take that risk. This morning, as he was finishing his breakfast there on that porch in Westlake, Reginald realized that he was done taking risks at all. He was going to make this last sale, he'd leave Los Angeles and not look back. His attorney could deal with the goddamn parole officer.

What about Jack, though?

Revenge wasn't a time machine. He'd never get back those years he spent in prison on Jack's account. But if Burdette was willing to let it go, then maybe Reginald was too. Which is to say, if Jack decided not to be an asshole, take his loss, and go live his life, Reginald wouldn't press. He'd just disappear like he wanted to. If Jack couldn't do that, well, Reginald would have the kind of money that he could hire the kind of people to make that problem go away quietly and forever.

They left the 105 by way of a serpentine off-ramp that reminded him of a child's maze and onto La Cienega. Lucio was turning right into the complex when he jammed on the brakes suddenly, throwing everyone forward.

"What the hell?" Reginald belted out.

"This fucking guy!" Lucio shouted, holding up his right hand. A car whipped around them at the light, cutting them and several others off, in order to make the light first. The car was a silver blur. By the time Reginald twisted his head around to follow the car's path, it was already down the long, palm-lined entry road and pulling into the traffic circle that was their destination. Reginald had a good idea who that was.

"Don't worry about it," he said. "Let's just get there."

Lucio cursed again, this time in Italian. Reginald didn't know what he said but recognized the word for "mother." They completed their turn and drove down that long, landscaped entry road. Reginald could see the 105 above and behind the cluster of buildings they were driving toward and above that, a plane on final approach to LAX.

Reginald opened his phone and pulled up the app WorldSecure had given him. The armored car was about three minutes behind them. Lucio pulled up to the traffic circle and stopped before the middle building, behind the silver Aston Martin that cut them off at the light. Carter LeMothe was getting out of the car. He was dressed in an azure blue jacket, white shirt, gray tie, and light gray pants.

"You can pull into that spot there," Reginald said, pointing at an open space in front of the building, just offset from the traffic circle.

They all got out when Lucio parked and walked over to where Carter was standing. Lucio and Tommaso made a show of buttoning their jackets in an official-looking way and taking up position around their "principals." Lucio touched his earpiece and softly said that they were moving.

Reginald silently admonished him not to overdo it, but this was probably a lot of fun for those two, pretending they were high-end bodyguards.

"Are we ready?" Carter LeMothe said, his voice a little too fast. "Let's *do* this!" He went to shake everyone's hand, shooting the cuffs so they could see how big his watch was. "Guess you can't shake hands," he said to Lucio and Tommaso, who thankfully just ignored him. Carter was speaking in an excited tone, everything a declaration. Reginald had done his share of coke in the eighties, and this felt a lot like that.

"How about we get this underway," Reginald said.

"Looking good, Mr. De Angeles," Carter said. "De Angeles in Los Angeles. Ready to kill it!"

Reginald closed the distance between himself and Carter.

"Are you okay?" he asked in a low but hard tone. "Are you on something?"

"I'm fine," Carter said, seemingly pulling himself out of orbit.

"Then get it to-fucking-gether," Reginald said. Carter blinked a few times but said nothing else. Reginald asked Lucio and Tommaso to wait for the WorldSecure car and then join them inside. He didn't think the guys at Pan Pacific would try anything, but there was nothing wrong in rolling heavy.

Carter LeMothe led Reginald and Vito inside the building. The lobby was stark white and chrome. Reginald looked over at Vito and smiled. "We've come a long way since Knightsbridge," he said.

Vito smiled, uneasily at first. Reginald guessed that Vito was surprised that he would bring that up in mixed company, but Carter was probably so high he wouldn't remember, anyway. Not that he'd know the reference.

The elevator arrived, and they rode it to the second floor. Carter stepped out first and immediately looked in both directions, trying to orient himself to the hallway. Reginald knew immediately that he'd never been here before. This guy might do million-dollar deals for breakfast, but he was still an amateur. By some miracle, "Cocaine" Carter LeMothe figured out the hallway's numbering system and led them down the hallway and around a corner to a door with a gray plate displaying "208" in white letters. The door was the typical office-park solid wood, but it had a logo on it of a stack of bars over an outline of the Pacific Ocean with the words *PAN PACIFIC METAL-LURGY AND MINERALS* beneath it.

Carter LeMothe opened the door and led them inside to the receptionist, announcing their arrival and their appointment with a Mr. Lau.

FROM THEIR PARKING SPOT, Jack and Rusty watched a silver Aston Martin DB11 Volante convertible rocket down the long entry road and whip around the traffic circle at a speed that should have invoked centrifugal force. The car stopped just in time to not blow by the building. Not long after, a black Range Rover pulled up and parked in a space in front of the building. The trees, berm, and other landscaping broke up the sight lines so even though they were close, Reginald would have to walk around to Jack's parking spot to recognize him.

"I've got Reginald, Vito, and two others," Jack said. He watched the four of them walk up to the overly animated figure that crawled out of the Aston. Jack recognized the two other men as the heavies Reginald and Vito dragged with them everywhere, but they were done up to look like professional security guards. Smart. Jack assumed all four of them would be armed. Reginald stepped in and said something to the fifth guy, and he looked to calm down. They departed for the building, and the two goons waited out front, presumably for the armored car.

As if on cue, the red-and-gray WorldSecure truck turned off La Cienega and onto the entry road.

Enzo texted them both in their secure app to say that he was stuck at the light but was on La Cienega, about to turn.

The parking lots on the side and behind the buildings were not very full. Though, it looked like the primary occupants of two of the three buildings were schools for working professionals, so they probably didn't get much business until after business hours. That was smart to put the meet here. Reginald was dealing with some savvy people. Worth noting.

The armored car pulled into the traffic circle and pulled around to the center building. The driver stayed in the vehicle. Jack didn't see the others exit the vehicle, but two guards approached Reginald's heavies, so there must have been a side door on the cargo compartment. They were carrying a strongbox; each had their left hand on the front and rear handle, respectively. Their right hands rested right next to their pistols.

A blur of motion in Jack's vision pulled his attention away.

He looked over to the main road and saw an SUV and a car approaching a fairly high rate of speed, certainly faster than what most drivers would take on that road. Both of the vehicles were heavily tinted.

"Rusty…"

TWENTY-THREE

The SUV entered the traffic circle moving way too fast and turned hard, going in a counterclockwise direction. The driver slammed on the brakes and stopped between the Aston Martin and the armored car. Tires screeched in angry protest as the SUV skidded to a stop, hopping the curb. The car entered the traffic circle equally fast and took the clockwise direction. They were boxing the armored car in. The car stopped at an angle, blocking most of the road. If someone was going around it, they were going to have to drive on a sidewalk, which was protected by bollards, or go over a fountain. The driver and passengers were out before anyone could react.

The WorldSecure guards reacted the way they were supposed to. They broke for the armored car with their strongbox without a moment's hesitation.

The gunfire started before Jack could even get a word out.

The trees in front of the car and the fountain made it difficult to have a direct line of sight. The action unfolded on the opposite side of the SUV and the armored car, but Jack and Rusty still had, more or less, a front-row seat. And that was not a good place to be.

Jack saw Constantino Fiore clearly as he emerged from the

Escalade, his face gaunt angles and sharp lines, his suit equally sharp. Fiore was overdressed for a gunfight. Three gunmen jumped out of the SUV and three more from the car. The WorldSecure guards and Vito's men were outgunned almost two to one. The armored car was blocking his view of the WorldSecure guards, but Jack saw Vito's men returning fire. One of them dropped a gunman from the car before he fell himself. His partner wasn't as lucky, and he was cut down right away. Apart from Fiore, the gunmen on either side appeared to be armed amateurs, given the number of shots Jack heard in a very short amount of time.

"They're going to take the box," Jack said quickly.

"Yeah, and they've got us two to one at least," Rusty snapped back.

SPECIAL AGENTS FUERY and Reaves sat in a small office inside 208. They had a folding table set up with recording equipment and headphones that enabled them to listen in on the conversation happening in the conference room. That's where that insufferable prick Carter LeMothe and his two sellers, Burton and De Angeles, were meeting with Chan Lau, aka Special Agent Victor Zhao.

The FBI had been renting this office space for some time, using it as a front for a much longer sting. That operation just concluded, but the government still had access to the rooms, so they were able to create the office space for Pan Pacific. Fuery and his partner chose this room because it faced the building's front entry. Fuery was shocked as shit to learn they had an honest-to-God armored car. That almost torpedoed the entire thing. When Fuery and Reaves briefed their section chief, Supervisory Special Agent Linda Abbate, on the plan, she pushed back hard on the idea that diamond thieves would be able to get an armored car. She said these companies vetted their clients, did income verifications and the like. They would also have to verify the provenance of the diamonds.

Fuery had to hand it to his partner. Reaves dropped a respectful "not so fast" on her pretty quick.

Reaves had that investigator's instinct to not inherently trust anyone until they've earned it. That went for everyone. Reaves had the foresight to call WorldSecure and attempt to open an account. He made up a legend that he was a high-dollar investor and was converting a lot of his holdings to gold because of "the world situation." He didn't even need to elaborate on *what* world situation that was. He was given a provisional account provided he could produce the gold and was assured he would be "thoroughly vetted."

Reaves's theory was that WorldSecure wasn't doing anything illegal, they weren't knowingly trafficking in stolen goods, but they also dealt with the superrich and it wasn't their job to ask a lot of questions. In fact, they even covered that in the paperwork they sent over to Reaves's dummy business email. They simply provided a safe, secure, and insured place for high-dollar investors to store their treasures, and if said investor was storing stolen or otherwise illegal items in WorldSecure, it would result in immediate termination of account, referral to proper authorities, and the list of potential repercussions went on. But Reaves was also able to get from his "executive account concierge" that they got a commission based on the dollar value of items stored, so that first line of defense was incentivized against asking too many questions when bringing new clients in the door.

Abbate was convinced, at least enough to let them proceed.

Fuery was watching the window for the armored car and spotted it on the long approach to their building. He couldn't see all the way to La Cienega from here, but he did have a good view of the main road. Fuery followed the WorldSecure car until it pulled up in front of the building and met a pair of private security guards that Burton and De Angeles hired. They'd have to stop that pair from entering the office; Pan Pacific policy was that there was no private security allowed on the premises. The receptionist was also an agent, and she knew what to do.

"All units, this is Fuery. I've got the armored car pulling up to the building," Fuery said into his radio. The building fell within the jurisdiction of the City of Inglewood Police Department, so they had several units on standby to establish a cordon in the event that Burton and De Angeles decided to flee. Or that the armored car was actually a con. The extra police support was purely a precaution, and Fuery expected them to release the officers within the hour.

Fuery had just gotten back to the table and settled to listen on the wire when the first shots broke out. Fuery looked over to Reaves. The agents jumped out of their chairs and ran to the window to confirm what they both suspected. An SUV and a car were positioned at opposite sides of the armored car, blocking a possible escape from either side. Fuery didn't have time to count, but the gunmen clearly outnumbered the guards. The gunmen were not practiced shooters, but they targeted the WorldSecure personnel first and numbers took care of the rest. Both of the WorldSecure guards dropped almost instantly. The gunmen shifted fire to the two hired security, one of them took out a shooter, but both were down fast.

"All units, all units, we have shots fired! Repeat, we have shots fired. Respond immediately!"

Fuery saw a gunman fall as the units on the radio rogered his message and confirmed they were moving in. He hoped the guards could hold out long enough for help to get there and that this didn't turn into the fucking Alamo.

"Let's go," Fuery told Reaves, turning from the window, but Reaves was already on his way out.

A SECOND GUNMAN DROPPED, one of the guys from the SUV, but Jack had no idea where the shot would have come from. Then he realized that the armored car's driver was still inside the vehicle. He must have had a way of shooting from cover.

"We should get out of here," Rusty said in a tone that was all edges.

"Not yet," Jack told him, though that was a reflex response. Even as he said it, Jack realized how insane it sounded. They were fifty yards from a gunfight that was going fast in the wrong direction. There were ways out of this, but none of them good.

Then the situation turned again.

A police car, all lights and sirens, burst through the access road between the second and third buildings at the traffic circle's nine o'clock, screeching to a stop behind the SUV. A second police cruiser tore around the building Jack and Rusty were parked next to, and a third came in from the access road at the traffic circle's twelve o'clock. The gunmen's car whipped around in reverse. Two shooters managed to make it into the back seat before the driver floored it. The police cruiser saw the escape attempt and tried to stop it by ramming the back quarter panel. The cop's aim was off and he just grazed the gunmen's car, but it was enough to break the vehicle's momentum and knock it off course. The car's rear end fishtailed like it was waterplaning, and the driver fought to maintain control. He made the traffic circle exit and accelerated onto the exit road, still fighting for control of the car. The police cruiser was right on his tail. Jack followed for the amount of time he had to whip his head around and watch the car try to make La Cienega.

"Where the hell did those cruisers come from?" Jack asked, turning back around. He didn't see them in the parking lot when they arrived. There was no way that they could respond that quickly—those things were here within thirty seconds of the first shot.

That meant they'd been waiting.

"Oh, Jesus," Jack said. "This is a setup."

The question was, for whom?

"Jack, we have got to get out of here, now!" There was real panic in Rusty's voice.

The shooters had partial cover behind their SUV and were engaging with the officers that had taken up position between their open car doors and vehicle's main body. Fiore was the only gunman Jack could see. Where did all of these guys come from? He couldn't believe that Cannizzaro could afford to send so many soldiers all the way over here, or that they'd be so well equipped. They had to be getting local support somehow.

One of the mafia soldiers moved out of cover holding a machine pistol or submachine gun—Jack couldn't tell and didn't know weapons well enough to know the difference. The man sprayed it in a wide arc, back and forth, aiming for the gap between the SUV and the armored car. The cop in the car in front of Jack, on the other side of the landscaping berm, fell backward, hit. Several shots hit the berm in front of them, sending dirt flying into the air.

One of the gunmen ran across the open space, probably going for the strongbox.

Constantino Fiore was looking for targets. Jack could see his eyes as they tracked across, looking to make sure that his man took that cop out. Fiore looked beyond the bullet-riddled police car, finding a black BMW...and he locked eyes with Jack.

Even at fifty or sixty yards, Jack could clearly see that cold, emotionless gaze.

Jack's mind flashed back to that bank in Rome. The Pink Panthers gave him a pistol because they wanted everyone else to think he was in on it, but it was empty. When Constantino Fiore emerged from his office to put a stop to the heist, Jack got the drop on him and bluffed his way to Fiore lowering his weapon, kicking it over to Jack. There was red hate there when Fiore realized he'd been had. But it was nothing like the look that passed over his face when the cop that was supposed to be on the Cannizzaro payroll just up and let Jack walk.

The recognition was there.

Fiore raised his pistol and started walking forward, ignoring everything else around him. Jack could see in his eyes that he was going to settle it.

Then Fiore's head snapped back.

It looked like a series of still photos.

His body jerked.

His arms flailed out to his side, gun flying, like he was electrocuted.

Fiore stumbled once, was hit twice more, and fell.

Two men in suits stood just outside the building's doorway, both of them in a perfect shooting-range stance.

Jack couldn't hear what they said, but he could see their mouths move.

The police turned the plaza into a killbox. They'd surrounded the gunmen on both sides, like the two arms of a *V*. Jack saw a couple of rounds go through car windows, the men behind them drop. But it was the two guys in suits that turned the tide. Once they saw Fiore drop, the rest caved pretty fast.

Guns thrown down, hands went up. Police moved out from behind cover and went to secure the shooters. One went over to check on their injured officer.

Two more police cruisers arrived on scene, and Jack could hear helicopter blades ripping the air above them. It orbited the scene once and then took off at a high rate of speed. That car must have been giving a pretty good chase for them to divert air support that fast.

The police officers started lining up the remaining gunmen. Jack didn't know how many there were total, but he could make out two from where they sat. The cops had them on their knees with hands behind their heads. The two guys in the suits were barking orders, motioning with their free hands because their weapons were still out. They would be securing the scene shortly.

"We should get out of here," Rusty said, resignation draped heavily on his words.

"Not just yet," Jack said and opened the car door.

"What are you doing?"

"Let's go. I'll take the lead, and you just back me up. This can still work."

"What can still work?" Rusty asked, his eyes tracking across the scene unfolding, police officers securing the gunmen and trying to make sense of what in the hell had just happened here.

"Our original plan," Jack said, irritation seeping into his own voice. There was a very small window to pull this off, and he didn't have time for debate.

Rusty studied him for a moment. Words were on his lips, but he didn't speak them.

He's giving me an out, Jack thought. When this all started, Rusty and Enzo thought Jack was hedging. It was Rusty who pushed him, saying that he couldn't have a foot in both worlds. If he was going to do this, he was going to have to *be a thief*. Later, Rusty seemed to have had a slight change of heart. He understood that Jack was at greater risk than the two of them and had much more to lose. Rusty suggested that maybe Jack shouldn't be here for this part, for the take, because they needed him to move the diamonds afterward.

Now, Rusty seemed to be giving him a chance to walk away entirely.

Jack understood. What he had in mind was dangerous and there was no safety net if it collapsed, no way out. It relied on the chaos and confusion of the moment, both factors he could not control. And he would have one chance. But Jack knew people, more importantly, he knew people that were part of systems and how that could be exploited.

This would really have been better with two people, but Rusty wasn't up for it. Jack understood now that all of Rusty's activities that flew well south of the law were all things under his control and with layers of security that he himself had set. Rusty only dealt with other criminals, and they were people who relied on him, needed his services, so the threat was relatively low. Jack didn't understand how someone who'd been a counterintelligence officer operating undercover against the Russians in the post-9/11 era, a world with perilously few rules even for *that* game, could lose his nerve on a jewelry heist.

But then again, maybe he did.

As an FBI agent, Rusty had a safety net. The US government was always there to back him up.

Until they weren't.

Jack thought he knew what was going through Rusty's head. *Were they ever?* That was an understandable shattering of confidence, and maybe he needed to give his friend a pass.

Whatever the reason, the window on these diamonds was open just a sliver and closing fast. Jack knew if they still had a shot at them, he was going to have to do it on his own.

"Give me the warrant you typed," Jack said.

Rusty reached into his jacket and pulled out a few pieces of tri-folded paper.

Jack pulled out his phone and dialed Enzo. He said, "*Noi non potremo avere perfetta vita senza amici.*" Then he hung up.

"What the fuck is that?"

Jack held a beat. "It's a distraction," he said. "Buy us some time to get away. Might involve running a red light and accidentally hitting a police car. People hear it on an open radio, they think you're talking about a band." Jack held up his hand. He was committed now, and he wasn't interested in opinions. Rusty was out of his element, and maybe bringing him along as part of the crew was a mistake, but they could sort that out later. "Meet me on that long street that runs north-south, parallel with the parking lot," Jack said, pointing to the west, beyond the building. "We have to get out of this parking lot before they seal it off, and that road is the only way out." Jack glanced back over his shoulder to the tree-lined street that led out to La Cienega.

"Isis Avenue, I think it is," Rusty said, voice still edging in on anger.

Jack didn't take the time to agree with him.

Rusty got out of the BMW with Jack and orbited to the driver's side.

Jack ran to the side of the building nearest them, which was the last one on the traffic circle, moving fast like a person looking for cover. He stepped from the corner to the sidewalk and quickly went to the other side.

"WHAT TIME SHOULD we be expecting the shipment," Chan Lau said. He had a rigid posture that spoke of a youth spent at an expensive boarding school and a diction that could only have been refined at Cambridge or Oxford. He also had an authority about him that Reginald didn't like. Something had felt off about this meeting since the moment he sat down, but he couldn't put his finger on it. He knew Pan Pacific was a front. This wasn't a real business, so he'd expected this office to look exactly like it did: out of the box. Still, there was something else that felt...fabricated, perhaps. He didn't expect Carter to know. That wasn't a guy who got far in life by asking too many questions. Questions led to messy answers. All Carter wanted to know was that he had a dumping ground for the gem deals that his company thought were too shady to move forward on. A savvier person would've seen this for what it was. This was too...organized for a fly by night. The generic artwork on the walls, the just-enough-staff-to-make-it-seem-like-a-business, the walls without scuff marks behind the doors, and everything laid out like it was described on a checklist.

Reginald heard a muffled, staccato ripping sound from outside the building. It was muffled but unmistakable.

That was goddamned gunfire.

And a lot of it.

"What the hell was that," Carter LeMothe said, dropping both of his hands nervously on the table and throwing his eyes back and forth as if the gunfire were in the room with them. "You guys stay here, I'm going to check this out," LeMothe said, half-standing. That guy had been so erratic since the moment he pulled up, it could only be because he was on something.

"Carter," Reginald growled, "sit the fuck down. I'm sure there's a situation where you're useful, but this ain't it."

Chan Lau gave LeMothe a cold stare and lowered his hand to the table, indicating that Carter should do the same.

More shots.

Reginald knew this could only mean one thing. Jack wouldn't even bring a pistol for insurance, let alone however many the hell guns Reginald heard outside. And anyway, Jack should be up in Van Nuys about now trying to con his way into the airport. Under different circumstances, Reginald would've allowed himself a smile thinking about Jack trying to fit greasy maintenance coveralls over a five-thousand-dollar suit. Vito's Italian friends had brought some heat with them and made their play. Somehow, they'd been able to track Reginald's moves, figure out that the deal would be going down here and now.

Yes, they'd been inside his apartment, but this deal didn't come together until after that. Did they have a tail on him the entire time? Found the place in Westlake? That didn't seem likely or within their specific province of ability. Unless the mafia figured out how to tap cell phones, which didn't seem likely to him, that meant they'd gotten this from the inside.

Vito, or one of his two idiots, was playing both sides.

Reginald stood and buttoned his jacket.

"Mr. Burton, please sit down," Chan Lau, the Pan Pacific guy, said. "I do believe that's gunfire."

"Welcome to Los Angeles, Mr. Lau," Reginald deadpanned and started walking toward the door.

"Sir, I'm going to have to insist you take your seat, for your own safety."

"Reg, what you are doing?"

Lau moved to stand, but Reginald made the door before he could do anything.

Sorry, Vito. Reginald didn't know how he was going to salvage this, but he sure as hell wasn't sitting around here. He found that he was genuinely saddened to discover that Vito was playing him. Reginald allowed himself the time it took him from the conference room to the hallway to feel remorse over it.

"Mr. Burton, please return to the conference room. We have an active shooter situation," the girl behind the reception desk said, standing.

That's what it was. No front desk girl at a fake company was going to bravely stand up and tell him to calmly return to the windowless conference room. She'd be hiding under the desk, videoing herself being "brave and strong" so she could post it later. Hashtag Inglewood Shooter.

Reginald said nothing to her and made the door before she was around the desk.

Goddamn it, Vito. This could've been beautiful, *man.*

Reginald wasn't giving up on his score yet. The mafia clowns might have numbers and guns on their side, but they were stupid and they didn't know shit about smuggling diamonds. There would be a way to get these still, Reginald just needed the time and space to work it out. He heard the "receptionist" in the hallway coming after him. Reginald opened the door to the stairwell and moved down it quickly. He made the first floor and entered the hallway near the rear door. The Range Rover was a no go, but they were only a block from the light-rail station.

If the customs paperwork held up, the FBI wouldn't be able to hold onto those diamonds for long and would revert the stones back to WorldSecure. Reginald would have them transfer the diamonds to one of their offices out of the country. It was a delay of a few months, but nothing insurmountable. But he was cutting Vito off. This mafia thing, that was his fuckup.

As Reginald entered the hallway, he saw a man in a gray suit and sunglasses walking with purpose pass just in front of him.

JACK MOVED around the back of the nearest building along the circle, across the access road, and onto the middle one. He chanced a look to his right down the road between the two buildings. It looked like one more cruiser had arrived even during the short walk from the

BMW. He made fast steps on the sidewalk, moving around that center building to the rear entry. Jack opened the door and entered a wide, air-conditioned hallway. There was a doorway to a stairwell immediately to his right, and he saw a bank of elevators on either side in the center of the hallway. There was a straight shot through to the other side, and he could clearly see the flashing lights of the police vehicles through the far doors.

Jack didn't remove his sunglasses when he entered the building. In part because if this building had security cameras, he would most certainly be on them, but also to convey a sense of character. Jack heard the stairway door open, saw it out of the corner of his eye.

FUERY AND REAVES issued instructions to the Inglewood PD on-scene commander, a patrol sergeant until one of their lieutenants arrived, and headed back inside the building. The police had this well enough in hand. The gunmen appeared to be a mix of native Italians and Italian-Americans. Some of them didn't speak much English or at least wanted to give the appearance that they didn't. They would know as soon as names were processed whether there was a connection to Italian organized crime (IOC), the Bureau's designation for the mafia.

They didn't have time to wait for the elevator, so Fuery and Reaves took the stairs immediately inside the doors. Fuery saw someone in the hallway, probably some guy that hadn't sheltered in place like he was supposed to. Well, the Inglewood PD would turn him back around if he was dumb enough to go out front. Right now, Fuery had to figure out whether they had enough to charge Burton and De Angeles. The fact that someone showed up and tried to take those things by force suggested that those two had some kind of underworld connections. *Maybe* they weren't dirty, but they probably had some associates who were. Everything would now hinge on that customs import paperwork and whether they could prove these diamonds weren't stolen.

"I'm going to start working on Burton and De Angeles," Fuery said when they were in the stairwell. "Can you call back to headquarters and talk to the OC guys?"

"You want to see what they know about our shooters?"

"Exactly."

"Okay. I'll call LAPD Vice as well."

"Good thinking."

They entered the hallway and walked fast back to 208. Fuery wanted someone to tell him what in the exact hell was going on, and he wanted it fast.

JACK IGNORED the person exiting the stairs, assuming it was someone that was trying to get away to safety. He was moving past the elevators when he heard that person opening the doors that he'd just come through, caught that same slight squeak of a hinge that needed oil. Jack continued moving to the front doors, opened them, and stepped outside into bedlam.

He counted five Inglewood police cruisers and twice that many officers, most of which were standing over the gunmen, who were lying facedown on the pavement, cuffed. There was an ambulance on scene now. He saw paramedics working on one of the officers, the one Jack watched Fiore shoot. That brought his gaze over to where he saw the mafia hit man fall. There was a body lying prone in a pool of blood. None of the paramedics had gotten to him yet, but he'd shot a cop, so Jack imagined that the police officers here might have waited just a bit for first aid. Fiore had fallen face first, but they'd rolled him over to confirm if he was still alive. Beyond him, there was a young patrolman putting up yellow police tape.

"Sir, this is a crime scene. You need to go back inside," a hard voice said.

Jack's eyes went to a Black police officer with sergeant's stripes (Jack assumed that's what they were) on his short sleeves. The cop's arms were so big, Jack had to imagine that even getting dressed in the morning threatened to cut off circulation.

"Little, US Customs," Jack said casually. "I'm reaching for my credentials." He pulled the badge holder out of his jacket pocket and flipped it open. He was a good ten feet from the cop. The guy just gave him a chin nod, and Jack put it away.

"This is still a crime scene," he said.

"You're goddamn right it is," Jack said with a voice of authority. "What's your name, Sergeant, is it?"

"Fulton, and that's right."

"Follow me, please, Sergeant Fulton." Jack walked over to Fiore's body. Reluctantly, the police officer walked with him. Jack looked down at the slain hit man, sightless eyes staring up into a heaven that would most certainly be denied him. "That," he said with a decisive, two-finger point, "is Constantino Fiore. He's a hit man for Salvatore Cannizzaro, an Italian mafia boss. Actual mafia, not this penny-ante shit we've got out here."

Jack thought about his friend, Giovanni Castro, and the last time Jack saw him. The night Fiore murdered him.

Rest easy, Gio.

Jack turned back to the cop. "This is an international smuggling operation. I've been after these guys for years, Sergeant. Can you tell me where the diamonds are?"

"Diamonds?" A cloud of confusion came over Fulton's face.

"That's what this is about. Diamonds. They were transported in that armored car there."

"Well, we've got a strongbox over there, but we haven't opened it yet. The forensics team has to have it first," he said, his naturally thunderous voice sounding strangely tentative.

"Sorry, Sergeant, but I can't leave it for them."

"But it's evidence."

"Yes, it is," Jack said flatly. "That's a small fortune in that box. I can't leave it just sitting here."

"Wait, you said you were with Customs?"

"That's right."

"I thought this was an FBI thing. I need to talk to Special Agent Fuery about this."

Jack turned to face the police officer. He reached into his jacket pocket and pulled out the tri-folded paper. "This is a joint operation, Sergeant Fulton. The Bureau is handling the mafia angle, that's their thing. Smuggling diamonds is mine." Jack unfolded the paper but didn't hand it over. "This is a search and seizure warrant from the federal magistrate, Sergeant," Jack said. He held the forged warrant for a few seconds, watching the cop's eyes as they scanned the text. When they left the document to meet his own stare, Jack knew he didn't have to flip the page. He folded the paper and put it back in his jacket.

"I'd still like to run this by Fuery."

"All I'm going to do is get these things inside. This place is going to be covered in newscopters, reporters, more federal agents than you can count, to mention a few. The last thing *any* of us want is for eighty million in diamonds to somehow go missing in all that chaos." Jack walked over to the strongbox before Fulton had a chance to formulate a rebuttal. He'd just put into the man's head the gravity of the situation and magnitude of the problem he'd have on his hands if something happened on his watch.

One of the WorldSecure guards had been killed outright. His body lay under a sheet where he'd fallen, just steps from the armored car. They'd almost made it. The other was on a gurney being attended to by the paramedics. The driver, shielded by armored plates and bullet-resistant glass, survived unharmed. Looked like Vito's men had been killed as well. Jack scanned the line of mafia gunmen. Even though they were lying on their stomachs, he could make out profiles, and some of them had their heads turned to the sides so that their faces weren't scraping concrete.

Bartolo was not among them.

"Sergeant Fulton," one of the police officers said. Jack watched Fulton hold a finger up, his attention on the strongbox. Jack knew that look. He was running out the scenarios in his head to see which was the one that was going to land him in the most trouble with management, the most paperwork. The last thing any city cop wanted was to be the piece of meat in a tug-of-war between two federal agencies.

"Sarge?" the kid said again.

"I said in a minute," Fulton barked back.

"The keys are probably on the guard's belt," Jack said. "I don't have gloves, but I'm happy to take a pair."

Fulton reached into a pouch on his Sam Browne belt and pulled out a pair of white latex gloves, which he handed to Jack. If this asshole from Customs was going to disturb the crime scene, fine, but Fulton wasn't going to help him do it. Jack pulled the gloves on, bent down, and lifted the sheet covering the dead security guard. Jack moved the sheet just enough that it uncovered the security guard's belt. It was a similar style tactical belt as the police wore, utility pouches, a radio, and space for two extra magazines. Jack opened a couple of the pouches before he found a set of keys on a red lanyard. He unclipped them and walked over to the strongbox.

Jack opened the strongbox. Inside was a carrying case made of ballistic nylon that was about two feet long. There was a thick handle on top. A heavy-grade zipper ran the entire length of the case, which would allow it to be opened flat. The two zippers were secured with a zip tie that had a WorldSecure badge on the end of it.

"You have a knife, Sergeant?"

Fulton reached into one of his pouches and handed Jack a folded tactical knife.

Jack was acutely aware of how much time this was taking. He didn't have much longer that he could play this out. At some point, Fulton was going to get tired of this and insist they talk to whoever this Special Agent Fuery was. But Jack also knew this was a critical part of selling the con. Any law enforcement officer would inspect the goods on scene.

Jack unfolded the blade and broke the seal. He collapsed the knife and handed it back to Fulton with a low, distracted, "Thanks." He unzipped the case. Inside, there were six smaller pouches that were all secured to the side of the case with MOLLE straps. Jack pulled one of the pouches out, opened it, and gently tapped some of the contents into his palm.

Several diamonds rolled out.

He had them.

Jack quickly returned the pouch to the case and secured it. Then he stood. "Okay," he said in a flat voice. "I'd better get these inside before it gets any crazier out here." Jack clutched the case handle in his left hand. "Thanks for your assistance, Sergeant Fulton. I'll be sure to note your cooperation in my report. What's your lieutenant's name?"

"Olivera," he said.

"Lieutenant Olivera," Jack repeated. "Good to know. I'll be sure to thank him. Good luck," Jack said and headed toward the building. He didn't look back.

TWENTY-FOUR

"Where in the hell are Burton and De Angeles?" Fuery thundered.

Special Agent Zhao explained that when the gunfire started, Reginald Burton got up and left. Because he was in a windowless conference room and didn't have the benefit of the radio chatter, Zhao didn't know that the armored car had arrived. He'd probably guessed as much, but he didn't *know*. Still, either the setup for the bust or the gunfight outside was sufficient probable cause for an investigative detention. It sounded like Burton just somehow got away in the chaos of it.

But they had De Angeles, and at least that was something. Though, it turned out he was an Italian citizen, and that was creating its own unique set of complications. They would have to notify the Italian consulate that they had him so that they could see if he was wanted for anything in his home country. They were also lucky to still have him. Once the gunfire started and Fuery and Reaves ran downstairs to assist the Inglewood officers, Reginald Burton took off. Zhao had tried to stop him, but then Carter LeMothe went into a full-on, crazed panic. Zhao had to restrain him. De Angeles slipped out of the conference room when Zhao turned his attention away.

Luckily, Agent Tina Terry, who'd been playing the part of the receptionist, was at the office doorway and blocked his escape. She'd started to go after Burton but then turned around when there was another burst of gunfire, going back to assist Zhao. She radioed to Fuery to advise him that Burton was moving, but Fuery didn't have a radio with him. He and Reaves had left them on the desk when they went to assist the Inglewood PD.

De Angeles said he was scared by the gunfire and just wanted to get out of there. Terry played along and assured him the safest spot was in the windowless room, and when that didn't work, she informed him that she and Zhao were federal agents and he was, indeed, "safest" with them.

Burton couldn't get too far, and they'd get prints off of his vehicle. It would only be a matter of time before they were both nailed, but Abbate was going to have his ass for this. Thank God they at least had the diamonds.

THERE WAS a six-foot-tall off-white brick wall that surrounded the complex, except for a pedestrian entry in the northwest corner. Here, the wall transitioned to a black metal fence that came up to the middle of Jack's chest, and it ran from the brick wall to a higher brick wall with anti-scaling bars that ran along the property's northern side. The fence was cipher locked, but Jack easily vaulted over it. Rusty had figured this would be the obvious exit for him and was waiting. Jack climbed into the car and said, "Just drive, man."

They'd done it.

Jack sank into his seat as Rusty accelerated away. The adrenaline crash rolled over him like a great ocean wave, and Jack was suddenly very tired. It didn't seem real yet. Of course, they hadn't escaped, not fully, but the diamonds were in their possession, and that was something. Still, it wasn't going to take the police—and, it would seem, the FBI—very long to figure out that there was no Agent Little with US

Customs, there was no joint operation, and those diamonds most certainly hadn't been brought inside for safekeeping. Jack figured that, on the outside, they had ten minutes.

The original plan called for them to crash at the Beverly Hilton. They had a suite reserved with a ghosted credit card. That was a place that respected privacy, and three men walking in with expensive suits, sunglasses, and light luggage wouldn't stand out from the scenery. Jack needed to fly back to Sonoma and get his passport. They'd decided that they would fly directly from Los Angeles to Rome during the planning here these last few days. Jack didn't have his passport with him and would have to return to Sonoma to get it. The others didn't know. The extra leg would add complexity to an already complicated thing, not to mention that they'd have to wait for him to fly up and back. Now, Jack wasn't sure the Beverly Hilton was a smart move. Nor did he think that he'd be able to sit still in a room for thirty-six hours. Rusty had them booked on a private charter that was leaving from LAX, but not until the day after tomorrow. Staying in Los Angeles was risky and dangerous. Keeping their original plan of flying out of an airport that was three miles away from the scene was suicidal.

Jack checked his phone. There was nothing from Enzo.

"Head north," Jack said. "Fast."

"That's what I'm doing," Rusty replied, irritated. Rusty guided the X6 past Los Angeles Air Force base and then picked up the 105. They hit the interchange right away and, from their elevated position, got one last look at the scene as they passed it. LAPD air support was back over the building, and there were two or three times as many patrol vehicles as Jack had seen when he was there just minutes ago. Rusty accelerated onto the 405 and took them north.

There was still much to process. Reginald and Vito had walked into a trap. Jack figured that this Pan Pacific was a front company, but he'd assumed it was for a criminal syndicate or just some shady businessmen, not for the FBI. This was very problematic. Reginald knew exactly the tune he would sing. The FBI might be able to prove that the diamonds were stolen, but they couldn't prove that Reginald knew it—not until it went to trial. They didn't *have* any diamonds, so they might not actually be able to charge him with anything. That would be the ideal scenario for Jack. He'd still have a threat to deal with and one who knew just where and how to hurt him, but Jack wouldn't also have to deal with the FBI.

"That was absolutely a setup," Jack said after a few miles of silence. Rusty had been off all day, distracted and short-fused. Jack originally put it to nerves. Most seasoned thieves couldn't pull off a score like this, and there were maybe twenty guys in the world that Jack knew of with the audacity and skill to do what he'd just done. Just walk in and con the police into giving him the evidence? But now that it was over, he expected Rusty to come down, get back to normal.

"Looks that way," was all he said, though.

"It wasn't just Inglewood city cops, Rusty. The one that I talked to said they were just there as backup. He said the FBI was leading the operation. I think Reginald stumbled himself into a sting."

Rusty mumbled something under his breath. Whatever it was, it was an outgassing of frustration and nerves and ultimately not intended for Jack's ears.

"We need to change our plans," Jack said. Whatever was going through Rusty's head, he was going to have to get over it. They had work to do. "We can't fly out of LAX now. It's too close, and if Reginald got nabbed, he will talk about us and they'll be watching local airports."

"I already booked the plane. We're going out of a private terminal."

"It's a credit card tied to a fake business," Jack said dryly. "I don't think we're worried about cancellation fees. Have them change it. We'll fly out of a different city. Vegas makes the most sense. It's close, and there's a lot of private plane traffic."

Unfortunately, there was no way to know what Reginald's fate was. If they had him, the FBI wouldn't announce it because they'd be shifting focus now to who stole the diamonds out from under them. There was a time that Rusty still had contacts in the Bureau, people who didn't agree with the Bureau sacrificing him on the altar of bureaucratic exigency, but those people wouldn't talk to him anymore. Once the DSS got involved, the people who knew him... didn't know him anymore.

"We're sticking to the plan," Rusty said in a flat voice.

"The hell we are, and it's not your call."

"I took two bullets over those stones, so yes, it is my call. We have a way out and it's safe. We're not deviating from it."

Jack had encountered thieves before who thought they'd invested more in a job than the rest of the team and therefore earned an unequal stake, but it had been a very long time since someone had questioned his plan, let alone tried to overrule it.

"Rusty," Jack started, forcing his voice into an even tone. "I appreciate the sacrifices that you made getting us here, but this is still my plan. If you are uncomfortable with that or if something else is bothering you, Enzo and I can handle what's next. I'll be honest, I don't want to go into this thing in Rome without you, but Enzo and I can manage. You'll still get an even split, but I'd rather—"

"It's fine, Jack," he said, his voice sharp. "Maybe you should drive," Rusty said.

"We're on the freeway."

But Rusty was already pulling over. Rusty hit the hazards and guided the BMW over to the shoulder. They hadn't cleared Inglewood yet, and Jack would be uneasy until they put a lot more miles between themselves and the scene. Rusty stopped the car and put it in park, opened his door. Jack got out as well and walked around the back of the vehicle. Cars rolled past at freeway speed, oblivious to the scene. It was just two men changing up drivers. A canal ran along the right side of freeway, though it was bone dry. The trees on the other side of the retaining wall were mottled green and brown and needed rain. Though the shoulder here was wide due to its proximity to an on-ramp, and there was a good five feet of sun-bleached asphalt between him and traffic, Jack cleared left before moving around to the driver's side. Rusty had gone the other direction so they wouldn't have to two-step around each other.

Jack had to admit as he climbed into the X6's driver's side that he didn't have any idea what was going through Rusty's head right now. Jack was glad to be behind the wheel, however. He didn't like being a passenger, ever, but now he'd feel like a little more was in his control at least. Jack also realized that he needed to put himself in his friend's position. Rusty was a fugitive now, and that carried its own weight, one that Jack couldn't ever truly appreciate.

Because he'd always gotten away with it.

But more than that, Rusty hadn't been back in the US since he fled. He hadn't wanted to come back here, but Jack had pressured him into it. That, and he'd forced Rusty into a role he wasn't comfortable with and hadn't played before. All while giving the appearance that Jack wasn't willing to make the same sacrifices that Rusty and Enzo were. Like Rusty told him, he couldn't do this job and have a foot in both worlds. If they were making a play for these diamonds, Jack had to be prepared to walk away from his other life, to run from it. He wasn't. Worse, he'd never intended to, and Rusty would surely have sensed that.

Jack put the BMW in drive and accelerated quickly along the shoulder, looking for a break in traffic wide enough for them to merge. The mountains that separated greater Los Angeles from the San Fernando Valley loomed much larger now. After a long, hot summer, they looked much more brown than green. Even from this distance, they looked ready to spark. Jack hadn't lived in LA for over twenty years, and though it had changed massively in those years, it was still a place that he knew very well. In his early days as a wheelman, Jack's role had been to get crews to and most vitally *from* the job. That required planning. Endless hours in stolen cars driving the various escape routes that they *might* use and committing those routes to memory. He got to know neighborhoods. Jack learned where he could stash a backup car and have confidence it would be there when he arrived, and he learned what neighborhoods he'd rather get caught by the police in than stop for the span of a stoplight. He learned all of the places that you could hide a car.

Jack exited the freeway at Wilshire, one of the last before the freeway cut through the mountains. This was also the route he'd need to get to the Beverly Hilton. He saw Rusty visibly tense when he turned right onto Wilshire, it was subtle and contained, but Jack noticed all the same. Then he understood why. The structure nestled in the armpit of the 405 and Wilshire was the Los Angeles FBI building. It was a massive concrete monolith that looked like a 1960s science fiction writer's vision of a dystopian future. Jack drove past it, and he could see Rusty relax. Again, it was subtle and not something most people would notice, but Jack knew how to read someone. They drove through the glass-and-concrete canyon of Westwood in silence, but when Jack turned right onto Glendon and into a faded pink parking structure, Rusty knew he was deviating from the plan.

"What are we doing?"

"We're getting rid of this car."

"The car is clean," Rusty said.

"The car was in the parking lot, and that parking lot will have cameras. The police *and* the FBI will be looking at that footage right now."

"We can change the plates," Rusty said. That was true, but it would take him time to find clean plates. Yes, they could take some off of any car and switch them out, but there was always the possibility that the owner would report them stolen. Being the subject of two BOLOs was not something Jack was willing to chance right now. He didn't know how long it would be before Rusty could get a new set of plates here, but probably it was longer than it would take for them to just switch cars and get out of the city.

Jack snaked his way through the parking garage, looking for a spot. He found one on the fourth level. This was almost perfect. It was an older garage and attached to a public library. The car would sit here for a week or more and no one would notice. Jack also didn't see the black domes indicating security cameras. Jack pulled into the spot and got out, popping the rear hatch as he did. In the distance, Jack heard the screeching of tires as a car rounded a corner. Rusty met him around the back.

There was a gun in his hand.

TWENTY-FIVE

"Slowly place your hands in the air and then lace them behind your head."

Jack stared at him, dumbfounded.

"Jack, your hands." Rusty spoke in a calm, practiced voice.

"What is this, a citizen's arrest?"

"Jack, I'm not going to ask again."

"Or. Fucking. What." Jack held his unblinking gaze on Rusty until the other man flinched and looked away. "If shooting me is an option for you, I'm going to make you do it. There's no way in hell that I'm letting you steal these diamonds from me." The next part he said through gritted teeth and with narrowed eyes. "Not without making you earn it, you fucking snake."

The corners of Rusty's mouth dropped into a sad frown. "I'm not trying to steal from you, Jack."

If this wasn't Rusty making his own play, then what in the hell was it?

Jack's options were few.

Rusty was at arm's length. Jack's hands were still at his sides. There was no chance he could reach, draw, and fire his own pistol in the time it would take Rusty to fire his. No one could miss at this range. Grabbing the weapon was an option, but not a good one, for the same reason as going for his pistol. Rusty was playing this smart. He was partially covered by the car next to theirs and his back was to the garage at an angle, so someone would have to be right up on them to see that he was armed. The pistol was close in, which was terrible for aim, but at this range it wouldn't matter. Jack would still have to step forward to make a grab for it, and Rusty would see the movement and shoot before Jack could close the distance.

Rusty had trained for situations like this. Jack had not.

Oh, Jack had taken a "combat skills for rich paranoids" that some ex–special forces type taught the eccentric elite because it was exactly the kind of thing Frank Fischer would do. In that class, the instructor taught him that a gun was not a force field and it wouldn't protect you if an adversary closed the distance between you before you could shoot them. Academically, Jack knew how to do it—drop back and to an angle, putting weight on the back foot while bringing your close hand up to push the gun away. The shooter would fire, but the round would just miss the target. Knowing how to do it and trusting that you could pull it off without getting a round in the chest were two different things.

"Hands in the air," Rusty said again.

"I told you. You want these diamonds, you're going to have to kill me to get them."

"I'm not robbing you, Jack. I'm arresting you."

Jack threw his head back and laughed. It was large, loud, and nervous, but it was a full-bellied guffaw nonetheless.

"You're arresting me," Jack said back to him, recalling a time not long ago when he'd said that it was a slow wit that said back the last thing they heard in a conversation because they were stalling for time. In Jack's case, he genuinely needed to say it again in an attempt to make his mind believe it.

He kept his hands at his side.

"That badge in your pocket is as fake as mine."

"They offered me a deal. I get a reduced sentence in exchange for turning over you and the diamonds."

"Who offered?"

"The DSS brokered it with the Bureau."

The Bureau. Does this mean Danzig knows about this?

"I'm getting a pardon, Jack. I'll have to stand for the passport forgery and some other things."

"Trading on your friends in exchange for what? Five years in prison? Some deal."

"My friends? That's what this is?" It was the first time in their exchange that the gun moved. "Jack, the Bureau and I had an understanding when I fled. They weren't going to look for me too hard as long as I kept a low profile and played by certain rules. I was even working with people in our own intelligence community, solving particular problems. And it worked. They did it because I know some pretty damaging things, and many in my chain of command were worried about what I'd say if I ever went to trial. But all that changed when I started working with you. First, Danzig somehow figured out my real name. How she got to *those* files, I'll never know. But once you started taking risks you shouldn't have taken, taking *jobs* you shouldn't have taken, burning through passports and ultimately getting jammed up with Aleksander Anđelić, that was the line for them. All those passports I forged for you, the bank accounts, the Bureau...*my* Bureau was worried that maybe I was actually playing for the other side. The Bureau came after me hard."

Rusty's emphasis on "his" Bureau meant the part of the FBI that dealt in counterintelligence, which he'd often said was almost a separate agency from the law enforcement side. It was a dark and covert world.

Rusty adjusted the position of the gun. "You think this is my real hair? You think that I've been living this easy life on the lam in Switzerland? I move constantly. I haven't spent three months under the same roof since Rome. Meanwhile, you get to live in some goddamn vineyard and preach about how others have to share in the risk. Fuck you."

Certain things made sense now. When this started, Rusty was the one that pushed the hardest, guilted Jack into going forward with it. He knew exactly the strings to pull on...like a skilled operator. Staying back from the grab today, if Rusty had turned into a CI, he was prohibited from committing a crime even to protect his identity—Jack learned that one firsthand. He'd thought it was nerves at the time. Rusty always played himself as the dashing rogue; Jack never once suspected that he was continually on the run, tired and afraid. He knew the man was a fugitive, but Rusty always portrayed that as a choice, almost a protest against a government that betrayed him.

Tires squealed against the garage floor on the level below them.

Jack waited a moment, but Rusty didn't say anything. He wasn't speaking any more than he had to. Smart. There was no apology, there were no salving words of remorse—*I'm sorry it had to be you, Jack, but this is how it goes sometimes.*

There was nothing but a pistol and a hard stare.

The stare...something was off about it. Then Jack realized that Rusty had blue eyes. He'd dyed his hair, and Jack never knew because he'd always had stubble on his head. But it took Jack this long to realize that he was wearing colored contacts. That was a detail Jack shouldn't have missed. It wouldn't have tipped him to this, but glossing over details was what got you arrested, got you killed.

"So how does this work, exactly?" Jack asked.

"I take you into custody, and you're arrested for attempting to sell a fortune in stolen diamonds, receiving stolen property, and bank robbery."

"Well, now, that's interesting."

"I don't have time for this, Jack. And I'm tired of talking about it."

"They're lying to you, pal."

"Who?"

"Well, the Bureau, it would seem. Again." Try to land the punch, see what he did. "Anything that happened in Rome was part of my plea deal, my trade for Anđelić. The Commerce Bank, *Vito* stealing the diamonds—remember, I wasn't there. He was also the one who shot you. Vito brought the diamonds into the country, not me. If anything, you should have made a deal to give them him." Rusty wouldn't know the details of Jack's plea deal, and the judge sealed the records because of the assistance Jack gave Danzig on rolling up gem trafficking networks in Europe. Anyone Rusty was working with would need to get those records unsealed, which would take a judge's authorization. Jack was stretching it a bit when he said he had a pass on anything that happened in Rome. He obviously didn't tell Danzig that they were stealing Bartolo's diamonds from the Commerce Bank.

That meant Danzig maybe didn't know about this thing, otherwise she never would have come to his place and asked him questions about Cannizzaro. Unless they'd brought her in on it. Jack forced himself to stop that line of thinking. Jumping at mental shadows was only going to make him paranoid.

Whatever Rusty knew, the FBI wanted to silence it and was going to some great lengths to keep it quiet.

Rusty tensing up as they drove by the FBI building a few minutes ago suggested that maybe this thing Rusty was involved in, whatever deal they offered him, wasn't being run locally. Otherwise, wouldn't Rusty just have turned Jack in at Pan Pacific?

It also meant, though, that there were some holes in Rusty's story, or in the story the FBI was giving him.

That was no longer Jack's problem.

"We're done talking, Jack. I'm going to cuff you now and then turn you in."

"Someone want to explain to me what the hell *this* is?"

Enzo Bachetti in a silver Chevy Malibu.

Jack had never been so happy to see someone in his life.

Enzo parked the car, still idling, just behind Rusty and Jack. His door was open, and he was talking to them over the roof.

"What the fuck?" was all Rusty said, shaking his head in disbelief. "I don't know what you're doing here, Enzo, but you should leave now. I'm not turning you in, but I will if I have to." Rusty's eyes went to the corners, but he didn't turn his head. The car was in his peripheral. His gaze returned to Jack.

"Turning me in? What are you talking about?"

"Rusty made a deal, Enzo. He walks on whatever he did before we knew him, in exchange for me and the diamonds." Jack turned his attention back to Rusty. "As for why he's here, that's what I meant when I called Enzo from the parking lot. The phrase was from Dante and was about the value of friendship, but back in Turin, we worked for someone that used to quote it all the time. He was a real asshole and had a way of not paying you what you were worth, so over time, Enzo and I started using it ironically. Eventually, it turned into a code we used to use, shorthand for 'I don't trust you.'"

Rusty looked genuinely confused.

"You were acting erratic all morning. I was worried that you might do something strange, but I didn't think you'd turn into a snitch."

"That's pretty clever," Rusty said, conceding the point. "The Bureau isn't interested in you, Enzo. You should leave now."

"That's fine," he said. "I'm not particularly interested in them. I am interested in my share of the diamonds, though."

Enzo stepped back from the car door and moved down the length of the front. Jack saw motion and Enzo brought his gun up. The gun. Rusty had gotten them the guns and the BMW. A deal like this would be a long time in the works, which meant it wasn't something that was offered when Rusty broke the surface tension of the US border. Either these were plants or Rusty was hedging his bets. If the cars and the guns were plants, the BMW would most certainly have GPS tracker on them.

Whatever its origins, Enzo's pistol was up now.

"After all that talk about how the government turned its back on you, how the Bureau hung you out to dry, you're still willing to go crawling back," Jack said. "Can you at least tell me at what point did everything you'd told us become complete bullshit?"

A short, mirthless "Ha" escaped Rusty's lips. Jack watched the corners of his eyes narrow. Rusty was getting impatient, getting nervous.

"That's funny coming from you, Jack. You're the Dutch Master of bullshit."

"I was never anything but honest with either of you. After the Carlton, when I needed your help, I trusted both of you with the name of my other identity, the name of my winery, so you'd have some collateral if you needed it. Even going into this thing, I was completely honest about what I was risking and why I didn't want to do it. I gave you all an out, a chance to back out if you didn't want to go through with it. But I guess by then you knew you had something to trade. Isn't that right, Scott?" Much like Jack had created Frank Fischer, "Rusty" was an alias, a persona that the fixer lived under. Jack landed a shot saying his real name and saw the man wince at its use.

Rusty said nothing. They all knew there was no response he could give.

One last try. "We can all still walk away from this."

"No, Jack, we can't. There's no deal without you." His eyes flicked to the corners again. "But I don't need to give them Enzo."

"You're not giving anybody anything," Enzo said, and he took one more step to the side.

"That's fucking far enough, Enzo," Rusty said.

"You know what I went through for those, Rusty," Enzo spat. "You saw what they did to me." Enzo had broken into Andelić's house while Jack, Rusty, and Vito were making their play for the diamonds. Enzo was caught and one of Andelić's heavies worked him over in a garage for hours while the lawyer, Castillo, watched and asked questions. With each set of them, the promise that it would end, but it never did. Not until Jack showed up and ended it for them. "You're not taking those diamonds from me." For some reason, Enzo's accent was especially thick when he said those words.

Rusty turned his head a quarter to look at Enzo. The gun was still pointed at Jack, and Jack could see Rusty's eyes flick to the right to make sure Jack wasn't moving.

There were things Jack could say. He could tell Rusty that there was a way out of this, and there was. Rusty could walk away now and still get his cut. Jack had no issue with that. Or Rusty could simply walk away. Disappear. From everyone. But Jack could see in Rusty's eyes that he wouldn't. Jack knew what it was like to have to run and he knew he didn't ever want to do that again. Rusty had reached his limit. Again, something Jack could understand. There were other deals Rusty could have made, if only he'd trusted Jack enough to talk this out with him first.

Instead, Rusty blamed Jack for his situation, and so he traded the one commodity he knew he had. Trust.

That, Jack understood as well.

Rusty's deal was based on his giving Jack over to the FBI. There was no trade Jack could offer him, nothing of equal value to them that Rusty could offer up in Jack's place. Maybe the diamonds, but Jack already stole those and impersonated a federal officer to do it. His fate was sealed.

Rusty was about to speak. Enzo cut him off.

"Last chance, Rusty," Enzo said. "Put the gun down."

"You can't shoot me. You don't have a deal if I'm dead, Rusty," Jack said.

"That's true," Rusty said evenly, and he corked his torso around to match the direction his head was facing, to Enzo, and the gun barrel followed.

Rusty knew Jack wouldn't shoot him. Jack had killed a man once before. It was self-defense and that man earned it, but it was still something Jack lived with every day. It was a human life and that had a cost. Maksim Radas was an enemy, a thief, possibly a war criminal, and a genuine threat to people. That was hard enough to live with. Rusty was his friend.

Jack went for his pistol.

Rusty snapped back and realized his mistake too late. Jack had his own weapon out now and braced for the reflex shot. But it never came. Rusty maintained his discipline, it seemed.

Two on one. Enzo and Jack had Rusty covered, and Rusty had a gun on Enzo.

"You both have about two minutes," Rusty said in a flat voice.

"For what?"

"For a car to come around the corner and see you two with guns drawn. They will call the police. I have an out. You don't."

"Yeah, but not much of one," Jack said. "I saw you tense up when we passed the FBI building back there. You might have a deal with someone in the Bureau, but it's not with anyone in this town."

"My problem is solved with a phone call. Yours is not. Enzo, they don't care about you. You could slip out of the country and go back home. The US government won't come looking." Rusty's eyes shifted from Enzo to Jack. "But Jack, your only chance is to give up and come with me. Right now, you have something to trade and an opportunity to come willingly. If I have to take you by force, it'll mean I'm turning in the diamonds, not you."

"Rusty, there's no turning anything or any*one* in. I'm going to explain this one time, and I hope you can appreciate it, even if you can't understand it."

"You'd better talk fast."

"Bartolo tried to kill me in 1997. He found out that Giovanni Castro was an undercover cop, and since I brought Castro into the School of Turin, he thought I was in on it. Obviously, I escaped, but I spent the next five years looking over my shoulder. Up until Bartolo was arrested for stealing these diamonds. He spent the next sixteen years in prison thinking about nothing but them. This is his life's work, and I'm taking it from him. I risked my life and my freedom for these. Enzo and you, I might add, both bled for them. So, no, I'm not giving up and turning myself in."

Jack's speech was interrupted by the squeaking of tires across concrete. Somewhere, in the bowels of the garage, a car was moving.

If the car left, it was no problem. But if it came this way, Rusty was absolutely right.

"Tick tock, Jack."

"I'm not turning myself in, Rusty. You can walk out of here or we can all fucking shoot each other, but I'm not turning myself in, and you're not arresting me."

There was another squeal of tires, this one closer.

Rusty's eyes, which now seemed to be someone else's once Jack noticed that the color had changed, were hard. The hair, grown out and colored, it was as if he were speaking to an entirely different person. Someone he couldn't reason with, someone for whom Jack's struggles wouldn't even register. A stranger. Rusty was, he saw now, a chameleon. He'd adopted one persona as the dashing underworld fixer and troubleshooter, perhaps as a way of distancing himself from the life he'd had as a federal agent. Jack saw now that it was just that, a persona, a role. Even the name was fake. He was now Scott Donners, a disgraced former federal agent, but *that* man knew what he'd given up or been forced to.

The tires screeched again. The car was on the level below them, and they could hear the engine now as well.

"What's it going to be, Jack?"

"I've given you the terms, Rusty. That's the deal on the table. There's a lot you have to offer up to your handlers, but Enzo and I aren't part of that bargain." Jack faced west, and he had a view on where the ramp up to this level of the garage was. He could see a white Lexus SUV through the concrete pillars. The driver would be a woman, professional, forty-five to fifty-five years old, and she would not take risks. She would deer-in-the-headlights freeze the second she rounded that corner, and the only pause they would have would be for her to panic dial 911 from her car.

"Put it down, Rusty," Enzo said.

"You first."

"Oh, for fuck's sake," Jack said, now unable to contain his anger. If a phone call went to LAPD, they were all of them done. The diamonds would be gone forever. The three of them arrested and Jack didn't know the nature of whatever Rusty had worked out with the Bureau, but he had to imagine that getting picked up first by the LAPD was not part of it. The one thing Rusty had to offer the FBI was his continued silence on whatever got him ousted in the first place. Once another agency got involved, the Bureau wouldn't know for certain whether or not Rusty talked.

Rusty's eyes went to the corners, toward the SUV. They had seconds. He lowered his gun. Enzo didn't.

"Enzo," Jack said through gritted teeth.

"He *turned* on us," Enzo growled.

"And we're not solving that problem in a garage in broad daylight with an eyewitness," Jack said. "A dead body only gets us revenge, it doesn't get a ticket out of here."

They'd been here once before, and Jack only now realized how dangerous of ground they stood on. Enzo Bachetti had learned to stomach a lot of unpleasant things in this life he'd chosen, but betrayal was not one of them. When Ozren Stolar double-crossed them in Cannes and murdered Gaston Broussard and Gabrielle Eberspach, when he thought he'd killed Enzo, Enzo and Rusty followed Ozren and his fellow Pink Panthers to Jack's safe house in Rome. Even though Rusty had Ozren covered and he was essentiality disarmed, Enzo shot Ozren in the face.

Twice.

Out of the corner of his eye, Jack saw Enzo turn his head to look at him. Jack was still focused on Rusty, watching for any sign of movement, of a change of heart.

Enzo lowered his weapon.

The Lexus rounded the corner, and it slowed when it approached. Enzo's Malibu was still in the middle of the lane. The Lexus driver—Jack couldn't tell if his profile had been right because the windows were very dark—slowed even further so that it could creep around the Malibu without scraping it. The Lexus edged around it and then put on a short burst of speed, just a touch of engine rev to show them the driver was annoyed. It parked in an open spot at the end of their row.

No one spoke.

A door slammed, and they heard purposeful heels clipping the concrete. Jack took his eyes off Rusty for a moment, they all did, to see a nearly six-foot blonde stomping away from the vehicle in the direction of the stairwell on the garage's northeast corner. She wore a white jacket, skirt, and handbag that matched the color of her car.

Before anyone could speak, Jack said, "Is the BMW yours, or did the Bureau give it to you?"

"Did I acquire it for this job, you mean?"

"I mean what I fucking said, *Scott*."

"It's not the Bureau's car," Rusty said.

"Good. Then you can call them for a ride." Jack turned his head. "Enzo, get in the car and drive. I'll call you from the road and tell you where we're going."

It'd be one of the last phone calls he'd make with this phone, too. Though they'd always communicated using a secure app so others couldn't listen in, Rusty had the number, so Jack had to assume that the FBI did too. They'd need new everything.

Jack had two remaining passports, one was at his home in Sonoma and the other was at a place he had in Tuscany, but Rusty had created them both.

Strangely and entirely against type, Enzo got into the car without another word. It was probably the only time the safe cracker had done something in his adult life without wallpapering it with profanity first. He started the vehicle, then pulled backward to let Jack back the BMW out.

"Tell me," Jack said. "Do you feel any remorse over this?"

Rusty had an expressionless face. It looked like he was wearing an actual mask. "None whatsoever." Then he said, "You can run now, Jack, but you can't run forever."

"Everybody runs."

Jack's eyes narrowed, just slightly. He nodded once and got into the BMW, locking the doors immediately. He kept the pistol on his lap. Jack backed out of the space.

Rusty stood, pistol at his hip, neither ready nor not ready, just...there.

Jack didn't know how long they had, but he wasn't waiting here to find out.

Jack pulled around, and Enzo followed him out of the garage.

They found the 405 and drove north.

TWENTY-SIX

Supervisory Special Agent Linda Abbate was not happy.

"I, and frankly others, are wondering how in the hell that a suspect managed to get past two of your agents, get down to the first floor, past *you two*, and convince an Inglewood Police Department officer to give him back the diamonds. *All in the middle of a fucking shootout.*"

Fuery learned long ago to look the boss in the eye during an ass chewing, though this one was particularly difficult. It was his operation, his responsibility, and his fault. Abbate was a tough boss, she had high standards and didn't tolerate cut corners from the agents under her command. Fuery had let her down, and it left a dark pit in his stomach.

There would be a formal debrief with all of the agents involved later. This one was so Abbate could get the facts straight for the briefing she'd have to give the Assistant Director. They'd just finished their first pass. Normally, a field office was run by a Special Agent in Charge, but given its size, the Los Angeles Field Office was led by an Assistant Director.

"We heard gunfire coming from the front of the building and

received a shots-fired call from the Inglewood PD. Kent and I responded. I neglected to take the tactical radio with me. I was thinking only about assisting the other officers, and I didn't believe I could hold a radio and shoot."

"Why didn't you inform the other agents that you were going?"

"There wasn't time. I notified Tina on our way out, but I did not tell her we were not taking a radio. Kent and I took the stairs and saw the Inglewood PD engaging approximately six perpetrators. We identified ourselves as federal agents, but at that point I cannot confirm if they heard us."

"Kent?" Abbate asked.

"That's correct. When I saw that Ray had the right field of fire covered, I engaged targets on the left. We were in the open and there was no cover we could take."

Abbate nodded and made notes. Fuery continued.

"You have to cut De Angeles loose," Abbate said at the end of their second run-through and after she'd informed them that she had enough information to brief the AD. "We've got nothing to hold him on."

"We've got PC to sell the diamonds," Fuery argued, though he knew it was pointless. He was making the case just to make it. "Unless he can prove that those diamonds are the property of his company, we can show they are stolen."

"But you don't have any diamonds, Ray." Abbate's tone softened. "Without those, there's no probable cause to do anything."

"Boss, I know it looks that way," Reaves said. "But I'm not convinced it was Burton who talked to the Inglewood cop," Reaves said. He and Fuery had gone over this on the ride over. Fuery didn't think there was any other possibility, but Reaves wouldn't let it go. Fuery said it was grassy knoll shit. He didn't agree with the theory at all, but he wasn't pissed that his partner offered it up. They were both convinced that Burton and De Angeles were dirty; they just needed time to work out how much and how deep.

"Say more," Abbate said.

"I want to go on record and say that Ray and I discussed this on the way over, and he doesn't agree with it. So, if it turns out to be bullshit, it's on me." Abbate nodded hastily and made the "get on with it" hand roll. "Burton wasn't going to brave a firefight unarmed, not even for those diamonds. I think we was cutting his losses and decided to escape. All he had to do was look out the front door and see that place was swarming with cops. I think he went out the back. Hell, he probably took a different stairwell and we just missed him. The other piece that doesn't square with me is that the Inglewood cop who talked to him, Sergeant Fulton, described the man as mid- to late-forties, dark hair, average height and build. The man presented himself as Customs. Burton is late sixties, gray hair, and a beard. The US Customs agent, Little, was in a gray suit and dark tie. Burton was in a tan jacket and black pants. There's no way he did that kind of a quick change."

Abbate nodded. That was the one part of this that Fuery couldn't reconcile. When they'd talked about it in the car, he admittedly was thinking about how they were going to explain this to Abbate and hadn't given Reaves's idea much thought after he initially dismissed it. They already couldn't explain how there was a shootout, and now they had to incorporate a *third* group into the calculus? That seemed like a long shot. But Kent did have a point, and Ray couldn't ignore the physical differences.

"Okay, I think it's unlikely that Burton was able to pose as the US Customs agent. And we've checked with Customs already?"

"Yeah," Reaves said. "They don't have an Agent Little assigned in Los Angeles and certainly didn't have one in Inglewood today."

"What if he's a backup?" Fuery asked.

"What do you mean?"

"Well, what if this guy, this Little, was there as a backup plan. If these guys really are smugglers, they're not going to let a fortune in diamonds out of their sight. If they got wind that the buy was a setup, they'd want a way out. If they're savvy enough that they can smuggle these things in from Europe and then con their way into an armored car delivery, they are a fairly sophisticated operation. The kind of group that would be able to fake federal credentials." Fuery saw emerging head nods from the other two. He was feeling it now, that moment when the investigator's instinct kicked in and the ideas started to flow. "They stage a guy in the parking lot. If Burton or De Angeles think something is off inside, either it's police or a setup, they text Little and he goes to intercept the diamonds. Rent-a-cops aren't going to question a warrant and probably couldn't spot a fake, anyway."

"Ray and I talked about the possibility of there being three separate groups involved," Reaves added. "But we both agreed that seems implausible. It just doesn't stick that people that appear to be as savvy as Burton and De Angeles would also have OPSEC bad enough that two other groups could figure out their plans and tail them."

"That logic fits with me," Abbate said, making notes. "Let's go with that for now. Where are we with the shooters?"

"There were eight total, including the drivers. Both of the drivers and one of the shooters were Americans. LAPD Vice has already identified them as members of LCN." Bureau shorthand for "La Cosa Nostra." While they'd always maintained a presence, the American mafia had never been big in Los Angeles. During their heyday, MGM studio head Louis B. Meyer was asked if he was worried that the mob was ever going try to take control of the movie industry through the labor unions the way they had with other organizations. Meyer reportedly laughed and said, "We already got a mob." La Cosa Nostra had seen declining influence everywhere following a nearly thirty-year campaign, led by the FBI and some courageous US Attorneys, culminating in the dramatic arrest and trial of crime boss John Gotti in the nineties. Here in LA, the mafia faced an uphill battle for territory and resources against other ethnic criminal organizations and, more prominently, the LA street gangs. Following the death of their last don, Peter Milano, in 2012, La Cosa Nostra's presence here was believed to be less than twenty members.

Fuery continued. "Of the eight, we have four that were killed during the shootout, and all of them appear to be Italian nationals. We have the three Americans and one Italian national who survived. They are downstairs now. While Kent was talking to Customs, I got in touch with our organized crime squad. They're getting their counterparts at LAPD Vice to come over and interview them."

"We can hold De Angeles forty-eight hours. It's Thursday evening now, so that means we hold him through the weekend. That's plenty of time to soften him up. It also gets a little more time to see if we get anything back from the consulate."

Fuery said, "I've got calls into our LEGAT at Rome, see if we can get their law enforcement involved." Fuery knew it was the middle of the night when he'd called the guy; he also knew that was part of the job. "It's a mess."

"What is?"

"Italian law enforcement. Seems like a lot of overlapping jurisdictions and missions and he said they aren't the fastest to respond. But he's got De Angeles's name and is going to run it down with them. As soon as I can get fingerprints on the two dead private security guards that were with De Angeles and Burton, he'll run those as well. He also told me something interesting."

"What's that?"

"There's a squad over there in Rome TDY right now that's working on a joint operation with the Italian antimafia police."

"Interesting," Abbate said.

"Yeah, so the LEGAT gave me the name of the squad leader, she's a Kristin Danzig. She'll give me a call, hopefully later tonight, our time, once she's up." Fuery anticipated Abbate's next question. "The time difference between here and Rome is nine hours. We'll see if she knows anything about the Italian mafia sending any of their people over here. Doubtful, but everything helps."

Fuery took a sip of lukewarm Philz coffee from the to-go cup in front of him. He suspected he'd need a lot more to carry him through the rest of the evening. It had been a long day already and far from over. Following the shootout, they'd had to debrief with Inglewood

PD and their detectives to make sure that everyone had the same accounting of events. Then they'd had to interview each of the police officers involved to find out what they'd seen. There were field interviews with the surviving shooters, none of which had born fruit, but a weekend in a federal holding cell had a way of loosening tongues. This generation of mafiosi were nothing like the old-school guys and their code of silence bullshit. They'd flip like a pancake to avoid prison time. The question was whether they knew enough to make it worth the Bureau's time. They were just soldiers, so Fuery suspected probably not. Still, it was something to run down. Fuery and Reaves had then had to do an initial use-of-force review with the local agents who were tasked with that responsibility. Any time an FBI agent discharged their weapon in the line of duty, there was a formal process to go through in order to ensure that the agents exhausted all options before opening fire.

All of that happened before he and Reaves returned to the FBI building. In most cities, the FBI's offices were downtown, usually in or near the federal buildings. LA, in nearly every way, was different. Their field office was on Wilshire about halfway between Hollywood and the ocean. They'd left just as the afternoon rush was getting into full swing and it had taken them close to ninety minutes to get from Inglewood to here. Once they wrapped with Abbate, Fuery and Reaves still needed to document everything that happened today so that an accurate record was made while the events were fresh in their minds. Fuery still needed to speak with Agent Danzig, probably between ten and midnight was when she'd call, depending on what their schedule was. His wife wouldn't love that, but she knew what she'd married into and was pretty easygoing about that sort of thing. He'd already called her to let her know that he was okay and jokingly said that the tie she got him on Father's Day last year was going to be on the five o'clock news.

Abbate looked down at her watch.

"I need to brief the AD in fifteen. I think I've got everything that I need from both of you, but let's go through next steps. We're linked up with the OC squad and LA Vice. They'll talk with the suspects and see what they can shake out. We're going to hold De Angeles for forty-eight hours, which will take us through the weekend. What's the plan with him after that?"

"The other option," Fuery said, "is we can try another interview now and start poking holes in his story. If it holds up, we can kick him loose now and see if he leads us to Burton. If not, then I say we hold him through the weekend."

"I'm fine with that," Abbate said. "You're talking with Katrina Danzig, hopefully tonight."

"That's right. You want me to call you if it's anything earth shattering, or hold until morning?"

"If there's a direct link, you can call, otherwise let's just plan to sync up first thing." She looked over at Reaves. "Kent, you're taking point on this US Customs agent, right?" Kent nodded. "Let's get an artist over to that Inglewood cop and get descriptions out to local law enforcement." Abbate closed her pen and slid it into the holder in her folio, then closed that and stood. Fuery and Reaves stood as well. "Gentleman, I'm not happy about the diamonds getting away, obviously. In all likelihood, those were stolen to begin with, but whatever the origin, they are certainly stolen now. We need to get a team looking into that. These things came from somewhere. I can pull Edwards and Moreno off that surveillance detail if we need to. Beyond that, I think you did well today. You made the right decision going to support the Inglewood officers, and I think your actions probably saved some lives. I will be very clear about that point with the Assistant Director. You should have had a radio with you, but I understand your reasons for not and I can't really fault them. In the heat of the moment, I suspect most of us would make a similar decision."

"Thank you," Fuery said. Kent nodded in agreement.

"So, it appears that we either have two legitimate businessmen or two con artists who were attempting to sell seventy million dollars' worth of diamonds of a currently undetermined provenance. We have members of the Los Angeles and Italian organized crime that attempted to take those diamonds by force. We don't yet know how the mafia knew about the location of the buy with us. That's something to run down with De Angeles, see if he's playing both sides. Then we have a third actor, who was aware of this and impersonated a US Customs agent, presented credentials and a search and seizure warrant to an Inglewood Police Department officer who didn't question it, and said that he was taking the diamonds inside for safekeeping and that he was part of the operation. He then disappeared, whereabouts currently unknown. Reginald Burton disappeared in the commotion. We have four KIA and four in custody, three American and one Italian national. That about sum it up?"

"Yes, ma'am."

"K. Boys, you have either lucked yourselves into a career case or a shitstorm of biblical proportions."

TWENTY-SEVEN

They ditched the BMW in the Burbank airport parking lot.

It took them farther out of their way than Jack would have liked, but he wanted to avoid the Van Nuys airport, even though it was right off the 405. Since Vito said that he and Reginald would be flying out of there when he tried to throw Jack off their trail, Jack couldn't know that they hadn't given that up to the authorities when they were arrested earlier that day at the office park. Assuming they had been. Jesus. There was a lot he didn't know right now and that made him nervous. They stopped at a Circle K in North Hollywood and picked up Clorox wipes, which they used to scrub every conceivable surface in the BMW before ditching it. Jack assumed the cleaner would be enough to destroy any fingerprints, but he had no way of knowing for sure if there was any residual DNA that a forensics team might be able to scrape off of it. They had to assume Rusty was giving their last known location and vehicle descriptions to the FBI right now. They also had no way of knowing whether Rusty had planted a tracking device on either of the vehicles.

Jack used his corporate credit card, the one that was tagged to a dummy corporation offshore, and rented a car. Rusty, of all people, would know of Jack's predilection for exotic cars (and his reasons for driving them), so instead, Jack chose a red Tesla Model S. With a 390-mile range, he couldn't get home on a single charge, but he could get close and charging stations were common throughout California. The Tesla was a perfect vehicle for this. They were now ubiquitous throughout eco-conscious California and would blend in. It also had a top speed of two hundred miles an hour and could accelerate to sixty faster than most production sports cars.

Jack looked off to the mountains to the east, just above the 5. The sky was dark with ash and smoke from the Wildwood Canyon fire and he was suddenly reminded that Reginald LeGrande, Vito Verrazano, and former Special Agent Scott Donners were not the only problems he had today. Jack powered up the Tesla, texted Enzo, and left the airport. They drove about a mile to a shopping center on Empire and left the Malibu in the parking lot outside of a Target. They wiped it down as well. When that was done, they tossed both sets of keys in a trash can, along with the can of wipes, and got back on the road. It was just about two o'clock in the afternoon. If traffic wasn't bad, Jack could be home by dinnertime.

They needed to split up. The FBI would put an APB out for two men traveling together and that would most certainly go to Highway Patrol to check the interstates. Unfortunately, dropping Enzo at an airport would mean doubling back, which Jack wasn't willing to do. Interstate 5 was the riskier choice, but it was also faster. They turned their phones off before getting on the road. Jack wasn't going to trash his until he knew he had a way of wiping the information on it. But he at least had his Frank Fischer phone so that Megan could get in touch with him if there was an emergency. Rusty didn't have that number. Still, he didn't call her to let her know he was on his way. He didn't want to tip his hand. If the authorities did call, better that she knew nothing.

No one spoke until Bakersfield.

"What do we do?" Enzo asked.

"What do we do about what?" Jack said, unable to muster any emotion for it.

"About fucking Rusty? He knows the plan."

"I know. But our choices are, we can hide the diamonds and pretend that Rusty is lying, see how far that gets us. Or we proceed with the plan and sell them to Cannizzaro. I don't see any other options, other than turning ourselves in. If we weren't going to do that back there, I don't see why we'd do it now. If you have other ideas, I'm open to it."

Enzo looked out the window at the sun-scorched central valley rolling by.

"That requires us to go to Italy," Enzo said.

"Yes, it does. I have two passports left, and Rusty got them both for me. I also have a federal conviction for passport fraud. If I get caught with a forged passport again, I'll get twenty years in prison." Jack stated it like it was a box score. "Cannizzaro made some kind of deal with a Russian gangster and is in over his head. That guy apparently needs a shitload of diamonds. If Cannizzaro doesn't get them, he keeps sending people after me until he does."

"Us, Jack," Enzo corrected. Jack could see out of the corner of his eyes that Enzo was looking at him. "Remember, I'm the one his people saw at Vito's house."

"Yeah, and most of those people are dead," Jack said, but that was a throwaway comment. They had to assume Cannizzaro knew about Enzo. For the first hour in the car, they'd listened to local radio news and learned nothing new. Jack suspected that the FBI wouldn't start leaking information to the press until later that night or possibly tomorrow, once they'd figured out their strategy. "Enzo, short of giving these things away and hoping Rusty has a change of heart, I don't see what other choice we have. I spent six years looking over my shoulder, waiting for Nico to jump out of a shadow. I'm not doing that again."

Jack assumed that Reginald and Vito were arrested, though he wasn't sure what they could be charged with, seeing as the FBI didn't have the diamonds. Neither of those two could finger Jack as the likely thief without implicating themselves. Legitimate businessmen wouldn't know the name of the world's leading jewel thief. Jack believed there might actually be a kind of insulation there. Reginald would only give Jack up if he was looking to burn everything down around him and believed there was no way that he could get the diamonds for himself.

So, that left Rusty.

Rusty's deal, at least as far as he'd told Jack, was that he gave the FBI Gentleman Jack Burdette and the diamonds. That was probably icing, though. Rusty's real value to them was whatever he knew about the operation that burned him as a counterintelligence officer. Rusty would still have to explain to his handlers why he didn't have Burdette, and that's where the problem lay. Rusty knew Jack's alias and, though he'd never been there, knew the name and the location of the winery. Jack also had to assume that his FBI file had Katrina Danzig's name all over it. That's where everything would fall apart for him.

If it wasn't for goddamned Rusty, this would have been perfect.

Jack was getting really tired of people double-crossing him.

"The only option that I see is for us to sell these to Cannizzaro and at least get him off our backs. Since he already controls a bank, we don't have the challenge of laundering it. We've got enough to run on that."

"Are you really going to do that?" Enzo asked sourly.

"Everybody runs," Jack said.

They continued driving in silence.

"We need to get new phones," Jack said. "And get you transportation. Do you still have that credit card I got for you?" Jack had set Enzo up with his own shell corporation a while back so that he could transfer the proceeds from their heists. There was a corporate credit card attached to that account, which Enzo should be able to use to get himself home.

"Olive Branch Global Services?" Enzo said, cracking a dry smile.

"We need to split up. I'm going to drop you here. You need to fly out of the country as soon as you can, before Rusty has a chance to give these passport names over to the FBI and they can get them to Customs and Border Protection."

"You're assuming he hasn't done that already."

"No, I'm assuming that the US government is a big, inefficient bureaucracy and that they just can't move that fast. You get out now. We can get new phones here in Bakersfield." Jack gestured at the low, dust-filled skyline ahead of them. "You can rent a car and drive to Las Vegas. It'll be really easy to get a flight out from there. You'll take half the diamonds with you."

"Hey." Enzo put both of his hands up. "I don't want to be caught with that shit," he said, and it was clear that his mouth was talking before his brain thought it through.

"Enzo, you're probably the only person on Earth that I trust anymore, but that only goes so far. I'm not taking any chances, and neither should you. We split the take here. At least this way, if something happens to one of us, the other one isn't out too."

"You better not be using me to test that passport theory of yours."

He said it in a way that Jack couldn't tell if he was joking or not.

Bakersfield was a long, low, dirty break on the horizon and didn't improve much as they neared it. They each bought a disposable phone and agreed to get new smartphones so they could communicate via a secure app. Jack said he'd find a new one to use since the FBI would know about the one they had been using. He knew that these apps had been built by people obsessed with privacy with the intent of having a form of communication that the government couldn't listen in on, but Jack was also not putting it to chance. Jack dropped him at a car rental place downtown. Enzo took his camera case with half of the diamonds hidden in it.

"This place has one of the highest crime rates in the country," Jack said. "Most of that is petty theft and property crime. I wouldn't hang around here too long."

"As soon as I have the car," Enzo said.

Jack said his goodbyes and told Enzo he'd be in touch with their next move. Enzo's assignment was to get Don Salvatore Cannizzaro's direct phone number however he could.

Jack hoped they'd both last long enough to make that phone call.

Jack had to backtrack across some desolate state roads to get back to Interstate 5, cutting across blasted farmland. By the time he'd made it to the Bay Area, they were already in the crippling height of San Francisco traffic. Even cutting across back roads, it was close to nine when Jack arrived in Sonoma. He dropped the car at the airport and took a cab to his house. Jack lived on a ridge with a west-facing view of the valley. He'd smelled the fire when he got to the airport, but it was so much more pronounced in the hills. Jack let himself into his house, locking the door behind him and walking straight through to the patio that faced the valley. Even in the dark, he could see that the air was thick with smoke, and Jack could see the glow of fire on the left ridge line as it slowly shifted between red, orange, and yellow.

Sleep didn't come easily that night.

Everything smelled like ashes.

JACK WAS the first to arrive at Kingfisher the next day. He'd called Megan in the morning to let her know he was back. She seemed upset that he didn't call when he'd gotten in, but Jack deflected, saying it was later than he thought. He couldn't face her and say that he'd come so far, only to have it all fall apart. Now, as he walked the grounds with his coffee, he felt like this would fall apart too. He'd slept poorly. It seemed that every time he closed his eyes, Jack sensed someone creeping up on him. He spent most of the night on the verge of sleep.

He gave up on rest early and started checking reports from CalFire.

Kingfisher was located at the northern end of Sonoma County, near the city of Healdsburg, which had been devastated two years before in the region's most destructive fire to date. Today, there was a large blaze between Chalk Hill Road and the Russian River, which at least was serving as a natural barrier. Jack could see that one burning when he looked west from his property, across CA 128. But a lightning strike had ignited a patch of dry underbrush in the mountains behind the winery, not far from Robert Lewis Stevenson State Park. Even in daylight, Jack could see the flames. There was black haze over the ridge lines in front of and behind the winery, and the sky looked like a yellow bruise.

Jack asked Megan to have the staff there by nine that morning, if they could. Megan was there about a half hour before the rest of the team. Jack found her waiting in the parking lot, leaning against her white Wrangler. She was in faded blue jeans and a light blue Kingfisher T-shirt, her auburn hair tied in a ponytail. She had a line of freckles across the tops of her cheeks, which bloomed like wildflowers whenever she was in the sun for long. Megan turned her head as Jack approached, and he could tell that she'd been crying.

The guilt he felt at that moment could not easily be put into words.

They needed him, *she* needed him, and Jack was nowhere to be found. Instead, he was pursuing a selfish fortune in stolen goods. He'd done it as much because Vito double-crossed them and Jack wanted revenge as because Jack wanted to show Niccoló Bartolo that he was the best. And he'd done it, just to find that his one and only choice now was to take those diamonds and run.

Special Agent Danzig had bailed him out once, but she'd been very clear that was a onetime deal.

The federal judge had said much the same.

Jack could turn himself and the diamonds in now, half of them, anyway, and could perhaps get some leniency, but that would be it.

He walked forward and took Megan in his arms. Jack held her for a long time, and he lied when he said everything was going to be all right.

MOST OF THE staff arrived at nine. A few people lived in areas that were under evacuation and hadn't shown. They had about thirty or so here. Jack surveyed the faces. Some were scared and some were angry and had every right to be both. They met on the patio, because that was the only place where they could seat everyone. Megan had brought a couple of large to-go carafes from a local coffee shop and some pastries. People drank, but no one was terribly hungry and the food went mostly ignored. Jack held a coffee in two hands and searched for words. The air smelled very much of smoke.

"I spent most of the morning looking at the latest CalFire reports and with county emergency services. So far, we are not under an evacuation order. That said, we can't predict which way the fires will go. For those of you that were here last time, fires made it onto the property." Jack shifted his coffee to his right hand and motioned with his left to the east. "These are a little farther out, yet, but anything can happen. Megan and I discussed it and agree that for the time being, we should stay open." There were a few murmurs in the crowd. "I want to give everyone the opportunity to work as long as they feel comfortable and safe, plus the county is going to need the additional revenue. Of course, if you are under a voluntary evacuation, you should feel free to go. I've also offered to help out any of the local wineries that have had to shut down already. If any of their people are looking for work, we can float them here as long as we stay open. That's what I know right now. What questions can I answer?"

"Where were you?" Corky said, and there was an angry note to his voice. "We needed you here, man."

A couple of people around the hospitality manager tried to hush him, but a few others nodded agreement.

Over the years, Jack had to find creative ways of covering for his trips overseas. For a long time, he'd been able to invent international wine conferences or meetings with other winemakers. As an up-and-coming winemaker and someone new to the trade, that wasn't a hard notion to sell. Then someone embezzled ten million from them and within a few months, an FBI agent fatally shot a Serbian criminal in their tasting room. Jack spun it all as an elaborate blackmail scheme, someone trying to take advantage of a businessman they thought was an easy target. It worked, but he knew there were doubts. The old where-there's-smoke logic. Jack winced at the thought and cursed himself for the analogy. His records with the FBI were sealed, that was one condition for his cooperation that his attorney had been able to secure. The idea being that if any of the international criminal networks he'd dealt with as a thief found out he'd ratted on them to the US government, Jack probably wouldn't last long. So, apart from Megan, his life as Gentleman Jack Burdette was a secret from his employees. Still, he knew that people here wondered where he was when something important was going on. Like, why he would leave for a few days right after they'd finished harvest and were starting the grape crush—and then wildfires.

Because I had to steal back a fortune in diamonds that I'd already stolen once before.

I won, only to lose everything else.

"Hey, he's right. It's a fair question," Jack said. "I had personal business, and I'm sorry." He wasn't going to lie, not to them. But he couldn't exactly tell them the truth. This was the only family Jack would likely ever have, and he honestly wondered if this was the last time that he was going to see them. He could also see in their faces that his one statement of dismissal wasn't going to mollify all of them. Corky had been with him almost since they opened, and if he was angry enough to say something, what could the others feel? But there was nothing else that he could tell them about where he was or what he'd been doing.

"Frank takes care of us," said a loud voice in the back. Lincoln. "He always has." Lincoln, whose title was vineyard manager, was in charge of keeping the grapes alive and, during harvest, managing the teams of seasonal pickers they used. Lincoln was the son of migrant workers and grew up mostly in California's agricultural central basin, the blasted near–dust bowl Jack had driven through the day before. Lincoln, who'd also been with Jack for close to ten years, was a good friend. Jack would go to his kid's little league games, though that was a long time ago. Kid was in college now. Later, he'd had his friend and attorney, Hugh Coughlin, help Lincoln's parents get their citizenship. "Whatever he has to do is his business." Jack could see the warmth and admiration in Lincoln's eyes. "Besides," Lincoln said, those same eyes lighting up with mischief. "Ms. Megan was here, and she's the boss anyway." There were some much needed ripples of laughter at that.

"He's not wrong," Jack said and looked over at her. The tone started to change. They spent another half an hour or so taking questions, and it was mostly about the logistics of whether the winery would close and what that meant. A newer employee, one who hadn't been through this before, asked if they would still get paid, and Jack reassured them that they would. "If we shut down because of the fire, everyone, *everyone*, will continue to get paid as though we were open. We'll keep that up as long as we can. We will supplement whatever you're getting from unemployment, so it's like you came to work." He paused another moment to let that sink in. "Corky, how are we doing on the weather?" Corky had come to him not long after Kingfisher opened, looking for something to do. He'd just retired from the Air Force as a weather officer and wanted something fun to fill the hours that had nothing to do with fighter pilots or Afghanistan. But with Corky's twenty-five or so years as a meteorologist, Jack tapped his experience every year starting in the late summer to help predict when they should start to harvest. Winemaking was a gamble every year. You wanted to push the harvest as late into September as you could to maximize the ripening, but there was always a danger that the autumn rains would catch you off guard. Anything left on the vine at that point was lost. Since he had a meteorologist on staff, Jack made good use of the expertise, and Corky was happy to help. He remained fascinated by the science of that job and was eager to apply that knowledge in a different environment.

"I think any day now," he said, somewhat sheepish after his outburst at the start of the meeting. "Obviously, we're really late for the year already, but there have been some isolated showers in the mountains." When most of the state was on fire, there was only so much humans could do to impact it. California's firefighters and those who traveled here from other states or even countries to battle the blazes risked everything to contain them and prevent loss of life, but so often it came down to when would the rains start?

Corky spent a few minutes giving an impromptu lecture on the meteorological mechanics of climate change's impact on the delayed start of the rainy season. It was over the heads of most of the people in attendance, but Jack felt it was important. And that's just what Corky did.

"Thanks, Cork."

Jack ended the meeting but reiterated to everyone that he would only keep the winery open as long as he felt it was safe. If anyone had to or wanted to evacuate, they should do it, and their job would be here when they got back.

As long as we are, Jack thought.

Jack realized that it was a Saturday about halfway through the day and was surprised to see as many people visit the winery as they had. It was still about half of what they would usually see on a weekend this time of year. Jack spent most of his day in the barn and the other two outbuildings, near the fermentation tank, the soon-to-be-filled holding tanks—where their wines were aged—and among the barrels that held the vintages from the two years before. This was Jack's legacy. It was the one good thing he'd done in this world. Now, he stood to lose it for reasons that were arbitrary and capricious, completely outside of his control. Jack, who had benefitted from enough luck to last three lifetimes, would never make an argument about whether this was "fair" or not, but it sure as hell seemed "wrong." He'd stand out here with a garden hose and keep the fires back himself if he had to.

Jack and Megan closed up so that people could get back to their homes and families.

"Follow you home?" she asked when it was all done. "I'll cook."

Jack put his arm around her. "Let's just order in. It's been a long day."

"Nothing hot has made it to the top of that damned mountain," she quipped. Jack relented, as he always did. They stopped by the market on the way home and picked up supplies for dinner. There was a lot of winery business they had to go over, but Jack hoped that could wait until tomorrow.

When he'd started Kingfisher, Jack established it as a corporation rather than it being listed in his name. The original purpose was to put as much legal distance between Kingfisher and Jack Burdette. His Frank Fischer identity was as good as they come, but it was still a fake, and though it would easily pass a state or a bank background check, if the federal government looked too deeply, they'd be able to figure out that the social security number had originally been assigned to a child who died in 1973. As the years went on and Jack became more attached to Kingfisher and the people who worked here, that corporation became a way of leaving something he loved to the people who mattered to him, should something bad happen. Hugh helped him set it up. Megan would get control of the corporation, and all of the employees would become partial owners. Obviously, that fell apart if there was ever a connection made between Frank Fischer and Jack Burdette and the money laundering he did, but if *that* happened, there wasn't much Jack could do but run.

Jack parked in the driveway and Megan parked on the street. He drove an Audi S6 most days but had a mid-90s Land Rover Defender, which he parked next to, that he was steadily restoring for the times when he needed to haul more than the Audi allowed. Jack's house was on a tight cul-de-sac, with each house getting a commanding view of the valley below. The logistics of it could be a pain, but Jack had never found a better spot on earth to watch the sunset. They made small talk as they approached the house. Megan had a bottle of a reserve Cab that a friend of hers just released, called "Implausible Deniability." The day she'd gotten that bottle, a week or so ago, Megan and Jack argued for a solid half hour on whether that label made any sense. Though they named their signature wines, they were all named for predatory birds, keeping with the "Kingfisher" theme. Jack wasn't sold on the increasing trend over the last ten years or so of coming up with clever names for releases. Beers did that. Jack always believed that the wine was its own marketing.

Megan cradled it carefully in her arms.

Jack one-armed a bag of groceries and held his car and house keys in the other hand. For a moment, he almost felt like life was normal.

They didn't see the form detach itself from the shadows and approach them from behind, but they certainly heard the voice.

"That's far enough."

There was no mistaking its owner.

TWENTY-EIGHT

Reginald LeGrande stepped out of the shadows with a gun in his hand.

Reginald's silhouette was framed by the shadowy black oak that dominated Jack's lawn and the fiery sky of sunset behind him.

"Go ahead and open up that door, old buddy," Reginald said with a dangerous nonchalance. "Careful not to drop those heavy things, now."

Jack interposed himself between Reginald and Megan and handed Megan the keys. "It's okay, Megs," Jack said softly. "Open the door. It's going to be okay," he said in a low voice. Reginald, hearing him, laughed.

Jack quickly thought through the situation.

The diamonds were in a concealed safe in his bedroom. As soon as Reginald learned that, he would use Megan as leverage to get Jack to open the safe, which he knew Jack would do. Then he'd kill them both.

Jack had a nine millimeter SIG Sauer P365 in a concealed holster underneath his shirt. It was a legally purchased gun, and he was licensed to carry it. Well, Frank Fischer was licensed to carry it, and that license was based on an ultimately bogus identity, but this wasn't the time to split hairs. He'd ditched the one he'd gotten from Rusty. Their only chance was for Jack to get a shot off before Reginald forced him to open the safe.

Megan opened Jack's front door and Reginald ushered them in with his gun, muttering with fake humor that it wouldn't do for the neighbors to see them. Megan walked into Jack's entryway and stopped, unsure of what to do next. Jack followed, flipping the light on as he went. He had an open floor plan. The living room was to the right of the entryway. The dining room was straight back with a wall separating it from the kitchen. The kitchen was spacious and open, connecting with the wall-length windows that ran along the house's western side, which faced the valley.

Jack stepped back toward the living room, giving Reginald room to enter. He made a mental map. There was a large Eames chair and ottoman about two feet behind him. Reginald stepped in and closed the door behind him, locking the deadbolt by awkwardly extending his left hand behind him. He never took his eyes off Jack.

Jack realized that he hadn't seen his onetime friend and mentor since his trial seven years before. Jack wasn't sure that he'd have recognized him if it wasn't for the voice. Reginald's once-blond hair was now mostly shot with gray and was longer than he'd typically worn it. Reginald had sported a mullet for years longer than it'd been fashionable (if that had *ever* been true), but it was now long and saltwater stringy, like a surfer gone out to pasture. He had a thick but well-trimmed beard, also gray. Reginald wore a brown jacket with a blue window-pane pattern, blue shirt, and tan pants.

"Back up, now. Can't be too close. Social distancing and all that."

Jack took a step back, and Megan, who was farther in the house, stayed where she was. Jack was now about three steps from Reginald. Too far to close the distance in time without a solid distraction.

"Mind if I set these down?" Jack said.

"Yes, I do," Reginald told him. "You know what I'm here for, so we can save the wasted time of you asking me. I have to say, I'm impressed that you pulled it off." Jack knew what he was doing. Reginald was going to make a point of describing everything that happened in Los Angeles because Megan was in the room. "Breaking into my house was uncalled for," he said, pretending to look around Jack's place. "But I guess this makes us even, huh."

"Do I have to listen to you talk, or are you going to get on with it?"

Reginald gave a forced half-laugh. "You have to listen." He smiled. It looked like someone pushing back the lips on a corpse. "It took me a while to figure out that you took the diamonds."

"You're a real dime detective, Reg."

"When they didn't mention anything about it on the news, I knew the FBI didn't have anything to brag about. Plus, none of the Italians got away, so I put it together that it could only have been you."

"You did that all by yourself?"

Reginald wasn't taking the bait. Instead, he was reveling in this. There was a smug, self-assured look that was smeared all over his face. "How'd you do it?"

"I walked up and took it," Jack said. "You didn't seem to need them anymore." He could deny it. There was nothing connecting him but conjecture, but Jack's assumption that Reginald would just use Megan to force him to do what he wanted was still correct. Jack wasn't going to take that chance, so he just admitted it. He also didn't think the extra few minutes of arguing would buy him anything.

"How'd you get past the police, is what I want to know."

Jack shrugged. He wasn't going to give Reginald the satisfaction of having Jack reveal how he'd stolen those diamonds in front of Megan.

Reginald laughed. "Always the ballsy one, eh?"

"Reginald, I'm not interested in bantering with you. I want to know what you're doing here, other than the obvious. If you're going to take the diamonds and fuck off into the night, fine. You can have them as long as I have your word that you'll leave us alone. But if you're going to just kill us anyway, I'd just as soon tell you to go to hell now and you can get on with it. I'll make you have to kill me."

"Jack," Megan said. "I get a say in this."

"Listen to the lady, Jack."

"Don't fucking talk to her, Reginald. Not ever." Jack knew that was a slip, even as he said the words, but his nerves were frayed, his control ground down to powder.

"Why don't you have her go fetch my things, and you and I can catch up?"

"They're in a safe," Jack said.

"Huh." And Reginald let his eyes slide over to Megan. "Too bad." Then he said, "You still didn't tell me how you pulled it off. How'd you just walk up to all those cops?"

"Speaking of cops, you sure sound like one. Asking all these whodunit-type questions. You wearing a wire, Reg? I mean, wouldn't be the first time, right?"

That got a laugh too, and if Jack didn't know better, he'd think it was genuine.

In 2000, Reginald was arrested for robbing a Beverly Hills diamond wholesaler. He didn't even get as far as the city limit. Reginald had tried to get Jack to go in on the job with him, but fresh off his narrow escape of the School of Turin bust, Jack passed. Reginald, Jack later learned, always blamed him for the failure of that score, believing that if Jack had been with him, they'd have gotten away with it. Seeing Reginald go up is what prompted Jack to develop the rules that guided his career.

Reginald got ten years for that job but only served a fraction of it. He turned snitch in prison, practically volunteering information to anyone who'd listen. Reginald got about seven years shaved off his sentence and spent the next decade as an informant to the California Highway Patrol, who also acted as the state police. Reginald helped them close dozens of cold-case robberies across the state. But mostly, he used his informant gig to set up rival thievery rings and take out the competition. The whole time he was working as Jack's fixer, Reginald was double-dealing with the state police.

It didn't seem plausible that Reginald could have escaped from that building with police closing in and the FBI already inside. Unless, of course, he was informing on them and they let him go so that he could lead them here. They wouldn't have let him have a gun, though.

"You've never been to prison, Jack," Reginald said softly. Though, sotto voce for him still sounded like a rock through a window. "So don't be too quick to judge what a man would do to get out. You've also earned a snitch jacket, if I'm not mistaken."

That was true, to a point. Jack used the FBI and the Italian police to set up Aleksander Anđelić in Rome. He felt no remorse over that.

"This is all fascinating," Megan said in a bone-dry voice. "But can you please get on with it."

"You heard the lady," Reginald said.

"No," Jack said.

"Excuse me?"

"You heard what I said. You never answered my question. If you're going to take the diamonds and kill us anyway, then fuck off. I'm not giving you anything. If you're going to take them and leave, we can talk."

"I guess you won't know until it happens."

"Not good enough."

Reginald shrugged and kind of smirked, though Jack thought it looked more like a pout.

"You have my word," Reginald said.

"That's *definitely* not good enough. Put your gun away, then I'll do it."

A short laugh issued from Reginald's mouth, and he growled a "no."

"You never told me why," Jack said, changing the subject.

"Why what?"

"Why you sold me out. I know you blamed me for getting caught in Beverly Hills, even though I had nothing to do with it. But why?" Jack had been holding that bag of groceries for a long time, and it was getting heavy. There was also the numbing sensation of whatever cold thing they'd purchased resting on the bottom part of the bag. He was starting to worry about his reaction time, if he needed it.

"You're stalling, but okay, I'll play along." Reginald wagged his gun in the direction of the table. "Honey, why don't you open up that bottle of wine in your hand, and we'll all have a chat."

Jack watched his eyes and could see that he was thinking things out. Reginald wanted to be clever, but he wasn't a stick-up guy and he wasn't used to having to control a crowd. Having Megan open the bottle of wine, an arrogant gesture intended to show how fully in command of the situation Reginald was, would do the opposite, and Reginald was now starting to realize that. Megan went into the kitchen for a bottle opener, and now Reginald had to cover both of them in two different parts of the house. Yes, she'd be in his line of sight, but her hands wouldn't be, and Reginald wouldn't know for certain what those hands were doing the whole time. Did Jack have a gun in the kitchen? He didn't know. It was a little far for a knife, but that would still force him to think about her as a threat, at least long enough for him to take his eyes off Jack.

"I'm setting this bag down," Jack said. Give Reginald something else to think about.

"You're fine where you are."

"No," Jack said. "You're not going to shoot me now or you won't get the diamonds. If you shoot her, I won't cooperate. That's the only leverage you've got." Jack slowly lowered himself to a squat while Reginald grumbled a "fine." Jack set down the bag and resisted the urged to flex his hand to get some feeling back into it. He didn't want Reginald realizing that it was numb. Jack stood.

Megan was to Jack's right, just out of arm's reach to him, and about five, maybe six, steps to the dining room table. Jack still had his back to the living room, and there was a large chair behind him. Reginald was near the front door but out of reach. Jack had turned on the entryway light when he'd stepped into the house. He pretended to do this out of habit, but he also wanted to put doubt in Reginald's mind about whether he could be seen from the street. Jack had a large front window, though the curtains were drawn. He had vertical blinds that ran the length of the wall that faced the valley, and those were open and filled the room with the fiery, if ash-hazed, sunset. That would be in Reginald's eyes if Jack could get him to take a few steps forward.

The entire house was filled with burnt-orange sunlight and would be, Jack knew, for the next thirty minutes.

"Can we get on with whatever the hell this is," Megan said, still cradling the bottle of wine in her hands. "Jack and I have dinner plans." Even in the face of a gun and an uncertain fate, though one that Jack couldn't possibly see as anything but bad, Megan still had her fire. Nothing, it seemed, would tamp that. You didn't really know a person until you saw how they reacted to stress. Most people folded when faced with possible death. That's why stick-ups worked. Seeing her stand up to Reginald like that, to not back down, just made him love her more.

And made him feel so much worse for what he knew was going to happen.

Reginald laughed again. It was that wet, throaty half-cackle. "Jack? So, she knows, huh?"

"You forced my hand on that."

"That right."

"You never answered my question, Reg. Why'd you sell me out? You set up Paul Sharpe to embezzle money from my winery because you wanted me to keep working. If my escape plan was slowly bleeding money, I'd still need you, need to keep working for you. But that doesn't explain why you sold me out to the police."

Reginald was quiet for a time before he answered. If Jack didn't know better, he might accuse Reginald of being almost thoughtful. "There wasn't some grand plan, if that's what you're wondering. Cops, they're like junkies, man. Always chasing that dragon. You give them information, they want more. What was general info about a landscape turns into needing specifics on jobs, on crews. You give them a robber, now they want a crew. You give 'em a crew, now they want the guy who set it up. You give them *that*, now it's a goddamn network, the logistics, where'd the information about the job come from. Every time you bump up a tier, you think that'll be enough, but they got you and they know it. They always hold that deal over your head, 'Gimme this or you go back to the joint.' They know that they got you and that you'd rather take your chances on the street for selling people out than go back to prison. Because *anything* is fucking better than that." Reginald didn't take his eyes off Jack, but they became unfocused and Jack knew he was looking at the past and not at him. "You were just the biggest fish at the time. They said I had to give them something worth their while. It'd been a bit since I gave them anything good, and it was time to jerk the line, make sure the hook was still set, you know?"

"So the Carlton job was always a setup? You promised the police a huge collar so you could get out?"

"No, not originally," Reginald said, his voice slightly wistful. "I was serious about that job. If you'd have taken it when I'd offered it to you, we'd have split that money and I'd have disappeared after that."

That event, in many ways, set Jack up to be exactly where he was now. He'd turned Reginald down because he thought the job was impossible when Reginald pitched it. He didn't know until he'd actually done it (albeit with a tremendous amount of inside help) that the security surrounding that collection actually was a joke. Jack often wondered whether it was actually Ari Hassar, the owner, who put the word out about the job. The Israeli diamond mogul was close to broke when he hired Jack to steal those jewels. Hassar claimed the insurance money and then quietly sold the stolen gems on the gray market after Jack handed them over. It would make sense that Hassar would've used a veil of incompetence and the very real seams in French law as it related to private security to make them a fairly soft target. Of course, Jack didn't know any of that until he told Hassar someone was coming for him.

When Jack turned Reginald down, Reginald had Paul Sharpe steal ten million from the winery's accounts. It was money that was supposed to be used for a tract of legendary Napa Cabernet vines. Jack transferred the money from his personal holdings to the winery, as Reginald knew he would, and Sharpe took it. But even after that was resolved, Jack had to keep working. They never got back what Sharpe embezzled from them, and Jack never made back the money that he loaned the winery for the purchase. That's what led him to Rome, into Aleksander Andelić's plot, to Vito Verrazano and the diamonds. It's what led him, ultimately, on a collision course with this moment. All he'd have had to do was take a job that broke his three rules, which Jack absolutely would have gotten away with, and he could have retired. Ari Hassar wouldn't have dispatched his ex-Mossad security team to hunt down the perpetrators, and Megan would never have known he was a thief.

Gaston Broussard and Gabrielle Eberspach would still be alive.

Shows what principles get you.

"Sorry, pal. It got to the point where I had to give them something...and only you would do."

"But why now?" Megan said, the anger in her voice boiling over. "I get that you tried to get Jack to steal things for you before, but why *now*? Why not leave us alone? Look outside, can't you see what's going on?"

This wouldn't help them. Losing their cool with Reginald was only going to show that he was getting to them, and that reduced their bargaining position even further. Desperate people didn't bargain.

"Lady, that looks like a whole lot of 'not my problem.'"

"Meg," Jack said softly, but if she heard him, she was past caring.

"Half of this county is on fire, and our place is right in the goddamn middle of it. Why can't you just let us be? What have you ever built? What have you ever done that wasn't taking something that you didn't earn from somebody else?"

He laughed again, and the sound was hollow and dry and horrible. "You're saying all that about me and you don't even realize you're in the presence of greatness. Honey, your boyfriend is the greatest thief of *all time* and you're yelling at *me* about taking things? So, yes, I am. But I'm not stealing anything that Jack here hasn't taken himself already. I've just let him do the heavy lifting."

"There's a special place in hell for thieves who steal from other thieves," Jack said.

"I'll let 'em know when I get there," he said, voice desert dry. "So, this was all fun, but I do have places to be. Also, the moralizing from you rings a little hollow, don't you think? How many people did you steal these things from, Jack?"

"I never intended to take them in the first place, but Anđelić pushed me into it. Everything after that was just me getting back what's mine."

"Well, then a fitting end to your journey is me ending up with what's yours," Reginald said with a leer. "Now, if you would be so kind."

"Let her go first, then I'll do it." Jack took a side step, moving him next to Megan, outwardly a reassuring gesture.

Reginald stepped forward, as if by a natural opposing force, in order to bring the menace closer, and the burnt-orange light of sunset lit him up fully. He squinted but wouldn't give Jack the satisfaction of having him close the blinds.

"That's sweet, but no."

"I'm not giving you a choice, Reg," Jack said in a perfectly reasonable tone. "She lives or you don't get shit. The diamonds are in a safe, which you can't open without me. I had Enzo pick it out, and he said *he* couldn't crack this one without a torch. So, you need me to open it, and I'm not going to do that unless Megan is safe. You'll have your diamonds but will just have to take your chances with everything else." Jack shrugged. "That's the deal."

"There's no dealing, Jack. That isn't what this is. Don't think I don't know what you're doing." Reginald's eyes dragged over to look at Megan. "I know how good of a con artist you are. Don't forget, I trained you."

Jack took another slow step backward.

"Stop moving," Reginald said abruptly. "The thing you're counting on, Jack, is that I want the diamonds more than I want to kill you. I've been in prison twice, now, and both on account of you. I think that's time enough for one man. And while I'd like to disappear rich, I'll sleep just as good knowing you're in the fucking dirt where you belong." Reginald punctuated it by closing the gap and raising his pistol from his hip to chest height. At this range, he couldn't hit anything *but* Jack.

The words of retort, the stalling tactic were forming on Jack's lips when Megan screamed.

It was a furious, feral noise, deep and throaty, cutting and raw. She charged Reginald, who'd been so focused on Jack he didn't even see her move until it was too late to do anything.

She'd changed her grip on the wine bottle she still held, gripping it by the neck, and swung that thing like a club for all it was worth. Megan, still roaring, brained Reginald with the wine bottle. It connected with the side of his face, and he made a strange sound that could only be described as pushing pain out of his mouth. His body caved with the blow, rolling inward as if pulling the energy transferred with the swing and carrying through. Jack watched in slow motion as a bright red spray of blood burst from Reginald's face, part of the bottle having connected with his nose.

Jack went for the SIG under his shirt.

Reginald fired.

Jack fired.

TWENTY-NINE

"This is Fuery," the voice said and sounded worn.

"Hi, Ray, is it? This is Katrina Danzig. I'm with the Gem and Jewelry Program, but I guess you heard I'm currently working out of the US Embassy in Rome. I'm sorry it took me so long to get back to you."

"Hey, no problem. Candle's got two ends, right?"

"That's right," she said, smiling into the phone and hoping the tone carried across the line. "Well, I got a quick rundown from the LEGAT here, but maybe tell me what's going on on your end. Sounds like we may be working different ends of the same case. Do you have time to compare notes?" It was early here, late there, but then time had a way of warping when you were in the thick of a case.

She heard Fuery exhale in the way that said it was just one more thing he had to do.

"Yeah, happy to. In fact, we're stalled out. I called Silva, what, two days ago, hoping maybe you guys had some more intel on *these* guys."

"I think there may be a lot of guys involved," Danzig said. "How about you just start at the beginning and catch me up. Then I'll share what I know. Does that work for you?"

"Sure thing. We're based out of the LA division, and my partner, that's Kent Reaves, and I were on the financial crimes squad for a long time, but recently they've shifted our focus to China. Not counterintelligence per se, more like trying to figure out what American businesses the Chinese are targeting. Anyway, there's a firm based here in LA, a brokerage house for precious metals, rare earth elements and gems. We got word about six months ago that their VP of operations was dirty, that he was setting up deals under the table for Asian buyers and taking side money for it. Guy's name is Carter LeMothe. Real asshole. Anyway, we get a wire up on LeMothe and find out he's meeting with these two who are allegedly diamond wholesalers. Story goes they leveraged their business for this huge gem buy right before the pandemic hit and then couldn't sell them, so they are looking for a buyer to take them off their hands."

Danzig smiled. "Any chance this business was based in Italy?"

"Matter of fact, it was. The principals, one American and one Italian. Their names were Reginald Burton and Vito De Angeles."

Goddamn it, she practically shouted in her mind. *That was it.*

"I think I know them," she said.

"Thank God somebody does."

"The Reginald, I believe, is Reginald LeGrande. Career thief and then started a second career as a fixer and a forger. We busted him for passports and money laundering about eight years ago. He's been in prison twice. The other one is Vito Verrazano. He's a thief, was pretty big in the nineties and has been in semi-retirement since then. The diamonds they are trying to move, we believe, were stolen from the Antwerp Diamond Centre in 2003."

"No shit," Fuery said, drawing the words out long. "That would have been useful to know last week." Then he said, "Hey, I'm not bitching at you. There was no way you could've known we had this going on. Let me just explain what went down and see where we're at. Cool?" Danzig said it was. "So, we have Carter set the buy up. We get a fake business going, websites, registry, the whole nine. Had a leased office space from another case. One of our agents here is a Chinese American, got him to pose as the buyer. Burton and De Angeles show up, and they have the diamonds brought in by armored car. That was the first indication that either these guys were on the level or they were really, really good con men. This is also where shit goes all the way sideways. Burton and De Angeles are meeting with our agent and the diamonds are being unloaded from the armored car. An SUV and a car come into the parking lot, full speed, and fence in the armored car. Cars unload shooters, three apiece, and an all-out gunfight starts. Reaves and I respond, take out two of them. They've gotten all of the private security, except for the driver, and our police assistance got another. We took four into custody. One was an Italian national and the other three were IOC. We figured out later after talking with our OC guys and LAPD Vice that the Italian nationals were told by their bosses back home to link up with LCN here in LA. So, while all this is going on, Burton…or LeGrande, I guess, slips out. He escapes out the back of the building and disappears. The location was right near a metro that also had buses and is literally in the shadow of the 105 and 405 interchange. By the time we knew he was gone, there were too many escape routes to chase." Fuery paused a moment. "LeGrande getting away is on us. My partner and I were so focused on backing up the Inglewood cops because they were taking fire, we didn't coordinate with our own. LeGrande slipped through the cracks."

"You don't need to apologize to me, Ray. I wasn't there, I've got no room to judge."

"Thanks," he said, and it sounded like he genuinely meant it. "Now get ready for the craziest shit you've ever heard."

And then Special Agent Fuery proceeded to tell her the craziest shit she'd ever heard.

Danzig listened as he recapped what he told her about the mafia assault, but now with the benefit of interrogation and assistance from the LAPD. He told her about an unknown suspect posing as a US

Customs agent convincing the Inglewood police's on-scene commander to relinquish control of the diamonds to his custody, apparently using a bogus search and seizure warrant to do so.

"Guy talked like a cop. Inglewood PD said that between the badge and the warrant, it looked totally legit to him. It seemed weird that he'd clear the diamonds from the crime scene before forensics hit it, but the PD, a Sergeant Fulton, said he wasn't about to question the feds either. 'Above my pay grade,' was what told us. Our leading theory was that LeGrande and Verrazano had a backup." Fuery said their names in a tentative way, as though he was testing them somehow for authenticity. "From what you're describing about their background, that seems highly plausible. Makes sense too, given how much was at stake. LeGrande and Verrazano are in with us and the diamonds get delivered. They've got cell phones. All they'd need to do is signal their guy that something sounds off, and he takes possession of the diamonds. Without the stones, we've got nothing to charge them with. Like I said, LeGrande slipped out, but we held onto Verrazano. Kept him over the weekend, notified the Italian consulate. They're checking into it, seeing if his passport is valid, but I ask them how long it'll take and all I hear is, '*Domani, domani.*'"

Danzig didn't mean to smile at his frustration, but she understood it well. Whenever you tried to box an Italian into committing to a time, it was always, "*Domani, domani,*" which meant "tomorrow." Tomorrow as relative to exactly what day was usually up to interpretation. She gave him a knowing half-laugh and said she knew what he meant.

"We're going to keep on Verrazano, see if he kicks anything loose, though I'm not optimistic on that. He doesn't seem to have a lawyer and hasn't asked for one. Hasn't asked for a phone call either. The lawyer thing is the only part of this that doesn't add up for me."

"How so?"

"Well, they had a fairly sophisticated operation up to this point, so we kind of expected they'd have your archetypal crooked lawyer on hand, but so far, nothing. Without the diamonds, I don't think we can hold onto him for long, but if it comes back that his passport was bullshit—and we think it is—that gives us some extra leverage. And you're sure that my Burton and De Angeles are your guys?"

"I am."

Danzig spent the next few minutes briefing Fuery on the sordid history of Reginald LeGrande. Danzig knew much less about Verrazano but shared what she knew—the School of Turin, Niccoló Bartolo, their bust at the hands of the Italian state police. And about Gentleman Jack Burdette. She told him about Bartolo stealing the diamonds in 2003, this time providing much more detail than she had earlier in their conversation, and how Verrazano stole them from the Commerce Bank and Salvatore Cannizzaro in 2019.

"Jesus Christ," Fuery said.

"I'm working with a CI in the Cannizzaro organization. He's their money guy. Verrazano was supposed to sell the diamonds to Cannizzaro, but instead he threw in with LeGrande and fled to Los Angeles. Even beyond the names, I'm convinced these are our guys. My CI told me that Cannizzaro had them tailed to the States when it looked like they couldn't make the grab in Rome. The goal was to pick the diamonds up and bring them back. That obviously failed, and now the diamonds are in the wind."

"Any idea why they didn't just ambush Verrazano while they were still in Italy?"

"The CI doesn't have a lot of firsthand information on this, but the guess is that Verrazano was already in the States by the time Cannizzaro figured out that he was switching sides. We don't know exactly how they learned this, but we can confirm they reached out to LCN in Los Angeles for support. Money was exchanged, our guy set it up. They got cars and guns, which matches what you've said."

Danzig could now confirm that the diamonds were in Los Angeles and that Verrazano and LeGrande attempted to sell them but failed. LeGrande and now a third accomplice, most likely someone he'd met in prison or, possibly an older partner. Verrazano was in custody, for now, and that was good. But she couldn't interview him herself. And she didn't think the situation was much changed. She had the word of an informant that Verrazano smuggled diamonds into the United States, but without a seizure, they couldn't actually prove it. Which meant they didn't have anything to charge him with, other than illegal entry and possessing a fake ID. But they could extradite him and let Bruni pick him up. That might be worth something.

"Where are you with the armored car company?"

"WorldSecure? They're stalling us. They're trying to pull some Swiss bank shit, claiming that they have to maintain the confidentiality of their clients' assets. But that's not going to last. A federal judge is going to order them to cooperate. We think what's really going on is that they didn't scrutinize LeGrande and Verrazano heavily enough when they agreed to take their diamonds, and they know it. They're just trying to buy time for their lawyers to get a defense together, but between you and me, they're fucked. They're looking at some huge fines and probably criminal negligence. We've already ripped apart this fake company that LeGrande and Verrazano created. As soon as we get WorldSecure to acknowledge that they received, stored, and transported diamonds belonging to these guys, I think we've got enough to charge them both."

"You may be on shaky ground there," Danzig cautioned. "This is my wheelhouse."

"Hey, I'm all ears. Help a brother out."

"Without the diamonds, a judge may not agree to take the case. Up until this point, all we have is intent. We need to have the diamonds so that we can force LeGrande and Verrazano to prove their provenance, which they won't be able to do. Unless you get Verrazano to cop to it or you find LeGrande."

"I see what you mean." Fuery was quiet for a time, thinking things through. "I doubt we're going to get much from Verrazano. I suppose there's a chance that we could get him to roll on his partner, but my gut tells me that's not likely. I'm leaning toward letting him go, making a big deal out of it, like, 'Hey, we know you're skating' and then putting a tail on him, seeing if he leads us to LeGrande. I can always arrest him once we get WorldSecure to confirm they stored diamonds for him."

Danzig didn't like it, but she had to admit it was probably the best option. It also wasn't her case.

Danzig couldn't tell him about Operation Flipside. She was barely cleared for it herself. All she could do was impress upon him how important it was that they recovered those stones. She would need to tell him that they would be seizing the diamonds immediately so that they could be used in the Cannizzaro/Sokolov sting, but Danzig couldn't tell him exactly why.

"Ray, I've got an idea. Our end of this is that my team is providing operational support to the Italian government to help them bust Salvatore Cannizzaro. In addition to being a mafia boss, Cannizzaro has a massive money-laundering and public corruption operation. But he's hidden it very, very well. And he's got a long track record of buying off cops and judges. I bring all this up to say, we need the diamonds in order to make this airtight." She paused a beat to let that sink in. "What if we offer Verrazano a deal. He gets us the diamonds and agrees to testify against LeGrande, so you make your case. Then he agrees to try to sell the diamonds to Cannizzaro. We serve that up to the Italian government, and they nail this fucker to the wall. Everybody wins."

"Do you really think he'll turn on his boy?"

"Hard to say without being there. I've never met Verrazano, I only know him by reputation. But if we can convince him that he's looking at prison time in the States or extradition to Italy for a conviction there—and I can tell you Italian prisons are no joke—he might just do it."

"Worth a shot, right?"

THIRTY

The room with filled with the fiery orange glow of sunset and the acrid smell of gun smoke, and no one knew what happened.

Reginald lay on the ground, half on the tile of the entryway and half on the carpet, blood pooling around him. Jack's shot hit him in the chest, and by the gurgling sound Reginald was making, most likely a lung. Reginald kicked his legs, probably for something to do, a reflex action. Something to take his mind off the pain. He was still conscious, though, his head lolled to one side, a complete wreck from where Megan hit him with the wine bottle. He gasped for breath in heavy, wet drags. Reginald had dropped the gun when he fell, and it was somewhere near his waist now.

"Are you okay, Megs?" Jack turned to her. She was on her feet, breathing heavily and still holding the wine bottle by the neck in her left hand. She didn't answer. She just stared at Reginald dying slowly on the floor.

"He was...he was..." Her breath came heavy and ragged, like she'd just run some great distance.

"Meg, are you hurt?"

"He was going to kill us," she said finally, ignoring his question.

Jack looked her over and didn't see any visible wounds. Then he checked himself.

Jack's shirt felt wet, and when he put a hand on his right side, pain blossomed out like an angry red geyser. Jack swore as the pain intensified. In all his long career as a thief, Jack had never been shot. He looked at his hand. It was covered in blood. He felt weak.

The orange sunlight that filled the room was starting to darken to red. Smoke from the pistols was still heavy in the air around Jack, as was the smell of expended gunpowder.

There was a sick, wet chortling sound expanding into the space around them. It took long moments for Jack to realize that it was Reginald laughing. There was blood on his lips, trailing down the corners of his mouth. Jack had seen men die this way. Reginald didn't have long, but whatever time he did have was more than he deserved.

Megan looked over and finally realized that Jack was shot. She sucked air in and rushed over, then stated the obvious. "Jack, you've been shot!"

"It's not bad," he said through gritted teeth. Breathing hurt. Everything on his right side was pure fire.

The room reddened and darkened.

Reginald laughed again.

"I didn't...I didn't...even think to check you. You were always such a pussy about guns." He grinned as he spoke. His teeth were framed in blood. "That's a pretty good hit," Reginald whispered, though it wasn't clear to Jack if he was referring to Jack's shot or his own. "How 'bout we call it a draw and you call me an ambulance."

Jack breathed in pained silence for a while. One hand was pressed over the wound, the other white-knuckled the pistol. He'd endured a lot over these last eight years, and much of that pain was caused by the man bleeding out on his floor. If there was justice in this world, this was it. But even in these last few days, Jack had been betrayed by someone he thought was a friend, and he'd won only to find out that really, he still lost. And now, in the face of all that, that thing he built and loved, together with the woman he loved, was going to go up in actual flames.

Jack found that among the dying light and the gunpowder smoke and the smell of wildfires that he could now see from his home, that he was all out of mercy.

The first shot was self-defense.

The second shot would be murder, and Reginald had earned both of them.

Jack held the gun out for a moment and then lowered it.

He wasn't going to do this, not in front of Megan. If he crossed that line, if he became that person, he would be no different than Ozren Stolar, Aleksander Anđelić, Clint Sturdevant. No different than Reginald.

And he wasn't going to give Reginald the easy way out with a quick death.

Jack knelt down next to him. LeGrande coughed, and blood spurted out of his mouth.

Jack leaned closer and lowered his voice. He hoped Megan wouldn't hear, but he couldn't help it if she did.

"You're going to die soon, Reg," Jack said. His voice was flat and even. "I could help you, but I won't. You deserve this."

"So, you turned into a killer anyway, huh? For all that lofty talk. You're just like the rest of us." Reginald coughed blood again. "Maybe worse...you...actually believe the lies you tell yourself."

"I'll never make excuses for who I am or what I've done. Those were all my choices. I could have walked away after Rome, let you and Vito have the diamonds, but I didn't. I thought you'd never leave me be. But, unlike you, I've done something, built something. It doesn't make up for the kind of life I've led, but it brings people a little bit of joy in a pretty fucked-up world. Maybe that's not so bad." Jack shook his head slowly.

"Filling a wineglass doesn't make you better than me."

"You'll only ever be a carrion bird, Reg. Picking at the scraps of better thieves."

Reginald coughed again, and it was an ugly, wet sound.

Jack stood up, and then he watched Reginald die.

It took the son of a bitch a long time to go. He sputtered and wheezed, but Jack could see the pool of blood beneath his body expanding farther and farther. It soaked into the carpet.

When he knew it was done, he didn't kneel down and close the eyes. Jack left him staring off into a heaven that would never let him in. He turned around and staggered over to the dining room table, where he set his gun.

"Jack?" Megan asked.

He pulled a chair and sat. He was very, very tired. "We have to call the sheriff, and I'm going to need an ambulance." Jack leaned his head against the back of the chair. Megan was already reaching for her phone.

"Are you sure you want to call the police?" she asked. "Jack?"

"We have to call this in," he croaked. "You did good, Megs. You saved us."

IT TOOK the Sonoma County Sheriff and an ambulance a little over an hour to get to Jack's house on the ridge. In that time, Megan got him a clean hand towel to hold over the wound and some water while she attended him with a first aid kit. Jack stayed in the chair with the gun next to him, just in case. Reginald had dropped his pistol when he fell, but it was still close to the body, so Jack had Megan kick it out of reach. If Reginald so much as twitched, Jack was going to empty the gun into him. But he didn't.

"What are we going to tell them?" she asked.

"We're going to describe it exactly the way it happened," he said. "But we're not saying anything about diamonds. There wasn't a lot of talk. Reginald told us to go inside, and we did as we were told. Reginald complained about going to prison, said it was my fault and that he wanted me dead. The fight happened exactly as it did."

Megan nodded.

There was the sound of hurried knocks on the door and shouts of "Sonoma County Sheriff" on the other side.

Jack and Megan sat at the table with the pistol next to them, the body of Reginald LeGrande between them and the front door, awkwardly sitting through the moment it took the deputies to open the door. Three uniformed deputies came in first, guns drawn and sweeping the room. Two of them covered Jack and Megan, instructing them to put their hands on their heads. Jack told them he was shot and couldn't lift his arms. Two men in suits entered after that. There were another few awkward moments as the deputies secured the room.

"Good evening, Mr. Fischer," Detective Sergeant Ted Navarro said. Navarro ran the Violent Crimes Unit of the sheriff's department. They must have sent him automatically when Megan said on the 911 call that there was a shooting and a man dead. Navarro had been in the job for some time. He and Jack first met when Danzig shot Milan Radić in the Kingfisher tasting room, after receiving an anonymous tip that Radić would be there. A tip Reginald called in.

"Hey, detective," Jack said.

Navarro and his partner spoke with Megan first while the paramedics were working on Jack. They told him he was really lucky. The bullet looked like it grazed him, but they wouldn't know for sure until they got him to a hospital and could X-ray.

There was a sheet over Reginald.

Navarro sat down at the table next to Jack. "We'll want to have a more detailed discussion at the office, once you're out of the hospital, Frank, but it's very important that we get the initial facts straight. Is it okay if I ask you some questions now, before the EMTs take you in?"

"Yes," Jack said. "And I understand."

"Great," Navarro said. The detective looked to be about Jack's age, late forties or early fifties. He had a light complexion, bushy black cop mustache that was now speckled with gray, black hair similarly dusted throughout. There wasn't a lot of violent crime in

Sonoma, but Navarro seemed much older than the last time Jack saw him. They'd interacted a lot in the time between Radić's shooting and Reginald's trial, and he'd even testified to those events. Jack had brought a case of wine over to the VCU when it was over. He said he wasn't sure if this sort of thing was appropriate, but if it was okay anywhere it would be here. Navarro said it was fine. "Can you tell me what happened?" he said.

"Megan and I came home from the winery. We'd just wrapped up shift and sent everyone home. LeGrande was waiting for us. I think he was behind the oak out front. I wasn't really paying attention. He stepped out and spoke, told us to open the door and go inside. I saw that he had a gun. We went inside, and he closed the door behind him."

"What did he say to you? Did he give you any indication of why he was here?"

Navarro was seated at the end of the table with his back to the kitchen. Jack's pistol was in an evidence bag in the center of the table. Jack looked off into the distance past Navarro. "Said it was my fault that he was in jail. He wanted to die a rich man but would settle for me being in the ground where I belonged."

"Then what happened?"

"He directed us farther inside, I was standing there, by that chair, and Megan was right here." Jack used his left hand, the uninjured side, to point to their respective locations. The front door had been open this entire time and now the room smelled like ashes and burned things. "I tried to get him to let Megan go, but he said no. I think his words were, 'That's sweet, but no.'"

"Did he ask you for money, valuables?"

"No," Jack said, and it was the first time that he lied to the detective. This time, at least. "I had the impression that he was just here to kill me."

"Were you aware that he was out of prison?"

"I was not. I knew that his sentence would be up soon, but I wasn't following the date. I guess I should have."

"And he didn't attempt to search you or Ms. McKinney when he entered the home?"

"No, sir. I had the pistol in a concealed holster. The weapon is registered, and I have a concealed carry permit."

Navarro nodded and made notes. He looked back up at Jack. "When did you get that?"

"In 2014. After the...well, after the other time." Jack followed it with a perfunctory half-laugh. Navarro nodded but otherwise didn't engage. He was very good, professional and even. Navarro didn't attempt to lead Jack in one direction or another; he just asked questions and took down the answers. This was dangerous for Jack because if he was only answering questions, responding to what was asked, he had no opportunity to steer the conversation. Jack knew Navarro would circle back and check on the answers later, come at it from different angles and try to poke holes in the story.

"Describe how the shooting happened," he said.

"Like I said, I tried to get him to let Megan go, but LeGrande wasn't having it. I had been able to set the bag of groceries I'd been holding down, but Megan was still holding that bottle of wine. My hands were full when he jumped us, which is why I couldn't go for my weapon at the time. Anyway, after he said no to letting Megan go, LeGrande stepped forward, closing the distance between the two of us and basically making it impossible to miss me. Megan screamed at him and swung the wine bottle at his head. He must not have seen her, or was only focusing on me. She must have hit him pretty good because I saw blood flying. I pulled my pistol and fired. Reginald fired too, I guess as a reaction. He fell. I didn't realize that I was hit until a few moments later."

"After you shot Mr. LeGrande, did you attempt to administer first aid?"

Jack paused, and again he looked off into the window far behind Navarro, beyond it. There was a time he'd have given a lot to save Reginald's life. Never his own—Jack had honed his self-preservation instinct to a keen edge early on. Though decisions he'd made over the last few years certainly could suggest that edge had dulled.

"No," Jack said with finality. "I didn't think he could be saved."

Navarro again wrote that down and nodded in his cool way. But this time he said, "Can't say as I blame you. Man did come here to kill you, and it wasn't the first time." Navarro closed his notebook and slid it back into his jacket pocket. He stood. "Thanks for your time, Mr. Fischer. I'll let these folks get you to the hospital now."

"Thanks, detective." Jack winced in pain, and it wasn't faked. "I appreciate your time." Jack gave him a half-smile. "I hope the next time I meet you, someone's not trying to shoot me."

"Well, word gets around," was all he said. "I'll be in touch next couple of days, let you know what's next in the investigation."

"How long until I get my house back?"

"Crime scene for now, but we'll wrap this up pretty fast. Day or two. Goes without saying, but I need you to stay in town next couple of days, least until we get this sorted out. Of course, if you have to evacuate, that's different. Just let me know."

The EMTs loaded Jack into the ambulance and took him to Sonoma Valley Hospital. X-ray showed that Reginald's bullet nicked Jack's rib and took a small chunk out of it but otherwise passed through entirely and missed all of his organs. They said he was extraordinarily lucky. If the bullet had been an inch to the left, it would have pierced his lung. A few more and would have severed his spine.

Six lives to go, Jack reasoned.

They kept him overnight for observation, and he was released the next morning. Megan picked him up.

She drove him into downtown Napa and a restaurant called Grace's Table, which was one of his favorites, so that he could have a nice meal. When she wasn't shifting gears on the drive over, Megan held his hand. They sat outside at a sidewalk table, drank late-morning coffee, and picked at grilled cornbread. "You don't have to talk about it," she said. "And you don't have to tell me anything about why he was there."

Jack's pulse jumped.

The diamonds.

They were in a safe concealed in a sliding floor panel in his bedroom. It was under a throw rug that ran alongside the bed, but it had been designed to perfectly match the existing wood paneling and was expertly done. If you didn't know what to look for, it would be very hard to find. There was a matching rug on the other side of the bed as well, so the rug itself didn't draw any attention. But that would deter casual burglars, not trained crime scene investigators. The sheriffs wouldn't be able to open the safe without a warrant and a locksmith, but if they found it, there would be the inevitable question of, "What was LeGrande really here for? Are you *sure* that he didn't demand something of you or know that you had valuables? What's in the safe, Mr. Fischer? If you've got nothing to hide, open it up."

Jack tensed suddenly, and Megan caught it.

"Are you okay?"

"Yeah," he said, but his voice was tight. "Sorry," he said through a forced smile. "I moved wrong and pulled it. Guess it'll take some getting used to." Jack took a sip of coffee. The historically sleepy downtown Napa was enjoying a resurgence, even with the wildfires. For years, there had been little traffic with most of the focus naturally being on the region's wineries, which were outside the city. Restaurants might last eighteen months and many specialty shops less than that. Even at this early hour, most of the street parking was taken up with cars, and people were walking the streets. It was great to see.

The air was yellow and gray with ash and smoke; it looked post-apocalyptic. Normally, the restaurant opened their windows once the morning chill burned off. Today they kept them closed. Jack had a view of Franklin Street up to First Avenue and could hear if anyone came out of the restaurant. "Is there anyone behind us?"

"No," Megan said, confused.

"Reginald was talking about diamonds. I think you gathered that much."

"Jack, you don't have to do this," Megan said, and Jack could tell by her tone that she meant it. "I don't want to know about it. It feels safer if I don't. What I want to know is what you're going to *do* about it."

"I just want to say this. These were stolen about twenty years ago in Europe—not by me," he added with a dead, humorless smile. "But they were never recovered, obviously. The owners were compensated by their insurers and never publicly acknowledged the theft. The insurance company wrote it off. I'm only telling you this because *that* job was something I'd never do. We got them in Rome."

"Does this have to do with what that Serbian gangster tried to make you do?"

Jack nodded and sipped coffee. "That's right. They were hidden in a bank that the mafia controlled."

"Jack, that sounds like details."

"Sorry. We got them, there was a bunch of double-crossing and guns, and Reginald's partner ended up with the diamonds. The reason I went to LA was to get them back. I thought Reginald had been arrested, actually. So, my partner and I have them now and need to figure out what to do with them."

"But they're illegal?"

Jack shrugged. "I guess, technically. Honestly, Megs, a certain percentage of the precious gems that end up in jewelry stores were probably stolen at one time."

"But you could just as easily let them all go, right?"

"Adjusted for inflation, they're worth about a hundred million dollars," Jack deadpanned.

"Or we could keep them," she said.

"It's not like anyone is looking for these. Nobody other than crooks, that is. I was planning on selling them off over a period of years, a little at a time. That's basically all the cushion the winery would ever need." In truth, the winery didn't *need* it. They were stable now and had been making a profit for the last few years. Jack hadn't recouped the ten million that he was forced to invest in order to keep it running eight years ago, but he cared less about that. What he needed was a vehicle to legitimize his money. This part was dicey because after Rome, Danzig told him that she wasn't going to send the IRS after his assets as long as he took the chance that was offered him and straightened out. This was not that.

"What would you do with the money?" she asked.

"A lot of it goes to charity. Always has. There'd be a pretty big donation to the California Red Cross, World Central Kitchen, some of the other groups that help out during times like this. I'd like to do some good with it. We've talked about buying more acreage so that we can grow different types of grapes. Could expand production." Jack took a long drink of his water, and their server appeared to freshen their coffee. "And I'm going to need to buy a new house. I'd never be able to live there knowing a man died on my floor."

They were both quiet for a long time, neither quite knowing what to say next. Megan's response surprised him, perhaps even surprised herself.

"I think I understand now," she said, "all the years that you justified keeping your money offshore and ranting about how you didn't want to give the government tax money if you didn't trust what they were going to do with it. I know a lot of that was for show, but I know you well enough to know there was truth in some of it." Megan lifted her coffee cup and held it in both hands, staring over the top. "They didn't help us, ever. We never got the money back that Paul Sharpe stole from the winery, just a bunch of bullshit excuses about 'the process.' That asshole from the state actually had the nerve to say 'at least justice was done' when they sent Sharpe to jail and looked at me like I had two heads when I asked him about the *money*." Megan shook her head slowly. She looked to her side, across Franklin Street, to the shops of downtown Napa that always seemed to be turning over. "I wouldn't go along with this if I thought you were stealing them fresh. I'd never support that, and the thing I told you before is still true. If we're going to have any kind of life together, you have to be retired. But if the owners of these diamonds wrote them off twenty years ago and you can sell them without getting yourself in trouble..."

The last words hung in the air like smoke, heavy and undeniable. "Let's let them work for us for a change."

Jack's phone started vibrating. He looked down at the number.

It was Special Agent Danzig.

Here we go again.

PART 3

A SUNNY PLACE FOR SHADY PEOPLE

THIRTY-ONE

"This isn't really the best time, if I'm being honest," Jack said when he picked up the phone. He'd told Megan who it was and excused himself from the table. Jack was now walking across the street and, in his mind, wondering if he was about to run.

"I can appreciate that," Danzig said, and there was hesitation in her voice. "Listen, Burdette, I need your help. I don't have a lot of time for our usual banter, so for a change, I'm going to skip the clever wordplay." Her tone was dry. "I also don't want to have to wave your deal in front of you, but I guess it's worth reminding you that part of that deal is helping out with jewelry theft investigations over which you have specific expertise."

"Katrina, I get all that." Her name sounded strange to his ears when he said it. Jack was used to referring to her only by her last name for so long and negatively. "Get on with it."

He'd also killed a man the night before and didn't have a lot of patience for government bullshit.

A stabbing pain in his side reminded him that he'd also been shot.

"I'm sorry," he said. "It's been a rough morning, and I'm a little thin on patience."

"I'll try not to take up too much of your time," she said in that same dry tone. "So, I have your cooperation?"

"I mean, sure. Whatever I can do," Jack said, annoyed. He started to calm a little, realizing that she wasn't calling to distract him while law enforcement officers rushed in to arrest him. Jack had gotten halfway down the next block, and he turned and slowly started walking back toward Megan.

"Okay. I just need to remind you that what I'm telling you is confidential. I shouldn't even be sharing this much, but I don't have another choice and time is a factor."

"I got it," Jack snapped.

Danzig ignored it. "When I visited you at your winery, I told you that Vito Verrazano had possession of diamonds stolen by Niccoló Bartolo in 2003. We were assisting an investigation with our counterparts in Italian law enforcement to arrest a mafia don named Salvatore Cannizzaro. We believe that Verrazano was going to sell those diamonds to Cannizzaro. Cannizzaro was using that to establish himself as a major player in the international smuggling world. Only, the deal never happened. Verrazano disappeared. Instead, he came to the US and linked back up with an old friend of yours, Reginald LeGrande."

Jack noted that in Danzig's speech, she didn't use the term, "we believe" when talking about Vito bringing the diamonds to the States. She implied they *knew*.

Danzig continued. "Reginald is out of prison. My team is trying to get in touch with the California attorney general and the Bureau of Prisons, but it seems as though he qualified for an early release. Reginald and Vito were able to smuggle the diamonds into the US and attempted to sell them. In truth, they stumbled upon a sting operation run by the FBI in Los Angeles. I won't get into that. They were about to make the exchange with an undercover agent when Cannizzaro's people showed up."

"What, here?" Jack said, feigning surprise. The relative calm he'd felt a few moments ago started draining away now that Danzig was approaching the event. Still, if she thought he was a suspect, they wouldn't be having this conversation, right?

"Yes, here. We believe that Cannizzaro sent his people here and they linked up with elements of Italian organized crime in Los Angeles. Part of me telling you this, Jack, is to warn you to be careful. With Reginald, Verrazano, and now the Cannizzaro mafia all in California right now…" Danzig's voice trailed off. She cleared her throat. "There was a shootout between the mafia and local police. Reginald somehow organized an armored car service, and the shootout started just as they were unloading the diamonds from the truck to bring them inside. You probably saw that on the news. Reginald slipped away in the chaos. But a third perpetrator approached the police after the shooting stopped, identified himself as a federal agent, and showed a fake warrant."

Jack's mouth went dry and his pulse skyrocketed.

He looked across the street to Megan, who waved in a kind of silly gesture, like it was the first time she was seeing him that day. Torrents of guilt washed over him because Jack knew he was about to run.

"This individual convinced the police he was a federal agent, took possession of the diamonds, and disappeared. We have Verrazano in custody now."

Jack could almost hear the stopwatch ticking off the seconds he had left.

"So, how can I help you," Jack said, his voice husky.

"There are a couple of ways. First, do you have thoughts on whom Reginald might be working with? I know that you two were close before he, well, before he did what he did. Are you aware of anyone he might have been working with? The man was described as a middle-aged white male with dark hair. He was wearing sunglasses, so the local police didn't get a great look at him."

"I'd have to think," Jack said hesitantly, stalling for time to think through the implications of this as much as trying to sell the idea that he was thinking to answer her question. "I mean, no one comes to mind, but it's been, what? Eight years since Reg and I worked together."

"I thought so, but it was worth an ask. Do try to give it some thought, though. The other area I wanted your help with is locating LeGrande. I need to recover those diamonds quickly. They are instrumental in our operation against Cannizzaro. We—"

"Katrina," Jack said. "Reginald is dead."

"What? That's impossible. We can place him in Los Angeles in an undercover buy on Thursday."

Jack spoke in slow and measured tones. "Last night he showed up at my house and tried to kill Megan and me. Said it was payback for all of the years he spent in prison. Apparently that was my fault, or maybe he just wanted revenge, I don't know."

"What happened?" There was a wild incomprehension in her voice.

Jack knew he had to be careful here. Yes, he had a concealed weapon that was licensed with the state, but that license was based on a false identity, which defeated the purpose. "Reginald hid outside my house, waiting for us to come home. He had a gun, forced us inside. I tried to stall, get him to let Megan go at least, but he wouldn't have it. He talked for…for a long time. Rubbing it in. Eventually, his patience ran out with my stalling. Megan distracted him, she hit him with a wine bottle, and then I shot him with a pistol I had on me. It was enough." Jack paused. "Reginald managed to get a shot off. He hit me, grazed really, nicked a rib. I was just released from the hospital. The Sonoma County Sheriff has the investigation now. I'm happy to connect you." Jack gave a short laugh, one without humor. "Same detective as last time."

Danzig was silent for what felt like a long time. Jack stood on the corner, somewhat awkwardly. A car rolled past and slowed, and he immediately looked to duck around a corner, the twist sending a shooting pain through his side. He realized it was just some person who thought he was trying to cross the street. Jack smiled and waved them on.

"LeGrande is dead," Danzig said, as though her mind hadn't quite comprehended it yet. "And you're okay?" she asked, finally.

"Hurts like hell. I'll live."

"I'm sorry," she said. "Jack, what I'm about to ask you is very important. I know that you've just been through an experience...and I know what that is like. It'll take some time to process. But what I have to ask you is very, very important. I apologize in advance because this is going to sound callous, and it's not meant to be. I'm in Rome. The agents in Los Angeles are looking for this third accomplice, but they have very few leads. So, I need your help..."

IT WAS INSANE AND SURREAL.

It defied all logic and reason.

Danzig wanted him to find the diamonds. She said if there's one person in the world who can, right now, it's Gentleman Jack Burdette. Her deal was simple, but it was absolute. Help her and she would process him as though he were in witness protection. She would arrange it so that his name was legally changed to Frank Fischer, and he'd be given a new social security number. Jack Burdette would be...dissolved, as though he'd never existed.

All he had to do was locate the diamonds, deliver them to her, and he would have his way out, for good.

Well, he had to come up with a convincing story that would show how he found the fictitious third partner, managed to steal the diamonds from *him* in a way that seemed shady enough to believe, and deliver the diamonds to Danzig in Rome.

He had forty-eight to seventy-two hours, she said.

Jack couldn't go home.

The Sonoma County Sheriff's forensics team had what they needed from Jack's house by the next day and would turn the keys back over to him. His gun was now evidence. Navarro told him it was going to take longer than he thought to formally clear the case, because everyone—himself included—was helping out with the fires. There were mandatory evacuations that had to be enforced and voluntary ones that had to be encouraged. Navarro did, however, tell Jack that he would be closing the case as soon as he could. Jack could tell how distracted the detective was when they spoke, his mind was clearly on two or three other things at the same time.

"I'm probably not supposed to tell you this," he said, "but it's pretty clear to me that it was self-defense. LeGrande had a clear revenge motive, and the gun he used had the serial numbers filed off. You and Ms. McKinney have the same story. Mostly, this is just waiting on me to finish up the paperwork. I'll get to it when I can, but it's hell around here. Sure you can appreciate."

Jack said he could and he thanked the detective for his time. Jack could pick his keys up at the station in downtown Sonoma. He told Jack that there were remediation companies that specialized in removing blood from crime scenes, though he might have to call down to San Francisco for one of those. There were plenty now that specialized in remediating fire damage, and they might be able to help him.

For the time being, Jack was staying with Megan.

After breakfast and his call with Danzig, they went back to her place and Jack tried to lie down, get some sleep. Eventually, he must have napped because when he woke up, Megan was gone. She left a note saying she'd gone into the winery. They both processed things differently, and when Megan was under stress, she needed to do something.

They agreed the winery would stay open through Monday, though the fires were getting closer and the staff was getting nervous. They could see flames in the hills behind the winery now. There wasn't anything on the property yet, though if the winds shifted that could change very quickly. Jack and Megan already made the decision that working was optional; if anyone wasn't able to come in, they understood. They would make a call Tuesday whether to shut down and let folks go home. It looked like that was what would happen. Some of the staff was forced to evacuate already.

Megan huddled the remaining staff on Saturday and told them what happened to her and Frank. It was difficult, in the moment and under stress, she told Jack later, to remember to refer to him as "Frank" in front of the staff. She told them that the man who was behind the embezzlement eight years before and had gone to prison for it showed up Friday night and tried to kill them. He wanted revenge. She said after the thing that happened at the winery years back, for those that remember, Frank carried a concealed pistol and shot Reginald LeGrande. If he hadn't, he and Megan would have been killed. She told them Frank had been shot, it wasn't bad, and he was already out of the hospital but would probably take a couple of days off.

Jack had at least that long to figure out what he was going to do about the diamonds.

Navarro's people had searched the house to verify Jack's story that Reginald was only there for revenge, and if they found the safe, they respected his privacy and didn't say anything about it. Jack thought the investigation might have been more thorough if there hadn't been the fires to contend with. He also thought that was bitter irony. The thing that would likely destroy the civilian life he'd worked so hard to build was the thing that protected his criminal one.

Jack drank in the dark.

Megan had gone to bed, but Jack told her he couldn't sleep and stayed up for a nightcap. He needed to think. Megan, surprisingly, had a taste for bourbon. She said after being around wine all day, there were times that was the last thing in the world she wanted to drink. Jack helped himself to a glass of Four Roses Single Barrel and brooded.

It was hard to believe Reginald was dead.

Harder to believe Jack had killed him.

And would walk for it.

After Reginald's betrayal eight years ago and Jack having learned about the long years of deception leading up to it, Jack had wondered about this moment. He'd dreamed about it. Wanted to see the smug, arrogant look on Reginald's face drain away like so much blood. In truth, Jack found, a revenge fantasy was much less satisfying.

He'd still killed a man. Regardless of the fact that it was Reginald and regardless of the fact that his mentor had earned this, Jack killed him, and that was not an easy thing to live with. He tried to force himself to think about what Reginald had done, to conjure up a justification in his mind. He thought about the ten-million-dollar theft from the winery that he set Paul Sharpe up to pull and how, even today, the aftershocks rippled through Jack's business and his life. Both lives. Jack tried to force himself to think about the harm Reginald had done so that he could ease his mind with what *he'd* just done. He thought about the two friends Reginald had ordered killed, or, at least, hadn't tried to stop. Jack wanted that to be insulation. But it wasn't. His mind went to everything else. To the long-distant memories of when they'd been friends. To the scores they'd pulled together, the reminiscing on Reginald's boat, and going all the way back to Jack's earliest days when he'd recruited Jack, a wet-behind-the-ears kid boosting cars.

It came down to a fairly simple calculus. Jack had killed a man.

That's what he thought about, alone and in the dark.

Not the hundred things Reginald had done to earn it.

It was the one or two things that made Jack feel guilty for having done it.

There was a time in the night, probably into the second bourbon, where Jack sat on the couch and stared at the door, waiting for it to bust open and for police to pour in.

But they never came.

The night passed slowly, and eventually Jack slept. He crashed on the couch so that he didn't bother Megan. He woke to the sound of her making coffee. While it was brewing, she came and joined him on the couch, gently taking his head in her hands and placing it on her lap. She ran her fingers through his hair but said nothing.

Jack took his coffee and went out on her deck to make a phone call.

Megan lived in Santa Rosa, a small community to the north of the town of Sonoma, about twenty miles from Kingfisher. The house was on a mountainside covered in black oak on the western edge of town, and her deck looked out over the valley. She had neighbors in the technical sense, but they weren't close. Jack set his coffee on the deck railing, under the thick clouds of the marine layer, and watched the sky, a universal gray slab, for a time. Then he called Enzo using the burner they'd bought right before they split up. It would be night in Italy. Jack also realized that he hadn't considered the fact that the phone wouldn't have an international SIM card and might not work in Italy.

So, he was actually a little surprised when Enzo picked up on the third ring.

"Hey," Enzo said, and his voice sounded rough.

"You okay?" Jack asked.

"No," Enzo said. "I couldn't get on the plane."

"You what? Where are you?"

"I'm in a hotel in New York."

"In the city?"

"Yeah. I was supposed to fly out of JFK yesterday, but I couldn't get on the plane."

"Why not?"

"Because I've fucking never smuggled anything before," Enzo snapped.

Jack couldn't fault him for that. Jack had never tried to hand-carry thirty-five million in diamonds either.

"I understand," Jack told him. Then, "Reginald's dead. He showed up at my place, must have gotten away from the police in Los Angeles. He was going to kill me."

"But you got him instead, I guess?" Just like that.

"I did. If there's a small measure of justice in this world, Reginald got what he deserved," Jack said, then was silent for a few moments. "Were you able to get Cannizzaro's number?"

"Ahhh, yeah. It took a couple of favors, but I got it." Enzo's voice was subdued and a little halting. "Let me know when you're ready."

Pressing the burner between his ear and his shoulder, Jack grabbed his other phone. Enzo relayed the numbers, and Jack typed it into a note using his thumb.

"Anything from Rusty?" Enzo asked.

"No," Jack said. That moment seemed a world away, but it had just been days. "I didn't hear from him." By now, Rusty would have checked in with his handlers and explained the situation. They were counterintelligence guys, not jewelry guys, but they would certainly notify Danzig of their involvement. Right? They would have to tell her that their source, Rusty, could place Jack in Los Angeles.

Jack pinched his eyes shut.

A week ago, this was such a simple job. They were just trying to get back what was theirs. Stealing something that was already stolen. But it had gotten so far out of control since then. So far past the point where he could have, *should* have walked away.

Jack thought about telling Enzo of his conversation with Danzig. On some level, Enzo had a right to know that. It foundationally and fundamentally changed how they went forward. Or if they even did. After all, this deal got Jack a way out but there was nothing in it for Enzo. He'd have come all this way and risked his life only for Jack to get a deal.

But that's not an easy conversation to have, even with a friend. *I've got a deal, you don't, but you should give me your share of the take anyway.*

"I think we just focus on how we sell these things. Rusty is really for me to worry about, I guess."

"If you're sure."

Was he?

In their conversation earlier, Danzig shared a version of Thursday's events that sounded to Jack's ears like an abstract painting being described by an unreliable narrator. Reginald's buyer was not a Chinese smuggling operation or criminal outfit but an undercover FBI agent. Jack established his alibi in telling her that he'd shot and killed Reginald, which she would no doubt verify with Detective Navarro. It seemed he was clear for the time being.

Until they broke Vito.

Aside from Rusty, Vito was the only one who could actually place Jack in Los Angeles.

Danzig had offered Jack a new deal, rather than compelling him into cooperating on the basis of his other one, and she used the only real carrot that she had left.

She'd make Frank Fischer permanent.

The other thing was that she'd request that Jack's previous conviction be amended so that Frank Fischer could hold a passport. Danzig didn't know that Jack had a place in Tuscany, just that he wanted to be able to travel.

He would get to be Frank Fischer for real and forever.

All he had to do was find the diamonds and deliver them to her in Rome in forty-eight hours.

The diamonds that were already in his possession.

The deal was predicated on the fact that Jack had been at home in Sonoma when Reginald and Vito attempted to make the sale and that there was an unidentified third accomplice, rather than Jack, who took the diamonds from that Inglewood cop. He had no credible story for showing how he could come up with that haul in the forty-eight hours she'd given him, and if he said he was involved, it would be a violation of the deal he already had.

Jack won, only to lose.

But Danzig was also pragmatic. Maybe she wouldn't ask too many questions about how he found them. Jack could just make up a bunch of bullshit about criminal networks and contacts and such. That sounded thin as he thought it, but there was, perhaps, a thread he could pull on. Maybe he could convince the FBI to let Vito out of custody on the premise that Jack would follow him to the stash. No, that wouldn't work, they'd just follow Vito themselves.

If this was going to work, Jack had to figure out a way to convince Danzig—in a way that would stand up in an official report—that he found the diamonds. The "don't ask questions you don't want to know the answers to" defense would work with a civilian, but it wouldn't fly with a federal agent. Or would it? Jack knew firsthand that Special Agent Danzig would push the rules to the breaking point if it served her.

The FBI let these things slip right out of their grasp, and if they could quietly get them back before the public found out the depth of the blunder, they would do it.

The thing Jack had learned about diamonds was that people never really wanted to know where they came from.

THIRTY-TWO

When Fuery told her the story of how one of LeGrande's companions stole the diamonds right out from under the FBI's and the police's collective noses, he described it as the craziest shit she ever heard. And up until that point, it had been true.

Vito Verrazano didn't want to deal.

Or at least Vito De Angeles didn't.

Because the entire time he was in FBI custody, he didn't waver from his story that he was Vito De Angeles and not Vito Verrazano. The one thing he did do was lay everything at his partner's feet. Reginald Burton organized the import of the diamonds into the United States, had organized the flight that carried them, and had arranged the sale with Pan Pacific. Did Mr. De Angeles think it was strange that members of an Italian organized crime family showed up at the exact moment of the sale and attempted an armed takeover? Of course he did, but he had no advance knowledge of that and didn't appreciate the insinuation that because he was an Italian that he had mafia connections. De Angeles did find it strange that his two "private security" men didn't have any identification on them or badges or anything that identified them as licensed private security. But again, he didn't ask too many questions.

He was an old man, you see, and simply wanted to close this deal and retire.

Mr. De Angeles didn't seem to deny much that he and Burton were running a shell of a company, which was not in and of itself illegal. Whenever they pressed on where the diamonds came from, De Angeles told them that he and Burton had acquired them through a series of deals over the years from smaller wholesalers, most of whom went bankrupt during the various global economic downturns of the past decade. They'd been holding them for the right time to sell, which seemed like now.

And he didn't know who the third person was and stuck with that through several rounds of questioning. De Angeles told them he started to suspect his partner might be trying to double-cross him once they got the diamonds into America and had them stored at WorldSecure. Obviously, they would want them in a secure location, but though the account was in their business's name, only Reginald Burton could access them. De Angeles asked to speak with the Italian consulate several times and continued to deny any knowledge of the identities of any organized crime figures that had attempted to steal from them. Nor did he know how *they* knew where and when the sale would be.

At one point during questioning, Fuery suggested that maybe if De Angeles thought that Burton was going to double-cross him, he'd try to flip the tables and make a deal with the mafia to bring his own heat. De Angeles got so furiously upset by this that Fuery admitted to Danzig in his recap of it that *he* was almost starting to believe that Verrazano was actually Vito De Angeles, mild-mannered gem broker.

Mr. De Angeles repeatedly denied knowing anyone by the name of Reginald LeGrande, Vito Verrazano, Niccoló Bartolo, or Gentleman Jack Burdette.

Monday morning, they had to cut him loose.

They couldn't charge him with smuggling diamonds. The

customs paperwork checked out, and they'd paid the import duties through their company. The FBI couldn't actually prove there had been any crime committed, at least as far as Vito De Angeles was concerned. They had his passport, and it wouldn't take long to prove that was fake, but the most they could do there was just kick him out. And that was a Customs and Border Protection problem, not an FBI problem.

The US Attorney agreed that the company De Angeles and Burton allegedly ran was bogus, the two security guards they had (now deceased) were most certainly hired muscle with illegal weapons, and the mafia connection between the diamonds and De Angeles was much more solid than he was letting on. But the US Attorney said they didn't have enough to hold De Angeles on and they couldn't keep him. He also wasn't interested in having the Italian government bark at him for detaining one of their citizens unless they could absolutely prove that he was complicit in a crime. The new administration was keen to distance itself from *that* legacy.

Fuery said they had to let him go but were going to follow him to see if he linked back up with LeGrande.

Choi shook his head.

"That is the craziest shit I ever heard," he said. He and Danzig were at their spot in the LEGAT office at the US Embassy in Rome at a table they'd been able to confiscate. They had a table that was barely able to accommodate their squad and a wall where they could tape up case information. It was late and there were a pair of empty Birra Moretti bottles on the table and fresh ones in their hands. Like most buildings in Europe, the embassy didn't have central air and it was stuffy. A fan lazily pushed air around the room. "So, where does that leave us?"

"Burdette," Danzig told him. "Something tells me that Verrazano wants out. The way Fuery described it, that guy just wanted out of the room and out of the situation. 'I'm an old man and I just want to retire.'"

"Like maybe his heart wasn't in it?"

"Or he's cutting his losses. He makes a play with Cannizzaro, decides not to do that. Cannizzaro now wants him killed. He makes a play with LeGrande and that falls apart. LeGrande is dead. I think the guy just wants to GTFO."

"Can we use him?" Choi asked. "Extradite him home and use him to help with Cannizzaro?" Choi took another sip of beer and then answered his own question. He was in chinos and a navy FBI polo, his feet were on the chair in front of him. "Though without the diamonds, I suppose what can he help with, other than affirm that Salvatore Cannizzaro is an asshole."

"He could testify that he intended to sell the diamonds to Cannizzaro, but unless we have them in hand, that doesn't do us any good. And it doesn't give us Sokolov. I could give a shit about a mafia boss."

"But our friends here do," Choi said.

Danzig exhaled and nodded. He'd been advising her all along to attempt to play nice with their Italian counterparts. For as much a festering asshole as Bruni was, obstructing his investigation did not serve the Bureau.

Choi knew they were alone, had been for some time, but still twisted his body around to check his surroundings. Their squad were the only ones in the embassy that were read in on Operation Flipside. "What gives you any confidence Burdette is going to play along?"

"Because I'm giving him legitimacy. That's what he's looking for. The setup would work like witness protection, but he's already got a name. It's a paperwork exercise."

"You talk to the marshals yet?" Choi asked, smirking.

"If it helps us get Sokolov, we'll get whatever we need. But it's still risky, I admit that." Danzig sipped her beer and was quiet. "And I'd only trust this with him. Burdette has too much to lose. He could have stolen those diamonds from Verrazano any time in the last two years, but he didn't. If he wanted them, he'd have taken them already and vanished. But that's not what he wants. You were there." Danzig tipped the end of her beer bottle toward Choi to emphasize the point.

"I don't know," Choi said. "But I agree that we don't have any better options. With LeGrande dead and this unknown in the wind..." Choi let his voice trail off.

Their lack of leads on this third accomplice bothered Danzig, but she didn't want to put voice to it. She was putting a lot of hope on Burdette and counting on him to be able to reverse engineer the plans of a dead man in a matter of two days, get the diamonds back, and then transport them safely to Europe. She could manage the latter, would have to, but there were a hell of a lot of "ifs" between now and that point.

"Is there a way to get Sokolov without the diamonds?"

Danzig laughed.

That line had become a running joke between them. Operation Flipside hinged on them being able to arrest Sokolov for attempting to traffic a reported hundred million in stolen diamonds. Choi asked at least once a day, usually to break the mood, if there was another way. The first time he'd asked, it'd been a serious question. They could approach him, "they" being a representative of the United States government, with an offer to help him out of his current predicament in exchange for the intelligence they were after on the Russian president. However, that mode fell into espionage territory and would be an operation better suited for CIA. The FBI's play here was already incredibly tenuous. Flipside was a bold, daring, and extraordinarily risky operation. If this went badly, the downside impacts would be catastrophic and generational.

Which was why Danzig was willing to take a gamble on Gentleman Jack Burdette.

If there was anyone in this world she could trust to steal something out of spite from Reginald LeGrande, dead or alive, it was him.

The question wasn't would he do it, it was could he do it in time?

THIRTY-THREE

Jack dialed Salvatore Cannizzaro's number from the burner.

He had to hold the phone in his left hand because his right side still hurt from the gunshot.

"Speak English, and I don't have a lot of time for bullshit," Jack growled. "Don't be stupid and hang up. You already know why I'm calling."

Cannizzaro answered the phone in Italian, which Jack spoke with near fluency, but the man he was impersonating did not.

"Is this LeGrande?"

"He's dead. And Vito was arrested. You don't need to know who I am."

"If I don't need to know who you are, then I don't need to talk to you. So fuck off."

"Sturdevant," Jack said. "Clint Sturdevant. You heard of me?"

Cannizzaro actually laughed at that. "Of course I fucking haven't."

"Good. I was partnered with LeGrande. Vito didn't know about it. The intent was always to cut him out. Shit went sideways."

"Is there a point here, Mr. Sturdevant?"

"I have the diamonds." Jack let the words just hang there. No one spoke for a long time.

"Are you asking me to congratulate you?"

"I'll sell them to you. Right now."

"What's your asking price?" Cannizzaro's voice was hesitant, tentative. Jack wished he could see the man's face because there was something in the tone that said he didn't completely believe him.

"I'll give you the entire load for thirty-five."

"Thirty-five million?"

"That's right."

There was another long pause. Jack heard a scratching sound that he thought was a hand going over a phone.

"Thirty. And you need to bring them here, to Rome."

"Ha," Jack scoffed. "So you can ambush me and take them without paying? Fuck that. And if you want me to smuggle them into Europe, that's going to be extra. I already know you have people here, or did they all get killed?"

"Choose your next words very carefully, Mr. Sturdevant," Cannizzaro said.

"I'll bring the diamonds to Europe, but I'm not going to Rome."

You've got an FBI informant in your organization, Jack said to himself. *You're lucky I'm stepping foot on the continent.*

"Neutral site, but close to you," Jack said. He forced a smile. "You're a businessman with many demands on your time. I don't want to inconvenience you." The Clint Sturdevant he remembered would never have been that diplomatic. "Monaco," Jack said. "It's close, and the police are, well, they're flexible if you need them to be."

There was another long pause, though this time, without the shuffling sound.

"I agree to your terms."

"I'm not done yet," Jack said, grinding out the words.

"As you Americans are fond of saying, you are pushing *your* luck and trying *my* patience."

"You need to pay me immediately or there's no deal. None of this 'half up front, the rest when you move the stones' bullshit. You want to try that and I'm better off selling for full price."

"So what do you propose?" Jack could hear in Cannizzaro's voice that his patience was running out.

"There's a bank I use in the Seychelles. They work with businessmen such as yourself. You set an escrow account up, and when I see that, I'll know it's safe to come to Europe with the diamonds. I'll meet you in Monaco and we'll make the exchange. You transfer the money to my account, and I disappear happily and you get a hundred and twenty million in diamonds for thirty-five."

"A hundred and twenty?"

"I don't think Vito was adjusting for inflation," was all Jack said. "You have my number." And he hung up.

JACK WENT HOME.

He needed Megan to drive him because he hadn't been back to the house to get his car yet. When they arrived, she twisted in her seat to face him, putting a hand on his. "Are you okay? Do you want any help?"

"No, I can handle it. Probably better that I do this myself, anyway."

Megan nodded and didn't pretend to understand him. But she smiled and said, "I love you, Jack."

"I love you too, Megs."

Jack got out of the Jeep and walked up to his door. There was heavy cloud cover that morning, and it was cool.

He'd always made a point of being long gone from a place before the crime scene tape went up, and it was jarring seeing it on the door to his own home. He didn't know if the police forgot to take it down because they were in a hurry or if that just wasn't part of the checklist. Jack removed the two strips of yellow tape, crossed over his doorway in an X. He balled it up and held it in his left hand while he opened the door with his right. Jack stepped through the doorway and dropped the tape just in the entryway.

The first thing he saw was the blood.

It was a big, dark stain on the carpet, dried now so that it was almost black.

Jack walked around it, as though the ground were somehow cursed. Reginald had died there. Long before LeGrande was his enemy, he was Jack's friend. He supposed. Thinking back on the history of their relationship and the legacy of betrayal, Jack wondered how much of that friendship was ever genuine. In those heady, early years, was it just because Jack was an exceptional driver? A kid with racing chops and no fear behind the wheel? Later, when he'd become Gentleman Jack and one of the best jewelry thieves and crew runners in the world, did Reginald just keep up a veneer of friendship because that's what the job was?

Given the ease with which Reginald sold Jack out to the police, it certainly seemed that way. Had any part of their friendship ever been real? The question bothered him more than it should and more than he thought it would. Jack long believed, long told himself that when Reginald died, he would just be gone, dried up like the rain on the sidewalk. But Reginald's ghost hung in that room, almost as if to say, *You're not rid of me yet.*

Jack wished killing him had been enough. He'd certainly dreamed about it for years. In his low hours, Jack thought about the different ways he'd exact revenge for the pain Reginald caused him. Would he make him suffer or would he do it quickly? But in all those moments it was orchestrated so that Reginald would know, he'd goddamned *know* that it was Jack pulling the trigger, it was Jack exacting some measure of justice, and his last moments would be that —the grim, bitter knowledge that he'd finally been bested.

Jack was denied that.

Reginald died knowing, sure, and he died knowing that Jack possibly could have saved him and didn't. But it felt different to Jack somehow. There wasn't that moment of surprise when Jack sprung the trap, revealed the elaborate plan. Instead, it was a wing shot that he was lucky to have made.

People threatened Jack with violence once, long ago. Rather, they'd threatened his family. Jack's father was swindled by a business partner and lost everything. Jack, then an amateur circuit racer about two years from going pro, quit racing to work to help his family make ends meet. Wanting to do *something* with cars, he got a job at a local garage near where his family lived in Cicero. Turned out that garage was run by the Chicago mob. They liked Jack and thought he was a good kid, asked him if he wanted to make some extra money? All he had to do was drive a car and not ask any questions. He did, and for a couple months it worked and it was good money, until he looked in the trunk and saw he was ferrying drugs. He made the kind of dumb decision that a good kid in a bad spot would make. The mob guys found out, of course, and instead of killing him, they told him to leave town immediately and forever. If he ever came back, they'd kill his family. The punishment was Jack had to live knowing that his family thought he was dead. A year after he left, the state declared him so.

People wondered why Jack abhorred violence, wouldn't tolerate guns on his crews, wouldn't take the kind of job that forced him to use the threat of violence to compel people to do what he wanted. It was because he didn't want to know that he was like them.

Reginald LeGrande forced Jack into a live-or-die situation. He forced Jack to make a choice. He forced Jack to choose violence, because he believed Jack would not.

The son of a bitch could have walked. He could have just disappeared. He'd gotten away from the police and probably could have kept going.

That old saying, dig two graves.

Reginald got the easy way out. Jack had to live with it.

The blinds were open and the room was filled with gray light. Jack made coffee. There was fingerprint dust everywhere.

He walked back to his bedroom, closing the door behind him. He didn't know why, maybe Jack didn't even trust silence anymore. He walked over to the far side of the bed and lifted up the throw rug, ran his fingers along the board until he found the right spot and pressed down. The spring-loaded panel released and opened, revealing the floor safe. Jack looked back to the door, making sure it was still closed. Then he opened the safe.

Inside was his half of the diamonds and a Swiss passport with the name Roger Southerland.

He collected the diamonds and loaded them into the Pelican case that was made to look like it carried camera equipment. He closed the safe and replaced the carpet. Then Jack hastily packed a suitcase, placing the passport in it.

Jack took his things and walked back to the front. He grabbed a black mug from the cupboard, poured himself a coffee, and walked out to the deck. Jack had long ago developed the skill to not attach himself to things. Mostly, it was a reaction to Chicago. But he knew that in this life he'd chosen, that was a survival mechanism. He had to be able to walk away, to run at a moment's notice if that's what was called for. He'd been in this house for nearly fifteen years, looking out from the mountains onto the valley beyond. This had been home. He couldn't ever return here, he knew. Whatever happened in the next few days, Jack could not live in a place with Reginald's ghost. One more thing Reginald robbed him of.

He sipped the coffee. It tasted bitter and burnt.

Jack flicked his wrist, sending the contents over the side. Jack set the coffee mug down on the table outside and left. He never looked back.

THEY AGREED they would close the winery today.

Jack drove in. He was two days out of the hospital and should be resting, but his ribs only hurt when he breathed and he'd be damned if the last person to look on Kingfisher wasn't him. They loaded up all of the cases of wine from the tasting room and the climate-controlled outbuilding they used for storage and distributed them among the employees' cars and a U-Haul that someone was able to rent. There was temperature-controlled storage available for rent and most wineries, including Kingfisher, had emergency rental agreements with those places. The barrels and cases would go there, but space was at a premium. Any loose bottles from the tasting room were distributed among the employees. They wouldn't have time to empty what was in the fermentation tanks, which meant they'd lose the entire 2021 harvest, but if that happened, it would likely mean the winery was gone anyway.

The one consolation was that they had just shipped their 2018s.

They decided to store the really rare bottles at Megan's. It wasn't that many, a dozen cases or so of their most limited releases that Megan just didn't want to let out of her sight. While Jack's place would have been ideal because he wouldn't be going back there, Jack and Megan both agreed that it felt wrong somehow. That bloodstain was on the carpet, it was tainted. They both knew it was as impossible as it was illogical to think that it would somehow affect their wine, but they also weren't going to do it. Megan felt better knowing their product, their legacy, would be in her direct control. They also felt like her house, while in the wooded foothills of Santa Rosa, was far enough away from where the fires were now.

It took the day to move everything they could save to the storage unit just outside downtown Sonoma or Megan's house, and that might be all that remained of Kingfisher. When everyone left, they opened a bottle of their first vintage of the Cabernet they'd made from the Sine Metu vineyard, in many ways the thing that set them on the path to this moment. Megan always said it was the best wine she'd ever made and one of the best she'd ever drank, from any vineyard. Then they made love, quietly but passionately, and stayed in Megan's bed until it was time for Jack to leave.

Megan didn't ask any questions when Jack left, and she didn't ask him to make any promises. All she said was, "Whatever happens, here or there, I love you, and it was all worth it."

Jack said, "There are things I would change, but only the things that would have given us more time."

Jack held her, kissed her, and said he loved her.

Then he left and drove to San Francisco for a red-eye to New York.

THIRTY-FOUR

Nico's cousin, the mafia don, was in a mood.

Bartolo was trying to keep his distance since he got back to Rome. He'd almost not come back at all after the debacle in America. But if anyone knew the value his family put on vendetta, it was him. He'd weighed the odds and figured that they were pretty good Salvatore would kill him for failing if he returned, but they were damn certain Salvatore would have hunted him down if he had fled.

Bartolo thought using the American thugs was stupid and a recipe for disaster, and that was exactly what they got. He was supposed to be in charge of the effort, but that idiot Fiore was more interested in undermining him at every turn. All that guy talked about was getting Burdette; it was almost like the diamonds were secondary to him. Bartolo tried, just once, to convince Fiore that Bartolo's reasons for wanting to see Burdette defeated and dead far outweighed getting disarmed in a bank lobby. After all, Burdette allowed an undercover cop into the School of Turin and destroyed years of preparation. Antwerp would have been much different if it weren't for him.

Fiore wasn't amused.

Nico thought it was funny as hell.

Bartolo told them the assault would fail. It was a stupid move. He'd never worked in the United States but he knew from stories—from Jack and others—how responsive the police were. Fiore thought everyone was half-assed like the Carabinieri. And if they did show up, Fiore said they had more than enough firepower to handle it. Obviously they didn't.

You couldn't tell soldiers anything.

Nico wasn't there when it went down. He wasn't even in the state. Nico learned about the debacle in Newark as he was waiting on his return flight to Rome.

There was small consolation knowing that one of the American cops had shot Fiore in the face. But even that, Salvatore acted like it was somehow Nico's fault. So, Nico kept his distance while he was back here. Nico wanted to stay at a hotel, but Salvatore wouldn't hear it. Nico knew that it was just because his cousin wanted him close by. Either to plan or to shoot. Both outcomes were equally likely.

So far, though, there hadn't been much of the former and obviously none of the latter. Salvatore was spending a lot of his time with his accountant, Mazza. There had been a phone call, but Nico wasn't privy to it, and so far, his cousin had not seen fit to share any details. After that, there were some hurried, angry conversations with Mazza. Nico wasn't privy to those either. So, he was content to drink by his cousin's pool and not be the focus of his anger. Nico was in one of the rooms with one of the TVs, nursing a glass of wine because he could, when Salvatore came in.

Nico was lounging on the large leather couch and perhaps making himself a little too comfortable, a little too at home. At least that was what he gleaned from the look on Salvatore's face when his cousin walked into the room. He walked into the center of the room and folded his arms. He didn't pour himself a glass of wine, didn't do anything other than look at the television and scowl. Nico took that to mean it was time to turn it off. He did. It was a little after midnight and Nico wondered if he'd been asleep, maybe he could've avoided this scene until his cousin calmed down. Probably not. Nico set the remote on the coffee table and stood.

"There's gonna be an exchange," Salvatore said.

"For what?"

"The diamonds. The guy that stole them before you could has them and is going to sell them to me. You're going to go get them."

Nico kept his feelings to himself, but he thought that, too, was funny as hell. Somebody stole the diamonds right out from under the police, posed as one of them. Either Vito and his American partner had a third partner or it was Burdette. That seemed like exactly the kind of vulture move that Burdette would pull. Let everyone else do the heavy lifting and come in and steal the score. That's how they got into this situation in the first place. Burdette could have been a part of the greatest jewelry theft in history, but instead he let a policeman into their midst. Then instead of seeking his own fortune, he chose to steal Nico's.

"Where are they?"

"They will be in Monaco."

"Why Monaco?"

"Because that's where he fucking said they would be," Salvatore snapped. Nico knew there was only so far he could push, and judging by his cousin's tone, that line wasn't nearly as far away as he thought it was.

Nico held up his hands. "Sal, I'm on your side here. I'm just asking a question."

"Well, don't."

Okay, so much for that.

"You're going to fly to Monaco with a couple of my men. You're going to make the exchange. He's going to call you and tell you when and where." As if anticipating Nico's question, Salvatore snapped irritably, "I already gave him your number."

Great, but how'd he get yours, Nico really wanted to know, but this didn't seem like question time. Maybe Vito decided to make a different play, double-cross his partner, and this third guy was part of that scheme. That would explain how this guy could get a mafia don's personal phone number. But if it was Burdette, he was working with Bachetti, and Nico would assume that unless he was totally out of the game, this was the kind of thing that Enzo could figure out.

"The seller, what's his name?"

"Clint Sturdevant," Salvatore said.

"When do we leave?"

"First thing in the morning. Fabrizio is organizing it."

"Anything you want done to the guy?"

"I don't give a shit about him. I just want the diamonds. As soon as you have them, I want you on your way back here, you understand?"

"Yeah, I got it."

Nico didn't ask if he was getting paid for this, and he assumed that he wasn't. What a bunch of bullshit. A week ago, he was looking at twenty million euros to the find the diamonds and bring them back. Now, he was just another errand boy singing for his supper. That in and of itself was an insult. These were *his* diamonds, and he didn't understand why none of these fucking people—Jack, Vito, Salvatore—could understand that. *He* assembled the School of Turin. *He* trained them. *He* planned the Antwerp job, and *he* fucking pulled it off. The mistake he made was not planning the escape better. Well, that and one of his people was a computer guy, not a real thief. He only stole things online and wasn't used to what it felt like to run. He completely fell apart and the escape plan unraveled. And in a matter of hours. The bitter irony was that asshole was never caught. But they sure as hell found Nico.

Nico realized, in time, that he'd been too clever by half. He was trying to throw the police off the scent by continually lying about how much he'd stolen, changing his story constantly. Eventually, the judge had enough of that bullshit and charged him with contempt of court and added more time onto his sentence. Six years—because they never found the diamonds—turned into ten. Then he did something equally stupid and violated his parole by going to the US looking for Burdette. They arrested him when he returned and threw him back in prison. Six years turned into sixteen. If he'd have kept his mouth shut, Nico would have done his time, gotten out, gotten his diamonds, and then retired an obscenely wealthy man. His wife might even have taken him back.

He'd keep his mouth shut now, though.

"Okay. So, I wait for his call and make the exchange. You haven't mentioned money, so I assume that's being done electronically?"

"That's right," Salvatore said.

"I'll go pack a bag. Fabrizio will have guns?"

"Yes, but only as a precaution. I don't want another goddamn shootout. I want you to get the diamonds and then this guy can fuck off to wherever he came from, you understand?"

Nico nodded. He understood very, very well.

THIRTY-FIVE

Jack landed at Newark at about six in the morning.

He was flying to Paris and from there to Nice in four hours, which was plenty of time. The Pelican case was small enough that Jack could carry it on with him. He grabbed his things and went to call an Uber. Then he texted Enzo from the burner and let him know that he'd arrived. Enzo, not surprisingly, was awake.

Jack didn't blame his friend for not wanting to make the trip. Jack had agreed to take both sets of diamonds, and he was nervous as hell. If the plan fell apart, if they were caught, this was where it would happen—at the airport, trying to go through security. It had been a long time since he'd tried to smuggle something through an airport, and he had to believe the scanning technology was much better than the last time he'd pulled something like this off. But it was the only option he had.

Jack would have felt safer chartering an airplane. He had a ghosted corporate card that he could've used, but knowing that the FBI had a plant in the Cannizzaro organization, they could easily learn that the buy would take place in Monaco instead of Rome. Then it would be simple investigation to look at chartered flights from the US to France. At least with a commercial flight, there were a lot more names to check. Sometimes, invisibility meant just blending into the crowd.

Jack met Enzo out front of the airport.

They would take separate flights to Europe, just in case. Enzo's left later in the day.

They cleared security easily. The TSA agent took one look at the expensive camera equipment and decided he wanted nothing to do with it, closed the cases up, and sent both through the machine. Then Jack found a family bathroom. It was early and the airport was uncrowded. Jack took both cases into the bathroom and consolidated all of the diamonds into one. When that was done, Jack gave Enzo the empty one. Afterward, they walked to a bar in Jack's terminal and got a drink. They both ordered beers and took them to a table by the window. There was no one else around, and they could stash their cases under a nearby table, out of the way.

"I'm sorry, man, I just couldn't do it," Enzo said in a low voice. "I just kept thinking about what I would say if they asked—"

Jack held up a hand. "What you were trying to do is the hardest thing. It's not like the other things we do. It's a different skill. Don't beat yourself up, okay?"

Enzo nodded, but Jack could read on his face how he felt.

Jack took a long drag off his beer. "Long way to go for us to just have to bring them back to Italy, anyway."

"You know how you're going to play it yet?"

"Straight, I guess. I'm not really worried about Cannizzaro trying anything. The money is already in escrow, and he doesn't get the diamonds until the money is in our account. Since the transactions are automatic, he can't cancel them and get his money back like if it was cash, so I think he's committed to paying." Jack shrugged. "I mean, there's always something he could try. I suppose he could try to kill me out of spite, but what does that get him? He's already out thirty-five million."

"I still don't like going into this without protection. We can stall for a day or two, right? I know a place I can get some guns, and I know a couple guys I can trust. Let's get some backup."

Jack shook his head. "That's just two or three more guys that know about this and want a split, maybe more than they think they're entitled to. Besides, the longer we give Cannizzaro, the more time he has to plan something. We're better off doing the handoff as quickly as possible."

Enzo lifted his beer, and looking out the window, he said, "You ever think about not giving the diamonds over to Cannizzaro? Maybe this Russian takes him out."

"Problem is, there's too many people that know we were involved. Not only that, but we don't know what happened to Nico. When I was looking at the people that the police had in custody back in LA, I didn't see him. He's still out there, and there's always the chance he teams up with the Russian for a cut. No, I think the safest thing is for us to give Cannizzaro what he wants and be done with it. It's the only way I see that we get to walk away."

"I understand why you want to play it that way," Enzo said, in the way that meant he got it but didn't like it. That was fine with Jack. The fewer people that knew what he was planning, the better.

Jack hadn't told Enzo about his phone call with Danzig or the deal she offered him, and he wouldn't. Not after Rusty.

Danzig wanted those diamonds in Europe, and that's exactly what Jack was going to do. There wasn't another way. Jack spent a lot of hours thinking about her proposal and what he kept coming back to was that he didn't have a convincing story to give her to explain where he got the diamonds. Vito would be followed when he was let out of police custody, so Jack couldn't use that as a story, and they knew about Reginald's movements. There was another angle to play, however. It was risky, but it might be his only chance to pull something off.

They finished their beers and Jack checked his watch. His side hurt. The last thing he wanted was to sit on a plane for seven hours. He outlined the plan for Enzo, the part that he needed to know. Enzo would be at a separate location on a laptop and he would confirm for Jack over the phone that the money had posted. Once it did, Jack would hand over the diamonds to Cannizzaro's man. Even though he was giving Enzo access to view it, Jack had the account locked down so that no money could be transferred out unless he called the bank. As soon as he was clear, Jack would transfer Enzo's half to him and it would be over. Roughly seventeen million each.

"Who did you say you were?" Enzo asked.

"Just some guy," Jack said.

He wanted to trust Enzo, he genuinely did, but there was something lingering, some holdover from Rusty that convinced Jack the less he said, the better. If he couldn't trust Enzo, he was well and truly alone, but maybe that was the best chance for them to see the other side of this.

The name he gave them, Clint Sturdevant, was someone he hadn't thought about or heard from in twenty-five years. Clint was a thief that had worked with Reginald, a dangerous and violent man they'd pulled that disastrous armored car depot job with. When the job fell apart, Sturdevant turned on them and tried to get Reginald's and Jack's split too. Reg shot him but not fatally. They'd only learned that when Jack went to look for the body and didn't find one.

Reginald didn't talk about Sturdevant after that but Jack knew he'd kept tabs. Reginald always liked to know where his enemies were. Jack didn't know where Sturdevant was now, whether he was loose or in prison, alive or dead, the only thing he did know was that the sick son of a bitch never found religion and became a priest. Sturdevant might be out there still pulling down jobs right now, he might be retired. In the end, it didn't matter.

Jack needed a name and decided to give one that the police could verify, just in case it made its way back to Danzig. His rationale was, if it was just an obviously made-up name, there was always the chance that the authorities would simply assume it was him. But if he gave the name of a known criminal, that would start some rabbit holing. Even better if Sturdevant had an alibi for that night or he was dead, that would waste all kinds of time. And it could never be traced back to Jack—Jack and Reginald were never identified on that armored car job, and Reginald and Jack were the only two who knew everyone's real name. Only one member survived to be arrested, the idiot who put it together, and he only had their aliases.

Besides, Sturdevant was a psychopath who'd tried to kill him. If Jack had to give a name, it might as well be his.

Jack arrived at his gate and hugged his friend.

"I'll see you on the other side," he told Enzo.

"*Bon chance, mon ami*," Enzo said.

Jack lifted an eyebrow. "You're speaking French now?"

"For Gaston," Enzo said.

Gaston Broussard, their longtime partner and friend. Gaston had been murdered by the Pink Panther Ozren Stolar, after the Carlton job. He and Enzo had been close.

Jack gave a wan smile and nodded.

"For Gaston," he said back.

Jack never made promises of retiring. Not to Megan, not even to himself. The only one he'd really told that to was Danzig, because when a federal agent asks you if you ever plan to steal jewels again, there's really only one right answer. Whatever the outcome, though, he knew he'd never work with Enzo again.

And he shouldn't.

Enzo would have more than enough to retire on, to live out his life on.

Jack's gift to his friend wasn't the money. Enzo earned that.

Jack's gift was making sure Enzo lived to spend it.

THIRTY-SIX

The small plane touched down in Nice.

Gentleman Jack Burdette exited the aircraft wearing a tan suit, navy shirt unbuttoned at the collar, and his Persol Steve McQueens. He was ready to steal a lot of goddamn money from some very bad people.

There was a luxury car rental in Nice that was supposed to have an Aston Martin DB11 Volante waiting for him outside the terminal. Jack checked his watch; the flight had been on time. First, he checked the reservation on the email address he'd used and verified that he had the correct time. Then Jack opened the burner phone, having used that number to make the reservation. Jack purchased a new burner with a European SIM card during his layover at Charles de Gaulle and notified his hotel and rental company of it. There was a voicemail from LuxeDrive instructing him to call as soon as possible.

It was early afternoon, and there was bright sunshine coating everything. The Nice airport was built along the coast, giving airline passengers a staggering view of the Côte d'Azur on their final approach into the airport. With his back to the building, Jack had an impressive view of the city of Nice. Not that he was particularly interested in the scenery. He wanted to know where in the hell was his car.

LuxeDrive catered to the traveling elite, and as such, Jack didn't have to step through the usual dialogue required with most French citizens where they pretended not to understand English until it was clear the transaction wouldn't proceed unless they serendipitously remembered. Apparently, eighteen hundred a day for an Aston Martin cleared a few hurdles.

"Bonjour, Mr. Southerland," the crisp but slightly accented female voice said. "I trust your flight into Nice was pleasant."

Jack slipped into character, though under the circumstances, it wasn't that hard. "It was fine, but there appears to be a problem with my car. Or rather, the lack thereof."

"Yes, Mr. Southerland. I do apologize. We left you several messages."

"I was in the air," he said. "For quite some time."

"Yes," she said tentatively. "I'm afraid we are unable to use the method of payment you supplied. Therefore, we could not authorize the vehicle."

"Impossible," Jack said.

"I am afraid not, sir."

She went on to explain that the credit card he'd supplied had been cancelled. It was a corporate card opened in the name of a shell corporation he'd set up to be able to travel anonymously. Jack's mind went through the possibilities. Was this Rusty's handlers working to roll him up? Was this Danzig? Or perhaps something else?

Jack told the woman this was obviously some mistake and that he would have his people sort it out. He disconnected the call.

The card was burned, so he broke it in two and dropped it in the trash. He had another he could use, but he wasn't going to do it here. Jack hired a car to drive him the thirty minutes to Monaco and to his hotel, the Monte-Carlo Bay Resort. There was a long, curved approach to the resort beneath rows of palms and a perfect azure sky. Jack checked into his room, a large room with a seaside view, under the Southerland name. He explained that he was changing payment methods and tried a new card. That one appeared to work, and Jack was shown to his room. He tipped the bellman and set his bags down but didn't unpack them. For the time being, he slid the cases with the diamonds under the bed.

Since he had a seaside view, Jack didn't have any apprehension about opening the curtains. In fact, that's why he'd chosen the room. He allowed himself a few minutes to stare at the splendor. Impossibly blue water beneath a differently hued but equally impossible sky. It was no wonder this was the playground of kings.

Jack picked up the hotel phone.

"How can I help you, Mr. Southerland?"

"I neglected to hire a car before I left and was wondering if the hotel could arrange one for me for the day. I have a few appointments in town."

"Yes, of course. Do you have a preference?"

Thirty minutes later, Jack accepted the keys to a cobalt blue Porsche 911 Targa 4S. It wasn't the DB11, but it would do. Reluctantly, he'd checked the camera case into the hotel safe. Having robbed places like this before, Jack felt reasonably confident in their internal security. The main thing he was watching for in the lobby as he'd done it was anyone watching him. Jack checked the rearview as he pulled out of the hotel to see if any vehicles detached themselves from the landscape.

Leaving the resort, Jack guided the Porsche around a large traffic circle, taking the nine o'clock exit onto Avenue Princess Grace, and then accelerated. As a boy, Jack had dreamed of this, driving a Formula One racer through the streets of Monaco in the Grand Prix. Now, he was finally realizing that vision in a way, but it was a bitter and ashen version of it, a cruel joke.

Jack had thought about not staying in Monaco, believing it might be too risky, that perhaps he should stay in a smaller inland town where he could guarantee no one would be looking for him. He'd decided against it, ultimately choosing a hotel that was ten minutes from the place he intended to make the exchange. If all went well, he could go back to his hotel, sleep it off, and head home tomorrow. If it didn't, Jack had a lot of potential escape routes.

He had two voicemails on the Jack Burdette phone from Danzig when he'd arrived in Nice. He closed the Targa's top and called her back, having paired the phone with the car.

"Burdette, why are you up? Isn't it the middle of the night for you?" she said.

"Having trouble sleeping," he told her as he passed a glittering resort hotel bathed in sunlight.

"How are we looking?" she said, her voice anxious.

"I have a couple of leads that I'm running down."

"We don't have a lot of time left, Jack."

"I know, and I'm sorry. I don't have a network anymore. What happened with Vito?"

Danzig paused and then sighed. "They let him go. With LeGrande dead, they don't really have anything to charge him with. Can't prove the diamonds were illegally imported, and without the diamonds, they can't charge him with the intent to sell them."

"Are you tailing him?"

"I can't get into that with you."

"Just wondering if I have anything to be concerned about," Jack said. "I've already had one person show up at my house and try to kill me. I don't have any desire to collect the set."

"I understand. If I hear anything, I will let you and the Sonoma County Sheriff know."

"I appreciate that."

"Listen, I can maybe drag this out another day, but if you can't find those diamonds soon, I can't keep this going."

"So, there's twenty thieves in the world that I know of who could have pulled that job off. Ten of them are in prison, and three of them are dead. Of the ones that are left, it's a matter of figuring out which one of them might have known Reginald or Vito. I'm leaning toward the former, since it's looking like Reginald intended to sell Vito out."

There was another long pause. "And I suppose you have a theory about that?"

"Do you know the name Clint Sturdevant?"

IT WAS a two-mile drive down one of the most expensive stretches of land in the world to Jack's destination. Fort Antoine was built in the eighteenth century as a fortress to defend the small principality. The Italian army occupied Monaco in the Second World War but were forced to abandon it when the Mussolini regime collapsed. The Nazis moved in and occupied it after the Italians pulled back. The fortress was mostly destroyed in 1944 by the Allies targeting the Germans. In 1953, Monaco's Prince Rainier III rebuilt part of it and rededicated it as an outdoor amphitheater. Jack turned onto Avenue de la Quarantaine, which wrapped around one of Monaco's yacht harbors, and as he rounded a bend he could see the remnants of the fortress, a single parapet that looked out over the sea. A cliff rose sharply to his right, its top covered in lush greenery. The fortress was almost hidden in the trees. Jack took the tunnel beneath the fortress, which ended in the entry ramp for a parking garage.

Monaco had two major problems for someone like Jack—cameras and geography. For the former, they were everywhere and, as he'd already seen, on every parking garage or tunnel that he'd come across. For the latter, one had to know this city well because roads were squeezed into every conceivable surface that wasn't otherwise built up. Navigating was incredibly difficult and required advance planning. Because of the serpentine construction of the roads (which made for exciting racing) and elevation changes, a street map resembled a multi-level labyrinth designed by a particularly malevolent urban planner.

Wary of establishing patterns, Jack turned the Porsche around before entering the garage and drove back through the tunnel. He drove along the base of the mountain until he found a road that curved inward and would take him up to the top. He gradually snaked his way up through a park, found a spot to park his car, and got out. He wouldn't be able to use this approach later on, assuming that the park would be closed, but this would suffice for his recon now. Jack first spent several minutes watching to see if anyone else had taken notice of where he parked. Once he was sure he wasn't followed, Jack toured the grounds for the next thirty minutes to decide where he was going to set up. He called Enzo to ask if he was ready. Then he called Cannizzaro's man and told him to be ready for his call.

With the sun hanging low over the Mediterranean, Jack got into the Porsche and drove back to the hotel.

It was time.

THIRTY-SEVEN

"It's fucking *where*?" Danzig shouted.

"Monaco," Mazza said in a harsh whisper. "I just found out."

"Well, who has the diamonds, then?"

"I don't know. He's not telling me. I'm to move money, when he tells me, into a numbered account in the Seychelles. I don't know how much money yet. He hasn't told me."

"When is this happening?"

"Soon. I don't know for certain. He's not saying much."

"You need to do better than that. I have to know who is making the handoff."

"All I know is he's sending two cars and they leave in the morning. I'm doing the best I can," Mazza said hurriedly. "I'm already risking my life."

"You're a mafia banker," Danzig said evenly. "Let's not stretch this too far." Running informants was a tricky thing. You had to establish, in their eyes at least, a dysfunctional codependent relationship. They had to believe that they needed you as much as you needed them, if not more. You had to cajole and belittle, demand, and then up the ante of satisfaction. But every so often, you just had to jerk the chain to remind them they were still on it. Sometimes you had to push them into dangerous situations in order to get the information you needed. How dangerous depended on the informant. If they were a whistleblower, that was one thing. If they were a mafia banker, that was another.

"Mazza, I expect regular check-ins."

"I understand," he said, sounding scared.

"But listen to me. I expect to know how much money and when. The instant that transaction goes through, you need to figure out a way to contact me."

"I will do this, but you have to get me out of here. I can't—"

Danzig hung up.

Danzig stood. "Listen up," she said in a loud voice. Every head in her squad (and a few that weren't) turned to face her. "There's been a switch. The sale is going down in Monaco. Could be today, could be tomorrow, the next day, we don't know for certain. What we do know is that Cannizzaro's people are leaving by car first thing in the morning." Danzig pulled up her phone and opened the map. "That's about a six-and-a-half-hour drive."

"How credible is the intel?" Choi asked. "Mazza get it firsthand?"

"As far as I know. It sounds like Cannizzaro is compartmentalizing. Mazza said he just wired money into an escrow account in a bank in the Seychelles. It goes from there into a numbered account once they get instructions from someone on the ground in Monaco. That's all Mazza knows. Dan, you and I are going to Monaco. There's an Air Force C-21 squadron in Germany. We can use them to fly us to Nice."

"We used them last time, I remember. I'll get the ask to the LEGAT immediately." Interagency requests usually took a long time to coordinate, but they did have fast-track procedures for extenuating circumstances. C-21s were militarized Lear jets the Air Force used for transporting senior military, Defense, and State Department officials around Europe. They were based out of Ramstein Air Base in western Germany, about two hours' flight time from here. "If they can't get something here first thing, we'll drive."

"I'll look into commercial options for you too," Special Agent Rawlings said.

Danzig looked to another member of the squad. "Pierce, you're on the bank. We have an American involved, so we have jurisdiction. The US government can make things difficult for them if they like."

"On it."

THIRTY-EIGHT

Money didn't sleep, and neither did the people who had it.

At least, not the ones who didn't have to do much to get it, which seemed like most of the population of Monaco.

One of the reasons Jack chose the spot that he did for the handoff was that there was a large port on the northern side of the peninsula the fortress was built on. There would be parties on the yachts moored there late into the night. It wouldn't be the same as a public spot, but it might deter someone from shooting. Jack thought about a public location but ruled it out because he wanted to be able to see everyone around him and know if someone other than who he expected to see was there. But being close to so many people, even if they were floating in the docks, gave him the level of security that he'd need.

"Nine o'clock," he said in a gruff voice after dialing the number that Cannizzaro gave him. "We'll meet at the amphitheater at Fort Antoine. There isn't a performance tonight. I checked. The gate will be unlocked. Be ready to transfer the money to me or the deal is off."

"It will be ready." The response came in accented English but was practiced and well formed.

"You will be alone. If I think anything is up, I disappear. You understand?"

"I understand. You gave the instructions to Cannizzaro, he gave them to me." The voice was irritated now. "It's not that hard."

"Then let's not make it that way," Jack said and hung up.

He ate dinner in his room but opted for coffee instead of wine. He didn't want to dull any edges. At seven thirty, Jack called Enzo from the burner.

"Are you in position?"

"I am," Enzo said.

"Any issues logging in to the account?"

"Nope."

As soon as Jack got away, he'd transfer Enzo's half of the money to an account he had set up, and then Jack would shut this account down. It was layered inside a Russian nesting doll of shell corporations only accessible by people who didn't exist. It would be nearly impossible to trace, even if the bank wanted to cooperate with the US government.

Jack pulled the case containing the diamonds out from under his bed. Then he dressed.

Jack put on a black Canali suit, white shirt, and dark blue tie. He was dressed for anything short of a night at the Monte Carlo. He didn't have a gun and, on the edges of his mind, was questioning that logic.

He buttoned his jacket and regarded himself in the mirror, nodding once. Jack walked over to the window, then drew back the orange curtains so that he could look out at the sea. It had become slightly overcast in the early evening, and now scattered clouds partially blocked out the moon. Even better. Jack closed the curtains and turned back to the bed. He called for the car and waited ten minutes for it to be brought around. Jack opened his bag, grabbed a set of lock picks, and slid them into his jacket pocket. He took both his Jack Burdette phone, silenced, and the burner. It was bulkier than he wanted to be, but he thought he might need both. Especially if he had to run. He also took his passport.

Jack thought a moment about taking his bag with him. He'd be leaving behind fingerprints in the event that the meeting was burned and he had to leave quickly. However, if he was in a situation that involved fingerprinting, that would mean he was likely in police custody and the whole thing was fucked anyway. Jack grabbed the hardshell and left the room, making his way through the elegant resort to the grand lobby.

Jack scanned the crowd as he walked through the lobby, looking for anyone that might be looking for him. This was one of the few places on earth he could wear a five-thousand-dollar suit and look like a pauper by comparison.

He stepped out into the warm evening, bathed in the bright glow of the overhead lights, flanked by palms and succulents. A valet walked up to him and handed him the keys to the Porsche. "Right this way, Mr. Southerland," he said and guided Jack to the idling Targa. Jack tipped the valet, said he could handle the case, and got in.

He accelerated quickly out of the loading area and to the long, curving road with alternating spotlights and palm trees that led him out to Avenue Princess Grace. Jack drove quickly to the fort. He passed by the large Port Hercule complex on his left, then the road disappeared into the mountain. There was another brief opening and then another short tunnel, the road going through the mountain upon which the fortress was built. The theater was all that remained of the original structure. Now it was a large park with a twisting labyrinth of wooded footpaths that snaked across the mountain in the shadows of Monaco's government building and a library named for Princess Grace. Jack slowed as the Porsche neared the exit of the second, longer tunnel. He saw a white-and-gray triangle-shaped checkered pattern painted on the street that read *BUS*, and here the road split. The street terminated in a massive parking structure that also doubled as the Formula Two racing paddock. According to the signage, buses and motorcycles parked on this level and cars stayed to the right, descending to the next lower level. Jack took his parking ticket and drove through. He easily found a spot near the exit ramp on the opposite side and parked.

Jack got out of the car, taking the case with him, and walked back up the exit ramp rather than taking the stairs, because he didn't know where exactly they'd deposit him. Once outside, he found a wide footpath of red clay that, in full daylight, would be a faded pink. There was a small, wildly curving stone staircase that descended to a tiny rocky beach no more than a few hundred feet long. Say this about the principality, they knew how to economize space. This ran along the mountain and had been part of the original fortress. Beneath the walkway, one could still see the stone masonry that formed the outer wall. He walked along the pathway, staying close to the sheer stone cliff that had vegetation and trees growing out from the cracks. It was about a five-minute walk to the amphitheater.

Jack passed the opening between the tunnels as he walked. Here, he could see the fort and the park looming above him, now just alternating patterns of light stone and dark trees. But like everything else in Monaco, the pathway and the fortress were brightly lit. The stairs leading up to the theater were just on the other side of the gap. Beyond that, there was the Solarium Beach, which were rows of tiered concrete benches that simply faced the sea. This extended to a long dock, jutting out like an angry finger, that formed the southern edge of the U-shaped Port Hercule complex. This was one of the locations where cruise ships docked.

Jack reached the stone staircase that led up to the theater, which was shaped like a tower at the apex of the fortress. The staircase zigzagged up the side of the tower; most of that four- to five-story climb was in the shade of a large tree that looked to Jack like a kind of cypress. That was good, as it would hide him once he completed the initial ascent and the stairs turned back away from the tower. Once he was safely in the shadows beneath the tree canopy, Jack slowed his pace so that his shoes didn't make as much noise. There was a wrought iron gate at the end of the path, blocking entry. He removed the set of lock picks from his jacket and popped the lock on the iron gate in seconds. Jack pushed the gate open, wincing as it creaked, and he slid through quickly, closing it behind him.

Jack entered the amphitheater.

It was a wide circle, with seven tiers of stone benches rising up from half of it. The other side was a tall hedge planted in a stone base that completely obscured the theater from outside view. There were spotlights surrounding the fortress and dotting the park above, but the theater itself was dark. It was the perfect place for a covert exchange, and there was only one way in, unless you were the staff. Beyond the wall on the north side, he could see the lights of Port Hercule and could hear the sounds of myriad parties happening on the yachts within it. He could picture the neat rows of boats reaching into the marina. The sounds and music of a score of different parties mixed with the salt air, carried in by a cool breeze from the sea.

Jack walked over to the tiers of benches and climbed up to the second row. Here, there was a small stone platform at the end of the seating area that held some landscaping beneath two large cypresses. The amphitheater was black, and he had a perfect view of the entry gate.

He texted Enzo to let him know that he was in position. Enzo replied again with, *Bon chance*.

Jack smiled. Gaston would have loved this.

The Frenchman, their former partner, had been a soldier and demolitions expert in the French Foreign Legion. He lived modestly, was never interested in big scores—what he loved was executing the job. When they'd worked together, Jack always avoided situations that called for this kind of cloak and dagger. They had fences they knew and trusted, as much as one could in this business, but by the time they got to the handoff to the buyer, the risk was largely over. Gaston would have reveled in the planning of this.

At five to nine, Jack heard the gate open and watched the dark outline of a man step through. The man closed it behind him.

So far so good.

Jack detached himself from the shadow and walked to the center. He stopped when he was about ten paces from the other person.

Then his heart stopped.

Niccoló Bartolo stepped into the half-light, and he had a gun.

THIRTY-NINE

Nico regarded him with a mirthless smile.

"Clint Sturdevant," he said coldly. "I'm not surprised Salvatore didn't pick up on it."

"Put the gun away, Nico. You were warned."

"Maybe I learned not to take chances."

"Maybe you didn't. You see those woods behind me?"

"So?"

"Enzo Bachetti is up there with a sniper rifle and a night vision scope. If anything happens to me, if anything goes any other way than how I precisely scripted it out, he's going to put your skull into orbit." Jack's voice was calm and even.

Nico craned his neck up, futilely searching the inky darkness for the invisible sniper. "What the fuck does Enzo know about a rifle?"

"He grew up hunting, for one thing. For another, you haven't seen him in twenty-five years. People learn new skills." Jack paused and let that sink in.

"So it's a standoff, then," Nico said, not making it a question. "I shoot you, Enzo shoots me, Enzo gets the diamonds."

"Only if you're stupid, Nico. You can walk away rich or die broke."

Niccoló Bartolo, master thief, onetime head of the School of Turin, laughed at that. Jack wished he could see Nico's eyes. Jack guessed that he was again scanning the mottled indigo and black mountainside, looking for a sign of Enzo in the trees, calculating his odds. The darkness was instrumental to his plan, but this was the one flaw. He couldn't really see what his opponent was doing.

Jack wished he had a gun.

His mind went back to that night in 1997 when Jack learned that his friend and fellow thief, Giovanni Castro, was actually an undercover officer with the Italian Polizia di Stato. When he learned that the target was Niccoló Bartolo and his School of Turin. When he learned that Giovanni was going to let him slip out because they were friends and because he jokingly said arresting an American would be more paperwork than it was worth. Jack made one phone call—to Enzo, to warn him. Everyone else, Bartolo, Vito Verrazano, they were on their own. By that point, Jack had developed a healthy fear of Bartolo and wasn't sorry to see him get busted. Jack had raced through the dark streets of Turin to the apartment he shared with Giulia Montalto. They'd flee together.

Only, Giulia had made other plans.

Apparently, Bartolo suspected there was a rat in his organization, he just didn't know who it was. He lured Giulia away from Jack, that wasn't surprising, Nico was handsome, suave, and charming.

Jack went to the apartment he shared with Giulia and found Nico waiting for him. Nico's suspicions were confirmed, and a gun was drawn. Bartolo acted too quickly; he didn't wait for Jack to get all the way in the apartment. Jack was close enough to it that he could slip back through the front door in just a few steps. The memory was no doubt clouded by the passing of years, but in Jack's mind's eye, Bartolo fired as soon as he saw Jack walk through the door. Jack stood there comically, foolishly, processing the scene. Bartolo next to Giulia. Giulia, dark-haired and stunning, not making a move for him.

Jack shot back and nearly hit Giulia. He dropped the weapon in horror, and it would be nearly fifteen years before he touched a pistol again. Jack was out the door by the time Bartolo got his second shot off, taking the stairs two at a time, a blurred image in his mind he still didn't remember. He sped off into the dark of Turin and drove until the car he stole was out of gas.

Nico escaped the state police sting, but the School of Turin was smashed and much of his stable went to prison. When it came time to pull the Antwerp diamond heist five years later, he was rolling with the B team, and it cost him. Nico blamed Jack for Giovanni's penetration, for the sting, and for not being present in Antwerp.

Sixteen years later, Bartolo was relegated to the role of errand boy, sent to collect the very diamonds he'd worked so hard to steal.

Funny how things worked out.

Then, still chuckling, Bartolo nodded.

"I'm impressed. I see you picked up a few new skills yourself. That makes me happy. I'm putting my gun away." Bartolo made a slow, exaggerated motion with his right arm. From this distance it was all a dark blur, but when his right arm extended out to his side, Jack could see it was empty. Presumably, Bartolo had slid the pistol into a holster in his jacket.

"Good. Now, call Cannizzaro and tell him to make the exchange."

"Not until I see diamonds."

"No dice, Nico. It's too dark out here to see them, anyway. Make the call or I disappear."

"If you think that I'm just going to take your word for it, maybe you haven't learned as much as I thought."

Jack thumbed the call button on the burner and dialed Enzo.

"Here," Enzo said.

"I'm kneeling down now to open the case to show Nico the diamonds."

"Nico?" he said.

"Yeah, it's reunion week," Jack said dryly. "Be ready." Jack knelt down, not taking his eyes off Bartolo. He opened the case, revealing the camera equipment. He popped one of the hidden panels.

Bartolo stepped forward and told Jack he was reaching for his phone. His hand went to his pocket and returned with a phone, then he activated its flashlight function. Bartolo knelt down and ran the light over the compartment, and the diamonds glittered like stars. As he was looking, Jack said, "There are three more compartments just like that. Now, make the call."

Jack closed the case.

Bartolo stood and dialed.

Jack heard Bartolo call and tell whoever was on the other end of that line to make the transfer.

"They're transferring the money now," he told Enzo.

A pause.

It took a few awkward minutes. Cannizzaro, or presumably his accountant, had to speak to a representative at the bank to authorize the transfer. Apparently, even in that place you couldn't transfer thirty-five million dollars just because you said so.

"I've got an inbound transfer," Enzo said.

"Okay. Look sharp, just in case they try something."

"Jack?"

"What?"

"This is supposed to be for thirty-five, right? They're not breaking it up into smaller payments?"

"No, it's supposed to be the full amount."

"This is only ten million."

Jack lowered the phone.

"What's going on, Nico?"

Nico, in the shadows but still visible, shrugged. "If Salvatore pulled something, it's news to me. But my guess is you're being fucked."

"Explain quickly."

"He doesn't have any cash."

"He owns a bank."

"But he can't use that for this because the government has been watching him ever since your little *attempted* robbery two years ago. All of his money is tied up in real estate and businesses. Well, and guns and drugs, but none of that is liquid, you see. I suspect that he knew that if he didn't meet your price, you'd just go somewhere else, and that would screw him with the Russian. I'm not part of his plans, but it figures."

A thirty-five-million-dollar payday was now ten.

"Hold on, Enzo," Jack said into the phone, then lowered it to his side.

His cut of seventeen down to five, off of what was originally a hundred-million-dollar score.

"So, the question is, Jack, what are you going to do?"

"Kill Vito, for starters."

Even in the darkness, Jack could see Bartolo's alligator smile. "Yeah, I get that." Then he said, "You've got three choices. One, you take the deal. It's less than you planned...a lot less, but you get money and you walk away with your life. Your second choice is you can leave with the diamonds. I'd try to stop you, and I think we know how that ends. The third choice is the three of us fuck *him*."

"You'd betray your own cousin? A mafia don, no less?"

"He tried to have me killed," Nico said flatly. "So, I'm defining 'family' a little flexibly these days. But I'm not getting a cut of this. He expects me to be the dutiful courier, do this for the privilege for being welcomed back into the fold. He doesn't care that without me, there wouldn't be any diamonds."

Jack hadn't closed the phone yet, and Enzo heard all of this.

"What do we do, Jack?" Enzo said.

"I'll call you back." He closed the phone and slid it into his pocket.

Jack pushed the case forward with his foot, the plastic scraping across the stone.

Jack stepped back. "It's all yours."

"It's not too late. We can take this and split it. You, me, and Enzo."

Working with a fence they didn't know, you'd lose sixty percent of the value. They'd be looking at a payout of only a couple million each and would double-cross a mafia don in the process.

That was easy math.

Nico was welcome to make his own play, but Jack wasn't going to be part of it.

"Five million and not running seems pretty good to me."

"Well, we'll see."

Bartolo stepped forward and picked up the case. Then he reached into his jacket and pulled out the pistol.

Every muscle in Jack's body tensed.

Then Bartolo flipped the pistol around and handed it to Jack.

"What are you doing, Nico?"

"Salvatore has two men at the bottom of the stairs. They're either for you or for me."

Jack took the gun. He didn't have a way of knowing if it was loaded or not, if Bartolo was bluffing him, if this was part of some kind of scam.

Or if this man that tried to kill him once had just given him a way out.

"Why," Jack said, not a question.

"You do fifteen, sixteen years in a prison...especially the kind they got in Belgium, you can do two things with your hate. You can burn the candle on it, but sooner or later that wick is gonna go out. If it burns out and you still have time to do, you don't have too much to keep you going. Or you can let it go."

Jack half laughed. "You let it go? What was that in California?"

"That?" Bartolo was close enough now that Jack could see him smirking. "That was for the cop. But we're even now."

"He's dead, you know," Jack said. "Your cousin had him killed."

"Guess that's a kind of irony." Nico picked up the diamonds.

Jack said, "Take care, Nico. That case is designed to fool any metal detector or X-ray machine." Jack paused, waiting for Nico to say something else. When he didn't, Jack said, "Don't spend it all in one place."

"You either."

Nico Bartolo disappeared into the night with the diamonds he stole almost twenty years before.

Nico faded from sight, and Jack didn't know where he'd gone. He didn't know of any other way out of the amphitheater, but perhaps Nico did. More and more, this was looking like something his old mentor had planned all along.

Jack racked the slide on the pistol, chambering a round.

This was the one thing he hadn't planned on. He'd promised Danzig that he'd get the diamonds to Europe, but he'd never told her how. Jack didn't know if she was going to hold up her end of the deal now; he suspected that she wouldn't. That was fine. That wasn't necessarily part of his plan.

Jack slid through the gate and made the stairs.

More clouds filled the sky, and the night seemed blacker than it was. Certainly more confusing. The burner in his pocket vibrated, it would be Enzo wanting to know what in the actual hell was happening.

Jack wanted to know that too.

He wondered if Bartolo had figured out that Enzo wasn't actually in the hills above the fortress watching him through a night vision scope or if Bartolo bought it. Enzo was at home on the southern tip of Italy, safe. He'd bled enough for these diamonds.

He took the stairs quickly but mindful that he was in dress shoes with less traction. The two shapes at the bottom stepped out of the shadows and started climbing. If Bartolo was to be believed (and Jack was having a hard time even reconciling that in his head), their instructions were to either kill the man without the case or kill them both. Jack closed the distance quickly. That is, if they were the mafia soldiers that Bartolo made them out to be. Anything was possible, really. Maybe he'd picked up a police escort and was trying to get Jack to do his dirty work.

Jack told them in Italian to back off.

The two men kept coming.

In the stairway's lights he could see they were dressed casually and both wore jackets. That was stupid and a great way to stand out.

Jack told them again to back off.

One of them put a hand inside his coat.

Jack fired.

He was about twenty feet away and Jack aimed low, hoping for a glancing shot on the steps in front of him. But instead the bullet must have hit him somewhere in the leg. The man cried out and fell backward, crashing into his partner. Jack heard a gun clatter to the ground. He moved in quickly. The one was groaning on the ground, his partner was a few steps below him and clearly in pain from having fallen. Jack couldn't make out features in the darkness—they were below the light—but they were both male, dark hair, and in pain. Jack leaped over the first and moved toward the second. He was reaching for something.

"You were warned," he said and kicked the man in the jaw.

It wouldn't kill him, but it might knock him out, and he'd probably be talking through a straw for a few weeks.

Jack had had enough of people trying to kill him lately.

He'd never know if they were cops or Salvatore's men. At this point, it probably didn't matter. He was trusting the word of the last person on earth he ever thought he should.

Funny how things worked out.

Jack made the bottom of the stairs and took off at a dead run for the Porsche. Jack sprinted as fast as he could in dress shoes and a suit, jacket having come open and flapping like a poorly made cape. He dashed along the side of the mountain, passing a pair of nighttime strollers who no doubt wondered what in the hell a suited man was doing running. He made the parking garage and raced down the ramp, again not taking the time to look for stairs. He tried to keep his head down and away from the cameras. Before getting in, Jack looked behind him to see if he was followed. It didn't look like it. He got in, fired up the Porsche, and backed out, accelerating up the exit tunnel. Jack assumed there was a camera on him, so he kept his head low, though he realized that the car was rented under the Southerland name. It wouldn't take an ace detective to trace Southerland back to the United States using his travel records.

Sloppy, Jack thought. *And stupid.*

He accelerated up the ramp and into the tunnel.

Then he saw a pair of lights appear on the far side, and another pair of lights pulled into his lane, blocking the exit.

FORTY

Jack hit the brakes, screeching the Porsche to a halt.

He threw the car into reverse and floored it. There wasn't room to turn without doing a time-consuming three-pointer, so he accelerated backward, blasting out of the tunnel in the opposite direction. Jack hit the brakes again and cranked the wheel, bringing the nose around and flooring it just as the two cars were nearing the end of the tunnel. Jack was on the white-checkered bus lane indicator where the road split. He put the accelerator to the floor again, and the car jumped forward, aiming straight for the oncoming cars.

The drivers reacted, instinct pushing them to self-preservation. One car broke right, crashing into the wall to its right, Jack's left. The second car broke left, angling toward the parking garage's exit ramp that Jack had just come up. That driver was luckier than his partner. He stopped before crashing into the lowered security bar. Jack hit the tunnel and continued to accelerate. The two cars behind him reversed, nearly hitting each other, and took precious moments trying to sort themselves out in order to turn around to continue the pursuit.

Jack blasted down Avenue de la Quarantaine with the mountain rising to his left and a long building on the right. The Porsche nearly hit eighty before Jack hit the brakes to decelerate into a turn. He checked the rearview to see lights behind him, but they were distant. Jack whipped the car around a descending U-shaped turn and then immediately reversed direction at the bottom, turning a hard left to accelerate onto Boulevard Albert that ringed Port Hercule. It was different in the dark, but after a moment, he recognized that this long building to his right was the Formula One paddock. Jack accelerated, but his velocity was limited by traffic. The boulevard was a single lane in each direction, and there looked to be a line of cars in front of him. Slowing down, he had more reaction time to spare and could hazard longer looks in the rearview.

There was a line of cars behind him now merging from the opposite side of the corner he'd just whipped around, and it was impossible to tell if his pursuers saw him make the turn or made it themselves. That didn't last long. He saw a large white Audi sedan with blacked-out windows rocket onto Boulevard Albert from the crazy S-turn chicane he'd corkscrewed around. It was now racing up the oncoming traffic lane. There was a line of cars in front of him. It wouldn't take long for the Audi, an A8 or S8, by the look of it, to reach him. Jack put the accelerator nearly to the floor and cranked the wheel to the left, shooting across the street and through the gap between two cars in the oncoming lane. He hit the opposite corner at an angle and cranked the wheel further left, tires screaming.

He flew up half a block, pumped the brakes and down shifted, engine revving in protest, and leapfrogged around the car in front of him, narrowly missing a Ferrari 488. The white Audi made the turn. Jack pulled back into his lane just in time, cutting off a Mercedes G wagon, and fishtailed into a right-hand turn, whipping around a corner. He was at the end of the block and turning right again by the time the Audi made the turn. Jack didn't see any flashing lights, so maybe Bartolo hadn't lied about that, at least.

Jack was now facing the sea and heading back in the direction of Boulevard Albert. He'd been here before, but as a tourist and didn't know the city that well. Because the principality was built on, around, and between the jagged sides of mountains that spilled into the Mediterranean, every available inch of land was used for roads and buildings. Streets ascended and descended, forked and converged, following the natural counters of the land and the contours forced by development. They disappeared into short tunnels that ran beneath buildings and larger ones that ran beneath the ground. A street map looked more like an Escher painting than an urban plan. Basically, he was driving blind.

Jack was also mindful of the ubiquitous cameras. The police here could be bought, but not for the money he had. The cameras were a real problem because it meant that Jack couldn't speed, a difficult thing to do if you were trying to win a car chase. Since he no longer had Rusty to procure things, like cars, Jack had rented the Porsche through the hotel using the credit card and passport he was traveling under—data points to link those things to him. Worse, the camera would connect him to being in Monaco on a forged passport. If the FBI discovered that, Jack would be in violation of his parole, not to mention breaking a slew of fresh laws.

So, he just had to lose his two pursuers in a completely legal way. Or, near enough.

While driving through a city that was mapped out like a surrealist's interpretation of a cityscape.

Jack rocketed through a large intersection where the road he was on connected back with Boulevard Albert. There was a statue in the center commemorating the Grand Prix. Jack whipped around the statue, racing around the traffic circle, and took a right-hand exit ramp, nearly clipping a van. He pulled hard left and took the second exit in the traffic circle. The first exit would have taken him on a descending ramp to a road that formed the northwestern edge of Port Hercule and was part of the Formula One course. The second exit kept him on the current "level," heading in the direction of the famed Casino de Monte-Carlo. He accelerated onto Avenue d'Ostende, which took him gradually uphill, chancing a look in the rearview and seeing the Audi similarly blast through the traffic circle, but with much less grace. A thin ten-story apartment building was to Jack's left, but the right side was open so the apartments would have an unobstructed view, and that meant Jack could be seen from the traffic circle below.

Jack drove in the direction of the casino, the Monaco coastline and the port, far below, flowing by him on the right. If it had been daylight, he'd have been able to see the fort and the theater on the other side of the port. Traffic was starting to thicken now as he got closer to the city center. It would be harder to move. The road split here, with the right fork going directly in front of the casino and the left wrapping back in the other direction. Jack stayed left. He'd slowed to thirty miles an hour now, keeping with the flow of traffic, but the further he moved into the city, the more it became a convoluted maze of permutations. If he could stay a block or two ahead of his pursuers, he'd lose them. There was a small park, about half the size of a city block, to his left and to the right, a massive excavation site where they'd just demolished several large structures and were just getting the new building under way.

He turned left at the park, looking up just in time to see the white Audi S8 shooting up the oncoming lane and forcing traffic to part like Moses at the Red Sea.

POLICE CAPTAIN COSSERIA was not happy.

Cosseria was a short man with a stocky build, thick hair, and a mustache that could have found a home on any number of scrubbing implements. He wore an expensive tailored suit that was a little rumpled from the day. Danzig understood his frustration. The American FBI liaison in Paris, whom he'd never met, called earlier that day to ask for his assistance, saying there was a massive gem smuggling operation happening in his city. The FBI could offer very little in the way of details, had almost no idea where and when the sale would happen, and asked him for his help.

"Help doing what?" he'd first said to Danzig when they'd met and she'd asked for his cooperation. She had to admit that she didn't exactly know herself. He was right—they were working off the words of an informant who only knew that the sale was going to happen here. She'd pressed Mazza to find out where the exchange would be made and he was now on the edge of panic, having asked Cannizzaro and others one too many times for information that he didn't need to have. Danzig explained the situation to Captain Cosseria and he was sympathetic, wanted to help, but reiterated: help doing what?

Cosseria explained that they'd had no intelligence supporting the FBI's theory and certainly, in the morning, he would make his officers available to her to discuss the matter, but there was little he could do tonight without more specific information. "This is Monaco," he told her with a wan smile. "Something illegal will happen tonight."

Danzig and Choi were leaving his office and walking toward the entrance of the police headquarters, discussing what they would do next, if anything. They didn't even have a place to stay. Captain Cosseria ran into the hallway, breathless, coat open. He said, "We've just gotten a report of shots fired."

JACK TURNED HARD LEFT at the park.

He saw the S8 surging forward in the other lane, and he accelerated through the turn, narrowly avoiding being hit. The Audi bounced over a concrete chicane. Jack turned hard left again, looping the Porsche around the park and back onto Avenue Princess Alice. The Audi was forced to follow the same path; there were too many cars for them to be able to turn back. That gave Jack precious seconds. The street snaked around the construction site and then past another park on the right. Jack made a hard left, turning uphill and then finding the road narrowed to a single lane. Jack rounded a corner and found a line of cars parked in a single direction on either side of the street and knew he was in trouble.

When he rounded the bend, he saw that the street dead-ended.

In a geography that could only be Monaco, the street terminated at the end of the block in front of a pink townhouse. Jack hit the brakes and reversed. He'd never make it back to the main street in time, but he could ditch the car and possibly throw them off.

What the hell was even happening?

Cannizzaro had already paid him, why try to kill him too?

There was an apartment building on the left that had a semicircular turnabout in front of it so drop-offs could be made on the one-way street. Jack pulled in there. That would let him turn around. He was just coming out of it when he saw the white Audi ripping around the corner. He'd already beaten them in a game of chicken once, he didn't think that would work twice, and this was already a narrow street. Instead, he parked in the half-circle and powered off the car. Maybe his pursuers would do the same thing that he had—narrowly focus on quickly navigating the tight street and not pay attention to the surroundings.

Or maybe not.

The Audi screeched to a stop, blocking his exit from the apartment.

Jack had the Targa's top open, so he just launched himself out of the car, leaping out the passenger side. He heard car doors opening behind him but didn't bother to look. There was only one option. He spotted a set of descending stairs leading to the street level below next to the carport and bolted for those. Jack raced down the stairs as fast as he could, nearly slipping as he did. Descending, he saw there was a store on his right with a covered walkway and decorative pillars. Jack hit the bottom of the stairs and ducked behind a pillar just in time to hear the first gunshot.

Jack swore in reaction. He heard shouts of panic behind him. It was getting late, ten maybe, but this was Monaco, and for most, the night was just getting started. The streets were full of both foot and motor traffic, diners in sidewalk cafes. Using the overhang as cover, Jack made the street. It was a single lane, with cars parked on both sides giving him ample cover. He ran in between two stopped cars and made the other side of the street. Jack hit the opposite sidewalk and tried to duck behind the cars. People on the street had heard the first shot but hadn't seen it, had no idea what was happening. Some were crouched, some were looking around, trying to see what was happening. Ahead of him, he saw a few people leaning over a low wall beneath umbrellas that must have been a restaurant.

Jack assumed everyone here would take him to be just another person fleeing the scene. He stayed crouched behind the line of parked cars and ran up the street. There was shouting behind him and a scream. Jack turned his head to see one of Cannizzaro's goons running across the street, gun drawn. Jack turned his head and ran as fast as he could for the corner.

He sprinted past the restaurant's outdoor seating, two rows of tables, that he'd spotted a moment ago. Behind that was a park that made up the corner of that block. Jack slid to a stop at the corner, getting no help from his dress shoes. He looked at the small park. There was a hedge that wrapped around it, large shrubs and trees throughout and a plaque on the corner. There was a large black-and-white picture beneath the words, "Princess Grace." He didn't have time to read anything else. Jack put a foot up on the waist-high concrete wall, stepped up, and dove behind a hedge.

Jack ducked behind a large bush so that he couldn't be seen from the street and took a moment to catch his breath and tie his shoe. He still had the pistol Bartolo gave him. It'd been banging around his pocket as he ran, Jack keeping a hand on it out of instinct but otherwise forgetting he had it.

TURNED out there wasn't one shots-fired call but two.

Danzig and Choi rode with Cosseria to the most recent one, which occurred about four or five blocks from the Monte Carlo Casino. That was on the opposite end of the city from the Direction de la Sûreté Publique. Cosseria said it would take them about ten minutes to get there. They grabbed a Citroen squad car parked out front, lights and sirens blaring, and Cosseria floored it. Danzig didn't speak French and couldn't follow the radio traffic, but Cosseria said they would have responding officers on scene in about two minutes.

Danzig explained the situation as best she could, knowing that Cosseria was also listening to the radio chatter and trying to maneuver them through the congested nighttime streets. She said that the FBI's involvement, apart from providing intelligence support to the Italian DIA, was that they believed one of the gem traffickers was an American. She didn't say anything about the Russians. She almost mentioned it to see what she could get but decided this wasn't the time and certainly not the occasion. Danzig knew from the Flipside briefings as well as her own knowledge that Monaco was a favored hiding spot for the world's untouchable villains. The dictators, the arms dealers, the people for whom the word "corruption" was just a tax write-off. There were several Russian oligarchs that maintained residences here, though Sokolov was not believed to be one of them. She wouldn't ask unless she first vetted Cosseria with the Paris LEGAT, who was also responsible for FBI activity in Monaco. Danzig would also need to clear that with the Flipside superiors—it was not her case, after all.

Cosseria wanted to know "why Monaco?"

Danzig didn't have an answer for that. All they knew was their informant in the Italian mafia organization said the buy would happen here instead of Rome, where they'd expected it to be. As for why Monaco, she could only speculate. The principality was contained within France and had a close border with Italy, creating jurisdictional complexities if law enforcement got involved. It was driving distance to major cities like Nice, Toulon, Marseille, Genoa, and Turin. There was a train station in the city, an airport within thirty minutes, and, depending on the resources of the criminals, a port. Given the dollar value of the exchange, escape by yacht was a distinct possibility. Danzig texted Rawlings to have him check with the Italians to see if they thought Cannizzaro owned a boat. They knew his heavies made the six-hour drive from Rome by car, but that's not to say Cannizzaro wouldn't dump those things on a yacht to bring them home. That would be the safest.

"I've got people on scene," Cosseria said.

JACK HEARD a crunch of shoes on grass and knew one of Cannizzaro's men climbed up into the park. Jack was crouched, kneeling behind a large bush that hid him from street view, but it was only about chest height. If he stood, he'd be seen. He heard several tentative footfalls on grass until the shoes struck pavement—there was a short, winding footpath that curved its way through the small park. There were a few steps, then it stopped, and Jack could hear the sound of shoes rotating. He was looking around now, body pivoting. He didn't see Jack and was debating whether he'd come the right way.

Jack squeezed the gun in his hand.

Then he heard the sound of sirens.

And they were getting closer.

Jack stood, gun out. Cannizzaro's man wore dark pants and a black moto racer jacket. Short black hair and a deep, natural tan.

More sirens added to the sound.

Jack held the pistol out in front of him and orbited around the bush. As soon as his first foot hit the grass, the man's head cocked to the side and his body started to follow.

"Don't move," Jack said in Italian. "Hands out to your side." There was a moment's hesitation while the goon calculated his odds, but he complied. "On your knees," Jack told him. Slowly, he knelt down in the grass. Now, Jack had the problem of what in the hell to do with him. Police would be here any moment and it wasn't like he could jump out of the bushes and declare he'd made a citizen's arrest.

Jack flipped the gun around and brought the butt down hard on the base of the man's neck.

The man cried out in pain with the impact, loudly, falling forward on his knees, cursing, again loudly. That was the opposite of what Jack was going for. With his left hand on the wound, the man turned his head. "What the fuck is wrong with you," he asked in Italian.

Jack honestly thought that would have knocked him out, but he realized as he did it that he'd only ever seen that work in movies.

There wasn't much time now.

"Take your pistol out, slowly."

"Fuck you."

Jack raised his own pistol several inches. "Your boss has a funny way of honoring his agreements."

Cannizzaro's man only sneered.

"I've taken out two of your friends tonight. Want me to make it three? Take your pistol out slowly," Jack repeated. There were sirens all over now. They didn't have long. "The longer you take, the less time you have to run."

The soldier slowly reached into his waistband and pulled out a pistol.

Gesturing with his left hand and keeping a firm grip on the pistol with his right, Jack said, "Throw it over that hedge, onto the street."

Jack knew he had to be prepared to shoot now. He had no reason to believe Cannizzaro's man would comply, and if he decided he was after a shootout, Jack would have to shoot first. He prayed that Cannizzaro employed at least one person capable of critical thinking. The soldier probably realized now that Jack didn't want to kill him, or he'd have done it. Even in the dark, the shadows between city lights, Jack could see in his eyes that he was doing math.

More sirens.

"You're losing time and I'm losing patience."

The heavy cocked his arm and tossed the gun, but not far, and it landed with a soft thud in the grass.

"You're a fucking idiot," Jack told him and took several wide steps around him. He thought about hitting him again but decided against it. Cannizzaro's man would be anticipating that, for one, and it might end up in a melee, the last thing Jack had the time for. Keeping his body and pistol facing his opponent, Jack rotated around him until he was on the other side. When his feet hit the footpath, Jack took several steps backward, turned, and ran.

The park was small, the space on the corner between two high-rises to the north and east. The footpath led between them, which Jack found took him back to Avenue Princess Alice, across the street from the excavation site. He dumped the pistol in a trash can.

Now, there was the problem of his car.

He couldn't leave it where it was parked now that there were police on scene. It wasn't in a legal parking spot and would eventually get noticed, then towed and fingerprinted. But even before then, they'd run the plates and trace it to the rental company, see that it was hired out to the Southerland alias via Jack's hotel. An APB would go out on that identity, and he'd probably never make it home. Maybe that was giving a little too much credit to the efficiency of the Monaco police force, but Jack knew the FBI had an informant in Cannizzaro's organization, that's why he'd insisted on the drop being here instead of in Rome. Danzig had probably called to alert the Monaco police already. Still, it was better than her being here.

There was a parking area the shape of an isosceles triangle between the buildings. Jack walked across that to the sidewalk and headed uphill, back toward his car.

Here was the problem.

When Jack reached the corner, having completed his loop around the block and now standing at the opposite end of the street he'd originally fled down, he saw the few things that he didn't realize when he'd driven through here way too fast to pay attention to them. The street split at this corner. The right fork curving up and to the right, which is what he'd taken, and the left fork going straight. Both of these were one-way, single-lane streets. Worse, the direction of traffic followed the path he'd run down, which was now closed off by the Monaco police. There was a car, lights flashing, and two uniformed police blocking off this street about twenty feet in front of him and two more at the other end of the block. Judging by the sound of sirens he heard at varying distances, more were on the way.

The police hadn't figured out crowd control yet, and traffic was already backing up on the street. Jack crossed to the opposite sidewalk and headed uphill to his car.

COSSERIA PARKED in an intersection that one of the uniforms blocked off with his car. There were two police cars in the intersection before they'd gotten here. Danzig and Choi got out but were careful to stay out of the way. She didn't bother hanging close to Cosseria while he got a debrief from the two police officers since she didn't speak the language. Danzig looked around to get her bearings. The intersection was in the middle of what looked to be a mixed-use neighborhood, shops and restaurants on the ground floor of most buildings with residences stacked on top. The street in front of them was one lane in one direction, with cars parked along both sides. There was sidewalk seating for restaurants on both sides. There was a small park on the corner, between two buildings. Danzig saw the uniformed officer pointing at that.

After a few moments, Cosseria walked over to her and Choi.

"Eyewitnesses said a man came running down a set of stairs there." He indicated to a point at the far end of the street. "That's where the gunshot was. One shot and the shooter missed. The shooter chased the other man, which no one got a good look at other than he was wearing dark clothes. They ran down the street and jumped into the park over there. One person, the shooter, emerged and tried to flee, but we had two cars pulling up as he did. There was a chase, but another car grabbed him." Cosseria pointed at a direction behind Danzig. "That's where we stand. We'll question the suspect and see what the hell he was doing, see if that's your guy."

"Any word on the person they were chasing?"

Cosseria shook his head. "Only one person came out of the park."

There was a restaurant in the building adjacent to the park with seating on the patio. They'd have had the best view of whatever happened in the park. Police were conducting eyewitness interviews now.

Danzig nodded. She knew there was nothing that she or Choi could do until Monaco's police confirmed that whatever the hell happened here tonight was related to her case, and it would likely be hours before that could be determined.

"What's up there?" she asked, pointing in the direction of where the chase had started.

"Pretty much what you see here. Shops and apartments."

"Mind if we take a look? I don't want to be in your way here."

"Be my guest. I'll let the officers know you're free to walk around." Cosseria said something into his radio.

"Let's go," Danzig said to Choi, and they started walking up the center of the street. It was crowded. People had emptied out of restaurants and shops to see what was going on, were now waiting to be questioned by police. There was also a line of cars on the street, some of whom were honking, probably unaware of why they weren't going anywhere.

"What exactly are we looking for?" Choi asked.

"I don't know. Some kind of indicator if these are our guys."

"You want to see if this would have been a likely spot for the handoff?"

"That's it," she said. They made it to the end of the street and turned, now facing the stairs that Cosseria talked about earlier. The stairs led down from what looked like an apartment building and a street above, maybe just a more convenient way of getting to the shops on this street than having to walk downhill, to the corner at the end of the block, and around. There was a store on the left side of the stairs and the exit of a parking garage on the right.

"We know from Mazza the exchange was set up in advance so there wouldn't be any negotiation," Choi said.

"Quick handoff," Danzig agreed. "Could happen anywhere."

"Parking garage is a nice, out-of-the-way spot for that." Three cars were lined up trying to get out of the garage with nowhere to go, probably had no idea what had happened and were honking.

"Why don't you check it out," she said. "I'm going to have a look up there." She pointed at the stairs.

JACK HUNG ON THE CORNER, outside the police cordon, for several minutes, trying to decide what to do. In that time, there had just been more and more police arriving. He watched a pair walk down the street in his direction, looked like a man and a woman, though from this distance that was about all he could make out. They walked unimpeded, so he assumed they were police, probably plainclothes detectives. He was standing in a growing swell of onlookers wondering what was going on here. There were several police officers standing in the intersection keeping people out, and one of them was trying to direct traffic. He wasn't close enough to the police to hear, but based on the hand gestures, Jack assumed they were trying to figure out how to clear the growing traffic jam.

Jack pushed through the crowd and headed uphill in the direction of his car. There was a thick cluster of palm trees of varying heights and bushes on the corner, so Jack lost sight of the stairs leading up to where he'd ditched the car. There was no sign of the Audi.

DANZIG WALKED to the top of the stairs. She didn't know what exactly she was looking for, but this wasn't it. There was an apartment building, a carport, and a dead-end street. That seemed fitting. What did she hope to find up here? Or in Monaco, even. They didn't know what Sturdevant looked like. Burdette's description of him was thirty years old. They'd gotten a hit in the NCIC system, but *that* was twenty years old. And "Clint Sturdevant" was an alias that seemingly hadn't been used since 2006 at least. Good reason to bring it out of retirement. But he could pass right by her on the street and she wouldn't know it.

Hands on her hips, she looked around in the cooling night and swore under her breath. Cannizzaro must have figured out that there was a leak in his organization. That's the only reason she could think of that they would pivot and make the sale here instead of in Rome. She supposed it was possible that it was here because Sokolov was here and they wanted to shorten the supply chain. Rawlings offered that one but retracted it almost immediately. Without knowing exactly where in the city it would go down, they had no chance to set up surveillance, nor did they know who they were even looking for. That, of course, was the point to the switch.

"Goddamn it."

This wasn't it.

As a handoff, it didn't make any sense. Neither did the garage. There was one way in and one way out for all parties. If someone decided to double-cross the other, they were stuck with each other. People savvy enough to pull off a crime like this would be better planners. An exchange like this would be fast and prearranged, possibly even a monitored dead drop. If it was to happen in person, the location would be secluded, such as a hotel room or some other controlled location. Sturdevant probably wouldn't go for that, would think it was a trap, unless it was his room and he had help.

What if it's a diversion?

Monaco had one of the lowest personal crime rates in the world. Violent crime was almost nonexistent. The probability that there was random gunfire was too low to even contemplate. What if the gunshots and the chase were staged to draw police to one part of the city and the sale was happening in another part?

What was that old saying? *It's only crazy if it doesn't work.*

You're grasping at straws, she told herself.

She stood there at the top of the stairs, staring at this blue Porsche that someone had left in the half-circle turnabout in front of the apartment building, probably took off when they heard the gunfire.

It was a long shot asking Burdette for help. He'd gotten his out and she understood how he didn't want to risk himself, plus there was the matter of that psychopath LeGrande. If Reginald hadn't tried to settle old scores, Danzig might have been able to convince Burdette to do it. Instead, she was in Monaco for reasons unknown, chasing someone with nothing more to go on than a twenty-year-old alias and a grainy mugshot, the date and time based on the words of a mafia accountant who would say literally anything to see the end of the week alive.

THAT MONACO COP had been hanging out by the Porsche for a long time.

Did she see something? Had he left something on the seat? Jack didn't think so. There was no reason to stare at that car other than to admire the paint job, so why was she? He supposed he could just walk up to the car and get in. No one in Monaco knew what he looked like, certainly not the police. He was just an American-born Swiss citizen that was here on business. The most she'd do was tell him that it was a crime scene and he'd have to get his car later.

Jack was standing on the sidewalk across the street from the turnabout. It was maybe fifty feet from him. There were no streetlights on this side, just a wall and Monaco's ever-present landscaping. Jack was in the half-light, shadows, he was just some guy on the street waiting for his car.

The cop still hadn't moved.

Maybe it was instinct, but he didn't want to touch his car until she moved. He was in the country illegally and, just two years ago, subject of an INTERPOL Red Notice. While it seemed unlikely, there was always the chance that a police officer would recognize him. It went up markedly for a detective. On the French Riviera, where Gentleman Jack Burdette was known to haunt...

Well, since he had time to kill, Jack decided he needed to work on his alibi.

And settle some old business.

He pulled the Jack Burdette phone out of his pocket and dialed Danzig's number.

Then he watched the woman across the street, the Monaco cop, pick up her phone.

FORTY-ONE

"What do you want, Burdette? Now isn't the best time."

"Well, I have information that I thought you might want."

"What I wanted from you was diamonds, Jack."

"You'll forgive me if I didn't think I could locate them, steal them, and fly to Europe without every cop between here and there busting me in a flat second."

"We could've worked that latter part out," Danzig said flatly. She wasn't in the mood for this. Danzig turned away from the Porsche and moved toward the steps. "What do you want?"

"I know who made the handoff in Monaco."

Danzig stopped. "Wait, how do you know?"

There's an instinct you develop as an investigator, sixth sense, intuition, call it whatever you like, but there is a sense you get, a feeling when something seems out of place. It's the *thing* that you can't put a finger on but you know is wrong, makes the hair stand up on the back of your neck, your skin tingle.

"Because he called me to gloat."

"Who?" He was drawing it out now, and that was starting to annoy her.

"Niccoló Bartolo."

"Bartolo called *you*? To gloat."

"He wanted me to know that he'd won in the end. He stole the diamonds the first time and now he just stole them back."

"How'd he get your phone number?"

"Come on, Danzig. He broke into a vault, I think he can figure out number tracing. I'm not exactly out of sight these days."

Danzig opened her mouth to speak but paused. Something about that phrase he used struck her as odd.

Why would Burdette call her *right now*? Of all times.

So, if Burdette said that Bartolo called him, then the deal must just have happened. That gunshot may well have been part of it. Maybe they decided to take out Sturdevant after all. Or maybe that theory about the diversion wasn't as crazy as it sounded.

But Danzig also couldn't shake that feeling that something was off. She'd seen a guy loitering on the corner, looking at her. She hadn't thought much of it. There were a lot of people on the street and all of them wondering what in the hell was going on.

"There's something else I need to tell you," Jack said.

"What's that?"

"Bartolo isn't going back."

"What does that mean?"

"His cousin sent him to Monaco to get the diamonds. Bartolo isn't bringing them back. He said they're his and this time they were staying that way."

"Did he say what he was going to do with them?"

Burdette had the nerve to laugh into the phone. "No. He'd never tell me that, but if I had to guess, he was going home."

"Where's home?"

"Turin. Good luck. I hope you get him."

"Jack, wait—"

But Burdette had hung up.

Danzig still had that uneasy feeling. Something was wrong about this whole thing, but she couldn't put a finger on it.

She looked across the street to where she'd seen the man watching her.

He was gone.

FORTY-TWO

Jack left the car where it was, walked several blocks, and called for a taxi.

Twenty minutes later, he was pulling up to the resort's main building.

Jack entered his room and opened a bottle of scotch from the minibar. He poured about four fingers' worth into a glass and drank half of that in a gulp. Then he pulled his jacket off and removed the tie. The shirt was sweat stained, and his feet ached from the run in dress shoes. Jack pulled his laptop out of his bag and sat at the room's small desk, then he activated the portable Wi-Fi puck and logged on to the Seychelles bank website. Jack used an application to randomize his computer's MAC address, and while it wouldn't make him completely undetectable, it would make him much harder to find, especially if he limited his usage.

The Republic of the Seychelles is a small island in the Indian Ocean, off the coast of East Africa. The island was batted like a tennis ball between competing interests of British and French imperialists until eventually becoming part of the British Empire in the eighteenth century, where they remained until declaring their independence in 1976. As an island nation with limited resources, as the country modernized they turned to international banking as a business. Ironically, though they ranked lowest among African nations on a "corruption index," due to their encouragement of foreign investment, generous rate of return, and identity protection, the Seychelles has become a haven for anonymous banking. In fact, it was one of the chief locations outside of Panama and the Caribbean that was implicated in the infamous Panama Papers.

While there would always be methods to move money below the watchful eyes of the world's governments and most of them perfectly legal, it was becoming increasingly difficult to move money as fluidly as he had in the past. Switzerland had been closed off for years, thanks to America's singular pursuit of terrorism and its funding schemes. After the disclosures of the Panama Papers, the US government, particularly the IRS, was again stepping up its efforts to close offshore tax shelters for its citizens.

Jack had been banking in the Seychelles for years.

Most of Jack's assets were in Vanuatu, but he maintained accounts in numerous banks throughout the world. Given their history with European colonialism, the Seychelles was an easy place to transact business with European banks. For a time, they wouldn't allow private citizens to open bank accounts, but for a corporation chartered there (and coming with cash) the rules were a little more malleable. So it was that the Indian Ocean Development Corporation opened an account with LCB Bank of Seychelles Limited and was able to accept a ten-million-dollar electronic transfer from the Commerce Bank of Rome.

One of the reasons Jack used LCB Bank was their disregard of traditional banking hours for their high net worth accounts. As a self-proclaimed "global bank," they operated around the clock. While Cannizzaro shouldn't be able to pull the money back once it had been dispatched from the escrow account, Jack also wasn't leaving anything to chance. He spoke with a man with a precise English accent named Victor, (who was probably more like Vikram and based in a Bangalore call center). Jack informed him of the situation, how his firm, the Indian Ocean Development Corporation, was entering into a joint venture with Amalgamated Services, LTD. Indian Ocean Development was partially funding this with an investment from a silent partner, and that was being transferred from Commerce Bank of Rome, hopefully now, and needed to be immediately transferred to ASC's holding account in the Maldives. Victor/Vikram understood completely and was only too happy to oblige.

Because the money was in escrow, the transfer was immediate, but Victor informed him that the Commerce Bank of Rome was attempting to pull the money back. Jack (speaking as Richard Hayes Montrose III) assured him that he had no idea what that was about but the purpose for using the escrow account was so the transaction could proceed unimpeded. Victor understood this completely as well and said it was more common than one thought. Board members disagreeing and such. Without an injunction, the transaction would proceed as planned. The money was already in Indian Ocean Development's account and would be available for use in the morning. Victor was only too happy to process the transfer to ASC's account with Mauritius Maritime Bank (Maldives) Private Limited. Jack thanked him for his time and hung up.

Jack then logged in to his account at Mauritius Maritime Back and set up a transfer for Enzo's portion as soon as funds were available.

Jack called Enzo. "Money will be in your account tomorrow. Cannizzaro fucked us. But five million each is better than dead."

After a short while, Enzo said, "I can live with that, but I don't think he can."

"That's not something we need to worry about," Jack said. "Thanks for your help. I'll see you around."

"I hope not," Enzo said, and Jack could tell in his voice that he was smiling. Jack wasn't sure when he'd see his friend again. This was probably the last time Jack would ever see Europe.

Jack picked up the hotel phone and dialed the concierge. He said he was embarrassed to explain that he'd been forced to leave the car they'd hired for him parked, possibly (he gasped) unlawfully in front of an apartment building. There was, if they could believe it, a shooting, and the police had turned that location into quite a scene. The roads were cordoned off, so he wasn't able to drive it out. Jack gave the concierge the address, who assured him the rental agency would pick it up right away. They were just glad he wasn't hurt and assured him this sort of thing never happened here.

Finally, Jack dialed Cannizzaro.

"I made the exchange. Your man has the diamonds."

"And you have been paid," Cannizzaro said in an irritated voice.

"You gave me a *down* payment. You owe me twenty-five million dollars."

"You'll get the rest once the diamonds are in my possession."

"That wasn't what we discussed."

"But it's what I decided."

"Forgive me if I don't believe you. I just checked with the bank and they said you tried to reverse the transaction."

There was a pause. Jack drained the scotch and reached for the bottle, then he set it back down. If he had to drive tonight, he'd need his faculties.

Cannizzaro still wasn't speaking.

"You had no intention of paying me, did you?"

"Not much," he said.

"You may want to rethink that."

"Why is that?"

"Because I'm benevolent. For now. For example, the two thugs you sent after me will only require a hospital instead of a morgue. I'm in Europe now, and that's not good news for you. If the rest of that money isn't in my account in two days, I'm coming for you."

Cannizzaro laughed. "I don't think so. You are only one man, and you have no leverage. I have the diamonds."

"Do you?" Jack said. "Think on that. You have two days to pay me what you owe me or I'm coming for you."

Jack hung up the phone and then he destroyed it.

He broke it open so he could access the SIM chip, which he flushed down the toilet. He then removed the plastic trash bag from one of the small waste bins and put the rest of the phone in that, which he filled with just enough water to cover the phone. Jack tied the bag off and dropped it in the trash can. He took a nervous shower, every drop of water felt like it was falling on borrowed time.

Jack didn't want to stay in Monaco tonight, but there wasn't anywhere else he could go. There would be no flights out or trains until morning.

If Danzig bought his story, then there wouldn't be police all over Nice airport and he could fly to Paris as scheduled. If not, there was either a train ticket or hiring another car and driving to Paris. He didn't like either of those options because of the time, but they would have to do.

Jack thought about checking out of his hotel now and heading to Nice. It was a thirty-minute drive, but being closer to the airport wasn't the issue, it was about breaking links in the chain. Unfortunately, this was Europe, and the things you could do at midnight were limited. He was in a fifth-floor room, so leaving via the window wasn't an option either. Much like the street he'd parked on, Jack was in a dead end. If they figured out he was here, there wasn't much to do about it.

He shut the lights off and checked messages. There were several voicemails and texts on his Jack Burdette phone. The one Jack listened to was from Megan, and it was three words:

Jack, it rained.

FORTY-THREE

Nico wasn't coming back.

It had been three days, and Cannizzaro had heard nothing from his cousin. The sale to Sokolov was supposed to have been yesterday. Cannizzaro delayed that as long as he'd been able but he'd run out of excuses.

He'd put Fabrizio in charge. *Make sure Nico gets where he's supposed to be and watch him. Then, as soon as the sale is done, fucking shoot that American bastard in the head for my troubles.* Don Cannizzaro had been very specific on that point. But all Cannizzaro heard back were excuses. Sturdevant picked some old castle for the exchange, a place where he could see them coming. It made it hard to plan an ambush. They'd tried to take him on the road, but apparently he'd outdriven them. More fucking excuses. Then Fabrizio let one of his men get arrested by the Monaco police. They still had him in custody, and God only knew what the fuck he was saying.

Somehow, in all that confusion, Nico slipped away.

The one thing that Fabrizio hadn't counted on was that Nico would take his own side. When the American, Sturdevant, fled and they chased him, Fabrizio assumed Nico would call for a pickup, as agreed, so they could drive him back to Rome with the diamonds. That call never came. Fabrizio called him, several times, but by then everything had gone to shit. They'd chased Sturdevant all over the city, Antonio, the stupid fuck, *shot* at him on a crowded street, and now that moron was in jail himself.

The don was surrounded by fools.

Then Mazza was telling him that he couldn't get Cannizzaro's money out of the escrow account. He'd put *that* idiot on a plane with a couple of his lawyers and sent him to the Seychelles to sort it out.

The don barked orders at someone, demanding to know if the car was ready. Was it loaded and why was he still waiting around here? Cannizzaro decided to leave Rome for a bit. He was going to spend a few weeks at his place in Lago Como until it cooled off a little here. Maybe longer, he didn't know yet. The idea was to move. The place in Como might just be a jumping-off point. It sort of depended on how pissed off the Russian was going to be that Cannizzaro couldn't produce the diamonds on time. That, and what Antonio spilled to the Monaco police. Antonio was a soldier and he didn't know much, but he would know that they'd gone up there to take possession of diamonds from an American. It wasn't like the old days when people just shut their fucking mouths. Now, they'd gossip like village women on the way up and he'd say whatever got him out of trouble up there.

"*Vaffanculo a chi t'è morto,*" Cannizzaro muttered under his breath, to no one in particular. Maybe everyone.

Perhaps Sokolov would be a reasonable man. If anyone understood how deals such as this could fall apart, it would be him. Cannizzaro would just have to leave out the part that it was his cousin that double-crossed them.

Cannizzaro was escorted out of his house, somewhat competently, to the black Range Rover waiting at the door. Two men would be in an Alfa Romeo in front of him and another four behind him. That should be enough for the lake house. Someone would close up this place later today. Cannizzaro walked across the large, circular carport, gravel crunching under his feet. He wore blue linen pants, an off-white shirt, and had a white linen jacket tucked under one arm. One of his men was just finishing loading his bags into the back of the Range Rover, another thing that wasn't quite done yet. Cannizzaro was going to have to make some personnel changes. Things had gotten far too loose lately.

Climbing into the back of the SUV, Cannizzaro checked his phone to see if there was any news on either Antonio or Nico, but there was nothing. He'd decided against sending one of his lawyers to Monaco. Instead, they would just deny they knew Antonio. After all, why would a prominent businessman, banker, and importer-exporter employ a semi-literate thug? He wouldn't. How did said thug get his name? It was common knowledge that Salvatore Cannizzaro, a respected legitimate businessman, was smeared in the paper by rivals as being "mafiosi." Of course, these allegations were ridiculous and untrue.

Nico was another matter, and he wasn't entirely sure what he was going to do about that. Cannizzaro had waited as long as he could for Nico to surface with some bullshit excuse. Now, the hunt would begin. He would put the word out as soon as he got to his place in Como. Cannizzaro would send people to Turin, and he also had people watching Giulia in case Nico decided to rekindle that. Cannizzaro called Nico's ex-wife to see if she'd heard from him, and she was surprised to learn Nico was out of prison.

The small convoy began to roll and went through the massive iron gate.

Where they promptly stopped.

"What the fuck now?" Cannizzaro muttered.

He leaned to the side so he could look through the front window and saw that there was a large delivery truck blocking the street. It was at a diagonal and looked like they were trying, quite unsuccessfully, to turn it around. What were they even doing here? Cannizzaro's property was on the outskirts of Rome, the small village was a mile from here, and no one else lived on this road.

Even the delivery men around here were idiots.

It was like Cannizzaro was in the middle of an epidemic of stupidity.

He cocked his head to the side when he heard a high-pitched whine of a motorcycle. This was a long, flat road, and sometimes the little shits would race their crotch rockets down it, but normally only at night. Well, he hoped they had good brakes.

Cannizzaro leaned forward to his driver. "Get that fucking thing out of the way."

Idiots. Everywhere.

FORTY-FOUR

Danzig and Choi rolled up on the scene in early evening.

It was still hot, and the sky was a scattering of pastels that would soon darken to night. They didn't have portable lights out here yet and there weren't any streetlights to speak of, just the lights from Cannizzaro's yard and from the assembled news crews.

They also hadn't carted the bodies away.

Instead, they were stacked in a row and covered with sheets. Danzig didn't know what the Italian word for "coroner" was, but there were two white Mercedes Sprinter vans with blue lettering that she assumed was it.

After forcing their way through the crowd, Danzig flashed her FBI badge that the Carabinieri didn't care much about, and they'd waited on the edges of the police tape until a DIA officer who recognized them waved them through. Danzig spotted Bruni in the fray, but he made no move to come over to them. No doubt, he'd seen them waiting at the edge of the cordon and decided they could continue to do so.

The Cannizzaro compound was on the right, with a ten-foot-high stone wall, well lit, and a massive mechanical iron gate. There were tall, cylindrical Italian cypress trees and the thin, mushroom-shaped Roman pines along the inside of the wall. Cannizzaro's property was inset a little from the road. There was no house on the opposite side of the street, just a large, empty field dotted with Roman pine trees.

The only eyewitness accounts were Cannizzaro's men, the ones that lived.

Details were sparse, but what Danzig heard was that at approximately one thirty that afternoon, Cannizzaro was leaving his compound. A truck blocked the way, stopping the caravan. Two motorcycles approached from behind. One rolled right up to Cannizzaro's SUV. The rider had a submachine gun inside his jacket and sprayed the back of the SUV, which was not armored. The second motorcycle, the theory was, was a backup in case the first rider didn't get Cannizzaro. He did, so the second sprayed down the chase car, killing three of the four occupants. They were gone before the driver of Cannizzaro's vehicle or the two men in the front vehicle could react. Then the delivery truck left the scene.

It was a thorough and professional hit.

There was no doubt who'd ordered it.

With Bartolo taking the diamonds from Sturdevant and now Cannizzaro getting killed, they had no link to Gennady Sokolov. Operation Flipside was dead.

She'd spoken at length with her boss in New York, and no one at the Bureau was blaming her or her team. In fact, the leadership behind Flipside praised her for her resourcefulness and ability to think around corners. If there was blame to go around, and there would be, her boss said it was going to fall on the Los Angeles division for letting Verrazano and LeGrande slip away. The fact that the latter then went and tried to murder Danzig's informant didn't look good for the LA squad either.

The Bureau unofficially paused the operation once the diamonds disappeared out of LA, a work of misdirection that had them all completely baffled. The prevailing theory was that Reginald LeGrande tapped Clint Sturdevant to act as a backup in case something happened with the sale to Pan Pacific. The Bureau assumed Verrazano had suspicions that Cannizzaro would send people to collect, as he had. The LA division OC squad, supported by LAPD Vice, said this was the only logical explanation. The theory went on to posit that if LeGrande hadn't sidetracked and gone up to kill Burdette, he and Sturdevant would have linked up in Los Angeles and hid out until they could line up a seller. The FBI still had Verrazano in custody at that point and could have used him to get to LeGrande. When LeGrande didn't follow the script, Sturdevant called an audible.

Danzig never shared the idea of having Burdette make a play for the diamonds. Better that she execute an audacious play and then tell everyone about it than to be the one who presents something so absurd it shouldn't be considered. Discretion was a hard lesson to learn.

While she understood Burdette's hesitation, to a degree, something about it was off to her. She just couldn't place exactly what. It was similar to the feeling she'd had in Monaco with that walker. Still, Burdette did have the LeGrande situation to deal with, and she'd spoken to the Sonoma County Sheriff's detective herself and knew he'd asked Burdette to stick around and help with any further questioning. Plus, he'd had the wildfires to contend with. Danzig learned that both Burdette's home and his winery were in the path.

She'd called her boss when they learned about Cannizzaro's assassination that afternoon, he was just getting into the office. Danzig had to stop using that word when she talked about this. "Assassination" implied a dignity Cannizzaro didn't deserve. He was a crime boss that was shot in the street. Danzig told her boss they'd wrap things up here and would head home soon. She'd get most of the squad out the following day, but she might stick around if there was any assistance they could be to the DIA, though something told her there wouldn't be.

Danzig had no idea how she was going to write a report for this.

"When I was here before," Choi said, referencing his time as the deputy LEGAT in Rome before Danzig had recruited him, "I made a lot of contacts with DIA, Guardia di Finanza, Polizia di Stato. A lot of people were after this guy. He had the local government so wired, was in so many people's pockets it was impossible to touch him. He had everyone's dirty secrets, seemed like. Bribery, blackmail, whatever it took. He'd keep whatever sludge he had in that bank of his. When they bust open those safe deposits, it's going to be like opening Pandora's box."

Danzig knew that Cannizzaro had a long campaign of manipulating judges and political officials and knew that the Commerce Bank of Rome was the central hub for it, but she was certain that she didn't know the depth of it.

"These guys always find a way to check out before accountability," Choi said, shaking his head slowly.

He was more right than he knew, Danzig thought.

Bruni stalked over to them, frog-faced and angrier than normal. They'd been on scene for about fifteen minutes before he'd acknowledged them. Danzig observed Bruni several times just standing around when he wasn't barking orders at people.

"You shouldn't be here," he said by way of greeting. "Your government no longer has an interest in this case."

"We just wanted to see if we could have assisted."

"If you wanted to help, you'd have given me the name of your informant. I could've prevented all this."

Danzig regarded Bruni for a long moment. This guy had been nothing but obstructive throughout their involvement. Most people in his position would have been overjoyed at the prospect of American assistance and the resources that came with it. Bruni was a sexist asshole and Danzig had had her fill of him long ago. All she wanted was to drop him in his place. But that would create a mess for LEGAT here, and she didn't want to do that to him.

"How exactly would you have done that? He didn't trust you. He was the money guy, so he knew everyone that Cannizzaro was paying off, which meant he knew which *cops* Cannizzaro was paying off."

Danzig realized as she said it that the implication was that Bruni would assume that would mean he was on the take rather than it being an indictment about the various law enforcement agencies that made up the DIA. "Bruni, I told you a hundred times that he didn't trust your government because of the number of people on Cannizzaro's payroll. But what would you have done if you'd had his name? Please, answer that question." Danzig's voice was calm, but she could feel her temper starting to bubble. She saw Choi shift on his feet slightly in her peripheral vision.

"You Americans are so goddamn smug. You just roll up in any part of the world you choose and think you can dictate terms."

"Your government asked my agency to assist you," she said flatly.

"Nobody asked me if I wanted your help. It's bad enough I have to try to arrest a man no judge will convict, now I have to babysit you people on top of it. But I suppose none of that matters now," he barked.

"Sergio Mazza."

"What?"

"Sergio Mazza is Cannizzaro's accountant. He manages the Commerce Bank. He's the informant. He is all you need to open up the bank and expose the corruption."

Danzig didn't just hand Bruni an olive branch, she gave him the entire orchard. But Bruni probably wouldn't recognize it for what it was. "The only thing that convicting Cannizzaro got you, beyond the *perception* of justice, was testimony on all of the people he paid off, and that only worked if he was given something to compel him to do it. In other words, a deal. But having Mazza and his ability to describe the depths of the political and judicial payoffs was truly how you roll that operation up."

Bruni's face twisted in a lemon-suck expression. "If you'd have told me that two weeks ago, we could have prevented all this. I'll make sure my report reflects that." Bruni turned on his heels and left.

Danzig was going to tell him, again, that Mazza's identity would not have allowed Bruni to do anything differently, nor would it have miraculously conjured the diamonds, but she wasn't going to give him the satisfaction of saying that to his back.

"What an asshole," Choi said.

Politically, within the Bureau, she believed they were covered. The loss of the diamonds were on the Los Angeles squad. That was too bad, she liked Fuery, but that was an uncovered angle. Bruni telling his government that the Cannizzaro murder was Danzig's fault would not help, but she thought she could steer around it. She believed she could defend the decision on not telling Bruni who the informant was and could also show that even if Bruni had known, there were no different or better actions that he could've taken. But Danzig did have a reputation for exceeding her authority, taking unnecessary risks, and not considering the consequences of her actions. Someone above her might look at this situation and accept Bruni's interpretation of events. After all, they portrayed the FBI in a negative light, another of Danzig's earlier sins.

"Bruni can say whatever he wants," Danzig said, still keeping her eyes on the crime scene in front of them. "But I'd challenge anyone to prove him right. The simple fact is, Mazza would've fled if he knew we were handing him over to Bruni. We have him on tape basically saying that."

"The truth isn't much good when what you're looking for is blame."

The sky continued to darken, and the Italians were finally getting around to loading the bodies onto stretchers to take them to a morgue. TV crews were still reporting on the incident. There was a small mass of civilians outside the police perimeter, gazing, as they always did, at the carnage.

Danzig turned and walked back to the car. Choi waited a moment and then followed.

FORTY-FIVE

Jack learned about Cannizzaro's death from Enzo.

The international press did not mince words.

Mafia Boss Assassinated

Cannizzaro died on a slow news day and got top billing in the Italian press.

Jack took no pleasure in that but had to admit to the intense relief he felt.

The plan worked, though not exactly the way that Jack intended.

Though a shadow of its horrible and violent peak three decades before, organized crime in Italy was a pervasive threat throughout the country. There was an entire branch of law enforcement dedicated to its eradication. But it was also a highly fractured thing. The gangs that operated in one region had almost no ability to affect matters in another region. In fact, to do so might be to invite war. Though some groups did have operations outside of Italy, such as 'Ndrangheta or the Camorra, and a number of those were quite extensive, those were largely constrained to Europe and other Mediterranean countries. Cannizzaro changed all that.

Not only had he established a smuggling operation throughout

Europe and the Med, Cannizzaro could also send his people as far as the US to exact his will. It wasn't a simple matter of buying plane tickets. Once they got here, they were funded and supplied. Beyond that, it was a matter of being willing to take the risk, to defy the reach of the American authorities who would carry the fight to his door if provoked.

When Jack learned that Nico was involved, he knew that Cannizzaro would have his name and almost certainly his home. There was no outcome where Jack was safe. If he succeeded in taking the diamonds from Reginald and Vito, Cannizzaro would simply come for him. If he failed, Nico would do the same for no other reason than revenge. Even Vito added something to the calculus. Jack couldn't count on what side Vito was going to play on, but he could always count on Vito using that knowledge if it got him something with Cannizzaro. Trade Jack's life for his. You could count on that like you could count on gravity.

So, Jack engineered a plan that he believed would eliminate the Cannizzaro threat for good.

What he hadn't counted on was Nico.

Jack believed that Nico fled after the botched attempt on the diamonds in Los Angeles. He wasn't among the killed or arrested, and the police eventually caught the car that fled the scene.

But in a bizarre and surreal twist, they found themselves on the same side, if just for a moment.

Jack *wanted* to take Danzig's deal.

Jack thought about how he could still satisfy his part even as he was driving to make the exchange. By the time he left to meet Enzo, Jack knew there was no way to accomplish this from home. There was no story he could craft that would convincingly explain to Danzig how he came across those diamonds in such a short amount of time. Even if she found a way to believe him, Jack didn't think it would fly with her superiors. Jack always found a way out, he always outmaneuvered his opponents and the police, found some slippery way to win. This would not be one of those times.

It came down to this—Danzig couldn't guarantee his safety.

He would never trust the government to protect him.

Oh, she'd have offered the platitudes, the reassurances, the claims that Cannizzaro wouldn't be able to harm anyone again. But this was a man who seemingly controlled half of the judges in Rome. Jack didn't fully appreciate the extent of his empire until recently; he doubted the FBI did. Even if the Italian authorities did manage to arrest him, Cannizzaro would be able to manage his operations from prison and he would always be a threat. What if he or a member of his organization gave Jack's name over to the Russian?

Danzig offered him freedom. Legally change his name to Frank Fischer, be assigned a new social security number, and become a solid citizen. He could hold a passport again. More importantly, that would have killed, once and for all, any potential IRS investigation into where his money came from. Allegedly, Danzig said she'd stopped that when he served up Anđelić, but he never believed any of that. Jack always figured that was a card she kept in her back pocket to play when needed.

Passing on that was the hardest thing he'd done in his adult life. But he had to, because that path almost certainly would've meant going into hiding anyway, leaving behind everything he took the deal to save. If Cannizzaro lived, Jack would always be looking over his shoulder for a mafia hit man coming for him or the people he cared about. At the time he was also, rightly, concerned about Nico for exactly the same reason.

Jack thought about that old toast they used in Turin, as young men full of bravado.

When all my enemies are dead.

Jack felt no guilt or remorse over engineering Cannizzaro's murder at the Russian's hands. Cannizzaro was human scum of the worst kind. He was a true villain, and the world was better without him in it. Jack would lose no sleep over that.

Reginald was a different matter.

Jack's relationship with him was much more complicated. Jack hadn't wanted to kill him, not truly. He'd have been satisfied if Reginald had just disappeared forever. Certainly, Jack would have wondered when Reginald might show up at his door to exact some manner of revenge, but Jack thought he could live with that over the guilt of shooting him dead. Not just that, but also watching him die and doing nothing to stop it. That action felt justified at the time, and Jack knew he could live with that too, but that didn't make it easy. Reginald's death was on his hands and always would be. Knowing that it was in self-defense *and* to save Megan's life took some of the edge off, but not much.

Nico seemed satisfied with his "victory." That was a nice speech he'd given Jack about what you can do with your hate. It was a good line, but that's all it was. He'd have shot Jack dead in an alley if that's what was called for. In the end, all Nico wanted was his diamonds and to live out the rest of his years in luxury. He'd do that now. Nico wasn't walking away with as much money as he thought he was when he'd accepted the briefcase from Jack, but it was still more than he could probably spend in the years he had left. Sure, Jack told Danzig that Nico ended up with the diamonds, and if she wanted to give that information over to the Italian authorities, that was her business. If Nico had to spend some of those years on the run, too bad for him. That was necessary to cement his story with Danzig and give her something she could use since Jack wasn't giving her the diamonds himself.

Jack hadn't heard from Danzig since Cannizzaro was murdered. He'd wanted to help her. That part wasn't acting and he hoped she believed it, not just for the self-preservation but because he strangely found himself on her side. Danzig gave him a chance at an honest life once when she didn't have to, which he'd (mostly) made good on. Jack believed he owed her at least that much.

But like so much of what the government does, good intentions eventually meet bureaucratic inertia and those good intentions lose their momentum. Jack would never trust his safety to that.

Jack walked out of a coffee shop in Sonoma Square. The

morning was cool and foggy, it had rained the night before and had nearly every day since Jack returned from Monaco. As they had the year before, wildfires got to the edge of the property where Jack and Lincoln had dug a firebreak. Learning from the lessons of 2019, they cut down the growth at the edges of the property and removed the grass. Many of the Alexander Valley winemakers had done the same in the last two years, and that helped the fires stay somewhat contained. It at least helped minimize the property damage. Rain and cooling temperatures took care of much of the fires, and the extraordinary work of the firefighters ended the rest. They were still battling some holdouts, but for the most part the threat was over.

Jack made several anonymous donations to the California Red Cross, organizations that helped out in wine country, and one dedicated to the families of firefighters who'd lost their lives battling these fires. In total, he'd secretly donated two and a half million dollars—half of what he'd gotten from Cannizzaro. The rest of it would stay in various accounts, should Jack ever find himself needing to run. That was the price of not accepting Danzig's offer. Jack wouldn't live as though he had a foot out the door, but he always had to be prepared to run. He wouldn't face a threat from Cannizzaro or Reginald, but he would live with the chance that the IRS's criminal investigation division would renew their digging into his offshore finances, and if that happened, Jack Burdette and Frank Fischer would have to disappear for good.

So, he had two and a half million left.

Less a little.

A year ago, Frank Fischer bought himself a present.

Jack found a company that rebuilt classic muscle cars. They'd licensed the original specifications from Ford and Shelby American and recreated some of those Mustangs, among the most legendary and iconic cars ever produced, using modern technology. The result was a 1968 Shelby GT 500 in a matte silver-gray with black hood intakes and a lowered, curved front valance that looked like a shark was grinning at you. They'd finished the build over the summer and delivered the vehicle to Jack just before he left for Los Angeles.

Jack got in and fired up the car, gassing it slightly to feel the throaty rumble of the engine.

He was staying with Megan until he bought a new house. They weren't ready to move in together permanently, though they had talked about it. For now, Jack was going to buy a new place, though Megan was looking with him, and the unstated agreement was that she'd get a soft vote. His place on Dry Creek Road would likely go for about two and a half, which was more than enough to find them a new home. It would have to, because Jack would have to pay cash. He wasn't sure how Reginald's death there would affect the price, but that was a manageable problem. He had plenty of money, and if he had to take a loss on the house, that was fine. The money Cannizzaro hadn't intended to pay him would be more than enough.

Jack backed out of his space beneath the tall trees of the square. The winery was shut down for a few days while they brought everything back from storage and tried to reorganize. Plus, it had been a traumatic and trying time for his employees and they deserved a couple of days off. Jack would head up there shortly just because there was nowhere else he wanted to be.

"Just drive," came a voice from the back seat, and Jack saw a dark form rise in the rearview mirror.

FORTY-SIX

True to his word, Lieutenant Colonel Bruni blamed Danzig fiercely, often, and in public.

Not the FBI, not America in general, not even her squad, but Special Agent Katrina Danzig.

He held a news conference where he explained that Danzig had an informant in the Cannizzaro organization and refused to share his identity with the DIA, despite numerous attempts at cooperation. Perhaps this all could have been avoided and the Italian people could have gotten the justice they so richly deserved if only Danzig had done otherwise. Bruni also informed the LEGAT in Rome of his feelings on the matter and said he wanted to issue a formal complaint.

Special Agent Max Silva, the Rome LEGAT, took Bruni's complaint. Silva assured the officer that it would be passed on to the appropriate offices in the FBI. He did nothing else with it. Silva told Danzig that his job was liaising with local law enforcement, a job which required strong, personal relationships and trust. If he believed that there were merits to Bruni's accusations, he'd have been bound to pass them on. As it was, Danzig kept Silva apprised of the investigation at every step. The only things she'd held back were the details he wasn't authorized to know anyway. Silva also understood why Danzig held back on sharing Mazza's identity with Bruni, an issue that Danzig and Silva had discussed at length several times.

Danzig asked Silva's opinion and advice as both a brother agent and as the LEGAT—potentially two different perspectives. She knew it would be a controversial decision and also one that would have consequences for Silva later on. Given the circumstances of the Cannizzaro organization's massive corruption scheme and their history of buying off law enforcement officers, including in Bruni's own agency, Silva agreed with her reluctance to share. He also didn't see how sharing Mazza's name would have changed the outcome. She was sharing the intelligence they got from Mazza, which is what mattered. Bruni was being petty. Silva assured Danzig that in his report back to headquarters, he would state that he'd have made the same decision. Silva would also put a call into his counterparts in Italian law enforcement, though he didn't expect much to come of it.

Danzig stayed in Rome for an extra two days after the Cannizzaro hit, mostly to package up their case files for shipment back to the US and to help Silva with the fallout. Most of that time, she was quiet and despondent. Though he'd died in the way his kind usually did, Cannizzaro escaped any measure of justice. What they'd learned about him over the last year and the extent of his criminal activities, branching into drug and gun smuggling and human trafficking, said that Cannizzaro got what *he* deserved but the Italian people didn't. Nor did Cannizzaro's incredibly long list of victims, one that would stretch back decades and could likely never be fully tallied. Worse, though, was Sokolov. He was human dirt, but his value as an intelligence asset was incalculable. More than that and the basis for Flipside's dual meaning, Danzig came to learn, was that if Sokolov didn't want to cooperate and provide information on the Russian president, they had a mountain of evidence with which to prosecute him for numerous cybercrimes perpetrated against American citizens. Sokolov's "media companies" were little more than hacker banks running digital blackmail schemes.

Sokolov was a big target, perhaps one of the most significant the Americans had gone after in decades. There were certainly other plays the Bureau and CIA were considering, though Danzig had no clue about them. Above her pay grade, as the saying went.

On the flight back home, she drank.

Danzig had official coverage but there was always blowback in any organizational failure. Bruni claiming the Cannizzaro end of this was her fault, while untrue, would only increase the number of times her name was associated with it and might just lead some Assistant Deputy Director, far removed from operational reality, to wonder *did Special Agent Katrina Danzig do everything she could?* Would another agent have done better? Was this just someone with a reputation for being hard to work with struggling to manage a complicated and important diplomatic situation?

Monaco weighed heavily on her mind during that flight, and she wondered about the decisions she'd made. Could she defend them? Burdette couldn't find the diamonds but was able to give her a name. They ran Clint Sturdevant down and found an alias that hadn't been used in fifteen years. Two-time bank robber, that they knew about, at any rate. In and out of the system most of his life. Connected with several murders, though none of them proven. There was no obvious link to LeGrande in his National Crime Information Center system file, other than Burdette's word, but she knew how well LeGrande compartmentalized, so that wasn't surprising.

There were two angles about Monaco that unsettled her, unquiet feelings she couldn't shake. The first was the location itself. Why there? Clearly, the reason was to draw attention and men away from Rome, but the question was *whose*. Was this to outmaneuver Cannizzaro or the FBI? They almost got there in time. The second aspect that Danzig had trouble with was the man on the street. Someone watched her. Not an uncommon thing, considering that there were shots fired on the street maybe ten minutes before, but she wasn't in uniform, had no outward indicators that she was a cop. So why focus on her? Danzig tried not to pay attention to him, and then when she did, she looked up to find he was gone. Knowing that you were being watched was an unsettling thing.

So was having dots that you just couldn't connect.

Burdette gave her Sturdevant's name, and soon enough they'd track him down and prove if he was the third conspirator in LeGrande's scheme. Burdette also shared that Niccoló Bartolo had been the one to receive the diamonds on behalf of Cannizzaro, then Bartolo apparently called Jack to brag about it. That seemed excessively flamboyant, arrogant, and stupid, but this was also a man who'd served sixteen years in prison because he was flamboyant, arrogant, and stupid, so perhaps it fit. Danzig contacted some old colleagues at Europol and INTERPOL so that they could pick up the hunt. She'd let Silva handle any communication with the Guardia di Finanza.

When Danzig reported into her home office for the first time in months, she learned that Vito Verrazano would be extradited to Italy. The only thing they could charge him with was entering the United States illegally and possessing a false passport. The Italian government might prosecute him; on the other hand, they might just say he was a seventy-year-old man and maybe it wasn't worth it.

Danzig's boss, Ed Dysart, told her they'd done great work, the best they could have done under the circumstances. Those words seemed to hang in the air around him, *under the circumstances.* That was the kind of left-handed compliment bureau-speak for telling someone they failed without actually saying it. He'd gotten Silva's report and said it was highly complimentary of her and her team—was just a shame they couldn't have gotten to Cannizzaro before the Russian did.

Real shame. He made a point of saying that twice.

Danzig amassed a lot of vacation time over the last year. She planned on burning most of it. Travel a bit and not have her phone on. When she came back, she'd figure out what she was going to do next. Danzig would have twenty years in the Bureau the following spring. Fifteen of those years she'd spent following the dark money trails the villains of the world used to finance themselves. Most of that time was in precious gems, a lot of it abroad. She sacrificed much for this pursuit. Katrina was not married, in fact she didn't even remember the last time she'd been on a date. The only men she knew were other agents or industry contacts or informants, and that's not what she was looking for. Her work already occupied all of her thoughts; she didn't want it to dominate a relationship as well. This pursuit also cost her advancement in the Bureau. Danzig wanted to chase bad guys, she wanted to be a *cop*. But that meant not taking certain jobs, the kinds of things that got you noticed. That was a conscious choice and one she knew would likely limit her growth and certainly her advancement. It was an easy calculus when you're single and in your mid-thirties, a little different when you realize that you're looking at forty-three and your job is the only long-term relationship in your life.

Danzig didn't know what would come next, but she knew it would be in a different division. She needed a change. Not every investigation resulted in an arrest, and she also knew that she and her team had done good police work. That mattered. To her, at least. Her boss was a bureaucrat and had been behind a desk too long. Danzig also had two high-profile arrests on her record—a Castro regime hit man who'd been hiding out in Miami and later, a Serbian war criminal. Her reputation had enough horsepower that she could make a good transfer when the time came.

She'd debated giving Burdette a call and letting him know the outcome of it all. He'd tried to help her, that was true, though with him there was always an angle. Gentleman Jack Burdette was no Samaritan, there was nothing he did out of the goodness of his heart. He certainly didn't assist FBI investigations out of some lofty notion of civic-mindedness. Burdette only gave her Anđelić because the FBI got to him first and because Anđelić was going to kill him.

Danzig didn't know exactly what Burdette's involvement in this case was, but she knew it was more than he was letting on. She also knew that whatever it was, it no longer mattered.

She put her leave request in and told Dysart that she planned to take a full month. No can do, he'd said, like he was an auto mechanic. Two weeks at a time was division policy. *Fine*, she thought, *I'll come back for a week and check email for two days and then leave again.*

Danzig was angry and justifiably so, but she held her tongue, a lesson she'd learned the hard way too many times. She guessed it finally took. Dysart was just the messenger. And that's not even what she was angry about, what she could feel starting to boil up in her blood. The shock of seeing Cannizzaro shot dead had registered at the time, she knew what it meant, but the gravity of it hadn't registered until just now when her boss told her that the policy was two weeks of time off. Long months of hard work, nearly a year, without any break were just gone. Enduring the petulant whims of a misogynist cop that obstructed her at every turn and then blamed her publicly for their collective failure. The one thing she refused to do was ask the question of whether or not she should have stepped aside and let a male colleague take the lead. That question would be asked, she knew. It was coming. *We understand that Lieutenant Colonel Bruni refused to work with a woman, and that's deplorable. We all object to it. We just couldn't help but wonder, for the sake of the investigation, would it not have made sense to let Agent Choi or another member of the team take the lead with Bruni? Perhaps that would have effected a different outcome.*

She'd done her job and done it well. She had a good squad and they did *their* jobs well. She almost looked forward to the asshole bureaucrat who asked the question of whether she should have stepped aside.

Danzig left that thought in her office. She told Dysart she was taking the rest of the day off, starting her vacation early. It was obvious she was worn out and jet-lagged, and he didn't fight her on it. She did think about Flipside and whether that might be an option for her. That seemed like the kind of thing she was cut out for. Bring Choi over if she could. But those were problems for another day.

Danzig wasn't sure what she was going to do next, but whatever it was, it wouldn't involve diamonds.

FORTY-SEVEN

"How'd you get in here?"

"You forget how many cars I stole on your behalf over the years?"

"What do you want, Rusty?" Jack's hand went to his waist on impulse, but as soon as he felt nothing, he remembered that his pistol was still tagged in an evidence locker at the Sonoma County Sheriff's Office.

"I came to explain why I did what I did."

"I don't care why you did it," Jack said. He was about to ask Rusty if he'd known what he'd caused but stopped himself. Rusty could be wired up, probably was. He couldn't deliver Jack before, so this was the next pass.

"I was tired of running, Jack."

"You mentioned that already." Jack drove through an intersection and rolled past the old, restored buildings of the square. He wheeled the car onto West Spain Street to take him out to Highway 12 and then north. "I've got things to do today, so if you don't have anything new to share, you can get the hell out of my car."

"I came to tell you that you don't have anything to worry about."

"I know I don't have anything to worry about. All I've done today is buy a coffee."

"They don't care about you," Rusty said after a few strained, silent breaths. "They weren't interested in you anyway, and after that shitshow in Inglewood, the Bureau—at least *my* part of it—didn't want anything to do with it."

"What deal did you cut, then? You couldn't just turn yourself in or you'd have done it, and you're obviously free now."

"I'm not free, not like it looks. But ultimately what they decided was that what I know was more valuable to them if I was on the inside than the outside. If I'm here, they can watch me. And I have to go back to work for them."

"So what, they're giving you your badge back?" Jack said, acidic irony oozing off his words.

"Not exactly. It's more like witness protection. But now that we're finally acknowledging that Russia is a threat again, I will have to provide some specific knowledge and expertise whenever they want. There is also some work that I did abroad that's useful to them now. That's part of the deal too. Otherwise, I have to work some bullshit job, live in a bullshit suburb, and pretend to be 'Eric Warner.'"

"If you're looking for sympathy, you got in the wrong car."

"I'm not," Rusty said slowly and softly. "I just wanted you to know that you're in the clear. I figured I owed you that."

"Until you need something to trade," Jack said.

"No. Counterintelligence is a different world, Jack. They deal with the worst of humanity to protect the rest of it from people that are even worse. All that to say, no one I know gives a shit about a jewel thief."

Jack made a left turn and followed it around a snaking road to a small shopping center. The buildings were dark brown and stood out in contrast against the wet, gray sky. Jack pulled into a parking spot, got out, and pulled the seat forward so Rusty could get out of the back. He did. Rusty's hair was brown now, and his eyes looked haunted.

"You saved my life," Rusty said awkwardly. "We both know Enzo's temper, and I wasn't sure which way that was going to go."

"It was a matter of logistics," Jack said in a flat tone. He wasn't letting Rusty off the hook. "I didn't have time to hide a body."

Rusty nodded. He understood, was one of the few people in the world who did.

"Listen, I hope you don't, but if you ever need my help." Rusty pulled a card out of his jacket pocket. It was a blank business card with a handwritten phone number on it.

"You can get into a lot of trouble just offering me that. Your new friends will say you haven't learned your lesson."

"Debts to pay," was all Rusty said.

Jack accepted the card and pocketed it. He didn't know why, exactly. Maybe that's what Rusty needed, and Jack understood absolution.

"What happened to the diamonds?" Rusty asked.

Jack only shrugged. "You know what they say. Once a thief…"

Jack got into his car and left the parking lot with Rusty watching him drive off.

At least, Jack assumed he did. Jack didn't look back.

INSTEAD OF GOING to the winery, he first drove home. Jack let himself in. The remediation company had done an excellent job. You could never tell he'd killed a man here.

Jack walked to his bedroom and collected a few things. There was a leather travel bag on the bed, which he'd packed with clothes and hadn't taken with him. He'd need these at Megan's. Then Jack walked over to the carpet beside his bed and pulled it back. His fingers found the nearly invisible seam and he pressed down, opening the panel and revealing the safe. Jack dialed the combination and opened it. Inside, there was a velvet bag weighing about two pounds. He pulled it out and opened it, just to stare at the contents.

A few diamonds fell into his hand, and they shone like stars.

The contents were probably worth thirty million dollars, about a third of the original take from Rome two years before.

What Jack brought to Europe was a little over half of what he'd recovered from Reginald. The plan was simple. He knew he had to give Cannizzaro's men something and he also knew they wouldn't be able to tell sixty million in diamonds from a hundred. If it looked like what they were expecting, it would work. They would deliver the contents to their boss, and he would come up short with a very unforgiving Russian crime boss who would do the sort of thing that unforgiving Russian crime bosses did to manage their disappointment. Of course, Jack hadn't counted on Nico showing up and stealing them, but the outcome had been the same. Probably better, because now Nico was content and Jack wouldn't have to worry about looking over his shoulder for him as well.

Meanwhile, Jack had thirty million in diamonds that he could slowly and quietly sell off every few years.

That, too, was why he hadn't taken Danzig's deal.

Jack gently tossed the bag in his hand for a moment and then gingerly replaced it in the safe. He'd need to find a place to put them when he sold the house, until he could get a safe built at his new place. He kind of liked the irony of a safe-deposit box at a bank.

Jack closed up the safe and replaced the carpet.

He smiled.

"I don't know why people keep taking me at my word."

EPILOGUE

Lugano, Switzerland

Vito Verrazano strolled along the lake and enjoyed the Christmas lights.

Riva Giocondo Albertolli ran along the Lake Lugano waterfront and the trees, mostly bare, were wrapped in white lights. The lake on his left, was a black void, an inky smear that seemed to suck in all of the light around it. The buildings facing the waterfront were four stories, baroque architecture, and loomed like gargoyles. One of them was a bank and next to it, separated by a walkway in between, a McDonald's. The night was clear and cold. He could see his breath. There was a trace of snow on the ground and a few flakes in the air, which was strange. Lugano had a unique climate for this part of Europe, much closer to southern Italy than Alpine Switzerland.

Perhaps Vito should have chosen a spot a little further from his previous home in Maggiore to hide out, but Carlo needed some time to sort out Vito's legal troubles, and for that, he needed to remain close. Still, Switzerland was a different country but close enough that he could get home if he needed to. Lugano had a very large expatriate population, much of that Italian, and he could blend in easily. Vito wasn't very concerned. The extradition was embarrassing, and he didn't want to come back here, necessarily, but after seeing what a clusterfuck of a country America was, he didn't want to be there either. Ultimately this amounted to a minor inconvenience. The Americans couldn't charge him with anything because *someone* stole the diamonds out from under them and his government had enough on its plate right now; they didn't particularly care if an old man had a fake passport. Carlo said the government lawyer actually told him that it took so long to process passports these days, he didn't blame someone for getting a fake.

Vito guessed he'd been right about Reginald trying to cut him out.

The FBI pressed him on who that third man was, but Vito didn't know and continued not knowing the entire time they questioned him. He understood that in America the police could only keep you for forty-eight hours unless they were charging you with a crime, but his extended a couple of days because it went over the weekend. Then they let him go, but they kicked him out of the country. Vito white-knuckled that entire flight. Eventually, his anxiety rubbed off enough on the person he was sitting next to and they talked to a flight attendant. Vito told the flight attendant that he wasn't used to flying, it made him nervous. The flight attendant spoke Italian, so they chatted for about twenty minutes. Vito remembered how to be charming. She gave him red wine in a plastic cup, and he went back to his seat.

Very different from the flight he'd taken to America.

The nerves didn't subside, but he controlled them better and resigned himself to the knowledge that Cannizzaro would have a man at the airport waiting for him. He'd be gunned down before he saw baggage claim. Not only did he make it through baggage, Vito made it a lot further. Carlo met him at the airport and explained that Cannizzaro had been murdered, *assassinated* according to the local papers.

Carlo suggested Vito stick around Rome so they could sort out this thing with the Americans. "Fuck you, I pay *you* for that," Vito said and left, not telling Carlo where he was going. If Vito had learned anything from this, it was that he needed to get out of the habit of trusting people.

He never heard from Reginald again and assumed that he had the diamonds. Good luck to him. There was the question of Bartolo, still, and Burdette. For that, Vito didn't have ready answers. He wasn't going to run anymore, and he wasn't going to live looking over his shoulder. He believed Burdette wouldn't leave the country again and God alone knew what paths Nico would walk.

Vito still had a little of the money from the Knightsbridge job, his *and* Reginald's, and it was stashed at a box in HMZ Bank, right here in Lugano. Had been for twenty-three years. That was enough to live on. It was cash and British cash at that, but the bank could convert pounds to Swiss francs and euros easily enough. It just took time, and he had to do it in smaller amounts. It wasn't diamond money, but he'd live comfortably.

Though Vito settled in Maggiore, mostly because it was still Italy, he'd traveled to nearby Lugano often and liked it. This would be a good place to live, he decided. He had more than enough from the sale of his house on Maggiore to afford a home here. He'd find that later. For now, he wanted a drink.

Vito walked along the lake beneath the lighted trees and enjoyed the solitude. There were a few other evening strollers, but it was a weeknight and quiet. He looked away from the lake and saw a man walking in his direction, also enjoying the brisk night. The man wore a gray coat with a slim, tailored cut that went down to his mid-thigh. The collar was turned up against the chill, though the jacket was open. His hand was inside the flap of the coat, probably reaching for his phone. He had a black watch cap and a face mask; people were starting to wear those again. Vito smiled at his fellow walker and said, "Good evening" as he approached.

It wasn't until the man was steps from Vito that he recognized his eyes.

RUSTY DREW the silenced HK VP9 from his overcoat, raised it, and fired twice. The two shots landed right in the center of Vito's chest and the old man crumpled inward, like a building collapsing. Vito fell on his back, head hitting the pavement with a soft crack. There was still light in his eyes, though it wouldn't last long. His mouth worked, questions that wouldn't make their way out. Rusty fired a third shot to the head.

He twisted the silencer off in one quick motion and then tossed it and the gun into the lake.

Rusty turned away, crossed the street at a brisk pace, and disappeared into an alley.

WANT TO STAY UP TO DATE ON MY LATEST WORK?

For more information on my latest work and upcoming releases, sign up for my mailing list. In exchange, I'll give you a free "Gentleman" Jack novella entitled, *The Robber*. This is an exciting story about a heist gone wrong and I really think you'll like it. https://dl.bookfunnel.com/ncz6clru2z

You can also find me on the web at: dalemnelson.com

Thank you very much.

Reviews are the most powerful tools authors have to get attention for our books and helping us reach new readers. I rely on readers like you to help others discover my stories by leaving honest reviews of my work.

If you enjoyed this book, I would be very grateful if you could spend a few moments of your time leaving a review: My Book. It makes a world of difference.

ALSO BY DALE M. NELSON

"Gentleman" Jack Burdette Series

A Legitimate Businessman

The School of Turin

Once a Thief

Stand Alone Works

Proper Villains

The Bad Shepherd

"Firewall Spies" Series with Andrew Watts

Agent of Influence

A Future Spy

Tournament of Shadows

All Secrets Die

Thanks to my wife for giving me the push.

ABOUT THE AUTHOR

Dale M. Nelson grew up outside of Tampa, Florida. He graduated from the University of Florida's College of Journalism and Communications and went on to serve as an officer in the United States Air Force. Following his military service, Dale worked in the defense, technology and telecommunications sectors before starting his writing career. He currently lives in Washington D.C. with his wife and daughters.

ONCE A THIEF

Copyright © 2021 by Dale M. Nelson.

All rights reserved.

No part of this book may be reproduced in any form or by any electronic or mechanical means, including information storage and retrieval systems, without written permission from the author, except for the use of brief quotations in a book review.

This is a work of fiction. Names, characters, businesses, places, events and incidents are either the products of the author's imagination or used in a fictitious manner. Any resemblance to actual persons, living or dead, or actual events is purely coincidental.

Milton Keynes UK
Ingram Content Group UK Ltd.
UKHW030831181124
451360UK00002B/408